KEEPER
of the
House

Also by Rebecca T. Godwin

Private Parts

KEEPER

of the

House

Rebecca T. Godwin

St. Martin's Press
New York

Copyedited by Barbara Perris
Design by Junie Lee

LIBRARY OF CONGRESS CATALOGING-IN-PUBLICATION DATA
Godwin, Rebecca T.
    Keeper of the house / Rebecca T. Godwin.
        p.   cm.
    ISBN 0-312-11405-2
    I. Title.
    PS3557.O3165K4   1994
    813'.54—dc20   94-21898
                                                                    CIP

First Edition: October 1994
10 9 8 7 6 5 4 3 2 1

The author wishes to thank the National Endowment for the Arts, whose grant helped with the writing of this book.

Books are available in quantity for promotional or premium use. Write to Director of Special Sales, St. Martin's Press, 175 Fifth Avenue, New York, N.Y. 10010, for information on discounts and terms, or call toll-free (800) 221-7945. In New York, call (212) 674-5151 (ext. 645).

To Deane—best friend, reader, teacher, partner.

Honi soit qui mal y pense.
   —from the frontispiece of the *Morte d'Arthur*

Honi soit qui mal y pense.
   —from the frontispiece of the New Orleans Blue
   Book, a directory of sporting houses

Author's Notes

While the characters and events in *Keeper of the House* are fictional, the idea for the novel was born of fact. Sunset Lodge, a world-renowned house of prostitution, existed on the outskirts of Georgetown, South Carolina, from the 1930s until the mid-1970s. Growing up near there, I became more and more fascinated by the notion of that house and that town existing side by side for all those years. It was not until about four years ago that the way to write about it came to me, in the person of Minyon Manigault. In deciding to let her voice tell the story, I was guided by the words of Eudora Welty: "What I do in the writing of any character is to try to enter into the mind, heart and skin of a human being who is not myself. Whether this happens to be a man or a woman, old or young, with skin black or white, the primary challenge lies in making the jump itself." (Preface to *The Collected Stories of Eudora Welty*, 1980.)

I have taken liberties with the Gullah dialect of lowcountry South Carolina, intending to convey the richness, music, and humor of the language while retaining its accessibility for people unfamiliar with its patterns.

In writing this book, I have been supported and encouraged by many. I thank my family first of all, from my husband Deane to my daughters Lissa and Carrie, my parents Bumpy and Carolyn, my sisters Lynn, Claudia, and Caroline, and an amazing extended family of around seventy or so, including Uncle Jim, who taught me that life goes on from here. Thanks to my writing and reading friends, especially Tracy, along with the Women's

Weekend bunch and many other Bennington supporters; Pinky and Page; Lisa and Jane; and still, always, Martha and Temp. Thanks to my ninth-grade English teacher Flo Hanold, wherever you are, and to Sammy Crayton, who sat with me in his Winyah Bay backyard and shared his wonderful stories. Thanks to the National Endowment for the Arts for support on this work and others to come. To my editor George Witte, my appreciation for your careful, good reading. And to Colleen Mohyde, my agent, boundless thanks for your feistiness, faith, and hard work.

PART I

1929

Setting Up House

chapter 1

"This here's the girl you wanting."

Why I'm standing here in the smack center of my Gannie's front room all bathed, combed, and Sunday-dressed up, I ain't for the life of me know. Just goes along with how strange she's acting lately anyhow, looking some elsewhere than in my eyes when she talks to me and keeping to her room more instead of right in the middle of all us like usual.

Now Gannie's old hand pushes square in my middle back. I feel her sharp knuckles digging in, never letting up pressure, pushing me, pushing. My eyes're shut so tight I got black and red swirls inside my head, with some yellow busting out now and again. I plant my feet hard on the floor against her pressure and study on the insides of my eyelids. I ain't looking, I ain't moving.

Sure can still hear, though. "Not much for looks, Missus, but she's strong and quick," says Gan. "Smart as all getout, too."

My mouth drops open, then—can't help it, on account of Gan ain't exactly one to be passing out such compliments on her grandchildren. Fixing to whip my head round to see how she looks after telling those words, but then I hear that one voice, floating on the air light as the perfume I been smelling ever since she and Sheriff Dawson came into Gan's house:

"Not really in the market for a looker, anyway, Mrs. Tucker."

Voice don't sound a thing like Mizz Gertrude's or her Yankee friends' who come to the big house to visit, which's the only white women I about ever heard. They got high, thin voices come out through they noses, sound like screechy birds. But this one says words like she's singing sweet, low music. And's calling Gan Mizz Tucker, which I never heard white folks do before in my life.

"How old is she?"

"Seventeen next month." Which rocks me down to my shoes on account of never hearing Gan lie before. Shocks me so I let up pressure a minute, I guess, because next thing I know, Gan's made me lose my hold on the floor and's pushing me forward where I got to open my eyes not to knock into something. I don't wide them up, though, just squint, and all's I see is white and red; but between the smell and the voice and the little bit I spy, I can't stand not knowing, so I open them all the way, to see standing before me the whitest white woman in the world, with a white dress on to boot, and red shoes and a red belt and a big white hat pulled down low over a long head of hair that's no color I ever saw or even dreamed of before—looks like the sun fixing to set, evenings. My mouth drops open, can't get a sound out. Scared soul-deep, like I'm seeing the devil, else the angel of God Preach's always talking about, coming to fetch me for my sins.

"What's her name?" She's asking Gannie, but looking at me the whole time, the ends of her mouth curling like she's fixing to bust out in a grin. Next her's standing a big old white man I know to be Sheriff Dawson, who's looking not at me nor anybody else, can't tear his eyes off that hair.

"Minnie," says Gan. When I hear that, inside my head comes a roar and my throat closes up like I'm fixing to choke. Feel like if I don't say it now, ain't gone be another chance, so I stand myself straight up as I can get, though my knees's knocking some.

"No, Missus." My voice sounds like Willy the cat's first-thing-in-the-morning meow, all rough and razzy. "It's Minyon." And I ain't know where to put my eyes so I close them up again. But I got to finish.

"Minyon, like the very best cut of meat, Missus. Dark and juicy and expensive." Been saying the same words about my name long as I can remember, on account of Gan told me they the very words my mama told when she named me that, before she went off up north, same as all Gan's children, leaving me and Clarence and our big brother Jesse. "Minyon Manigault."

Her laugh rings like bells, makes me open my eyes back up. "Hope you're not too rich for my blood, Minyon Manigault."

She turns to Gan, and I squint through closed-up eyes to watch her lips move—looks like the inside of my baby brother Clarence's mouth, where the skin's shiny-wet and red.

"I believe Minyon here will do just fine, Mrs. Tucker." And for one second I don't think about what that might mean, just wondering how in the world I manage to do just fine for this fancy white woman.

She keeps looking at Gan. "Pay is two dollars a week." Behind me Gan draws her breath in sharp, like she's scared.

"And of course, she'll be fed and clothed, and so forth. Kept up."

"Take her with you now." Gan's voice sounds like some stranger's, rough and mean, makes my heart sink to my feet. "And don't be letting her visit none."

Too much for me. I turn on my heel to see Gan's face. Pinched and thin, like stone it looks, color and life draining out before my eyes. Makes me want to bawl like a baby, that pale stony face. How can it be that the one I figure to love me most in this world's gone shed me like old snakeskin, tell me to not even come visiting?

"Gan," I cry, finally, that name tearing out my throat. But she only turns eyes away and stares at the door behind me.

"What'd I do, Gannie? How come you so mad?" She says not one word, just keeps looking past me, skinny self trembling like a leaf in a windstorm.

White lady tells me, "Get your things, Minyon." I take a last look at my Gan, who just shivers and stares off.

A cold-as-winter wind blows through me. "I got nothing, Missus." Which ain't exactly true, I got some drawers and my day dress, but I don't want a thing from here now, except for away from this old woman who don't want me no more. Ain't gone cry, neither.

I stand stick-straight and stare at the lace and frills on this lady's dress, not at her face, on account of Gan says white folks don't like us looking them eye to eye.

"What you want me to do, Missus?"

"I want you to call me Miss Ariadne, for starters. Or Miss Fleming, if you'd rather. And I want you to go get your things." Something in that voice I ain't even thinking about arguing with.

Not looking at Gan, I turn and walk down the skinny hallway to the room where me and Clarence and our cousin Farina sleep, along with Aunt Millie's baby Christina, just got sufficient big to get out her crib. Right in the middle of my sleeping mattress is a squared-up bundle that I untie to see's got my clothes and a toothbrush and a brand new comb, black and shiny, all put together inside the pale soft blanket Gan made me when I was a new babe, that I slept with ever since.

Out the one window of my room I see the dirt road runs through the mid of Little Town, the only place I ever lived from the time I was born, fourteen years back, right upstairs in the room Gan sleeps in; where my brother Jesse was born, too, and my mama and the rest of Gan's children, and Gan herself; where our people's lived since slave times, Gan says—her mama and daddy both belonged to the white folks that owned this plantation called Arcadia. That was back before we was free to come and go as we please, she says. Now some please to go far away as New York, like my mama and her sisters, who don't come back but sometimes send a reminder of themselves, like when Clarence showed up with Lally's sister passing through, sent by my mama for Gan to raise up. Then there's those of us's stayed behind, who ain't tend to go much of anywhere, besides to Jameston some Saturdays. Got what we need right here, Gan says, no need to go looking for trouble some elsewhere.

So why's that woman set to send me off from the only place I know? My eyes fill, I can't help it, and I fall to my knees next to my bed, cover my face in this old blanket to keep crying in. Holding softness to skin, I think on Gan's softness, how she makes all her hard skinniness go round-edged when I crawl up on her lap—still do, big as I am—and she goes to rocking and crooning, singing sweet songs I ain't ken the words to, songs come all the way from Africa, she says. That's the soft side of my Gan. The hard side's the one keeps after us to read our lessons and never miss class where Mizz Ruby Kinross teaches us mornings, in our little church by the river Waccamaw; to tell the truth every chance we get, to stand up straight and proud, to be strong, especially in the face of what she names adversity. Trouble comes with the territory, Gan says. Never too early to learn that.

I tie this bundle neat once more and stand myself up again. Out the back window of this room's the loblolly woods that's been my ground, where me and Farina's played since we could walk, where Big Robert and Preach and the rest of the men work—now even Jesse—timbering the land for Mr. Waldo Carnelian, that rich Yankee who came down here and bought up all this land and woods and Little Town too, I reckon. Not us, though, Gan says. Not us, ever again.

"Min." Gannie's voice ain't sound a bit like her own, seem like's coming from deep inside a well, thin and hollow, and it strikes my heart hard as a pick. Holding my worldly goods before me, I walk back down the hall and stand straight as I can, keeping eyes right at frill level.

7

"Please go and get into the car, Minyon. It's out front."

"Godamighty." That just slips out. If Preach heard it, he'd cuff me good. So'd Gan, before. Now she says nothing.

But godamighty, I fixing to ride in a car. And for just a sec, that one thing makes me forget all else.

I don't turn to Gan nor change words—two can play at this meanness. My legs move me to the screen door and it slams shut behind me, makes our dog Mingo set up and take notice.

And here it stands, parked in the dirt of Gan's yard—the sheriff's car, named so on the side. I've seen it before once, when they hauled Junius off that time he cut Lutie wide open, her big as a watermelon with somebody's baby. Seeing that, I'm all a sudden wondering if I'm going to jail for something, and my head runs wild trying to think what; then I know not, on account of this particular lady's got nothing to do with jail. She wants me for something—what I ain't know yet—but it ain't jail.

So out I go and look that car over a minute. Fine looking, even though's some dirty. I ain't know the best way to get in, but the window's open and that seems easy and quick. And just as I clear it and go head first into the back seat I hear something, look over by the side of the house, and there's standing my brothers Clarence and Jesse and about six or eight other children. My cousin Farina's got one hand clapped over her mouth, eyes shining white at me. Rest of them's laughing and slapping they knees, except for Jesse. He's the biggest of the bunch, eighteen now, and the look on his face puts me in mind of a snake, eyes burning into my head till my breath comes short.

Then the screen door slams and out walks the white lady and the sheriff. Quick as spiders them children draw up tight together and push against the house where you can't hardly tell they there, unless you know where to look. But I see them—even Clarence's little burr head smack in the middle of the rest. Sucking on that thumb again, already got his teeth sticking straight out from his mouth. If I was over there, I'd slap that hand away, and he'd look up at me with those big browns, and grin. But who'll take care of that now?

The white lady gets in the car and turns herself around in the seat. On account of thinking about thumbsucking, I'm near to crying, eyes swimmy.

"If you don't want to come, Minyon, say so now." Voice's cool as winter marsh grass, ain't he. She looks at me and I look at Sheriff Dawson's ear on account of he's looking at her. "I don't have the time nor the patience for tears."

Blinking like crazy, trying to hold in. I turn my head back to the house a little. Can't see Clarence now, just a dark blurry circle of arms and heads by the side of Gan's house. Tall Jesse still sticks out, though. And through the screen door seem like I see the outline of Gan's head. While I watch, it droops forward like she's maybe studying on her hands, or the floor, or the ground beneath.

I look back at Sheriff Dawson's ear, it seeming a safer place to rest my eyes.

"No, Missus." Voice comes out croaky, but I sit with my back straight as a rod, how Gan taught me a long time since, and I blink, blink, blink. "Ain't gone be no crying here."

Then the sheriff's ear moves and my head's full all a sudden with the noise of this car—which, godamighty, *I am riding in*—and then we're moving on down the road, out of Little Town first, past the big house, then loose from Arcadia altogether, and onto the wide road.

And I ain't looking back.

chapter 2

Don't know if's haints in this place or not, but might be, so I pull my knees way up close to myself and wrap my arms round tight. Preach says that's a sure-fire way to keep old ghosty haints out, nights—wrapping yourself up to where they can't find a way to creep in. That, or else keeping a pure heart, he says. So just in case, I grab a tighter hold of my knees and squeeze my eyes shut.

Never had a whole bed to myself before, much less a whole room, though this really's a porch. Still—to myself. I'm more used to fighting arms and legs all night, listening to Clarence's thumbsucking, or Christina's crying, or else Farina's teeth grinding back and forth, back and forth, else one of our cats stealing in and out the room, quiet and secret as haints. Else Jesse.

Not gone dwell on such, though.

Last night I was too tired to dwell on much of anything. It was dark by the time we drove up anyhow, after we left Sheriff Dawson in Jameston and drove out here in another car, big old black, rich-smelling one, must be hers. Never saw a woman drive before.

"You'll sleep here for now," she said, pointing to this bed.

Then out she walked, leaving me. I didn't even change words, just lay me down to sleep, holding my Gan's blanket close up to keep me safe and hoping not to dream.

First light, I woke like a shot, had next to no idea where I was. Saw the sun trying to shine through bushes, heard one dove calling sad and low to her babies, else maybe to her mate. Then I recalled yesterday, and Gan. Remembered car riding and how the sheriff's ear goes round and round like that big seashell Gan keeps the door propped open with.

Sadness swept over me like a wave; but in the meantime, my belly was growling about no supper the night before, and my head was saying I got to see where I am. Trying to keep both them quiet and hold that sad far off as I could, I got up for a look around.

My bed was pushed up against the house on a little porch with screen wire all round. Couldn't see out, on account of high bushes. Ain't much breeze getting through either, and already's hot as the hinges, still and piney-smelling.

Feet stepping light as they could, I crept round the bend of porch, and directly found another porch stretching wide and grand cross the house front. Still there's high bushes I couldn't see around, all the way to the door at the end, where the steps came up. Slipped myself down there, floorboards squeaking every step. Wasn't anybody anywhere.

The yard's big, with grass grown high as me, most. When I peeked round the corner of the house, I spied some shanties out in the side yard, round back. They're grown up, too—weeds climbing the sides like they looking to hide something ain't supposed to be there.

Peered through the window of the house, but even pressing my nose flat against it, it's too dark to see much of inside. Door squeaked fierce as floorboards as I opened it, but I wasn't about to quit now. Anyhow, my belly was making as much noise as the floor and the door put together.

Inside was a big dark room. Two windows, but still not much light—not much light anywhere round, far's I could tell. Room's about big as Gan's whole house, though not much furnishings in it—one big old couch and a couple chairs. Smelled old and lonely.

I kitty-cat stepped through, into a long hall, dark as pitch, but with a light coming from a door at the back. Floor squeaks counted time with me. Seem like the house breathed round me—in, out, in, out—whining soft and steady every time I stepped on it. Made the hairs on my neck rise up.

Opening the door at the end of that hall, I was greatly glad to find a kitchen. On the table by one wall's a bowl with apples in. Ready to cry, I appreciated that so. Good and hard, too—first bite set the juices in the back of my mouth to squirting, jumping for joy. Gobbled that down fast and grabbed another, taking my time.

By the back door stood a tall white closet. When I opened the door, cold air rushed out at me. Icebox's what it was, but no ice in it; which beat all, but I was too hungry to wonder overmuch. Inside was a bottle of milk and a hunk of cheese, and when I held that bottle to my lips the milk was so cold and sweet going down, I thought to myself I'd made it to heaven without having to go to the pain and trouble of dying first.

Broke off a hunk of cheese and headed back down the dark hall. It's so quiet I was wondering if I was the only one round. Didn't seem near as scary with food in my belly, though.

Sat on one end of the big couch, gnawing on the cheese, letting each bite get soft and warm in my mouth so I didn't even have to chew. Old couch, looked like, but pretty cozy. My mind went wondering what my folks's up to over there in Little Town, Gan and Farina and those. Little bub Clarence, even Jesse. Balled myself up tight, and in a minute my eyes got blinking slow, and I reckon I fell asleep.

"Didn't come to this stinking hole in the wall to set up shop in a fucking fleabag." Heard a woman's voice, not much more than a whisper, but mean and bitter. Foul-talking. "Fucking tricked us, is what."

I stayed still as a turtle, opened one eye to a bare slit. Standing over by the front door's two white ladies. From the light behind them, I made out that one's little, the other big.

"Honey," the large one put her hand on the little one's shoulder. "We just got here yesterday. She told us there'd be some setting up time."

She touched the little one's dark hair. "Give it a chance."

Little one jerked her head back. "What fucking choice we got? You got enough money to get back to Chicago?"

Big one chuckled, said, "No, Chantal. But I'm sure I know how to lay my hands on some."

"Well." Seem like the little one relaxed some. She looked toward the dark hall. "Place gives me the heebie-jeebies, though." I ain't even sure what that is, but it put my neck hairs at attention right off.

The little one turned her head from the hall and looked slowly round the room. By when she got to where I was, her head quit turning. I stayed stiller than death. Ain't believed she saw me, it was so dark and me so quiet. She stared. I didn't breathe.

She saw me, though.

"Jesus Christ!" She screamed the Savior's name high enough to break glass. Sent me straight up off the couch, screaming too—not as high as hers—she got the highest one I ever heard. Then the big one whipped her head round and screamed too. Her scream's much deeper than our two. At that, the little one hollered even higher, the three of us screeching most in three-part harmony, loud enough to raise the multitudes.

Maybe we'd of screamed till Judgment Day, left to ourselves. As it was, though, I heard a snap, the room filled with light, and over by the hall door's standing the Missus, looking like the angel of God, with her long white gown and goldred hair puffed out past her shoulders.

We all stopped screaming at once. In the back of my head I was marveling at electric lights, which I only saw one other time, when Gan snuck me into Mizz Gertrude's house to show how they work. The other two's standing with mouths stock open, but no sound coming out.

The large one fetched up her voice first. Looking over at me, she started laughing, said, "Why, it's nothing but a pickaninny, Chantal."

That Chantal one looked hateful at me, then stared down at the floorboards like she's studying straight lines.

"Didn't know this was going to be a mixed house." She just muttered it under her breath, but I reckon the one who's supposed to hear did. "And ugly at that."

"If you have a problem with how things are around here, Chantal," the redhead stared straight into the top of that little dark head so hard I was afraid it'd split open from the pressure, but Chantal only looked harder at the floor, "feel free to pack your bags." Words were a little changed, but everything else reminded me of the offer she made me the day before.

When the Missus moved, seem like gliding—couldn't see no feet, and her white gown swept and swirled all round her. She floated over next me.

"I suggest you be nice to Minyon, girls. She's going to help us out around here. Word is she's a real hard worker."

"Minyon?" The big one sputtered my name out. "Her working name's Minyon—that scrawny little thing? That's rich."

My turn to study floorboards.

"It's her real name, Bess," said the Missus. "She's our live-in help."

First I knew what it is I am round here. Still not sure what and all it means.

"Well, Minyon, welcome to the house, then." That Bess seem to think a lot of things're humorous I can't see the funny in. I kept my head down, peeping over sideways. She held her dress out, made a little dip at me. "I'd be honored for you to empty my chamberpot, anytime."

"Chantal." The Missus' voice had no fun in it at all. "You mean to stay or go?"

"No place in particular to go." The little one still didn't look up. Room was quiet as Monday morning church. In a bit, she turned her head, eyes glinting with something. "I guess I'm staying."

"Don't guess, Chantal." Missus didn't raise her voice, but it was scarier than hollering, hard as a rod.

"I'm staying, then."

The room went quiet, like everybody's thinking.

"Smart girl." Missus' voice was all business. "Minyon and I've got our work cut out for us, the next few weeks." She almost touched my shoulder, but didn't. "You two have a job, too."

The two of them looked over at her, Chantal seeming like she was fixing to complain.

"Starting this morning, this place will be filled with workmen and tradespeople. In a town this small, word of mouth advertising is going to make or break us."

She glided over near them. "Your job, girls, is to make us. Get pretty," she reached out and almost touched Chantal's hair, "and see that you stay that way."

Not that I believe I'm any kind of judge about white-woman pretty, but it struck me these two had a big job ahead of them. Chantal's no taller than me, and most as skinny—chest flat as a boy's. In the face she resembles a scared little mouse, with big-lidded eyes, dark circled all round, sketchy little black eyebrows and lips so thin the top one's near invisible. Hair's dark and spread out round her face like a fan, then cut off sharp at the chin. She's got a crooked part down the middle, where her head shines white through. For some reason, that part gives me the willies, bad.

At least Bess ain't so sour-faced. Big as a man, though—shoulders door-wide, big old hands, and a mouth takes up most of her face. Pale skin with washed-out looking brown hair to go with, freckles standing up like bugs all over her wide face and bare arms. Looked like a farm worker, from where I stood.

Not that I figure to be any kind of judge.

The Missus set me to working, and before long, just like she said, the place was full of men: yard men, carpenter men, men on the roof, delivery men—even two men hooking up, praise Jesus, real bathrooms with flush toilets. Whole place bustled and stirred how Little Town will on a summertime Saturday evening—folks getting ready for some kind of *occasion.*

The Missus showed the men around, signing things, pointing out jobs, just plain bossing everybody in sight—seemed very good at it, too. And me, in between working my tail off, I took it all in.

I was in one of the upstairs rooms, scrubbing down the dust of ages top to bottom, when I spied the door opening on one of the shanty rooms out back. Through it came two those white girls. And if I hadn't seen them going in, swear to Jesus I wouldn't of known them coming out. Wasn't nothing short of a miracle.

Chantal stepped out first. Dressed in red, looked like a firecracker when the sun hit that fine shiny cloth. Shortest skirt in the world—way past her knees, held up on the shoulders by little straps made of what looked like jewels, and low enough to show even that pitiful bosom she's blessed with. Hair waved fine and close to her head, eyes painted dark, mouth wet and full, shining red like that shining red dress. Hot and dangerous, she looked.

Out behind her strolled big Bess, on the highest high heels you ever saw—that girl looked six foot tall from where I stood. She was wearing a pale blue wispy something, resembled a fancy nightgown more than a outside dress. Hair piled up on head, dangly earrings catching the sun, and a set of bosoms big enough to take your breath.

About took mine, and for sure I wasn't the only one. By that time my head was practically stuck out the window, taking them two in. I heard something sounded like a huge caught breath, and looked round to see that all a sudden wasn't a man out there working. They'd froze in place like salt licks in Sodom—one halfway up a ladder, one with his hammer raised but not struck, one about to fall off the roof of the shanty. Whole world quit moving, seem like. My heart went to pounding inside me, and I knew something, right then: a powerful spell'd just been cast on us all.

Bess was the one broke it. Looked over, saw me hanging out the window, hollered up at me, "Better stick it back in, Minyon, before it falls out!" She laughed. I heard eight or ten white neckbones swivel my way, made me pull back so quick I hit my head on the top window. It slammed shut hard enough to shake the room, and next I knew, I was flat on the floor. Seeing stars.

Lying there, putting two and two together, what I came up with was something Jesse told me about once, where men pay women to lie with them. I shook my head, trying to shape meaning from it. Best I could figure, though it didn't make a lick of sense, my old sweet Gan'd sent me to a hellacious bad place—my churchgoing Gan, who don't truck with sinning, wouldn't even let me talk to Lutie after she jumped bad like she did. Who tried for all she's worth to keep Jesse out of our sleeping room. She must not know what this place is, was all I could believe. If I could once get back to her and tell her the truth, she'd be bound to let me come home.

Right then and there, I made up my mind to get back to Little Town the first chance I saw, make things right with that woman I missed so bad.

Directly I got up. When I looked out the window, standing off to one side so nobody'd see, everybody was back to business out there. No sign of those two white girls. But I knew what I knew.

By evening I was tired as'd ever been. The Missus told me I could fix a plate when I liked, the food's laid out on the kitchen table. It was some fine spread, too—sliced ham and turkey, fat slabs of fresh smelling tomato, hard white cheese, bread. Wasn't nobody round. I heaped a reasonable amount on my plate, headed for the side porch where my bed stays, and commenced to eating.

In a minute came the Missus round the corner. Her eyes wided up when she took a look at my plate, which all a sudden did seem pretty full, after all. Mouth was full, too, but I reckon I know what's polite.

"Care for some, Missus?" Ain't even sure she could make out the offer, on account of me trying to talk round the food in my mouth.

She didn't answer, just picked up a chair from alongside the wall and sat down across from me. I chewed for all I was worth.

"Your granny was right, Minyon." She leaned back in the chair and crossed one leg over the other. In her one hand's a small glass of something pale she sipped along on. Her perfume smelled jasminy. There was just enough evening glow seeping through the bushes to light up her hair. I thought to myself if the angel Gabriel was a woman, he must would look something like that. Gave me the dry throat, couldn't get my food chewed down good.

"You really are a good worker." She looked at my plate, glanced at my working jaws. "Good eater, too, I guess."

She laughed then, and I smiled through my food. She looked away quick. "Probably smart enough to have figured out by now what kind of business we're setting up here, right?"

I nodded. Food finally got itself down my gullet.

"Well?"

I looked off to the bushes behind her, fixing to parade my smartness. "Hoe house, ain't he, Missus?"

She moved her head a little when I said that. In the darkening light, her eyes gleamed and shone. Took a little sip, then asked, "How old are you, Minyon?"

"Fifteen next month, Missus," and before it was out my mouth good I felt bad about telling the truth, on account of it made Gan out a liar.

She didn't seem to notice, though. Just sighed a little. "That's how old I was, Minyon, my first year as a working girl."

She leaned back in the chair some, stared up at the ceiling. Voice was low and soft, most crooning in the evening air. Reminded me how Preach's voice gets when he loses himself in Bible storytelling.

"Fifteen," she said, "and alone in this world." She heaved up a sigh, and I settled back to hear the tale I know's coming.

Outside the crickets rubbed they legs, whispering singsong at us. A bullfrog cleared his throat, urging, tell on, tell on.

"Mother died that year—a weak heart." Her voice caught. She angled her face down and swallowed hard; but for all her seem-like sadness, they was something removed about it, like she'd said it all a hundred times before, or maybe like she's making up a story for me to hear. "And I never knew my father at all."

Who does, I could say, but didn't. Didn't say nothing, just listened for all I was worth.

"See, we have that in common, Minyon, you and me. Being alone in the world—a pair of orphans, aren't we?"

Startled me, to think about us two having anything in common, but I wasn't about to disagree. "Yessum," I nodded.

"I wasn't as lucky as you, Minyon—I didn't have a grandmother to make sure I didn't get myself into trouble. What I had instead was a man who made sure I did."

The Missus took a big swig, near-about finished that drink, heaved up another big old sigh and closed her eyes. "No point in going into the whole thing, Minyon. Suffice it to say one thing: if you let them, men will be your downfall. Remember that. Keep yourself for yourself."

She slit one eye open over toward me. I forgot not to look at her, I was so took up with her storytelling. Instead of thinking about how she's a sinner and so, I just saw how sad and lonesome she seemed. Needful.

"All I ask, Minyon, is that you work hard for me, do your best." She sat up, leaning close enough so's the sharp tang of her breath snaked up my nose.

"You can learn a lot from me, Minyon. We can help each other." I lost myself in green witch eyes, ready to study.

"Are you with me, Minyon?" She's so powerful it was hard to catch my breath.

"Yessum, Missus," was about all I got out.

She drew back, seemed satisfied. "Good girl." That's all she said, and I was right glad to be called it.

She stood. The moon was out by then, crickets praising the Lord for the light of it. She turned to go, then looked back.

"And Minyon—call me Miss Ariadne. Got that?"

"Yessum, Missus."

She said nothing, just stared down at me.

"Yessum, Mizz Addie." About close as my mouth'd consent to go round all them little sounds. Hoped it was close enough.

Seemed so. "Good night, then."

And off she stole in the shadows, shimmering and blending and fading, leaving me to wrap myself tight as I can against whatever haints may or may not be round here.

Right this sec, when I close my eyes, my head goes swimmy and I see things swirling round: Gan behind that screen door, head drooping; bug-eyed, thumbsucking Clarence; the sheriff's round-about ear; Chantal and Bess with they magical changement; tall Jesse's dark shadowed face; my own self, curled up in a ball. And over us all, Mizz Addie spread large and thin, watching and moving us how she wants us to be.

Coolish nights like this, Jesse used to come sneaking in between me and my cousin Farina, with his sharp boy smells and his big man pecker, trying to get with us. Started years back, when we all stayed in that same room, and kept on even after Gan changed our sleeping arrangements how she did. It got to where I'd take myself out the bed, and later, after he's gone and I'd creep back, Farina'd sometime cry quiet, keeping to herself. We didn't talk about it, after. I got plenty of curiosity about what all goes on with that, but remembering the one time Gan caught Jesse trying to creep in with me—how she screamed and hollered to the Lord about mortal sins and eternal damnation raining down on us all—that about cured curious, far's me.

Anyhow, Farina showed me how to take the edge off curious with my own hands. This might be what Mizz Addie meant, keeping yourself for yourself.

So doing what I'm told, I finally fall asleep.

chapter 3

"Child, this ain't no place for the likes of you." That's what Ophelia said to me this morning, when I showed her my new room. She comes every morning now to pick up the cartload of laundry those two girls manage to mess up in a night. She's the biggest, strongest, sturdiest woman I ever saw, can wad sheets, tie them tight up in a ball and lift it with one hand, balancing it over her head. She is something else. Even Mizz Addie seems admirous.

I reckon it is a wonderment that somebody like me's got a room like this. All mine—not a porch cot, not a little closet-size one to share with however many more. Four square white walls, a real bed with a clean cover, sheets, my own pillow. I'm situated at the short end of the outback building—that's what Mizz Addie calls this place I'm lazing a little this afternoon, where I'll sleep tonight and every night from now on, where Bess and Chantal earn they living. Outback.

She chose a name for the main house, too. Hazelhedge, on account of the bushes grow tall round the porch. They'll keep prying eyes out, she says. Got a wooden sign made up with the name carved on it, painted red and gold, and stuck on a post in the front yard grass.

You ask me, that name ain't half fancy enough to suit. Ain't anybody asked, though.

This's been the busiest three weeks I ever lived through. And what's happened to this Hazelhedge in the between-time's about as wondrous a miracle as that change came over them two hoes. Which Mizz Addie says I ain't supposed to call them, but in my head I tend to.

Mizz Addie's big on proper names for things. "*Ladies*, Minyon." That's what she wants me to call them. "Sporting ladies, if you will." According to her, this ain't no hoe house, either—it's a sporting house.

The last bit of furniture got delivered today. Mizz Addie took me round to every room, teaching me proper names, telling what I'm supposed to do. Keeping it all straight seems like one big job.

Like the light in the front parlor—so big it took three men to hang. "One hundred and twelve crystals, Minyon." She pulled over a chair and stood on it, reached up and unhooked one of them. Light sparkled like splinters in the room.

"Twice a month, Minyon, take these down, one by one. Soak them in vinegar, scrub them thoroughly, dry them to within an inch of their lives, and put them back up." She hung the crystal back.

"One hundred and twelve, Minyon. And they've all got to shine. No point in having a chandelier, otherwise." My head filled with points and sparkles and the bigness of the job. I felt relieved when she turned the light off and the room settled back to daytime dark.

Two marble tables in the parlor need just once-a-day wiping with a damp cloth, she told me. Brass tables and trays and the spitting bowl—spittoon, she names it—got to be polished every week. Silver, too. "No sense in having nice things, Minyon, if you don't take proper care of them." Real big on proper.

And dust—Lord, never seen so much stuff got to be dusted every day: lamps with green and red shades, hanging from chains, fringes swinging long and low; fancy paintings with gold frames where the paint stands up thick enough to feel with your finger; mirrors about everywhere you look, with carved gold frames got plenty nooks and crannies for dust to hide in; big vases Mizz Addie says come from clear round the world, place named China.

That ain't all I got to do, either—not even close. In the cleaning department, they's sweeping every day, and scrubbing two toilets plus this one special one made just for cleaning your cooter. And washing the dishes they dirty up at night. Glasses take forever, how she makes me do—one at a time in the sink, same as chandelier crystals. She's awful big on one at a time, too.

Then's the sheet situation—enough to keep a body hopping all night. Every time Bess or Chantal get through with a customer, I got to run up, rip off sheets, and put on a fresh set before the next show starts. Seem like the biggest waste in the world to me—sometimes ain't a wet spot nor a stray hair on them.

After seven or eight times a night, I'm wore out with it and ain't even half through. The linens make a huge pile in the kitchen, so every morning when Ophelia comes and takes a look, she shakes her head, rolls eyes to heaven, says something like, "Lord, those girls been *too* busy last night." Then she commences wrapping the sheets up to take home. Every day she brings a clean load, takes home a dirty one. Mizz Addie says clean linens's the surest sign of a first class sporting house. Which this one surely must be.

Ophelia don't stay but about an hour, getting that laundry together, and sometimes she's come and gone before I get to see her. Which I'm sorry for, on account of they's something about her comforts me, with her big old wide self. Makes me want to crawl up in her lap, quit cleaning and changing sheets and polishing and learning the proper name for everything in sight.

Two other coloreds work here now, but don't none but me live in. Sarah the cook, she comes round four of an afternoon, cooks the one real meal we eat, which I'm generally starving plumb to death for by then. I eat on the side porch cot used to be my bed, a heaping plate of good food every afternoon except Sunday, when we pretty much got to scrounge for ourselves.

Sarah's the blackest woman I ever saw, with hair pulled back in a bun so tight it makes her eyes slant up. Ophelia told me she's a good woman, tends to a sickly mama and a passel of brothers and sisters. But her face's never once cracked a smile since she's been here—maybe since she's been born, for all I know. She's so dark and fed-up looking, I do my best to stay right out that kitchen when she's in it. I ain't know what that woman's so mad over, but I ain't particular about getting in the way of it.

Then they's Frank. He comes in time for supper most days, and two times now he's sat with me on the side porch. We don't talk much, just sit together for eating. He fixes drinks for the customers, nights, and generally makes himself useful. "You have to have one good man in a proper sporting house, Minyon." That's what Mizz Addie says. "Keeps everybody honest."

I reckon Frank is one good man—ain't been round him enough to say for sure. He's one big man, anyhow, most has to stoop to come in the door. Got him a wife at home, Ophelia says, though he ain't yet mentioned that. Got nappy hair close to his head, turning white some places, so must be's got some age to him. Strong as a mule, too, picked up one heavy old chair Mizz Addie calls damask and moved it clear cross the room one afternoon, like it's nothing. Cleaning in there the next day, I pushed against that thing with all my might, couldn't even budge it. I basically plan to stay on the good side of Mr. Frank, too.

Mizz Addie don't limit her teaching habits to me. She's all the time teaching Frank about the liquors he's in charge of—they got proper names, too, naturally. She tells them to Frank, makes him repeat them back to her. French names, she says. Best wine comes from there, else Germany. Bourbon from Kentucky. Don't make no nevermind about gin, she says.

Wednesday's bootlegger day. She and Frank meet him at his truck, checking what he got, arguing about the price of this and that. First time he came, in the midst of price-haggling, Bess came yawning out her room, round three in the afternoon, half dressed, looking for coffee and a smoke. Bootlegger's jaw dropped open when he caught sight of one large bosom about to come loose its wrapper.

Mizz Addie ain't slow. She caught him looking, said something low; he nodded, then she waltzed over to Bess; and in no time flat, hoe and bootlegger'd disappeared into Bess's room. Ain't as much trouble about pricing since, and Bess's got Wednesday afternoons booked regular.

Not that regular bookings's a problem, anyhow. The problem's more that they's too much business for just two hoes to handle, I believe. Hard as I working, I surely ain't hankering to trade places with them.

Those girls' days start much later than mine—generally by two or three they up, Chantal whining for coffee, Bess looking like what Mizz Addie calls the wreck of the Hesperus. She tries to make them stay close if anybody's around, on account of she don't want possible customers making judgments based on they daytime looking selves.

Starting somewhile after supper—which is breakfast for them—around four-thirty or so, they get into their fixing-up routine. Sometimes, when I'm on break a minute, they let me watch. Chantal paints her pointy little nails blood red every day. Bess's nails're bit down to the quick, but she's got some long purple ones she glues on right before she goes into the parlor. I sometimes find one of them nails in a bed when I change sheets. Gives me a real start, every time—like Bess's losing parts of her own self in there.

Chantal, she likes bickering—all the time picking fights with Bess. They screech a minute, sometimes Chantal throws a little something, and then before you know it, they make up, and Bess's piling Chantal's hair high, making little curls round her neck, arranging her long feather scarf just so. Sometimes Chantal makes Bess's face up for her, saying Bess don't know how to do it right. They try on this and that, telling each other what looks good and what don't. Then fight some more, then make up.

Mizz Addie don't allow liquor in off-time, says drink leads

sporting ladies down the wrong path, but they generally manage to lay hands on some anyhow—specially with Bess spending her Wednesday afternoons how she does. So they take a little nip along and along, while they fixing up.

Then round eight, they troop on over to the main house parlor, drape themselves cross the furniture, play records on the victrola. Chantal, she likes the blues. Bess likes just about everything. And round about nine or ten, work starts.

How they stand it, jumping in bed with any old man's got the money and inclination, I ain't know. In between changing linens, I now and again catch sight of customers. They every kind of man you can think of—saw one so fat he had slits for eyes, fingers like wild hog sausages, following close behind tiny Chantal, who's leading him off to her outback room. Some smoke big fat cigars Mizz Addie keeps in carved wood boxes, and they drink till you can smell the trail of them, stale and smoky, follow it with your eyes closed up tight. They're loud and sometimes mean, I hear Chantal and Bess talk about that, how sometime they treat them so rough. It gets bad enough, they's Frank around. So far nothing's got that bad, though.

All night long, those girls traipse back and forth between parlor and rooms, with me right behind, tearing off sheets, making up beds. One night I made up twelve beds for Bess. Next day she groaned and moaned; Mizz Addie said twelve's about the limit for a high-class sporting lady, on account of health reasons. Though how she knows I ain't sure—she never does the serious work her own self—just glides round the parlor, making sure every man's got a full glass, and the music's right, and they blood's getting up.

Mornings, round three or four, the place clears out and I get to go to bed. Sometimes they's another customer or two still making time, but I ain't responsible for the last change of sheets. Those girls tend to sleep in the last set, anyhow—too tired to care, I reckon.

So my job might be about to run me ragged, but I am greatly glad not to have theirs.

Mizz Addie says we all got to do double duty right now, on account of just starting up like this. "Hazelhedge will be the finest sporting house on the east coast, Minyon. People will come from far and wide, just to see what we're all about." She tells how houses like this're what she calls a vanishing breed, since New Orleans got shut down, since what she calls the big boys done moved into Chicago, which is way up north. "We will make history here, Minyon."

Ain't know about history, but I made me six dollars here. Keep it in my dresser drawer, right by the bed. Open up that drawer, pull out them six bills, smell them, rub them, think what all they can buy.

Then I think of Gan, her head so still and drooped behind that screen. Our ramshackle shanty, fatback and rice. How fine I'm eating now, got my own clean room, this money. About how Clarence needs somebody to keep him from thumbsucking, how I miss my cuz Farina, our loblolly days, our whispery nights. My eyes fill then, can't keep from, and I hold Gan's blanket close like it's some bit of her here with me.

A car door slams outside. I open my door one tiny crack, see a huge, shiny, black car, with a silver medal on front. And who I see standing beside it makes my breath draw in sharp.

He's in a dark suit, hat pulled low and to one side some. Ain't seen him but three times, but that's enough. I know him. It's Mr. Waldo Carnelian himself, the one owns Arcadia, and Little Town, where my folks been left behind. He's standing right in this Hazelhedge yard, like my thinking about home's done conjured him from thin air.

I feel a hard stab at my heart, want to run right out, call to him: How's my Gan? Clarence still sucking that thumb? Farina's cat have babies yet? Jesse got himself in trouble with the boss again? Course, even if I did, he wouldn't know the first answer— he don't much truck with us. Seeing him here, though, I all of a sudden feel more like I been gone from home three years, instead of three weeks, and I miss my people something fierce.

Mr. Waldo, he just stands there looking at Hazelhedge,

hands in pockets. In a minute, he walks over to the sign, runs one finger over the raised-up wood part. He turns to head over my way now, seem like's looking straight at where my eye shines out from this door crack. My palms go sweaty and I'm fixing to slam the door shut and lie down in my bed like I been napping all along, when I see Mizz Addie come round from the front of the house. She tippytoes up behind him while he walks on, must don't hear her. She steps right up and puts her hands cross his eyes, knocks his hat right to the ground, and I think to myself, uh oh, gone be the devil to pay now—when Mr. Waldo turns quick, picks her right up off her feet and swings round with her. They both commence laughing to beat the band, her arms round his neck and Mr. Waldo looking like a sixteen-year-old schoolboy instead of something closer to fifty, and one of the richest men in the world, according to what Gan told.

He puts her down, and they stand out there in the yard and kiss like's not a bit of shame in it. Watching, I picture Mizz Gertrude—that's Mr. Waldo's wife—with that thick-as-a-treetrunk waist and what Gan calls her overabundance of chins. Still, she's been pretty nice to us—passing along her old clothes and sometimes sending down this or that leftover party food. All I can think of right now, though, is that Mr. Waldo'd have his work cut out for him, trying to lift that woman and twirl her, how he's just this minute doing Mizz Addie.

By now the two of them's walking round the place. Her arm's through his, and they strolling like Sunday promenade time. She points, he talks, she talks back, gazing up at him. Every now and again, he just looks down at her face, and even from this far, ain't no mistaking that he's crazy-fool in love. Mizz Addie's hair's all wild and gold round her face, and she's dressed in some wispy something where you think you see skin here and there underneath, but ain't sure if it's that or just a trick of the light. She glows like sunrise, and he's helpless as a whipped pup before it. Near makes me sorry for him.

Coming close to outback now, maybe close enough to spot one shiny eyeball, so I close my door quieter than quiet and slip over to my bed. Hear them now, passing by. Rumble of his voice, then her low music.

"She's fine, Waldo, really. A good little worker. You were right."

Pondering what that means a minute, losing track of they talk, when I hear his voice clear as if he's in the room with me: "Old Gan Tucker's going downhill fast," he says.

They sufficient close now for me to hear the crunch of feet on dirt, the rustle of clothes. I stay so still I hear my own eye blink.

"She knew it, too—tough old bird—when she came to ask me about finding a place for Minnie." Feet pass right by, walking on. I hear her ask something, don't make out what, but when he answers back, seem like I hear Jesse's name spoke, though I ain't sure.

As I lie here looking up at the ceiling, it all fits together—how it is I come to be here, and Mizz Addie, too. Mr. Waldo's part of the answer for us both: Mizz Addie's here on account of him being so fool in love with her and rich enough to do something about it; I'm here on account of him, too—him and my Gan together.

One at a time, everything that's happened slips into place in my head—*click, click, click*—till it's straight as a cornrow. The last part falls with a bang: my Gan's bad sick, for sure.

Which knowing makes me sit straight up in my bed, reach over to my dresser drawer, pull out six crisp dollar bills and stuff them in my shoe. Going to the door, I see Mr. Waldo and Mizz Addie disappear round front. Got a pretty good guess where they headed. All's quiet from Bess and Chantal's rooms—they busy fixing up. Frank's not here yet, Sarah's cleaning up after supper. And me, I'm out of here, slipping quick and sly from my door to the woods, smelling my own sweat and the pine straw, six bills in my shoe, a whiff of Mizz Addie's French perfume, and something like freedom.

Got just one thought in my head. Gan's going downhill fast, and I got to run like the wind to get there before she reaches bottom.

chapter 4

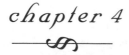

"Farina!" I whisper-yell to pitch blackness, my head stuck through the window of my used-to-be room, which for all I know's empty as my stomach that's been growling and groaning this last couple hours, ever since the sun left good. Ain't no moon to shine the way, nor a stick of starlight showing.

"Cuz?" Not even the sound of Clarence's thumbsuck, and in my head comes a picture of what might be happened since I been at Mizz Addie's—maybe they all picked up and hit the road for New York, else a terrible sickness descended, how Gan said came before, and wiped them out, every last one. Back of my neck goes to goosebumps the second I think that, and I pull my head back into the night air so the window can't fall and cut my head off while I'm busy whispering "Cuz" to a room full of ghosts.

Gan sleeps in the upstairs bedroom, only one up there, says she's got to have relief sometime from us kids. Stairs're so rickety, they squeal like stuck pigs when you step on them. In the living room's maybe Jesse and some them other boys, so I got nowhere else to try except right here.

"Farina?"

What's that little fool doing? She's the hardest sleeper—Gan says she might could doze right on through Judgment Day. Be sorry then, I reckon, but that don't help now.

I'm flat bushed myself. Seem like days ago I left Mizz Addie's, instead of hours. Feet hurt bad—my dogs're killing me, is how Bess calls it, after a long night of prancing and dancing in the parlor, then traipsing back and forth to outback. She claims a hoe spends more time on her feet than on her back, contrary to what folks might think, and it's the feet gives the most worry.

Mine's giving me plenty right now, what with all that walking and having to tippytoe up to this window. My legs complain so hard I got to pay them mind, so I lay myself flat on the ground beside Gan's house to rest, which feels comfortable enough to do me a sec.

I was wrong about the moon—lying here looking straight up I see a teeny slice of its pale self, like a half pie crust's had all the good ate out of it. Most the good's done spilt out of me, too, feel like.

Surely did take me a trip today. Can't wait to tell Farina all about it—I can picture her eyes getting bigger and bigger, then she'll clap one hand cross her mouth and rock, she'll wonder so. I'll tell about stepping through piney woods, keeping the big road in sight all the time on account of I know it leads to Jameston and once I got there, I figured I could get back on to Little Town without too much trouble. Thinking I could keep to pine woods all the way, but forgetting what I know, because all a sudden the woods ran out and so did the land and only then I remembered the river that cuts through. And ain't nothing but one narrow bridge carrying cars cross, and wagons, and me, if I was going.

Ain't know the name of that river, but it's fast, one white-head wave pushing hard at the heels of the next, hellbent on getting where they headed, home to mama-ocean, I reckon. It's some darker and meaner than my river Waccamaw, where Arcadia and Little Town sit, where we catch fish and the wild hogs wash themselves, where Mr. Waldo's rich Yankee friends come to hide in tall marsh grasses and shoot the greenheads when they fly, where we sometimes go for a swim, in the parts where gators don't laze false-sleeping on the banks. Dogs ain't smart nor lucky as we about that—somebody loses at least one every year or so to old stick-dry, slow-looking gator, moves his big slime jaws in a eyeblink.

Anyhow, I got over that first river by not much looking down or to the other side, where automobiles went by, one sufficient close to make my arm hairs stir in the breeze of it. Fingers cramped up from grabbing the hot iron sides, and inside my hands's stained red by when I reached the Jameston side. But reach it I did, and pretty proud on account of it.

So I reckon I felt about ten feet tall, strutting toward Jameston right on my own, like I never did before. Passed the paper mill that opened up last year, looks like a town to itself, it's so big. Gan says Mr. Waldo had something to do with bringing that here—supposed to save this town from poordom. Can't wait to tell Gan what else Mr. Waldo's brought.

This ain't the side of town I'm too familiar with, but pretty sure about where I had to head: Water Street, where all the stores sit, down alongside this same river. When I got to the end of that street, seemed like all I'd have to do's turn away from the water and walk till I reached the Waccamaw, then straight on to Little Town. I was figuring to do me a little shopping along the way maybe, spend some the cash's burning a hole in my shoe, then head on home before nightfall, if all'd go as planned.

Course it didn't. First off, when I got to Water Street, dusk's already setting in and all the stores were closed up tight. I was disappointed enough to cry, on account of I planned on buying Gan some little something, and maybe me, too, and now I couldn't. Still, the whole thing was pretty stimulating, walking by myself downtown. Always'd been with Gan before, else Sylvia, Mizz Gertrude's snooty white housemaid, sometimes took me along to carry things. By my own self sure felt different.

So down I strolled broad Water Street, not a car nor wagon

to stir its dust—just me, window looking, thinking what and all I might buy me, next time I come to town.

I was about square in front of the Jefferson Davis Hotel—three stories high and years back, about as fancy a hotel as's likely to be this side of Charleston, according to Gan, though ever since Jameston lost all its good cash crop called indigo, the hotel changed hands oftener and oftener, till's nothing but a shadow of its former glory. That's what Gan tells, she knows that kind of history.

Still seemed pretty grand to me, though I admit the last three weeks did largen my idea of grand some. So busy trying to peek in through the dark windows, see what I could see, that I didn't know I had company till one big white hand clamped down over my shoulder, scared me so bad I jumped and tried to whip round. That hand was heavy, though, and held me still.

"What you think you're up to, girl?"

Turned my head sideways, but he's too far behind to catch clear sight of. Then I saw him reflected in the window I faced. Police, one of the Jameston ones, not county.

Tried to open my mouth, but ain't know exactly what to tell I was up to, so nothing came out.

"Talking to you, girl. Where you from?" He spinned me round, and I saw he ain't all that much older than me, maybe twenty or so. Had a serious grip on my shoulder, but I could tell right off he ain't mean through the eyes like some. Still, he asked one hard question—where I'm from?

Even though I thought I was froze up, couldn't talk nor think, my training kicked right on in. Hunching up my shoulders how Gan and the rest do when they talk to white folk, specially white folk wearing a uniform, I looked at a place halfway between his chin and shoulder.

"Right round here," I said, mumbling and running words all together, letting my mouth go some loose and glazing my eye over. Looking stupid. Good at it, too. In a sec, his hand eased up on my shoulder, his chin relaxed, mouth went to curving up. Then he dropped his arm altogether.

"Get on back there then," he said, but still not too mean. "Before you get your high black ass in trouble."

"Yessir," I mumbled and started off, letting my feet drag just right. "Thank you, sir. I sure will do that."

He walked off whistling, seemed happy enough. And I was free, though my heart thumped inside my chest hard enough to bust loose. On account of I just realized what being free might mean—having no fall-back at all: no Gan or Little Town or Arcadia behind me, to explain me or keep me safe, no Hazelhedge nor Mizz Addie neither, to pay me wages and feed me. I was all a sudden scared to death of free, running down the road toward Little Town fast as my feet'd carry me, till my breath came in big heaves and I had to stop under a oak tree by the road and rest.

Didn't anybody else mess with me on the way, but I had one more bridge to cross, the narrow, rickety one over the Waccamaw. My dark river ran swift and quiet underneath, seemed like looking up while I passed over, saying: welcome back, girl. Gurgled like it's glad to see the bottom of my feet.

Then dark fell—*boom*—like eyes shutting fast, and nothing but blind memory got me to Gan's house, that and the lights I saw shining at the big house, helped me mark my way.

All that, and now nobody's here to tell. Pretty well disgusted about the whole thing, I tiptoe up once more, go to whisper out one last, lonesome "Cuz," when over my open mouth claps down a hand. And right before I scream I stop, because I know that smell. It's Farina hand, and I'm so happy and startled my knees give in again, and I'm once more flat on my back, seeing stars.

Straight over me, one headful of wild frizzed hair darker than night sky creeps out, blocks my heaven-view. One high-pitched whisper asks: "Minnie? That you, Min?"

"Who you think, fool?" I pick myself up, put hands on hips. "The haint, come to pull you out of bed in the middle of this night, take you to ride?" I laugh out loud, forgetting myself, filled up with hearing that voice I ain't known till right this minute how much I missed.

"Sshhh." Even in the dark, Farina's big eyes gleam.

"Sshhh your own self." I creep closer. "Help me up."

"Naw, Min, wait. I'm coming there." And quick as she says the words, she's out the window and standing next me. Can't wait another minute now, I reach out and hug this slim cuz of mine, and she me, and it makes me know something: this's the first time anybody beside myself's touched me since three weeks ago. Makes my throat close, knowing that.

Ain't no time for crying, though. Farina leads me away from Gan's house, out past where Preach and them stay, and Big Robert, and Lutie's mama. Then I know—we headed for the stump, our in-the-woods place, where we been playing and sharing since we wasn't tall enough to see over it.

Now we two's sufficient big to sit on the rough top of it, and it broad enough to hold several more. Just us tonight, though, and me impatient as all getout. Farina acts strange, if you ask me, and I've just about had it with her. Hadn't I been gone three weeks, walked all day, starved near to death—and ain't she standoffish? What in this world's she thinking about?

"Farina." Fixing to ask straight out, but she's too quick, interrupts out-of-breath me.

"Oh, Min," she cries, then puts her head down into both hands and sobs like her heart's fixing to bust.

Mine, too. I got to know. "Is it Gan, Farina? What?"

But she just keeps crying, doesn't answer; I watch, till directly I got to keep her company and start up myself, even though I don't know the history of any of it yet. Just can't help it. So we two sit on our stump in the woods, me crying about things in general, she in particular, till she can quiet enough to tell.

Finally: "Gan's sick, Min. Preach says she's sick unto death, for sure."

On my feet fixing to go, when out whips Farina's hand, holding me back. Her voice comes, high and scared. "You can't go, Min. She's sleeping, too sick for company. She won't be happy to see you, anyhow."

That stops my feet and heart. I sit back down, feeling low as low. Still wondering—what is it I did, made Gan so mad?

"You know what it is, don't you, Min? It's Jesse." Me and Farina's so sister-close, we sometimes see into each other's head, answer things ain't been asked.

"He's real bad since you been gone," her voice quavers how Gan's does at hymn singing. "He told Gan she can't get you far enough away—said you're a Little Town nigger, his blood-kin nigger, and he gone get you back."

Her whites gleam at me, then close up and disappear. "He says no sister of his gone get no high-faluting hoe house ways."

It's all a sudden very quiet in these woods. No bugs nor nothing, everything holding breath still, while I take it in: if Jesse knows where it is I been sent, then Gan must, too.

"Gan says how it's bad enough, what Jesse's been doing with me all this while. Bound to make us terrible trouble down the road, she says." Farina's hand lays itself over mine.

"But with you, Min, she says it's much worse. Jesse lying with you's mortal sin, hellfire forever on you both." She slips her arm round my shoulder. "That's why she ain't be so happy to see you, girl. She's afraid for you, loves you too much to let you spend forever-after with the devil, she says."

Lord, ain't I tired. My mind opens up like a wide blank space. Inside there I weigh a load of things at once: eternal hellfire, Jesse's plan for me, Mizz Addie and her hoes, scary freedom I had me a taste of. Way in the back part, other things jump, hoping to be noticed, too: aching feet; empty stomach; good, strong Farina-smell. And then they're all shut out, disappeared, and all I see in there, taking up every last bit of space, is that outline of Gan's head through the screen door, last time I laid eyes on her. Fries my mind, and before I know I'm planning to, I'm up, running a downhill race straight to Gan's house.

Time I get there, I'm some winded but don't stop. Straight to the front door—*screee*—on the hinge. Breath comes ragged as I ease myself in, but that noise seems the least of my worries. No sound from the front room as I walk by—ain't know if Jesse's in there, but it don't much matter, all that does right this minute's at the top of these stairs. Squeak, squeak, squeak—I two-at-a-time them till I'm on the landing, opening the door to Gan's room.

And ain't it dark—but my eyes're used to that now, and where Gan's bed is I see a tiny lump must be that woman, don't hardly take more space than messed up bedclothes. Whole room's filled with Gan-smell, dry and soury-sweet, makes my insides ache for lonely, even though I'm right here in the room with it.

"Gan." Creep forward now, but that lump don't move. And now I get my own lump, deep in my throat—growing larger by the second, every step I take forward. "Gannie?"

Standing right beside now, and don't that thin sliver of moon decide to help, shine its weak self square down on this thin sliver of Gan's face, showing above the sheet. Her hair's so wisp and spare I swear I see head skin under, maybe the bones holding it together, too. Get down close, close enough to see her face looks more like a baby's than old woman's. I lean forward and press my lips to that forehead, where the skin's thin and grainy as ash.

Cool to touch, like she's done halfway or more to where she's heading. Afraids me to think that, but I do. When I draw back, though, her eyes're open, looking steady at me. She don't move, nor me—we just stare face to face, breaths mixing between us; then a stream of wet starts at her one eye and soaks directly into the pillow. Ain't no sound to it at all. After a bit comes a little moving under the covers, so in I reach and find her hand, which I hold till it goes still and her eyes close, though the wet still comes steady. Lay my head down next hers on account of I'm so tired, too.

Next I know, I feel Gan trying to speak—Lord, she's too weak—and up comes my head, watching them little lips done dried up to next nothing, trying to get round some words, croaky little whisper. No way to hear better, already closer than close, so I watch her lips move in this pale moonlight, see can I guess. She don't pause, says the same two words time and again, like it's the most important thing in this world. And directly it comes to me, fills me up with joy and surprise.

"Happy birthday." That's what my Gan's trying to tell, with all her near used-up might. And she's right—it *is* my birthday, though I clean forgot myself. But Gan didn't—about gone from this world, and all she remembers is her Min's birthday. And don't I see right that second how loved I am, and don't I feel it clear to my toes?

Too grateful to praise God, I praise Gan instead, kissing every inch of that wisp-haired head. And she all the time keeps moving those lips, celebrating me.

"Min!" Farina's sharp whisper's at the door, though I ain't heard her come up the squeaky stairs. "You got to get, now!"

Gan's lips quit moving. Peaceful looking, and I know it's true, what Farina says, know that's what Gan wants, too.

Ain't gone see my Gan again, that's a truth I feel in my heart; and I hold my head very still one minute to clear it out and make one good clean memory-space for skin, hair, lips, eyes, nose, cheeks, head-bones; for one-of-a-kind Gan smell, whisper touch of thin-bone hand under sheets, pale breath sound, taste of skin on my lips.

"Min!"

It's done, and I'm gone from here. But not empty now, carrying this new Gan-space inside me for all time.

Down loud stairs creak me and Farina, but I'm past worrying about that now, ain't thinking about Jesse, on account of being filled up with Gan. Farina's face's so worried though, I'm quiet and quick, for her sake.

We're on the porch outside in a skinny minute—two dark ghosts, ain't we, stealing still as smoke through woods and houses in dead night. I tap Farina to tell her so, but when she turns to me, her face freezes, at the same time I hear the screech of screen door behind.

"What the fuck's going on out here?" Deep voice don't bother with whispering, on account of he thinks he's the boss of things. Ain't boss of me, though: I'm my own.

I swivel round to face him, discounting Farina's frozeup scaredness. Look straight into the face of my brother Jesse, who stops in mid-yawn, one arm half-stretched in the air. His face changes from sleepy to shocked to mean and something else, so quick it's hard to track.

"You!" he roars, about knocking me backwards with his loudness. That outstretched hand comes down and grabs my throat—his one-hand fingers're about sufficient long to close round it. "Where the hell you think you been to, girl?"

So surprised, I can't answer, plus his thumb's pressing pretty hard against my Adam's apple. So I just gurgle, which don't please him much, on account of he takes his free hand and frams it cross my face, sets my cheek to burning and stinging something fierce. Behind me I hear Farina cry out like she the one been slapped silly. Then I don't hear much else, because Jesse's hand's coming back round, turning my other cheek hot and red. I feel my feet lift up off the porch floor, and between kicking thin air and trying to breathe, the night turns all a sudden darker than pitch and my head goes plumb blank.

Come to on dirt ground—ain't know how I got off that porch—and the air all round's filled with yelling I ain't got sense enough to hear for a second. My throat's burning and it's hard to swallow, but I can, for which I am greatly glad.

Staying still as death, I open eyes up one tiny slit. Standing on the porch's Preach and Big Robert, holding Jesse back. Farina's up there, too, still yapping and sobbing so loud, and Preach's hollering about Jesse must be lost his mind, what's he think, acting so when Gan's upstairs, close on to meeting her Maker.

"Ain't none of your fucking business, old man." Never heard nobody talk like that to Preach. His voice gets high and wild and—*crack*—he slaps Jesse's face. Then Jesse lights into him, Farina screaming, Big Robert getting in between, windows banging open all round, doors slamming, high-pitched screaming, low cussing, moaning. I start creeping my small self right along next to dirt, praying I'm dark enough to pass and they too busy to notice—inching cross the clearing of Little Town, then scrambling for all I'm worth into pine woods, loud roar lingering in my head, the feel of Jesse's fingers still strong on my neck.

Never spent a night in the woods before, but no better time to start. With big old loblollies blocking sky, I can't see past my hand, and'm all turned round anyhow, might could end up in bed with gators, if I ain't careful. Else them wild hogs live in these woods, meaner than gators, though you can't tell it by the taste, sweet and stringy when Big Robert guts them just right and cooks them all night on a slow spit.

Just thinking about one dripping hunk of that plopped down between two pieces of light bread, sopping up the sweet hot gravy Big Robert makes so good, and the back of my mouth squirts, like I fixing to light into a plate of it. Ain't I starving, ain't I tired and sad? Sleepy, too.

Next I know, the palest bit of morning light's shining through tall pines. Must've slept, but don't remember falling. I open both eyes quick, recollect where I am, and don't move till I can figure what it is woke me.

Nothing but pine woods to my front. I swing eyes to one side—same story. When I swing them to the other, though, I laugh out loud, on account of being about spitting distance from the big dirt road leads into Arcadia—like I been camping by my way home all night. Must be some smarter than I know.

Thinking about the miles I got to go, eyeing a pine cone and wondering how it might be to gnaw on a while, when it hits me what shook me loose from sleeping: a car's coming. I peek out round a myrtle bush and see Mr. Waldo's car, the big one he never drives himself, got Lawrence for that, with a special driving hat he wears. Don't take no thinking on my part, my legs got they own mind: I run out in the road, right in front of that large black automobile, arm-waving like the star sinner at a tent revival, fixing to be saved. Which one way or the other, I reckon is a fact.

Car stops short, dust clouds up round it and me. After it clears a bit, Mr. Waldo rolls down the back window and leans his head out, asking, "Why, what have we here?"

Reckon he ain't smart as he looks, else the dust's in his eyes, so I help him out. "Me, Mr. Waldo." In case that ain't enough, I keep on. "Minyon Manigault."

He blinks and starts to say something or other, but I hurry up. "Can I please catch a ride to Mizz Addie's house called Hazelhedge?" And in case he's thinking about telling me no, I sweeten the pot a little. "It's my birthday, Mr. Waldo—and my dogs're killing me. Please?"

Who knows what he might say then—not me, on account of, for the third time lately, my knees give plumb out, my head spins, and darkness grabs me in close.

Now ain't I smack dab back in my own outback place again, with Mizz Addie not saying much about me running off, just her and Mr. Waldo talking low by the car and then her sending me to my room and in a minute Ophelia out here with some food, tsk-tsking when she gets a look at my neck, and Sarah coming out sometime later, saying I best rest up today, on account of's lots of work needs doing, not saying much else, just looking at my neck, looking mean, like them finger marks's my fault.

That's how this day goes by—me just lying here in bed, drifting in and out, one folk and then another coming by to check. And now it's night and still Mizz Addie ain't made me work, and I'm scareder than scared she ain't gone want me no more, I'm gone be free.

And don't my big toe reach down and push hard against the iron footboard that holds my bed together, pushing, starting up my own night rhythm. Rocking, how I done long as I can remember, used to make Farina groan in the night and kick at me sometime, tell me: stop that damn rock-rocking, all the time rocking, Min. Farina don't rock—but ain't grinding your teeth how she does some way the same, setting up some kind of rhythm, to help you get through the night? Like Clarence's thumbsuck, that's his rhythm.

Outback here and in the main house, they's rocking rhythms going on about anywhere you care to look. In the parlor they rocking, listening to blues, rocking back that dark liquor, letting it fill them with that feelgood sleepiness comes from rocking; rocking they jaws, making words come, sounding good, make them look good, leading up to the rocking they come here for after all, Bess and Chantal's kind of rocking, all them men trying to get inside, rock themselves right back to where all the rocking starts anyhow; and don't I have in my head that hum-hum-humming sound Gan used to make back most before I got memory, when she'd rock me in that old porch rocker, same as she rocked Clarence when he come along; and ain't that humming rocking, like as the whushy noise my Waccamaw makes, rock-rock-rocking along, longing to get back with that ocean.

I push myself back and forth, back and forth, on account of rocking's comfort past knowing, and we all got to do it, some way or other.

chapter 5

"So then he says to me—and he's got this whiny little voice, Min, makes you want to slap him—he says, 'Just this once, Bessie, one more time, please, and I won't ask again.'"

Bess takes one big sip of her dark drink and looks sideways over where I sit on the bed. I don't say nothing, never much do when she's trick-talking. She's satisfied I'm listening, though—leans forward and straightens the mirror on my table, puts one more coat of paint on her eyelash.

"So I says, 'Let me think about it,' and act like maybe I will, maybe I won't, while he sits there twisting his hands. That's his favorite part, the waiting. His little bald head gets red and wrinkled up and worried looking." Bess stops with one eye, sips a little, starts working on the other. She laughs under her breath.

"Then I heave a big sigh, and I get up and start pacing around the room some, like I'm trying to decide, and he gets real antsy then, his hands fluttering, neck jerking—he can't stand the suspense." She grins at me, though it's not the kind of grin makes you think about laughing.

"Timing, Min. Half of being a good whore's timing." Now

she opens her case of purple nails and that little gluepot, starts dabbing and pressing, talking all the while.

"Finally I says, 'Oh, all right. Get on the floor.' And he starts shaking so bad he can hardly get down there, the whole time saying, 'Oh, thankyouthankyouthankyou, Bessie.' I say: 'Don't call me Bessie.' And he's laying himself down on the floor, apologizing, fumbling, all over naked as a baby. I say: 'Did you bring it?' And he reaches under the bed and pulls out the folded up rubber mat he hid under there when he first got in the room, and pulls it underneath him.

"And I finally do it, starting down by his toes, stand over him and dribble a little on his feet, and say, 'That enough?' And he can't even answer, he's moaning and shaking so, and I move up to his knees and let a little stream go—it takes a lot of control, Min, *finesse*—and then up to his wong, which is straight up now, looking me right in the eye, so to speak, and by the time I get to his face I let go, and so does he—gone to heaven, hollering, 'Yes, yes, Bessie, thankyouthankyouthankyou,' and crying."

Bess studies the hand that's got the long purples. The other hand's still a bit-up mess. She shakes her head. "Ten minutes later, he's folded up his mat, cleaned himself up, dressed, paid me my five-dollar tip, and walked out, looking for all the world like the fine upstanding Jamestonian he is. And the best part is, I don't even have to take anything off but my panties."

She sips right along, near finished with this glass, but got her flask tucked inside her brassiere, which has to be a right snug fit. "No wick-dipping, no muff-diving—just good, clean fun. That's my kind of john, Minyon."

I think to myself that white folks surely got funny ways of doing things.

Which I certainly know more about now than I used to. Partly on account of Mizz Addie, but more because of Bess, who's been spending break time in here with me ever since the two new hoes got here last month, ever since Chantal took up with that Katrina, who calls herself Swedish but who Bess claims's more likely from Podunk, Kansas, wherever that is.

"*Katrina.*" Bess spits that name out like it's something nasty on her tongue. "Cow name—she couldn't do better than that?" How Bess tells it, hoes don't ever use they own name. Bad form, she says—bad luck, too—can't even *tell* the real one. Every hoe's got to make herself up one.

"Bess is the common name for a queen," she tells me. "And I consider myself as royal a common piece of ass as any." As usual, Bess laughs about stuff it's hard to see the funny in.

Ophelia says I'll get tainted, listening to Bess's trick-talk. Not that she's even round here afternoons, but Sarah or else Frank must of told her how Bess comes hanging round my room.

"Child, just do your business and keep to yourself and your own kind," Ophelia tries to boss me, even though she's only here a hour or so in the mornings. I act like it chafes me, which pleases her and me both. "Mixing never leads to nothing but trouble, Min, best be remembering that."

Who Ophelia thinks I'm fixing to mix with, I ain't know. For sure not one of these white tricks round here. That's not my job, and besides, I stay plenty busy without.

Did get invited to, though, about two weeks back.

I was passing between outback and kitchen, my arms full with two bed loads of sheets, thinking about nothing except how fast hoes can mess a bed and how my work's doubled since Katrina and Sal started hoeing in them upstairs rooms. It was Friday night, the whole place's rock, rock, rocking, and me hustling to keep up. By now I'm pretty good at it, too. Even Mizz Addie says so, heard her brag on me to Chantal—who was probably complaining about how slow I tend to bring her coffee. Good enough for her.

Anyhow, my mind was solid on work, when stepped in front of me's a white man—tie on crooked, shirttail half out, glass of bootleg in one hand. Looked lost to me, I figured maybe he'd been taking a piss in the wood and can't find the way back.

"Parlor's up that path, sir," said I, in my best maid voice. Mizz Addie gave me lessons on how to speak to what she calls customers and the rest of them call tricks. Which I ain't yet figured out for sure who's tricking who in this game.

He said nothing, just stood in my way, wobbling some. Leaned up close to me and put one hand on top my sheets, his stinking breath strong and hot enough to fry eggs. "Yeah, but where's your room, honey chile?"

Truth of it is, I ain't caught what he meant till I felt his other big paw reach round the side of me and clamp itself down hard on my behind, squeezing.

"Always heard a good piece of dark meat'd change a man's luck, honey. I sure could use some of that."

I was fixing to open my mouth to tell him polite as I knew how that I'm just the maid round here, not a hoe, this ain't no mixed house, when he swung one of his legs round behind my knees and gave a little push. Directly I was on my back, he on my front, the sheets in between, and him wrestling with his belt.

"Sir," I started out, but just that sec he let out a big bust of air, then lifted clean off me, clean off the ground, matter of fact. I looked up to see his pale self dangling from the dark hand of one Frank Washington.

"Looking for the parlor, sir?" Frank's deep voice sounded interested and polite as could be. Trick didn't answer, just wheezed some, and kicked his feet around. Frank let up on his collar then.

"Follow the path to the left, sir. Parlor's straight ahead." Sir didn't look round nor change words, just headed off where Frank pointed.

"Min?" Bess's face's all a sudden right up close to mine, so close I see more than I want—the hundred or so pits in that pasty skin of hers that she's all the time trying to fill with powder never quite matches up right, those pale eyes that get glazy when she sips enough old dark drink. "Where's your mind off to? You're not going to get weepy on old Bess again, are you?"

I ain't cried but once in the whole four months I been at this house, and Bess's my one witness. She ain't tend to let me forget it, either.

46

It was a Tuesday afternoon then too, me taking my evening rest and she assembling her hoe getup, when we heard a car out in the yard. Both us went to the window, on account of we don't get deliveries or regular visitors on that day, as a rule, Tuesday afternoons being one of our quietest.

Faces pressed to windowpane, we saw Mr. Waldo step out his car. Driving his own self, so evidently's planning to stay a while—when Lawrence is with him, it means he's just on his way to or else from Charleston where he catches the train north. He likes to check in regular.

Mizz Addie must of known he's coming, on account of she was waiting on the porch, came flying down to meet him. He held out both arms; she ran straight into them. Both they faces's so wide open and happy, it was hard to recognize them from they everyday selves. Mr. Waldo looked like a young man, and Mizz Addie for once ain't all business. Or seemed so from here at least.

My breath fogged the bottom part of the window, and right up behind me Bess heaved a big old wet sigh. "That's what every whore dreams of, Min, but few ever get—a rich-bitch sugar daddy to set her up and keep her honest. Give her good reason to open her eyes in the morning and her legs at night." She heaved again, and the uptop of the window steamed up too cloudy to see past.

"I just hope Miss Ariadne Fleming knows how lucky she is, that's all." She leaned back from the window, shoulders drooping heavy, mouth corners down-turning. "Wasn't for him or one like him, she'd be humping, same as the rest of us."

Those two headed into Hazelhedge. I settled back down on the bed—had about fifteen minutes before evening work started up—and Bess got herself back to business. I watched her face and it changed too—that sad part she generally keeps covered up, it stole down over, even though she's humming something under her breath while dabbing on the brightest, bluest eye paint you ever saw, whole time humming, humming. Can't carry a tune worth a lick, so it took some time to know the song. "Ain't we got fun" it was, one of the songs they play on the victrola over in the parlor, and laugh loud and hard to, nights, their laughless laughs.

Just then came a hard knock. I was so busy Bess-watching and she so busy mirror-looking, that both us jumped straight up like we'd been caught in the act. Bess ain't hardly had time to hide her glass by when the door opened, and Mizz Addie's gold head came shining through. She looked pretty serious, and I was afraid she's fixing to fuss about Bess being in here, or else tell it's time for me to get working, else ask how come we two's spying out the window.

Didn't none of that happen, though. She didn't even look at Bess, seem like, just me. "Mr. Waldo's here, Minyon."

If she turned her head and glanced at the window, she'd of seen what's left of two big breath-clouds that'd tell her I *been* knowing he was here. She didn't, though. "He'd like to talk to you a minute, Minyon. Out here." She glanced over at Bess then, but I couldn't tell what she's thinking.

"Yessum." I got up and walked where she was, body all a sudden lead-heavy, feeling like it took forever and a day to get to the door. Mizz Addie drew back when I finally got there, and I saw Mr. Waldo standing out under the oak between the kitchen and outback. For some reason, I couldn't go no further, just stopped there, like if I didn't go over and he didn't speak, whatever it was he had to tell ain't happened, not till he said it, and I heard it.

"Go on, Minyon." She did what she always does: instead of touching me, she came just sufficient close to make me believe she did it. It was enough to get my feet moving. And ain't it long to cross, that dirt between him and me.

"Min," was all he said by when I finally got to him. Tears'd been falling down my face from about the halfway point, made me deep ashamed, on account of that's one something Gan taught me: never let them see you cry nor laugh, Minnie—got to keep the real you hid under a bushel. Mizz Addie knows it, too— says it some different, but it's the same thing: keep yourself for yourself. Even Bess and the other hoes, with they madeup names, they know it. And here I was, coverless, spilling myself down my face, for the world and Mr. Waldo to see.

No help for it, though. He opened his mouth to speak again and I wanted to lay my dark hands cross that white face, jam them hard down on his thin-lipped mouth, keep that voice inside. But that I wasn't able to do, and here those words came, sounding just like I knew they would: "Your grandmother passed on, Min. Last week."

I stood looking at him, took a minute before the "last week" part set in, by which time he's already explaining it.

"She asked me especially to come tell it. Asked me to wait until after the burying." He studied his own hands. "It's done, Min."

"Is she resting next to Cap?" It was the first thing came to my mouth.

Mr. Waldo's face went blank, and I saw he ain't got the slightest. "I don't know the details, Min." He at least had the gracc to look sorry.

Gan always told how she wanted to lay next to Cap when she went, same as she lay twenty years before he gave up struggling, heart exploded in his chest. "Pentup hate, Minnie, that's what killed your granddaddy Cap. Pentup hate, and plumb uselessness." I remember her sad head-shaking. "That same hate your granddaddy held inside till it killed him, Min, that's the hate your brother Jesse carries round with him on the outside. It's gone kill him just as surely, too, unless some something happens to change it."

Jesse—he knew about Gan's burying wishes. "Did Jesse see to the putting down?" The tears still flowed like sprung well water down my face, but I was well past worrying about that.

Mr. Waldo's face got even seriouser. He waited a minute, then just told it. "Jesse's gone, Min. Left the day your grandmother died. Nobody's heard from him since."

He reached across the distance between us then, patted my

shoulder, mumbled, "I'm sorry." Doing the best he could, I reckon, which I appreciate, but the milk of his human kindness runs some thin for my lonesome self.

There he left me, standing in the oak tree shade, while he joined up with Mizz Addie by the porch, and in they went together to Hazelhedge. And I was all a sudden filled slam up with hate for they in-love selves—couldn't swallow nor breathe, crawled to the bushes by the house and threw up my just-ate supper again and again, till I was emptier than air.

Up behind me where I knelt frozen came big old Bess. She lifted me, carried me to my outback room, lay me in my bed. She was crying too, black and blue mixed and falling down from her one painted eye. Then she went to stroking her hand cross my forehead, over and over stroking, like maybe how so she could rub the sad right out of me, smooth my skin till the black turned to white bone, too dry for tears.

After while I hushed crying, wore out with it. And besides, they's work to be done, ain't he.

But Bess ain't let me forget it. She's so desperate for friends, she's chose me, and I got to let that be.

So here we sit, one more Tuesday afternoon, me and Bess—her trick-talking and readying for nightwork, me letting my mind wander to other same afternoons—when just like before, we hear a car door. Just like before, both us rush up to see what we can see. I feel hairpricks on my neck, and I some way know another bad something's fixing to be, know it even before I see it's Sheriff Dawson's car in our yard this time, instead of Mr. Waldo's, even before I know it ain't never gone be Mr. Waldo's car again. Not in this lifetime.

Just like before, here comes Mizz Addie down from the porch. She ain't running or laughing, of course, just her usual glide-walking, her everyday madam-face on. Sheriff's watching her close—like always, looks like he could eat her alive. She's oh-so-polite, ain't she, every inch—you can see it from here. She knows and he knows she ain't much care for him—but ain't business business?

50

Off comes his hat when she gets right up to him. Above my head Bess's making fog on the windowpane again. Me too, and we don't neither one say nothing.

It's all over in a minute or two. Reminds me of the one picture show I ever saw, where you ain't know what folks's saying unless you read the cross-bottom words, piano music playing the whole time for background noise. In my head's playing Bess's old ain't-we-got-fun song, while I watch Sheriff Dawson's lips move, while I watch Mizz Addie's paleness go paler yet, her swaying some back and forth, saying nothing, his lips still moving, till her eyes close one time and don't open back, knees give way and down to dirt she goes in a crumple.

Both us suck in sharp breath, still don't talk, while Sheriff Dawson makes no move to break her fall, just lets her go, then bends down slow, movie-silent. As he goes to pick Mizz Addie up, he slips one fat hand down inside her blouse, so quick and sly you might could miss it if you's to blink. Then up he lifts her close to his face, turns that whorly ear of his and heads for the house.

Halfway there, and here comes Frank out the back door. Got on his sheriff-shuffle, blank-eyed and shy-acting. White and black men now both move lips some, back and forth, in which meantime Mizz Addie rouses herself and's let down.

She shakes the sheriff's hand—don't his finger linger on skin—and seem like I see Mizz Addie all over shudder, how a highstrung horse'll sometime do. Then he's off to his car and Frank's walking next Mizz Addie and into the house.

"Whew!" Bess lets out one big bust of air. "Wonder what the hell's up now?" She bustles round, finishing up. My work's calling me too, but I ain't wondering what's up, been somehow knowing it, knew best when that fat white hand stole skin from sleeping Addie. What I'm wondering is how we gone get through it.

Mizz Addie don't come out her room this night. Frank says she's resting, told him to put Katrina in charge for the evening.

Her blond self loves that job, all prissed and puffed up with it, which makes Bess poutier than ever.

I finish my work, bring in one last sheet load to the kitchen. Must be round three or so, still pitch black out. In walks Mizz Addie, whiskey-reeking, hair haywired, wrapper open, naked as a newborn under.

"Need something." Mumbling and stumbling, don't seem to even notice me. Makes her way to the refrigerator, opens it, and stands in front—stands, doesn't move to get food, just soaks in that coldness I can feel from way over here. Ain't no question she needs something, but I ain't believe it's in there.

"Mizz Addie?" Don't turn nor start, just keeps soaking up cold. And in a minute she takes to shaking, starts up at her red-gold, wild-headed top and works its way down through till her toes pick up the rhythm. Kitchen floor takes it up, sends it over my way, shaking up through my feet into my head.

I go over and close that cold door, look at her face and see she ain't know I'm in this world. She's not looking like some down-to-earth angel now—more like a little lost girl, most young as me. Moves like an old woman though, while we make our way through the hall and into her bedroom, while I help her back into bed, pull the covers up and tuck them in. Find myself humming, humming that one song like Gan used to—Hush little baby, it goes, talking about mockingbirds and papa-love.

Her shaking keeps up even after she falls asleep, body taking it in spells. I set myself on her lounging sofa—chaise, she calls it—and watch those covers tremble, trying not to think what it might mean, if Mizz Addie's really nothing but a scared little girl. Fall asleep to that worry.

Wake up to the sound of scritch-scratch-scratching, dry as bones. Ain't till I open one eye that I remember where I spent the night.

Mizz Addie's out the bed. She's sitting at her carved wood desk, got her back to me, and the scratching noise is her, putting words to paper. She writes quick, arm moving back and forth, whispering under her breath as she goes. I can't hear what she says, though. Directly she quits writing, whispers some more, then balls up that paper, throws it down, and goes to pen-scratching again.

"Minyon." Her voice saying my name out the clear blue makes me start up three inches. She ain't turned nor looked round—how'd she know I'm up and watching?

"Please bring me coffee." She sits straight enough to most bend backwards, and I'm all a sudden worried she's gone be mad with me, done slept my black self on her lounger, breathed her same air all night.

"Yessum," I say and sneak from the room feeling thievish. She ain't look up.

Glad to see Ophelia's large self in the kitchen, acting just like usual, bundling sheets, humming to herself. She stops when I come in.

"Lord, child, must be one long night. You are a mess!"

"Big trouble, Ophelia. Something with Mr. Waldo."

"That's right, girl. I know that, mm hmm." Then she commences with the laundry again, and humming. I ain't know what to do except get to making coffee, which I do.

Ophelia says nothing till the coffee smell's thick in the kitchen. Then she quits her bundling, comes to stand next me. "Mr. Waldo's dead, Min, and that's the truth. But you ain't, nor me, nor Miss Ariadne Fleming in yonder. We're here, kicking still. We may be got trouble, child, but ain't that life?"

Then she puts one large arm round my lonesome shoulders, feels like a warm, soft blanket I'm praying not to give up. Makes me think about Gan, about adversity, which this surely is. "Us living ones," Ophelia says, "we got to stick together."

By when I get to Mizz Addie's room with hot coffee, she already looks like her own self—hair combed and pulled back neat, day dress buttoned up tight.

"Thank you, Minyon." Lord, her voice's high and mighty. Still ain't mentioned where I slept last night, though. Maybe she ain't noticed.

"Go wake the ladies, please. Tell everyone I want to see them in the parlor."

My mouth drops open, then winds itself back shut. No point in arguing, even though it's not but eleven, same as middle of the night for hoes. Still, when Mizz Addie means business, that's all they is to it.

Those girls sure can cuss a person, though. That Sal tends to throw things, too. But I get it done, and by the time a half hour's gone, they're sitting in the parlor, yawning and growly, snappish as all getout. I bring in coffee and get set to go on about my business.

"Stay, please, Minyon. I want everyone to hear this." So I hang by the door. The four hoes sprawl pretty unladylike on the sofa and a couple chairs. The room ain't been cleaned yet, still smells of whiskey, cigars, perfume and us all, plus some randy, leftover man-smell.

"I have bad news." Don't horse around at all, stands straight in front of this sleepy-eyed bunch and gets right down to it.

"Our friend and benefactor Mr. Waldo Carnelian is dead." Voice don't quiver, even when four hoes suck breaths in all at once and Bess lets out one quick sob.

"I wanted you to know it from me, first thing, and to know what it will mean to Hazelhedge and all of us." She ain't reading from no paper, but I know she's seeing words writ from short time back pen-scratching.

"This place is ours, ladies—and we're going to keep on doing what we're doing, what we always planned." They sit up a little at this—this notion of "ours"—and seem ready to hear what it is they always planned.

She goes on: "We're going to make it the finest sporting house in the country, a house people will talk about in Chicago, in San Francisco, New Orleans, New York—even in Paris, maybe." Voice's quiet, but somehow's got a certain ring to it, makes it seem big and grand and true. Hoes's is wrapped up in it—Sal and Katrina done lost their sleepiness, Bess's a goner—

don't take much for her dreamy self. Even Chantal's sour face lights some.

"Whatever it takes, ladies," and with the word they seem to straighten some, trying to fit it now, "we've got to be prepared to do." She looks round the room, even at me. "All of us."

We stay quiet. Behind me, traveling from the kitchen, down the hall, to the doorway where I stand, comes the sound of Ophelia's humming.

"We can do it." Her voice's strong music, sounds like when she's storytelling to sway folks to her way of thinking. Just that sec, the sun chooses to slant his bright morning self through the window behind Mizz Addie; and when the light hits that head of hair, it about blinds us all. "Together, we can," she sings out, and it's all I can do not to holler hallelujah and fall to the floor.

By afternoon, we're all going about our business like nothing's changed. It is, though. We got ourselves a mission now.

Along round five, Sheriff Dawson's car comes pulling up. He steps out, takes off his hat. I watch Mizz Addie go out where he is. Their lips move, first his, then hers. And I ain't one bit surprised when she takes his beefy white arm and leads him into Hazelhedge, smiling up into his round face like he's the very one she's been waiting all her life for.

Far as me, I work in the parlor. By the time I finish, the shine on the brass hurts your eyes, the wood gleams dark and silk-smooth, the overhead crystals sparkle like new-made knives.

chapter 6

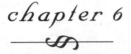

"Death comes in threes, child." That's what Ophelia said, this morning. "Mark my words." That large woman's all the time telling me to mark her words.

Still, they are floating round inside my head this dark early morning, while I make what I hope and pray's the evening's last trip from outback to kitchen this go-round. Got two loads of linen, Chantal's and Sal's, and figure everybody's up with their last trick for this night. Parlor lights're out—that's my usual sign—and the bicycle Frank rides to work's gone from next the shed.

Most November now, and black air's got some bite to it, reminding me who's just round the corner, fixing to chill my bones.

Death comes in threes—the words hum round and round. Can't hardly see over the sheets I'm carrying, keeping to my path by feet-memory. One owl hoots when I'm most to the kitchen, makes me draw in breath sharp and gaspy, then laugh to myself. Ain't but half that laugh out when it all of a sudden stops in mid-throat, on account of something traps it there, something hard and cold as steel, tight round my swallowing spot. Right next to my ear comes a hiss of breath, and my nose fills up with the stink of bad bootleg.

I drop the sheets and dig my elbow back, hard's I can, how Frank taught me. Don't catch nothing but thin air, though, and then that arm's grabbed up behind me, hard. One arm's left, and little breath, so I put all I got into it. This time my elbow connects up solid. The tightness round my throat and arm lets up a minute, and I whirl around, free.

The light from the kitchen reaches just far enough to help me see for sure what I already reckoned by smell and feel.

"Jesse." Name croaks out from my sore throat.

Holding his middle, he looks over at me. Light catches his eye, but don't give nothing back, seems black and deep as a pit with no bottom. His breath's some short, too, but it ain't a problem making out what he says: "Minyon." My name sounds dirty on his lips. "White man's whore."

Then he goes for me again, but I jump quicker, making for the kitchen steps. Almost there, too, when he grabs hold my dress and pulls me back. He's wise to my elbow trick this time, and keeps clear. Quick as blinking, I'm on the ground looking up at my brother straddling me, his one hand tight round my neck so my best talking's no more than a whisper.

"I ain't a hoe, Jesse." Try to turn my head side to side, let him know I'm whispering truth.

He leans down close. "Ain't gone be one anymore anyhow, Minyon. You coming with me, girl. Then when you go whoring, it'll be on my say-so. Not white folks'."

Jesse's hated white folks from the first time he laid eyes on one. Gan tried to sway him, told him flat out it's gone kill him one day. "You got to work around them, boy. They's ways." But Jesse has his own ways, don't care to learn anybody else's.

Ain't no future in arguing, far's I can see, so I try another tack.

"I can't hardly breathe, Jesse." Which ain't no more than the truth of it.

Hand loosens some. I take heart, fish up a grin.

"How's everybody at Little Town," I whisper, sociable as possible from flat on my back.

It takes him back some—he stares down at me.

"How's Clarence?" I say, pretty sure I'm on the right track now. Fingers loosening more—he must be remembering we're kin. "How's our cuz Farina?"

When Jesse laughs low and tightens up his hold, I know I just some way miscalculated, bad.

"Farina's just fine," he says, squeezing my neck with one hand and reaching with the other to loose his pants. "Farina, she's big as a sow, fixing to have old Jesse's baby before too long." He pushes my dress up, shinnying his pants down at the same time.

"Yessir," he grins, leaning forward to position himself better, strong bootleg breath in my face. That extra weight on his hand against my throat makes my eyes flip back in the sockets some. Colored lights go to swimming, and seem like his voice's coming from way far off, a dream chant.

"Jesse's done left his mark on Farina, and now he's gone leave it on Minyon, stronger and longer than any white man's mark."

Mark my words, Ophelia's morning voice floats through my head along with Jesse's whisper-words. How can that large woman know so much? *Death comes in threes*—and I go to kicking my legs when I recollect those words, on account of I ain't ready yet, got things to do yet.

But my legs're some tired, ain't they, and I'm all a sudden not so much gasping for air as feeling sucked down in some powerful dark dream place—it's calling me, and maybe I see the outline of Gan's head, calling, and my eyelids go heavy. I feel Jesse on me but don't feel him, too, on account of I'm floating now, I'm in the dream now, I *am* the dream now.

Then Jesse grunts and flops his face down close next to mine and I begin slow waking from that dream. I feel his breath push up through him and blast into my face, stinking of rot whiskey and something else, and his whole body goes limp and heavy. They's a high little wheezy noise too, which it takes a minute to know's my own breath, trying her best to get loose from my tight-up throat.

Jesse heaves another big sigh, wet and long. Must've done had his way with me, but I ain't remember and can't feel nothing. I'm still living, seem like. And the air all round's filled up with some new smell I ain't know the name for.

I open one eye, and for a minute all I see's something looks like gray clouds. I think maybe I ain't made it after all, maybe I'm on my way somewhere—when the clouds part and I seem to see the porch light shining on Mizz Addie's red head, glowing like's a fire round that pale face, which doesn't make a lick of sense, so maybe I'm still dreaming, else gone on to the next world. I let my eyes close back—it's hard to breathe and my brother's heavy upon me, and I'm tired near unto death.

"Minyon." This Mizz Addie look-alike angel-ghost's got hold of my name somehow. My eyelids fly back open.

"Get up." Does she mean I'm to rise and meet my Maker? I hope so, in which case Jesse must not of finished his business with me, on account of the devil ain't gone have a messenger looks like this.

"Coming, Missus." That's what I mean to say, but no word leaves my dry, hurtful throat. Jesse's dark head yet lays next mine, and he's quiet too, stiller than still. Then the Mizz Addie-haint leans forward, disappearing from eyeview for a minute. Comes a grunt, and directly the Jesse-weight leaves me and I feel light, lighter than air maybe, like I might rise right off the ground and float straight to heaven. So grateful, I close my eyes and wait to go.

"Get up." I open them back, and the Mizz Addie-thing's standing right over me, looking down. I ain't floated off after all, and the whole front of her white wrapper's all over splotched in black, don't seem like angels should be messed up so.

"Hurry." She bends and whispers to me. Where'm I supposed to hurry to, Missus?—I want to know, but my voice ain't working.

"Hurry, we've got to hurry." She whispers over and over, and I turn my head to see what Jesse makes of this dream we having. I ain't even mad with him or scared no more, just sad.

"Jesse." Move my lips to call his name, but in that very same sec I know he ain't about to hear me, whether I whisper or scream.

He's lying crumpled on one side, facing me, and out his open mouth's spilled so much blood that the ground where he's lying's soaked black with it. His eye stares blank ahead, blind to this world, and the first thing comes to my mind is, will he fetch eternal damnation, how Gan was scared of?

Studying my brother, I let my one hand travel directly to my woman part. It comes away blood-sticky, showing me it's only death he spilled on me. I send a message to Gan, who feels so close right now, to tell her she can quit that worrying.

"Hurry, we have to hurry." Mizz Addie's trying to lift me. I would help, but this heaviness's hard to fight, and every inch of my flesh aches.

Still, don't one foot seem to move in front the other at the most surprising times? Before I know it, I'm standing up, looking over at my brother Jesse. His pants're down, his bare behind's gleaming, and sticking clean out his mid-back is the hilt of one large Hazelhedge kitchen knife, fine blade Mizz Addie says come all the way from a place called Europe.

"Hurry, hurry." It's all she says. I can't talk, just able to do. She grabs Jesse's feet and goes to dragging, motioning at me to help with his top part. I can't, though; so on she goes, dragging, and he starts twisting onto his back. I'm afraid the tip end of that knife's gone come clear through to his chest, the way she's got him knocking and bobbling along on the ground, leaving a trail of his own blackness. So finally I help, got to, hold up his shoulders while she takes his feet. Backing into the pine woods she goes, me following, Jesse our in-between. The wind blows low through the loblollies, mixing their sound with her whispering words. "Hurry, hurry." My head fills with whispers and we walk, walk, walk, I ain't know how long, till at last she says, "Stop," and lets go.

I do what she tells, past knowing anything else.

"Stay here, Minyon. I'll be right back," and she and her whisper disappear, leaving just me and Jesse and tall dark pines, speaking their own secret talk.

Ain't but scantest light, but my eyes're done used to that by now. Just like in this barest bit of time, I'm already used to Jesse's dead and goneness, this body part all that's left.

Looking at his face, I remember my used-to-be brother Jesse, instead of the one tried to do me. At the swimming beach, how his skin sparkled dark in the sun. The smell of his boy sweat at supper. That church-meeting voice of his, raised so sweet and true, Gan swore his singing could make angels clap hands for joy. All that's gone now, swallowed under and stilled by the hate that ate him and one Hazelhedge kitchen knife.

Jesse's pants're twisted down round his knees, got his manhood exposed and shamed-looking. My one arm's sore as a rising, and his limpness's heavy, but ain't no way to let him go like that, is they—so I turn him on his side and wrestle his pants up to where they button. Then I put my both hands on the hilt of that blade still sticking out my brother's back and pull. Don't come easy, I got to pull with all my might. When it finally takes leave of him, they's a hiss of something comes out with, and I think it's Jesse's spirit, the good Jesse, which I hope and pray is free now.

"Minyon." On my knees, bending next to Jesse, and ain't heard nor seen her coming, but here she stands, with a lit-up lantern, spade and shovel. Ready to do business. She watches me a minute, doesn't blink nor twitch, while the lantern casts one moving shadow after the next across that whiter than white face.

Finally I say, "Yessum," but don't move, holding her fine sharp knife over the deadness of my brother like I'm the one done him in.

Together, without changing one word more, me and Mizz

Addie set to fixing a place for Jesse. She's slipper-shod, which slows her down some, and my sorenesses got me slow moving, but on we keep, she starting at one end, me at the other, right next to where his body lies, so we won't have to move him far.

This morning's cold to frosting, ain't he, but I work up a sweat, rises on my skin like early dew, and Mizz Addie's hair's pasted to her forehead. No sound but we two breathing hard, and once an owl hoots, gives me a start, makes me wonder if it's that one same bird and he's seen all that happened this night.

Can't dig that hole standing on the up-top but just so long. We still don't talk, I just look over where she stands, resting a minute, then I jump right down into where Jesse's gone finally rest himself, and go to digging more. After a while she spells me, then me her, till it feels deep and long enough.

Jesse's started stiffening up, I feel that when I grab hold of him again. We drag him, both seeming to know at the same time one more sad thing: ain't no way to lower this boy sweet to ground—the hole we dug's too deep for that. One last time we lift together, hold over that pit and let go. The dirt falls on him, his face, too, and already my brother's blending with brown earth.

I can't quit staring, and can't move. Mizz Addie comes over, takes my shoulder and pushes me back from that hole, sits me by one of them loblollies, while she goes to putting things back how they were. Shovel rhythm soothes me some, and when I squint my eyes I can't see nothing but a blur of white rocking back and forth, keeping time to shovel-sound.

Directly that quits, though, and I open eyes to see her leaning by her own tree across the way, weary and worn. I go over and take the shovel from her. Our eyes hit smack on and I don't blink, nor she. We break at the same minute, and I go to shoveling. After while, over she comes and stands on the other side. Takes off that white wrapper and the slippers she's wearing, marked dark with Jesse-blood, and drops them into the hole I'm filling. Then she points to my dress and I look down, surprised to find myself wearing that same gore. In goes my dress, shoes and socks too, and naked as a newborn I finish, till the dirt's mounded dark and raw.

Then—I ain't know why, it's just what I got to do—I squat right down, fill my hand with Jesse's grave-dirt, and hold it to my mouth, nibbling, see can I catch a taste, understand something more. Mizz Addie still says nothing, just watches, but a strange look fixes on her face and a shiver starts at her feet and goes up and out.

Me with shovel and spade, Mizz Addie with cold lantern, we bare two start back to Hazelhedge. The path's well marked with brother-blood, which Mizz Addie scuffs up and covers with pine needles as we go, till looking back, you can't see where we been, only where we're headed.

Ain't till we finish covering up that large spilled darkness in between kitchen and outback that Mizz Addie speaks more than a word or two.

"Minyon." Naked roundnesses shine in the morning light as she faces me. "What had to happen, happened. There's no turning back from such a thing, you understand?" Measures out words like medicine. "No turning back."

What in this world I gone turn back to, Mizz Addie?—that's what I want to ask but don't, because I know she's right: this is now and life's gone go on from *here,* not some before-time that don't matter now no more than if it ain't never been.

And the cold that ain't bothered me till now drops itself hard down on me, ice-shawl, and I hear a terrible sound like rattling bones, which turns out to be nothing but my own teeth, setting up rhythms, drumming they own song.

She don't change another word, just turns and glide-walks through the kitchen door, disappearing into Hazelhedge so quick I wonder if it ain't all been a dream, starting with Gan's old hand pushing me forward and ending with a pile of dark new dirt somewhere in those whispering woods.

Under covers I fold knees to head against haints old and new, blowing my own life breath into the coldness of my self, till I get warm enough to sleep. Before I go, I pray not to dream.

PART II

1937

Harder Times

chapter 1

"It don't matter how careful he slides them off and tries to hide them under the bed before I can get a peek—I still know."

That new girl, calls herself Belle, spends more time in my room than her own. Some's like that, especially early on, lonesome and looking for somebody to tell things to—how they got turned out, how their daddy or their brother or their uncle hoodooed them or their mama didn't care or they're just doing this till they get enough money or schooling to do something else. All got a story, all sound alike after while. Not much I can do about it, far's I can tell, except listen.

"My daddy wore cardboard on the bottom of his brogans, too, before he up and left. It's got a particular shuffle to it. Can't miss it."

She's a pretty one, Belle, not much over eighteen's my guess, straight off the farm. Ain't been here long enough to hurt too bad yet.

Through nail-polishing now, so she turns her baby blues my way. She just got a permanent wave yesterday, three of them gone to town for crimp and color, Mizz Addie calls it, so this afternoon Belle's brown hair fits round her fresh pink face like a curved-up frame.

"What I don't get, Min, is how come they do it—the poor ones I mean, like that Charlie, with his old cardboard soles." She swivels round and studies on herself in the mirror, wetting one finger to slick eyebrows, how she sees the others do.

"Not enough money to put three squares on the table, but he'll come sniffing round here once a month, regular as clockwork, plunk down his fiver and shuffle upstairs with me."

She's so close to the mirror it fogs up when she lets out her breath big. "Don't take more than ten minutes, usually, from cleanup to cleanup."

Blows some on her fingers, watching her own pouty mouth in the mirror. "Don't you think it's terrible sad, Min?"

Well, I sure do think so, and plenty else besides. But if it's one thing's not my job to do round here, it's spread the gospel of sad.

"Ain't so sad as might be, Belle. Gets what he comes for, doesn't he?"

She laughs a little—don't take much to cheer her up. "Well, that's a fact, Min, ain't it?"

She grabs up that little beaded makeup bag she spent a heap of money on last week and sparkles a big smile at me. "Besides, it's romantic, don't you think?—how I'm the one he always wants?" Belle's big on romance, reads *Screenland* and *True Confessions* when she's not tricking, fixing up, or talking to me. Or else writing home—she does that once a week, sometimes comes in here and reads the letters to me, asking do they sound like truth. How'm I supposed to know, I wonder.

"Got to get, Min." She's up and out, voice floating back from the door she fails to close. "Saturday night doings, you know."

I do know. Fact is, I got to get my behind to work, on account of Saturdays Sarah generally needs a little extra help in the kitchen and I got to make sure the dining parlor's just so: silver shining, chandelier sparkling, table linens clean and soft, champagne chilling. Saturday nights round here's what Mizz Addie calls insurance nights.

"The key to success, Minyon," she's told me I can't count how many times, "is laying the proper groundwork." That woman's all the time laying groundwork, ain't she?—hard to see how she ever gets anything else done. Still, she must be doing something right—going on eight years we been keeping house here, without a hitch, and I reckon part of the reason's these Saturday night groundwork layings of hers.

And we're doing better than most these days, ain't we? There's even times when Mr. Fitzwater Clemons, who owns the only Jameston bank that's managed to stay open for any kind of business, comes round here to get enough to keep going. Money, that is—sometimes needs cash to float him, Mizz Addie says. He's way too righteous for much else, anyhow. Brings the Episcopal minister with him when he comes, so nobody'll be thinking he's got something dirty on his mind. That old preacher sits out there in Banker Clemons' Cadillac, looking down at his hands the whole time the banker carries on his business with Mizz Addie. And what I wonder is, is that old man out there praying for all us?

"Business is business." Mizz Addie's all the time trying to bring me along, make me see how come things are how they are. "As long as we understand our place in this town, Minyon, how our business fits in with its business—we're going to come out on top." Sometimes on top, sometimes bottom, sometimes even upside down, according to how the hoes tell it. But I don't pass along that bit of funny to Mizz Addie—eight years round here's taught me to say less to her, keep more to myself.

It surely does bring me up short, thinking about eight years, sometimes seems no longer than an eyeblink, sometimes lies like a lonely stretch of road's got no end. Lord, we have seen us some *stuff* in here. Comings and goings, goings and comings. Can't begin to count the men that's been by—hard enough to even keep track of the girls's passed through on their way from one somewhere to the next. The longest we ever kept one was about a year, that Claire, who Mizz Addie had to finally near boot out the door on account of she took to boozing so bad and showing the tricks pictures of her family instead of the good time they paid their money for.

Hard money to come by, too, these days. Hard enough to where Mizz Addie had to what she calls deep-discount prices, for some folks at least—the paper mill boys and the army-navy ones. The rich ones, though, who come from Charleston and sometimes even further off than that, she still charges them through the nose, as a general rule.

General rules's something Mizz Addie's strong on, for sure. Like no talking to customers about family. And no boozing, unless it's with a customer, and then the liquor's so watered down, they tell me it doesn't taste like much of nothing. Course, just about all the hoes drink like fishes, and Mizz Addie sure does know it, but she looks the other way unless it gets out of hand. That's just the way things go round here.

She won't catch me boozing, though—I can't stomach the smell—and got next to no family to be running on about, do I? Jesse's long gone, with nobody besides me and Mizz Addie knowing where, and us not talking about it, not even to each other. Farina lit out for New York City a long while back, which I found out from Big Robert when Mizz Addie drove me out to Little Town to see what I could see about what's left of my real family. My eyes filled up when he told me where my sweet cuz'd got to, I was so scared and proud for her, way off up north like that. Free of here.

Big Robert and Lally's been good to my family—they took my baby bub Clarence to raise. I send money out there every month for that. But on that same long-ago visit to Little Town, Big Robert took me to one side, talking sad and serious, told how it'd be better, circumstances considering, if Clarence didn't get hooked up with me on account of where I work and all. Hoe houses and little boys don't exactly mix, he said, kind as he could. Pained my heart, but I reckon I heard him. And ain't been back to Little Town nor laid eyes on my brother since.

But I suppose we got us some kind of family out here at

Hazelhedge. It's a funny one—Sarah the evening cook, tall Frank the bartender and general round-the-house and yard man, Ophelia the sometime laundress, and me, Minyon the maid. Except Mizz Addie calls me housekeeper lately, and's saddled me with that scrawny not-good-for-much Luella to help out, evenings.

There's one more to name, of course: Mizz Addie her own self. But she's not so much like family—she's the string-puller, makes us all dance to whatever tune she's got playing in her head.

"Minyon?" Must be conjured her—that voice and knock happen so close together I ain't sure which comes first. My feet touch the wood floor at just about the exact sec that gold head pokes round my open door. She's got that surprised look on her face, how she always does when she's fixing to let you know you ain't quite lived up to what she hoped.

"Is there a problem, Minyon?"

"No, Missus." I sometimes call her that to rile her, which works about half the time, but not today. She keeps those penciled-up eyebrows high and doesn't flicker.

"Just finishing up my dinner." I pick up the empty plate by my bed and bustle toward the door. She says nothing, just looks hard at her watch and then heads off to see about who else might not be up to snuff. That's her job, I reckon. She sure is good at it.

Frank's bicycle's by the tool shed plus one more besides, but I don't think a thing about it till I get to the kitchen. Frank's in there, jollying Sarah—he's the one can make her smile the most and Lord, she is one pretty colored girl when he gets her going like that.

Standing next to them, grinning and watching, is a boy I ain't seen before. When I come in, he turns his face my way, and I see he's not so much a boy, probably closer to my age. He grins, and I feel the white of his teeth slam down to my toes, most makes my neck snap back.

"Well, there she is." Frank leaves off with Sarah long enough to speak. "Minyon. Just who I been wanting to see."

He plops his big old hand down hard on that boy's shoulder. "This here's sister Rose's boy, my nephew Winston." Pushes him forward a little, "Tell her hey, Winston."

Paying no mind to the teasing in Frank's voice, he looks straight into my eyes and tells me, "Hey, Minyon."

Time either stops or I lose track of it, along with my breath, as I look up into chocolate eyes swimming in whites so pure they're almost blue. I take in cheekbones high and dark, hair curled close round a good-shaped head, and a set of teeth that flash bright enough to blind. Never seen anything so fine in my life. Before I know what's hit, the plate's someway gone from my hand, we two's out the door and into the yard, and he's asked me something I ain't heard proper.

"Huh?" Sound like a perfect fool, don't I, but can't get collected to save me.

"I say, been working here long?" Brown eyes flick once to the house and then back to my face and then down one time real quick and back. A hotness starts in my belly and pushes up through my neck into my face. A sweet evening breeze's building, but I all a sudden got the serious sweats.

"Eight years," I sputter, pretty well pleased to get any sensible something out my mouth.

His eyes go some wider. "Eight years!" He brushes his hand light as wind cross the top part of my arm. "You way too young for that, girl. Tell the truth."

Truth is, my arm's tingling and twitching where he touched it, and what little breath I have managed to hold onto's about gone. Good thing I'm leaning against the back stoop, on account of if not, I'd likely keel over backwards.

He's chewing on some gum, and when he leans in close, the air turns thick with wild fresh mint. "What's it like," he starts— then his eyes flick over past my head and his face freezes. He stands up straight and nods his head one time at whatever's behind me. "Evening, Missus," he mumbles.

Ain't got to turn around to know who that is. She doesn't say one word to him—got eyes, ears, and mouth only for not-working me.

"I assume your taking yet another break indicates that your evening's work is completed, Minyon. Is my surmise correct?"

When Mizz Addie gets mad she doesn't puff up and go red in the face like she might pop, how some white folks do. She gets quiet instead—like a snake she hisses through teeth nearly closed shut, and her voice goes so sweet, seems like it'd clog your veins, just listening. Talks fancier than everyday, too.

"Nome, Mizz Addie. I just . . ."

Frank comes busting out the back door right that second, talking up one side and down the other, explaining how his sister's boy's here for a visit and he thought the yard needed some extra work and Winston here'd be just the one could get the job done right and cheap. Cheap—now he's speaking her language. On and on he talks, and already Mizz Addie's face's softening up—it's hard to resist Frank Washington when he gets smooth-talking. Off I slip, and when I get inside the screen door, I turn back to see Frank's arm draped round Winston's shoulder while Frank explains what a fine upstanding young man he is and how he's gone get the elaeagnus and crepe myrtles in shape and clear that patch of bramble near outback. And I have to agree: he surely *is* one fine upstanding young man.

"Best get yourself to work, girl." Sarah's voice comes so close to my ear I about jump out my own skin. "Keep your mind on your business."

The business on my mind's got nothing to do with the work at hand, but I know Sarah's right, and I ain't particular about inviting another run-in with Mizz Addie this evening. Can't help but heave one big sigh, though, and take a last look out.

"He's not long for here, girl. No use pining after what you can't get; that's just asking for trouble." She goes back to basting tonight's ham, doesn't look round while she hands out advice nobody asked for. "It's getting late. Luella's in the dining parlor—you'd best go see is everything about ready."

Who died and named her housekeeper? Going down the hall I mumble under my breath about know-it-all Sarah, who'd best stick to her work and let me get on with mine. At the door of the dining parlor, though, I stop dead. The chandelier's got the room lit like Christmas and that skinny colored girl's in there prancing before the big sideboard mirror like she's queen of the ball, swishing this way and that, holding her housedress out to one side with two fingers and humming to beat the band.

"I guess you're through with your work, Luella Cathou, judging by how you got time to sashay about so."

Her thin self jumps like she's shot, then she grins my way, silly smile fading some when she catches sight of stony-faced me.

"Sorry, Mizz Minyon. Just finishing up." She goes to laying out the rest of the silverware, how I taught her. I watch closer than close a while, making sure the napkins get tucked up just so, making sure she feels my eyes hard on the back of her nappy head. Then out I slip, without changing another word. And don't I know she'll believe my eyes're still there long after I'm gone?

The hall's dark, but I don't light it, just feel my way to the linen closet, open the door, and slide in. Seems like the coolest, sweetest place in the house—cedar shelves six-high, stacked up on two sides with clean white towels and fine cotton sheets. By morning this room'll be most empty, all this whiteness sticky and stained with men and hoe juice, mingled. But right now it's pure and fresh as Ophelia knows how to make it.

Mizz Addie won't switch to the laundry in town, even though Mr. Walker's been out here two or three times trying to get her business. She says nobody can do linens sweet as Ophelia. Ain't that the truth.

I lean back and breathe in, my mind drifting to whiter than white teeth, sweet mint breath, touch of one hand on one girl's arm. I whisper his name, *Winston,* and a hard shiver shakes me head to toe. Never felt like this before, and it's some scary. I'm queasy, my belly riding high and wild like I might throw up.

High heel shoes clip-clipping through the hall bring this wild belly back down to earth quick. A light shines under the door. Time to get on with this evening's business.

I slip out and pop my head into the front parlor. Frank's behind the bar, setting up. I run my eyes round the room, check the wood cigar box to make sure the Havanas line up straight, then act like I'm just gone zip right back out. Can't help but catch the big old grin Frank flashes, though.

"What?" I put my hands on my hips, how Mizz Addie does when she's put out sometimes.

He towel-polishes one cut crystal glass, holds it up to the light, squints at it like it's the most important thing in this world.

"What you mean, what?" Sparkles shoot between the crystal and the chandelier. I stare at Frank while he studies the glass so hard he can't pay me no mind.

"Nothing," I say. Got better things to tend to, anyhow.

I'm half out the door when Frank clears his throat and says, low—like's talking to himself—"Mm, mm. That's what my nephew says about that girl. Mm, mm."

I don't even look round.

My cheeks're burning hot, though, by the time I get myself to the kitchen. Sarah's got the ham sliced thick, juicy and pink on a platter, her special-made honey mustard gleaming gold and sliding down the sides. On the stove's steamed rice and limas. Mm, mm—that's what's in my mind, so Sarah can't even trouble me with her scowly self.

"Need another platter for tomatoes," she mutters, and off I float to the dining room, happy to fetch her one. Luella's finished in there except for candle-lighting, which Mizz Addie doesn't want done till the last possible sec anyhow.

Passing back through the hall I meet up with Belle and Faith, dressed to the nines, cheeks colored high, eyes shiny-bright, nails flashing like red knives. Their perfume's mixed with liquor-breath smell—must be Belle's, on account of Faith's no drinker. She's got religion instead.

The other girls're already in the front parlor, must be, all their voices and laughs with that nighttime edge they get. Luella steps out the linen closet just then, a stack of fresh towels in her arms. "Get set, Luella Cathou," I call down the hall. "We're gone jump tonight." And it's true, it's in the air. Saturday night.

Sarah's bending to pull her biscuits out the oven and I'm savoring that smell and some other one besides, thinking my own thoughts, when in walks Mizz Addie. Lord, she looks fine, with her goldness piled up round that pale face and a long purple dress wrapped round her, shows off her bosom and what waist she still lays claim to. Truth is, she's curved up nowadays some close to plump, but she cuts one fine figure still, done up like this. She's got her Saturday night shoes on, too, what she calls brocade and has to order special from New York City. Woman does love her shoes, now.

"Mr. Cunningham and the sheriff just pulled in, Minyon. Are we ready?"

Ready's our middle name—heard one hoe tell that to another one time. "Yessum, Mizz Addie. All but the candles. I'll go light them."

Sheriff Dawson and Lawyer Cunningham are already in the room before I get the candles going good. They don't say a thing to me, of course, and I don't change words with them either, just finish my work and leave. It's not like they're unfriendly, or me either; it's nothing personal, just how things are at Mizz Addie's. "We observe the formalities," she says, which comes down to me being not so much Minyon Manigault when I wait on them as just a way things get done.

Before I start serving up that hot, fresh food Sarah spent the af-ternoon fixing, I got one more job. I stop in the hall by the full-length mirror, take a cloth out my skirt pocket, and dust the glass clean from top to bottom. Good luck, Ophelia taught me—stuff she someway knows about. "Every night, child—don't fail. It'll bring those girls luck, and us, too." Fuck luck, one of the hoes named it, some years back. Everybody calls it that now, and they all worry about will I forget. Which I surely won't, on account of, how I see it, all our luck's tied pretty much up together.

By the time I start serving, they're all there, the ones Mizz Addie calls Jameston's movers and shakers. Joining up with the first two's three more—Mr. Lafayette Prevost, owns a big restaurant downtown and half the land in James County; Doc Thayer, takes care of the hoes every week plus Mizz Addie when she needs it; and Mr. Billy Ray Bryan, who's got the only car lot and finest white undertaking establishment in town. Sometimes we have one or two more regulars and sometimes a special guest— big boys from Columbia or Charleston and every once in a while some from Washington, D.C., itself. But this is what we got tonight.

Mizz Addie turns the phonograph on to play sweet slow music, no singing, no jazz. "Swing comes later, gentlemen," she always promises, "classical is music to dine by." Dine they surely do—these boys can eat. And under every one of their plates is some extra little something—don't know how much, just see Mizz Addie slip it there, Saturday after Saturday. Except for the sheriff; he takes his extra in madam-skin. And after that comes dessert, which I don't serve. The hoes take care of that part.

Insurance nights. Ground layings.

By midnight, the movers and shakers's generally gone home to the bosom of their families and the girls get down to other business as usual. By four this night, I've done all I'm going to, crawl in my narrow bed and try to block the sounds of Faith, two rooms down, who swears she's got to praise God and holler hallelujah when she brings release to one of her customers. Scares some of them half to death from time to time, too. But she's got the ecstasy, don't you know, which ain't the worst thing a hoe can have. At least it's not generally catching.

Warm tonight. I curl up in a ball and feel my own sticky sweat where my body touches herself. Even so, I hold my old Gan-blanket close, for safekeeping.

Same thing happens every time I lay me down to sleep—

visions come, one after the other. Folks I know, or used to. Can't stop them, best thing to do is just look and try to keep in mind they ain't real, just visions. They can't reach out and grab me, pull me into the dark. I'm just the watcher.

Tonight the first one up's that new girl Belle, how I saw her a little while back, her last trick of the evening walking close behind, hungry, watching her body move through her thin silk dress. She only passes by in my dream, flicks eyes up once at me then down again and on she goes to her outback room. But I see clear as sky that empty something I've seen too much before.

My heart's sick inside me, when here comes my cuz Farina, clip-clipping by. Ain't laid eyes on that girl all these years, except in my nighttime visions. She's dressed in New York clothes, must be, head flung back, laughing for all she's worth—and my heart fills with missing her, wishing I was there, too; laughing, too. Now here's thumbsucking Clarence, must be about grown, probably doesn't even do that no more, but still it's how he visits my dreams, still a baby bub. Comes a faint outline I know's Gan, shaking her head, all sorrowing sad at where we've got ourselves to, wishing things were different.

My brother Jesse's shadow creeps in, too. He's my every-night visitor—stays sometimes shorter, sometimes longer, but never misses. Dead one visit, alive the next, but always eat up with the hate that killed him. To keep him off me, I got to get up sometimes, pass through the way me and him and Mizz Addie passed that long-back night and visit his resting place out there in the loblolly woods. Eat dirt for sorrow.

I go to trembling, but tonight Jesse barely makes a show, on account of here comes Frank's Winston with his fine self, makes me sweatier than ever, half in-half out of sleep, watching how that boy walks, how the light shines on his skin, how his ears lay close and sweet to his head. Mm, mm.

He starts to turn that head my way now, and my heart goes to thumping with waiting on two pair of eyes meeting. Then half there, he stops and freezes, looking at pale goldness dawning somewhere between me and him. Addie-colors everywhere, and can't anybody get a breath in edgewise.

"Lord have mercy!" Faith calls out, commending one more tricky soul to heaven.

Amen, says my curled-up half-asleep self, sinking down past where any of them can reach. Amen.

chapter 2

" 'Dear Mama. Things are going real good here. We made more than our quota last week, so we got us a bonus, and everybody says we're fixing to see the last of these hard times before long, which may or may not be true, Mama, but still, here's ten dollars.' "

Stops her reading and looks over at me. "How's that, Min? If you's my mama, would you believe it?"

Sometimes I feel old enough to be this child's mama, even though I got less than a half dozen years on her. And ain't either of us had enough sleep last night—her young self looks rough as a cob.

"Reckon so, Belle. Got no reason not to, does she?"

Instead of answering, Belle reads on.

" 'My supervisor says if I keep up the good work I might could move on to the shirt department soon.' "

She gazes at the page a minute, admiring. "Give 'em details, Min, that's what Francie says. Details and money, and they won't ask no questions."

Why would they question ten dollars, anyhow? Poor farm

folks, scratching out a living, the daddy gone to see is there a better chance out west, the mama with four head of children, trying to feed them all, sending this oldest out to get work. Far as she knows, this child works at the dress plant down the road—she's got no way to know they don't pay but six dollars a week and ain't hired new in years, not unless somebody knows somebody. Who Mizz Addie knows's Mr. Millwood Schneider works down there, sends likely looking girls her way. Every time we get one like that, Mr. Millwood gets him a free month of Sunday afternoons round here.

Mizz Addie's big on trade, calls it the backbone of the business.

Not that it always works out as good as she expects. Like two weeks ago, when Rainey Belune, works for Cap Lachicotte down at the fish house, came by, how he does from time to time. He gets horny—the hoes say it's on account of he's too ugly for even his wife to want to mess with—and'll come round with some leftover fish to peddle. That day it was shad—Mizz Addie's big-time partial to that bony fish. It was a Tuesday afternoon, our slow day, which Mr. Rainey knows, of course. He showed up at the back door, speaking his old geechy-talk to Mizz Addie, sounding enough like colored to pass, if you closed your eyes.

"Evening, Mizz Fleming," he said. "Interest you in a little changy for changy today? Fine fresh shad." That's how he always makes his offer.

"How many, Rainey?" she asked.

"Seven or eight good-size ones," he claimed. "Just hauled in."

"Pretty hot out there today, Rainey. Are you certain they're fresh?"

Hairy old head bobbed. "Course, Mizz Fleming. You know I ain't gone hoo-doo you."

"Fifteen minutes, then," she said, and he went to making tiny jumps on the balls of his feet. She called Jeannine, they got on to outback, and that night we had shad for supper, Sarah-fried, gold and crispy.

By midnight, though, every hoe in the place was sick as a dog, me too, and Mizz Addie near to dying; folks's throwing up right and left, and all the tricks got sent home with money still in their pockets. Cap Lachicotte came out here himself the next day to apologize, on account of Rainey Belune being too scared to show his face. He's one white man's off Mizz Addie's trade list, for sure, backbone of the business or no.

" 'My landlady Miss Fleming watches out for me and the other girls who stay here. We go to church Sundays, and we eat good, too.' "

Belle wrinkles up her forehead, worrying over it. "Think it's a mortal sin to lie about church, Min? Faith says it is." Doesn't wait on my answer, won't risk it, takes her pencil and scratches that part out.

" 'I'm making me a lot of new friends, too, Mama.' " She looks up. "You like Maureen, Min?"

Maureen's the new girl, been here less than a week. She's a strong talking hoe, a Yankee, with pushy kind of ways. I reckon it'll be interesting to see how she and Mizz Addie get along. Far as me, I don't have much feeling about her one way or the other. She's just another one of these hoes, comes and goes. Ain't my business to like them or not.

"I like her just fine, Belle."

"She's pretty smart, Min. Says she's gonna be a madam herself one of these days, run a house like this—even better, she says."

Can't help but snort out loud on that one. Hazelhedge's famous all over the place for being one of the finest houses on the whole east coast, so Mizz Addie tells, and we hear it otherwise, too. And this Yankee girl's gone go it one better? Uh huh. Nothing I ain't heard before though, on account of any hoe with a grain of sense in her head's got madam intentions.

Belle pays me no mind. She's bent on finishing up. " 'Kiss Mary Beth, Annie, and J.W. for me, Mama, and take care. I miss you and I will write again soon.' " Her voice gets some fuller. She swallows hard, then goes on. " 'Your loving daughter, Hallie.' "

Hallie Oakes—that's Belle real name. She told me it the first week she's here, even though I tried to warn her about how it's bad luck, telling the real one. She says she can't stand it, not one person knowing who she really is. And I'm just the one she chose to tell, Lord knows why.

Quiet in here now. Belle's still letter-gazing, and I'm mending one of my black skirts. Tuesday afternoon quiet's all around.

Fixing to get louder, though. We hear her voice before she opens the door without so much as a knock.

"Belle?" Maureen stands at the door, acting like she's the one owns this room. "What're you doing in here? I've been looking all over for you."

"Reading Min my letter to mama, is all. You need me, Maureen?"

That noisy girl sets herself down on the foot of my bed and leans back against the wall, settling in. Uninvited as you please.

"Just jumpy, kiddo. All jazzed up and nobody to talk to, you know?" Still wearing her robe and slippers, even though it's almost three o'clock. Her yellow hair's matted up on one side, and there's about a pound of makeup streaked under her washed-out eyes. Cup of coffee in one hand, cigarette in the other, and she's got it right—jitsy as a cat fixing to come loose its skin.

"OK if I park it here a while?" First time she bothers to turn her head my way; I watch this needle slip in and out of black, content myself with one little *hummph* under my breath.

Thick-hided as a gator, though.

"Writing your old lady, eh?"

Belle folds up the letter, smooths it over with soft fingertips, then slips it into her pocket, keeping quiet.

"Mine'd drop dead, probably, if she ever got a letter from me." She goes to studying Belle, who doesn't look up. "Aren't you jittery, kid? Don't you just want to *do* something?" She leans forward. "Tell you what—let's get ourselves gorgeous and catch a ride to town. See what trouble we can scare up."

Belle's head jerks up like she's shot. "Oh no, Maureen. We can't do that. It's against the rules. Miss Fleming . . ."

"Fuck rules. I can't believe you take all that seriously. What're you—born yesterday?" She leans back, takes a deep draw off her cigarette. "Look, every whorehouse in the world's got rules, kiddo—no drinking, no lezzing around, no freelancing, no pimps—and every whore worth her salt breaks them. That's how the game gets played."

Belle looks back down at her lap—not even close to convinced about all that.

The Yankee girl gives out one big sigh, pulls out a Pall Mall and lights it off the one she's most to the end of. "Some fancy joint—dumb farm girl, a holy roller, couple of lezzies, bunch of . . ." looks over my way, sneery, ". . . *rules*. Why I left the finest house in Troy, New York, to come clear to the end of the earth, I'll never know."

Me and Belle ain't know either, I reckon, since neither one of us offers up a word. I'd just as soon she get her northern behind back on up there, myself, or at least out of my room, which seems like's turning blue, between all her smoking and cussing.

I stab my finger through the cloth, suck in my breath and watch redness soak into black. And just that sec comes a door slam, sounds like a truck outside. No delivery's scheduled, so I know I best go see what's up—part of that housekeeper job, keeps getting bigger every time I turn around.

Delivery truck's out there, sure enough—Arnaud's Amusements, it says on the side, out of Charleston—and two boys round the back of it's fixing to let something down the ramp.

I'm priming to question them, when out the house steps Mizz Addie, seems to know what they're about, so I keep my mouth shut. Behind me comes Belle and Maureen, and from one outback room flies Jeannine and Francie—those two girlfriends spend all their spare time together.

So here we all stand and these two delivery boys're hard put to keep their minds on business. One of Maureen's bosoms's fixing to fall out of her wrapper, and Jeannine and Francie's not but half dressed either. Nobody says anything, on account of Mizz Addie's here, and we're naturally quiet round herself.

Out of that truck those two bug-eyed boys roll a wide box near tall as them. Mizz Addie points to the house, saying, calm as a cuke, "In there, boys."

She leads the way and they follow, the rest of us bringing up the rear. The boys can't figure whether to look forward or back. That box's so big, it barely makes it through the front door, but finally it's in and they go to unpacking it, all us meantime standing round waiting.

Finally they finish and stand back. We feast our eyes on a big wide box, half made from high-polished dark wood, looks like mahogany, the other half all shiny chrome and glass.

"A jukebox," Maureen whispers, like in church. "A Wurlitzer." Even her smart-alecky self's impressed most past words.

"The finest piccolo this side of New York City, ladies," announces Mizz Addie, proud and quiet, like she's making introductions. "Boys, plug her in."

In she's plugged, and lights like glory. Mizz Addie tips the boys, who stumble their dazy-eyed selves toward the door while the hoes crowd round that music machine, squealing and hollering out names of songs and bands. Mizz Addie offers up a purse full of nickels, saying, "First time's on me, ladies." Out she slips, then, leaving them to it. And in no time flat, the front parlor's filled up with the sound of swing.

Never saw such dancing. Seems like these girls's got so much saved-up energy, they been dying for something to do with it. And this's it.

Maureen jitterbugs to beat the band one minute, takes a shag lesson from Jeannine the next. Belle moves to the music any old way, looks pretty good for that, too—head flung back, hips going to town. Francie's all over the room herself. They're wild—whooping and laughing, too, not just dancing. Pretty soon Faith slides in, drooping her pale self off in one corner, Bible-reading, trying to look holy. But when the Big Apple comes on, she can't stand it. Joins the circle, Maureen calling out steps—still bossy—and all the rest doing their level best to follow, one after the other: "Charleston!" she hollers, and "Black

Bottom!" and something called the Suzi-Q. Their faces're flushed and red, sweat pouring, clothes coming loose. They all a sudden don't seem like hoes to me—just pretty young girls, wild spirits, filled up with joy, using their juices.

My own juices're squirting every which way themselves, but I've been with Mizz Addie long enough to figure what's proper and not. Housekeeper dancing with hoes ain't. That woman may be's gone from this room, but I sure do feel her in here yet. Freezes me up.

I slip myself out the door, fixing to finish mending and get ready for this evening. Rounding the corner, I find Sarah, who must of just got here and's brought skinny Luella with her. Still filled up with good music, I holler to them, "Hey y'all, we got us one fine piccolo!"

We can't hear it but slight out in the back yard, but when we go into Sarah's kitchen, there's no mistaking that Count Basie beat, comes up most through the floorboards. And proper flies out the window, far as we three.

Luella goes to dancing first, then me. Ain't long before even Sarah joins in, flinging her scowl-face off like a mask she wears to keep protected. The music goes round and round, so says the song. And it does, and we do. Pure moving—truckin', how that Big Apple song calls it. And we are *good.*

I don't know how long we go, but those nickels must run short finally, on account of the music stops for more time than it takes to change a record. Seems like we three women're waking from a dance-dream, looking round at ourselves and smiling shy, like we're thinking, "Was that us?" Sarah tucks in, Luella puts her shoes back on, I smooth my hair off my face.

Sarah's having trouble locating her stern look, mutters, "Best get supper going," and goes to slicing squash for all she's worth. Luella peers over at me, raising her little black eyebrows high, and I can't help it—I grin at her, big. Makes her face light like Christmas.

"Lord, Mizz Minyon, you sure can dance!" Her words please me so I can't hardly speak.

Sarah's got no such problem. "Best dance your black self to outback and dress proper, get this place ready for tonight."

Must be I'm still in the spell of swing, feeling nervy and full of something. "Sarah Besselieu," I move over by the sink so I can see that dark face. "Why you always got to be so mean?" I don't look at Luella, but I hear breath suck in and I know her mouth must be dropped wide. I'm right astonished myself.

Sarah stops her chopping, but doesn't look at me. The room goes stiller than still and I'm purely regetting I ain't on my way to outback. Light glints off the sharpness of the knife blade in her hand. I flex my toes, ready to haul, if it comes to that.

It doesn't, though. She laughs, instead. Not a good laugh—a low, bitter one, no funny in it.

"Mean?" Shakes her head, then turns to me, her face straight serious, eyes resting sad and clear on mine. "How long you been knowing me, girl?"

"Eight years?" Hoping to get back in her good graces for getting one thing right, at least.

"Right. Eight years. And this is the first time you got the nerve to ask me why I got to be so mean, right?"

I only nod, seems safer.

"That's why I do, fool." Turns back to chopping a minute, but doesn't stop telling me stuff. "It ain't called 'mean,' girl—if you got to call it something, say 'smart.' This here's white folks' place, not mine—yours either, even though you're living here. You got no call to be yourself here."

Turns back and leans her face very close to mine, like she's giving out secrets. Her dance sweat smells sweet and true. "Best be knowing that, girl. *It ain't your place.*"

She takes one hand and cups it under my chin, and I feel a hot rise of tears, comes from nowhere.

Sarah turns away for true then, back to her sink and squash-slicing. "Best get yourself a smart face to wear, Minyon, if you planning to make it in this world."

Room's so still I don't know how we miss footsteps, but

without us hearing him climb the stairs, Frank's here, his dark shadow spilling into the kitchen through the back door. "Evening, ladies." Rich voice fills us up, and Sarah's face goes soft how it does whenever she gets round that man. Kitchen spell's broken now. We all say hey, act like we're bustling. I look past Frank to see is there one more somebody out there in the yard. Which he naturally doesn't let me get by with.

"He didn't come today, Minyon." I'm too flustered to come back quick with something, how I'd like to. "Had to run some errands for his mama."

I try dredging up my best Sarah-face, finest Mizz Addievoice. "No idea what you're referring to, Frank Washington." Squeeze past his large self. "Reckon I got my hands full enough round here without trying to make head or tails of your mess." Off I stomp, righteous.

But putting on my mended skirt, tucking in my white shirt, fitting my feet into flat black shoes, good for all the walking's got to be done, I can't help but think about Winston Laurette. That boy's been hanging round here off and on more than a month now, working in the yard, helping Frank haul wood, clearing out the shed. We ain't had that much chance to talk; sometimes I bring him a lemonade and visit a minute, but I always feel Mizz Addie's eyes on the back of my head. She don't much truck with me having fun, that's sure. Anyhow, I can't fetch up much more than a stutter or so when he asks me something, on account of my insides shaking. Is that love? I ain't know, and got nobody to ask. All I know is, I can't keep him out of my head.

If it's up to me, I wouldn't worry about talking much anyhow; I'd rather be quiet with him, go lay us down somewhere still and hush, and me run my fingers all over him and he over me, not making a sound, besides breathing.

I shame myself, thinking this way. Makes my breath come short, too. That boy's leaving soon anyhow, him and his mama off to New York, got family there. What's he got to do with me? Nothing, that's what.

But inside my head some little voice pushes at me, calls: go, girl, go; this's your one chance.

I catch sight of Luella checking outback rooms, reminds me it's about time for the hoes to be fixing up now, and for some reason, ain't one of them left the main house yet. Best see what's keeping them.

I grab a broom for porch sweeping and head round the side of the house towards the front parlor. All the windows're open wide, and before I get to the door I hear talking, makes me slow-step, for some reason. I hold my broom and stop. Maureen's telling something.

"Counting, that's how I get by. Backwards from a hundred, keeping it spaced out as even as you can—a hundred constitution, ninety-nine constitution—you're counting in real seconds when you say constitution behind the number. Keeps your rhythm right, too. Works like a charm, girls." She stops a sec, and I can almost hear the sly in her smile. "Of course, if you ever get all the way down to one-constitution, why, you're either having yourself a real good time, or you're doing something wrong." She gives a short, barky laugh. "Back at Mother Faye's, where I come from, we used to keep a record, write it down, how many counts per trick. Then at the end of the day, we'd add them up and compare, see, and whoever got the lowest number won, because it meant they took the fewest humps. How about it, girls? Want to get that game going? It does take your mind off things."

"I'll have you know this is the Lord's work, Miss Yankee Maureen. You best not go belittling it with games." Faith's voice comes high and pure. Crazy as a bedbug, but doesn't seem to bother nobody much. "Suffer them to come unto me, saith the Lord. That's our mission here, we've been chosen to be Mary Magdalenes to all these poor, soul-starved boys, looking to be released." Her voice gets even purer, wondrous. "Why sometimes, sometimes, I swear the moment they're released, I feel the sweet breath of Jesus on my very own cheek, like a white cloud of pure spirit."

"Yeah," says Maureen, "I get stuff on my cheek, too, only I never thought it was so sweet, Faithie-girl. Just sticky."

"Darla," Belle interrupts quick with her own two-cents' worth. "Darla—she was here before you, Maureen—she made up names for different kinds of tricks, put them in groups, said it kinda helped you know what to expect, gave you something to think about while you're waiting for it to be over. Quick trick, that was one—like one of them scared-to-death cherries we get sometime, else one of them old ones, skin hangs on them like a bad set of long johns—that's what Darla used to say. You know the ones—sometime can't even wait till they get inside, groaning while they're walking behind you—seem like they ain't been touched by human hands for years? Wham-bam-thankyou-mammers, she called them. Anyhow, they're the best kind, right? Then she had other ones—hick trick for rubes, slick trick—them fancy ones, think they know stuff. Lick trick. Called that Irish boy, Sean, from the paper mill, mick trick. And then there's sick tricks, how we get every once in a while. Scary ones."

"They're all sick," pipes in Faith, "they come here for us to heal them."

"Nope, dope, you got it all wrong—they *are* heels. Heels, suckers, good-for-nothing good-time charlies. Meatballs."

"You will go straight to hell, talking like that, Miss. And I for one will not mourn your passing."

"Look here, girlie, if you think . . ."

Time to get these girls moving, ain't it? I open the screen door, and they are a picture in this world, all kind of sprawled out—Jeannine and Francie collapsed in a heap against the sofa, too worn out to even talk, Maureen lying sideways in the big armchair, propped up on one elbow, finger pointed, fixing to give holy Faith what-for, Belle stretched full-length on the sofa, face still red from dancing, hair sticking to her forehead, Faith sitting bolt upright in the little armchair, prim, prissy, and sweaty as a hog.

"Coming on evening, ladies. Y'all ready for it?"

And I don't know about them, but far as me, I hear piccolo

music in my head all evening long and well into the morning hours when everybody's taken care of their business and's asleep—not like actual playing, but like we heard it the first time, and danced to. Just us, just for ourselves—not counting backwards or conjuring up smart faces—just on account of glad to be alive and kicking.

chapter 3

"Minyon—you ready yet?" Belle sticks her head round the corner of my door. I swear, a soul's got no privacy round here, to speak of.

I sigh some, to show how I'm feeling. Not that she notices. "Well, I just about am, Belle. Got to get my hat."

She stands at the door, fidgeting to beat the band, watching while I look in the mirror long enough to fix my hat proper.

"You look good, Minyon, dressed up some. Ain't never seen you in nothing but your uniform."

When I got call to wear anything else, girl? Could ask that, but don't. Just get my bag instead.

"I'll go fetch Faith and Maureen," and off she flies. Like a child she looks, with her full long skirt, those shoes and socks.

I grab a sweater, on account of it's coming on November, and might be chilly by the time the show lets out. Stepping from my room, I smell the crisp in the air—always so full of promise, ain't it? Fall. Fine Sunday afternoon, fixing to have us an outing; got money in my pocket, hat on my head, Sunday dress. Yessum, feeling just fine, thank you.

By the back door of the house something flickers, catches my eye. Could be a trick of the light, but isn't. Directly, Mizz Addie opens the door and stands there, holding her wrap around her shoulders, looking over at me. Across this yard we face the littlest while, how we sometimes do, measuring the space between. It's like we don't have to talk, each one remembers every shape and sound and taste and smell of all the things that's happened in our time together, all leading back to one terrible one, and before that her white dress and the sheriff's whorl, Gan's drooping outlined head.

This afternoon I got the devil in me, so I hold out till the very last second, when I see her shoulders fixing to gather themselves. Then over I stroll.

"Minyon, you must watch the ladies at all times this afternoon, you understand? They are your personal responsibility."

"Yes, Mizz Addie." Don't look up. "Watch them best as I can, from the balcony."

"And not out of your sight any other time, either. Is that clear?"

As mud. "Yessum, Missus." She sucks in breath and I smile without moving my lips one jot.

I know one thing: it purely galls her, letting these hoes go off with me. She doesn't generally let them go to town without her being along, and then usually not more than two or three at the most together. But she can't be everywhere, can she—and right now she's got her hands full with Jeannine and Francie, those girlfriends's having a cat fight, plus that new girl Geraldine, who ain't got the hang of things round here yet. So I'm taking these ones off her hands for the afternoon, put their high spirits to doing something harmless while she gets the rest of them straight.

Her voice comes syrup-sweet. "Here're the car keys, Minyon." Down she drops them, too quick for me to grab hold of. I got to stoop to dirt to get them. Which I do, like I ain't proud about anything that silly. If's not but one person playing, ain't no game, is they?

She is put out with me now, for sure. Got that edge to her voice. "If anybody questions you, tell them you're from here. Tell them to call me. You hear, Minyon?"

Like there's a soul in James County would mistake who we are—brand new Packard with couple three hoes in back and a colored girl housekeep driving. "Yessum. I sure will do that."

I get to the Packard and open the door quick before she can tell me one something else. I close it tight behind me, and *I am in.*

Mm. Car smells fine. Rich. Cool leather curves up round my back and against my legs, smooth and sweet as buttercream.

This isn't the car I learned to drive in, of course. Mizz Addie's big on automobiles, gets her a fine new one about every year— same sort of turnaround as our hoes. But Frank's the one taught me to drive, in that old black truck of his. Handcranker. Mizz Addie made him do it, said she can't be the only one to run errands when he ain't around. Chose me as the likeliest suspect, I reckon, on account of I'm the only other one lives out here. Except the hoes, and she sure ain't want those girls driving her car.

Seems like it was months of bucking and bumping before I got the hang of that truck. When I did, one day, finally, on a dirt road Frank practiced me on—when I all of a sudden did, that day, stop worrying about how to do it and just did it, why, it felt fine. It was early spring, the breeze blew nice, the sun shone, and I was at the wheel, for once knowing what to do with it. Frank said we could go on a real road, and we did—Highway 17, toward Charleston. The air smelled so sweet and I was feeling like I was the one in charge, don't you know, with the road stretched out before me smooth and straight. I pressed my foot down on the gas pedal and felt full with that road moving under us, the truck doing what I said. I turned to Frank, who'd got hold of the dash and'd turned some paler, seemed like, and hollered, "Don't this feel just fine, Frank? Free!"

And it was looking at his face that gave me my first notion, even before I felt the truck start shaking, even before I turned my eyes straight ahead to see we were headed for the ditch bank, even before I slammed the brakes too late and we were all a sudden sideways in the grass. Both fine—just sideways, me picking myself up off him, him managing to get us out of there right by his strong self, me helping some, and him never saying a word to Mizz Addie about how that side of the truck got stove in so, just saying to me, later, safe and sound back at Hazelhedge, saying to never forget about how free might be one thing, but keeping your eyes on the road's something else again.

I slide the key in and turn, and this sweet motor turns too, humming. Here comes those three, squealing and laughing and piling in the back seat. Even holy Faith's having fun, got a little color to that pale face.

"To the movie house, James, and don't spare the horses." Maureen puts on her best high-toned voice and the other two giggle like she's the funniest thing ever came down the pike. I straighten my hat, clear my throat and come close as I can to a Frank-voice. "Call me Minyon, Madam."

Back there they hoot at that. Maureen says, "Yes, Minyon Madam," causes more hoots. I back the Packard out, and we're off, down the dirt road through the pines to Highway 17. I never once look back to see if she's standing there, willing me to do right. Don't have to, do I? My mind sees clearer than eyes ever could.

The Camelot Theatre's on the far side of Water Street, down from the old Jeff Davis Hotel. Every time I come through here, I remember one tired skinny colored girl, thought she's running away, years back. Remember her like she's somebody else—who knows where she ended up?

We park in front of the movie. *Dangerous* the sign says, and I hope it ain't what Ophelia calls an omen. Just in case, I turn around to speak to these girls firmer than firm.

Lord, ain't they something. Belle with her fresh-faced self; Faith's hair fluffed all round that little face and those big pop-eyes she's got; even sharp-faced Maureen looks softer and pretty today.

"Mizz Addie says, if y'all ever want to do this again, y'all got to be perfect ladies. Don't make me tell her y'all been anything but, hear?"

Like they're one instead of three, they open mouths together, sing out, "Yes, Minyon Madam," and laugh to beat the band. I do, too, and we're ready as we ever will be.

Sunday afternoon matinees ain't the most popular round Jameston. That's one reason Mizz Addie let us come. Just a few old couples hanging round so far waiting to go in, plus one group of girls look like high schoolers. They check us over good—the car, too—and I hear whispering, but not much more. I get my girls in line behind them, they pay they dimes, then I mine. Before I head in the side door that leads to the upstairs colored section, I tell them one more time: "Perfect ladies, y'all remember?" In they sweep without a look back, through with me for now.

The minute I start up the stairs, the dark swallows me, and the movie house smell gets in my nose. Only been twice before, and it always smells the same to me: stale food, sticky soda, dirt, sweat, and something else, something lonely. Upstairs ain't crowded, I see that once my eyes get used to darkness. The colored section doesn't hold more than about twenty, and ain't a quarter full. I find a seat in one corner where I can lean out over the rail, keep an eye on the hoes. The newsreel starts up and still's no sign of them and I'm getting antsy, when here they come, parading their hipswinging selves down the aisle, got popcorn and drinks and who knows what all else. When they finally settle in once and for all, I do, too.

Lord, ain't it fine to sit back and watch folks mess up and know you ain't the one's got to clean behind them? That Bette Davis girl up on this screen—reminds me how Faith looks some—she is one drunk hussy I'm glad not to deal with. Leave that to this slim boy who gets cow-eyed every time she looks his way. She's telling how she's a jinx, brings bad luck wherever she goes, and I'm thinking, wouldn't have to tell me but once—but he lights her cigarette and she fixes him with eyes that're about to

pop slap out her head, big lids coming down slow and then easing back up. I shake my head some, on account of I can tell that
boy's a goner now.

Right in the middle of all that somebody sits himself in the
seat next to me—why folks got to crowd up when there's plenty
of places other to sit, I ain't know—but I just keep leaning up,
half watching Bette Davis playact and half keeping eyes on my
hoes. About the time she tells him she's gone dance over the cliffs
to destruction, I start to feel something crawl up my back. I reach
one hand around to slap it down, but nothing's there. In a minute, right in the middle of that boy telling the good girlfriend he's
not marrying her on account of being crazy about that bad one,
here it comes again, tiptoeing along my spine. I reach my other
hand back and *whap*—that hand's grabbed and held fast. My
heart gives one big thump, lodging itself right up in my throat,
seems like. Round whips my head, a scream fixing to squeeze
itself past my full throat. But when I see what I see, that scream
dries up to nothing, my heart gives one more thump and drops
itself right down to toes, and my voice box manages to squeak
out, high and whispery, "Hey, Winston."

Next thing I know, that boy's pulled me back from the railing
and I'm settled in close to him, his one arm snug round my shoulders. The air smells of mint and Winston.

"How'd you know I was here?" My whisper comes out right
loud, on account of me not being so in control as could be.

"Shhh," is all he says, and puts his finger right against my
mouth, holds it there. In a minute, he goes to outlining the shape
of my lips with that soft finger, round and round. My whole face
tingles, and in my belly's a funny sliding kind of feeling.

Finished with lip-tracing, he moves fingertips cross my cheek
now, over to one ear, tracing whorls, then the other, down jaw to
chin. Big Robert's mama, Mizz Suzie, over at Little Town?—
she's blind, used to feel faces with fingertips. That's how this
puts me in mind of, what mind I got left, anyhow. A blind feeling
in the dark to know something.

I don't know what this boy's getting me into, all I know is I have been hungry so long for this touching, I ain't got will enough to stop it. I soak it in, drowning in it, like somebody dying of thirst taking in cool, clear water.

One arm around me, tips of fingers from the other stroking, Winston shifts some, blocking me and him from other folks up here. His fingertips slide down my neck, trace the hollow bottom part. I lean my head against his arm and the seat, everything in me going loose like I got neither bone nor muscle. No words, just breathing. Folks're still talking on that screen, but I long since got no idea about what.

Keep my eyes shut, like if I don't see, can't anybody blame me for this. Don't need to look anyhow; my body feels what's gone happen next, like it's something I memorized a long time back and just now am remembering. Don't even know my blouse's unbuttoned till I feel his warm tips touch my own red-brown ones. Between two fingers he rolls them, gives a small squeeze, causes my throat to make a noise it's never made before. He leans over and licks my lips, light as air, brings his mouth to my ear, says, "Shhh." And I try to hold groans in.

Then smart fingertips make their way to legs. My skirt lifts some and a warm hand grazes my calf, then knee. Lying floaty against the seat now, my breath comes shallow, my head swims.

Then his fingers touch the inside of my thigh, way high. When they do, oh, when they do—here comes some other something altogether, clamps itself down hard like a door slamming shut, bears down on all these lovely fluttery feelings and tramples them to the ground, roars though my body like a freight train, jerks me straight up off that seat and comes barreling out my mouth before I know any of it's gone happen or even what it means: *"No!"*

Every head in that balcony swivels our way—hear them do it, together, like one. My chest's heaving, knees wobbly, can't make myself turn sideways to look at him or those other faces, staring froze and gape-mouthed. From downstairs floats up one single white-girl voice. Belle, peeved: "We ain't even *doing* nothing, Min."

98

Between buttoning my shirt with fingers that most forgot how to work and fetching my hat where it fell behind the seat, I don't catch Winston leaving. Time I'm nervy enough to look around, folks' eyes're back on the screen and that boy's gone, the seat next to mine as empty as I feel.

The rest of the movie only parades past my eyes, while I look inside to wonder, did it all happen or was I dreaming something real enough to shout about? Did I really holler out at all?

That question gets answered soon enough.

Those three's gathered in a clump, waiting on me, when I get down the stairs. Outside, the late October sun's still bright enough to squint against.

They bustle on over. "They started it, Minyon." Belle's the chosen speaker, that much's clear, the other two nodding heads, up and down, like they're on pulled strings. "We wasn't looking to make no trouble," heads go side-to-side shaking now, "even after they threw popcorn—wasn't any co-cola left in Maureen's cup, anyhow, mostly ice, and besides, it didn't even reach where they . . ." Her voice dies off when she sees I ain't paying the kind of attention she's expecting. "How'd you know, anyhow, Min?"

"There's all kind of things I know, Missie. Best be remembering that." But my heart's not in it, and they know it.

Once we're in the car, Maureen pipes up, pushing her luck. "Let's go get a soda."

"Please, Min, please," Faith and Belle chime in.

Don't I know Mizz Addie's watching the clock, looking for us to turn into that dirt road right about now? "I reckon so, ladies. A quick one, hear?"

I pull in front of Prosser's drugstore, and out they pile. "You coming, Minyon?" Maureen turns to me.

Belle looks surprised. "She can't, Maureen. She's a, she's colored." It's Maureen's turn to be surprised. Belle looks past her shoulder, asks me, "Want us to bring you a soda, Min?"

"Strawberry," I say, and settle in to wait, hoping to collect myself. But they're back out in a blink, holding sodas in paper cups.

"Maureen said why don't we get them to go, and take a ride while we're drinking," Belle says as she climbs into the back seat. "Here's yours."

"Thank you," I say, and when I back out, I catch Maureen's pale eyes in the rear mirror.

We ride to the end of Water Street and on down to the Boulevard, where the land flats out to water and the blue bay sweeps wide over pale brown marsh grass and on to the ocean somewhere past.

"Let's park," Maureen says, and we do, just looking out and sipping. In a minute Belle heaves up a big old sigh, says, "She could of had him, don't you reckon, if she didn't go turning good, there at the end?"

"Yeah. Just goes to show you where being good'll get you," says Maureen, her old hard voice in place. "You heard what Bette Davis said—'a bad woman's got something a good woman doesn't.' Smarts, that's what."

"She was noble," Faith's thin voice is pretty sure of its holy self. "She saved herself by saving him."

"Oh, save it for the preacher, why don't you," offers Maureen. But ain't no heat in it.

It's quiet in the car a minute, while we sip on sodas.

"Maureen, you ever been in love?" Belle sounds young as she is, wishful.

"Naw. Love's for saps. Suckers." Her straw rattles, and I turn so's to catch a side view of their three faces.

"Well, maybe I was after all, kiddo, once. My first john, I guess. The one who turned me out." She laughs low. "See, that's what love'll get you—honest work.

"It's why I moved down here, kid. He was no good for me, taking most of my jack while I worked my ass off, if you know what I mean, seven days a week at Mother Faye's. And she knew it and knew your Miss Ariadne Fleming and Hazelhedge, so she set the whole thing up, see?" Voice comes quiet. "And I'm better off without him, see?"

Maureen doesn't look near so hard in this light, and I surprise myself by aching for her old Yankee girlness. She sees me watching, though, and must be catches something through my eyes—she loudens up her voice and looks bitter and hard at me. "And I'm going to have my own house one day, make a pile of money, take care of myself. Maybe even be famous."

Belle's voice comes soft, her eyes some sad. "I remember one time at a church dance, Johnny Hamilton swung me over in a corner and pushed against me and whispered in my ear he loved me. First time that ever happened. I didn't love him, though—he had pimples and smelled like tobacco. Said he wanted to marry me, but I think he just wanted to get in my drawers." She makes a loud slurp on her soda. "Still, wonder what it'd of been like, married to Johnny, three or four head of younguns to tend to, baking pies like my mama, helping run his daddy's farm . . ."

"Stupid. It would've been stupid, Belle. Why'd you want to spend your life taking care of some snot-nosed kids and their randy-ass daddy—for free! Wise up, kiddo. At least now you get paid for what you do." Maureen's got pentup mad in herself now, itching to get out.

"Yes, we do indeed," Faith comes dreamy into the talk. "We're paid each time we release those boys' essence from their earthbound bodies and serve it up to the Lord," she says. "I know I am well rewarded, when I see their pure souls go ascending to the Lamb." She sighs, "Praise God."

"That isn't their souls, Faithie-girl. It's man-sweat, steaming up, probably, off their backs. Assuming, that is, that a girl like you prefers missionary position. Better watch out, girlie. If they're sweating that much, they're working too hard—you're going to wear yourself out early."

Faith doesn't favor smartmouth Maureen with any answer past one loud soda slurp.

"Still," Belle's on her same track, worrying it like a dog with a scrawny soupbone. "I do wonder what it might be like, not doing this. Watching them town girls at the show today—"

"Bunch of stupid high schoolers, Belle—sweet little virgins, every one—don't know their ass from a hole in the ground. You're chasing after that?" Maureen's pure disgusted.

"All's I'm saying is, there might be some somebody somewhere a girl could fall in love with, and have babies." That face is so young, about makes me want to cry. And inside me's asking the same one question—*is* there some somebody?

Maureen turns away, toward me, where I'm looking back at them. "How about it, Minyon? You fall for this crapola? You ever been *in love?*" Spits it out, like salt in her mouth.

Why Maureen's decided I need to be part of this conversation, I don't know. I sit myself straight up, face back round and fix my hat. "Time to get, ladies." Start the engine and pat the gas. "We're gone be in hot water as it is, and it's coming on time for dinner and y'all readying y'allselves to sit for Sunday night company."

Dark's falling for sure, now, as we head through town.

"You kind of like that Winston, don't you, Min?" Meanmouth Maureen's got Belle interested now, and the whole thing's way out of hand, far's me.

Don't turn to face her, just work like crazy to push back thoughts of soft fingers tracing lips. "All I like's doing my job, Belle. That's all. Which I've been some slack at, seems like."

"Maybe Minyon here's a virgin herself, Belle—maybe she's saving it for her very own hot-blooded, dark Prince Charming." Maureen laughs, unsweet sound. "That'd be rich, huh? Colored maid keeping a house full of hustlers, keeping herself pure as, as—why, pure as charcoal."

Far enough. I pull the car to one side of the road and turn myself halfway round. "You may keep your smart mouth to yourself, Miss. Unless you care to stop here and truck your Yankee behind back to Hazelhedge on foot."

Quiet now. In place of where used to be three young girls in the back seat sipping sodas and thinking on what might be, there's nothing now but a pack of pouty hoes I'm ready and anxious to get back to their place of business.

I pull out, and we none of us say a word. Before I turn down Hazelhedge road, I put my hand back for their empty cups and throw them and mine out the window. Ain't no need to call attention to the fact that we been some elsewhere than Camelot.

When I park the car, they open doors and pile out, two of them bustling off fast to outback. Before she gets out, Maureen leans up close to me in the dark front and says, low, "Sorry, Minyon. I got nothing against you—just got, you know, hot about things."

Ain't had much practice hearing sorrys, and it takes me back some. By the time I turn to be gracious, she's gone already, swallowed up in Hazelhedge's dark.

Sarah's not here Sundays, nor Frank either, so I throw some cold cuts and bread on a platter and leave out for whichever of the hoes wants to fix hers. I stuff a sandwich in my mouth while checking parlor, linens, liquor, glasses. No sign of Mizz Addie still. The girls start gathering and it's time to give the hall mirror her lucky once-over. I'm bending down, cleaning the bottom part, when here she stands, reflected on the glass about an inch from my face. I straighten and turn. She doesn't smile, looks full in my face, seems like drawing truth from me, pulling it out in a string and taking it all to her pale self: balcony touching, one loud No, marsh grass, soda talk, one white girl's sorry—every last bit.

Her mouth opens and the doorbell rings at the same exact second. "I'll get it," I croak. She silent-steps one leg aside. I pass—too close, but safe for now.

One night around here's pretty much like another, and this one's no different. Just harder, on account of skinny Luella's not here to help. Lighter traffic, like most Sundays—I figure left-over churching must keep some away. Mizz Addie's cleared out early this night, gone by three without a word, leaving me to work it by myself and ponder what she's thinking. Which I try hard not to, clearing the last ashtrays from empty parlor, fixing to get my weary self to bed and hope not to dream. Then I hear it: screaming, coming from round back, behind the main house.

Through the hall and kitchen I fly, my feet scarce touching floors. From the kitchen stoop I see them, two hoes screeching and clawing, end over end in the dirt between outback and kitchen. And over by the walkway's standing one mister somebody, too dark to make out who from here, hat in hand, looking like he's fixing to turn tail any sec now.

Ain't no question about it: this's what Mizz Addie calls a disgrace, and it most surely is against the rules round here.

"Maureen!" She's the only one I can make out for sure, that white blond hair she calls platinum gleaming under porch lights. In two seconds flat, I'm out there between them, shorter than both but stronger, too—fixing first Maureen, then that new girl Geraldine, with what Ophelia calls the eye. They're out of breath. Geraldine's got three deep scratches marking one cheek, and in her hand's a hank of blond hair.

"Stand there and don't move one muscle, if you know what's good for you." I fix them both once more. They resemble statues, now.

Casual as I can muster, I stroll over to the tall white man in the shadows. When I get close enough, I see it's Mr. Linwood Clary, owns the Rexall on Cater Street. He's been a regular of Maureen's long as she's been here.

"Nice night, ain't it, sir?" Careful not to call his name, on account of Mizz Addie says it makes them jumpy. I pull up beside him and start walking toward the front, hoping he'll just naturally follow. He doesn't though, but tears glazy eyes off those two and looks at me.

"What?" Maybe he's wondering to himself what business one thin colored girl's got with him. Maybe he ain't taking too kindly to it either, but what choice I got but pressing on?

"I said, getting on coolish, eh, sir? Best be getting inside somewhere, safe and warm."

He looks down at me, puts his hat on his head, jams his hands in his pockets.

"Don't worry yourself about that mess, sir." I'm all bright and breeziness. "Those girls're just exercising. Wearing off extra energy they got, don't you know." This time when I move forward, his feet get going, too.

"We do this kind of thing all the time, sir. It's what we call tradition, round here. It's just for show."

I see him to his car and stand waving like this's my house and he's been by for an evening's visit. By when I turn the corner to outback, the whole Hazelhedge gang's gathered round: Geraldine and Maureen still faced off, just like I left them; Faith, Jeannine, Francie and Belle all goggle-eye watching; and up on the porch stoop is Mizz Addie her own self. Who opens her mouth just as I round the corner, saying, "We'll take this up in the morning, ladies. Right now, get yourselves to bed."

Fixing to do just that myself, crossing the yard and my fingers at the same time. Don't bring much luck this go-round, though.

"Minyon. I'd like to see you inside. Now."

Certain as Judgment Day, ain't she? "Yessum."

Figure we'll have it out in the kitchen, but she only stops there long enough to ask me do I care for some tea, which she herself fixes while I stand on, dreading.

"Come on," she says, handing me a cup of tea which she's sugared and stirred, too. "We can talk in here."

Her bedroom. Have mercy, what in creation's going on now?

She motions me to the chaise and sets herself down at the desk, turning the chair to face me. She sips, studies me, and starts to open her mouth. That's when I know: she's fixing to fire me. I way overstepped one colored girl's bounds this day, and'm fixing to be on the street, heading back to Little Town or New York or wherever I can think to go. Half of me's fear-frozen, the other half's hallelujahing. I sit straight up to meet it, don't flinch.

"I've been watching you lately, Minyon." Not exactly news to me, Missus, eight years of watching. "And I think you're ready for a change."

Here it comes. I take a sip and hear my own throat bob, trying to keep tea down.

"I'm giving you a raise. Two dollars extra a week."

The tea most forces its way back up on that. Mizz Addie gets up, goes to the safe beside her bed, and opens it, bringing out her black book where she keeps house accounts. Makes a mark in it, and looks at me, saying "Done," then sits back down.

"I want you to play more of a role with the ladies, the way you did tonight, Minyon—manage them, make them your personal responsibility. Keep them happy, and doing their jobs."

She sits back, sipping, taking her time. There's a certain look she gets on her face when she's fixing to tell me stuff, and she's wearing it, and here it comes. "The way you handled yourself just now proves something to me, Minyon—you understand what we're about here. You have grasped the value of discretion and respectability." She laughs a little under her breath at that, looks down into her cup and whispers, more like talking to herself than me: "Respectability." Shakes her head and squares off at me again.

"Hazelhedge exists because we have a place in this town and in this state—in this world, for that matter—and we know exactly what it is. And the minute we forget that—that's the minute we're gone, Minyon.

"I need people around me who understand that. And I think you do."

She puts her cup down and leans forward, keeping her eyes on this froze-up face of mine. "See, Minyon, you might not know it, but you're very good at this. And what you've got here at Hazelhedge is something a girl like you might look all her life for and never find: a position. A career, Minyon—a calling, one might almost say. A future, certainly."

But even while she's talking, my mind's conjuring one very other future for this girl. New York, maybe, and dark brown eyes.

She looks away a minute, then brings her eyes back full force on mine. Must be's read my mind. "I know you've had your eye on Frank's Winston, and yes, he's young and handsome. But, Minyon, don't fall for that trap. He's here now, but he'll be gone tomorrow—no question—and you'll be left with less than you had before. Maybe a lot less. You're too smart for that."

Rising, she sets herself beside me, close enough so tea breath and Addie-smell smoke up my nose, make my head swim. "Hazelhedge is where you belong, Minyon. Something special: it's your *place*." Then she actually touches me, pats my hand with her butter-soft one, nods like it's all been decided, and stands.

"It's almost four-thirty, Minyon. Why don't you get some sleep."

Who in the world can sleep now? "Yessum," I say, and don't look back, just slow-step my way to outback room and bed.

Don't believe I'll dream the first vision tonight: no parade of Jesse, Gan, Farina; no baby bub. Too dead tired to more than drop. Still, before my head hits the pillow, one clear something does make itself felt clean through weariness: Hazelhedge ain't the place I want to be no more, raise or no raise. Nossir, I'm ready to get shed of it, one way or another. Get out, make a place for myself. Be free.

And the last thing my head knows before sleep is a certain angle of light shining upon the face of Mr. Winston Laurette.

chapter 4

"If you don't sit still, Minyon, it'll just hurt worse."

Hair's flat being pulled out of my head, and this Yankee girl expects me to sit still?

"It's looking positively gorgeous, isn't it, Belle?"

Just in case that's anything resembling truth, I got no choice but to sit, holding my lips tight together to keep from hollering out.

Belle moves closer just when Maureen gives one pull even harder than the rest. In front of my eyes comes floating a hank of my own frizzed hair.

"Hard to work with, though, ain't it?" Belle's not even particular looking at me, just at my hair, like I'm a storefront dummy they're fixing up.

"A real corker—never saw anything like it." Next yank about lifts me off this stool she's got me sitting on, and here comes more floaters. She's gone snatch me bald, for sure.

It does feel funny, having somebody mess with my hair, especially this white girl, Yankee at that.

Belle stands back to look at whatsoever Maureen's up to with my hair. "I believe Winston's gonna sit up and take notice today, Min."

Surely hope so. That's the only way it all makes any kind of sense, letting these two talk me into this on an afternoon when I'm supposed to be in charge on account of Mizz Addie's run off to Charleston how she does every week or so, seeing about some of her own private business.

"Hazelhedge is your personal responsibility this afternoon, Minyon. I'm relying on you to take care of things." Off she glides in her big old Packard, looking in the rearview mirror till she's lost round the corner of pines. And ain't thirty minutes before these two's come up with a plan for me, which I couldn't manage to rally a big enough *no* against. Tired of all this personal responsibility Mizz Addie keeps trying to heap on me, anyhow.

Fact is, I ain't been able to put behind me what happened, or almost happened, or didn't, those few weeks back at the movies. Even though Winston still comes round most afternoons with Frank, he doesn't pay me much mind—polite and all, but eyes don't meet eyes. I can't get my mouth round words to tell how come I acted so fool at the show, nor how much I'm craving that same touch of hand one more time. Mizz Addie's keeping a sharp eye out, too, and every time I turn around, she's sending scrawny Luella out to take that boy a sip of something when he's working in the yard. The two of them don't seem to have trouble talking; I see them laughing and running their mouths to beat the band. Got to make sure I keep that girl otherways busy, for certain.

And all the time I remember how fingertips felt on skin. Makes me itchy and crazy. I heard Frank telling Sarah that Winston's leaving soon, too; his mama figures to be in New York City by Christmas time. And maybe I figure to be there too, if he wants me. But how's he gone want somebody who acts fool as me?

I've been pondering it ever since *Dangerous*. This morning I made up my mind to take it up with Ophelia.

"Is sex something we're supposed to like?" Worked up to asking it for days, and never lit on nothing politer.

"Supposed to?" Ophelia raised her head from the pile of laundry she was busy sorting long enough to study on my face some. Then she just shook her head, lowered it, and went to tongue-clucking.

Standing there looking at the top of her head where gray hairs're fast getting the jump on black, I felt a big lump in my throat, on account of Ophelia's the only one I got the nerve to ask and here she was, about disgusted with me. What now?

She looked up and rested her eyes on my face again, then hers went soft, she quit her sorting and came over. "What is it, Min?"

Grateful for that kindness, I busted out crying. Ophelia took me in her arms and covered me round with clean laundry smell. Rocked us both some—reminded me of Gan, which made me cry harder.

After while I got hold of myself, but Ophelia kept her strong, soft arms wrapped right round me.

"Ain't no suppose-to's about sex, honey. It just *is,* like breathing. Strong enough to make the world go round, I reckon. Or at least us, in this place."

Took both shoulders, held me back from her to study. I couldn't seem to raise my eyes. In a while, she let me go. And though that woman sure enough is a comfort, I ain't ended up knowing much more than before, have I?

"Here, Minyon. Drink this." Some pale pinkness in one of Mizz Addie's best cut crystals.

"We're not supposed to have those glasses out here." That comes out first, automatic. "What's in it?"

"Something to make you feel good. Relax, Minyon. Try it."

Even tastes pink, don't it, going down? Light and bubblish. I take a little bigger sip, letting it slide down my throat. Doesn't taste one thing like personal responsibility.

Maureen fixes one more something on top of my head from out that bag of tricks she brought to my room. Stands back, hands on hips, judging. "Yes," she says, taking her own big swig of drink. "That'll more than do."

She rummages round in her bag again. "Now for some color." Casts eyes my way. "It'll have to be something dark, to show." She grabs up a little pot of rouge, comes toward me. I take one big gulp of pinkness. Mashing her middle finger down into that pot, she brings up a blob of redness, dark as blood, and goes to rubbing my cheeks.

If Maureen's hands on my hair made me feel strange, her fingers rubbing my cheeks go way past that. Can't keep my eyes open, on account of got nowhere to look, while Maureen colors my face red, first one side and then the other, rubbing, rubbing her white girl fingertips into my black girl skin. When she finishes I take a large enough gulp to clean polish off my drink.

"How about get us some more drinks, Belle, would you?"

Maureen's right about one thing: this drink seems to make a girl feel much better. After the door closes behind Belle, I heave one relaxed sigh and open my eyes. Maureen's over by her bag of tricks, eyeing me.

"Never done it before, have you, Minyon?"

I know just what she's talking about, though how she knows's beyond me. She pulls out another color pot, sky-blue this time, and comes over next me.

"Want some tips on how to please your man?"

I say nothing, just close my eyes and wait. In a minute, I feel cool fingers, light as air, smoothing my eyelids. Her breath's close enough for me to smell the pinkness of her drink, soury-sweet.

"Here's the trick, Minyon. From a girl who knows." She stops smoothing and gets quiet and I can't keep my eyes shut. Flip them open to find her face just a inch or so from mine, pale eyes lacking that hard hoe look she mostly carries round in there.

"Give him *everything*. Don't hold one thing back. Open yourself up wide to him."

She dabs more blueness onto one white finger. "Close your

eyes again." I do, and in my mind I'm opening myself up to Winston Laurette, wider than wide, turning inside out, taking him into me, *becoming* him—that's how open this girl's gone be.

Maureen goes to whispering now, even though's not but us two in here. "Can you keep a secret?"

Sure can. My job, ain't he? Keeper. I just nod my head easy one time, so's not to mess her up.

"My man's coming, too. Tracked me down all the way from Troy, New York. He called yesterday."

I remember that telephone call, Maureen telling Mizz Addie it's her brother, there's some family trouble or other, and Mizz Addie hanging round the phone like she's got business; but everybody knew she was just listening in—doesn't much cotton to hoes phone-talking without her say-so.

"He loves me, Minyon. Can you beat it? Him trucking all the way down to this godforsaken hole?" She sighs. "Winston'll come around, just like my Jackie, if you do like I say. Don't hold back."

She's through dabbing now. I hear her move across the room, then come back. "Open," she says, and I do, my eyes heavy with the blueness she's laid on them.

"Don't blink," she tells me—like a person can hold back from something like blinking, comes natural as breathing. Especially when some white girl's messing with her eyelashes. Still, I got to do my best, look my best. I'm fixing to have my one shot at it, is how I figure. Winston and New York City and out of here. Free.

"Ooo-wee." Belle's back, standing at the door with a pitcher full of more sweet pinkness.

"Don't just stand there with your mouth open, Belle. Give us a drink. We've worked up a serious thirst."

Belle pours us both a drink, and it's true, I'm thirsty as all getout, take a couple of large sips right off. My head's starting to fizz up pink inside itself now. Feeling very sweet indeed, ain't I?

Belle and Maureen stand back, checking me out. "What's she

gonna wear, Maureen? She can't wear *that.*" Belle talks like my usual housekeep getup's a pile of rags.

"Nope." Maureen taps one finger against her lips while she looks me over.

"Got it!" She points that finger my way. "Got a dress I bought off a peddler up north, never could pull it over my hips. I believe it'll be just about perfect."

She turns to the door. "Be right back. Don't move, Minyon." Like I got any mind at all to get up and go on about my business.

Belle can't keep her eyes off me, walks round one way, then the other. In a minute, she comes near, brings her baby-blues up close, asks me, soft: "Can you keep a secret, Min?"

Head's spinning by now—and'm hearing one same question over and over. My answer's no different, either, and no need to even nod this time. Belle's so full with having to tell it, it's about to spill out before she's finished wondering about my secret-keeping worth.

Her round soft face comes closer still. She's so quiet, I more see her lips move than hear actual words. "I think I'm p.g., Min. Done missed two periods now."

That knocks a good bit of fizz right out my head. I've been round here long enough to know what's down the road for Belle. She hasn't, though.

"Min, reckon if I tell Charlie, he'll want to marry me? I'll tell him I think it's his." She stands straight now, got hands on a belly's not large enough yet to give up secrets.

"It might be, too. It could be."

No call to ask her how come she didn't do like she's supposed to—take the potash douche every time, right after, that Doc Thayer taught'll keep them from this kind of trouble. Too late now, for any of that. Not but one thing for Belle now.

"Won't be a secret long, Belle. You got to tell, so they can . . ." Heart and words fail me.

She turns dreamy eyes my way, rubbing her flat belly.

"Charlie'll want to marry me, Min, you just wait and see if he don't."

"See if he don't what?" Maureen's in the doorway, toting a pair of shoes, a dress, and the big mirror from her room. We're quiet for half a sec, then Belle bustles to the door. "What you got there, Maureen?"

"Something worth seeing, and something to see it in." That Maureen swears she's got a way with words.

She props the mirror up by the far wall. "No fair peeking yet." She hands over the dress, which feels cool and silky-soft. "Put her on, and let's have ourselves a look-see."

There they stand looking, waiting. I'm past worrying about this couple of white girls now, though. Slipping off my skirt, then blouse, I go to pulling that dress on over my head.

"No, Minyon. That's not the kind of dress you wear a slip with. It's the kind you don't wear a stitch of anything else with." Maureen laughs. "Except maybe perfume."

Cold in here all a sudden; goosebumps raise themselves, head to toe. I let my slip fall in a heap around my feet, unhook my brassiere, and drop it to the floor. Slow-moving, like in a dream, I seem to be. My nips're so hard with cold, they ache.

Keeping eyes on my own body—don't need to be looking up to meet white-girl stares—I pull my underpants down and step out. The cold could kill me now, seems like, it's that strong.

Still bent over, I reach for the dress. This time, I don't stand straight like I might want to, raise my arms to sky and let the dress fall down over my eyes while this body waits naked to take on colors. Instead I feet-first into it, keeping my eyes down on the pinkness of it, keeping my mind on how it glides on, like the soft leather gloves Mizz Addie passed on to me last year. I reach behind myself for the zipper—neither of them's offered once to help—and pull it up. Then, and not before, I finally coax my eyes into looking over where they stand, staring.

Both them's wide-eyed, their drinks halfway to open mouths, their eyes shining. I stand straight as I can. None of us says a

word; it's just them looking at me, me at them, all of us understanding some new something about the other.

Maureen's naturally the first one recollects herself. "Shoes,"
she squeaks out, dropping them on top of my heaped-up under-
stuff. "Step right up, why don't you?"

I do, and she comes up close, giving my neck a cold sweet
spray. "Chanel Number Five, Minyon—only the very best."

She stands back, taking a survey. "Lipstick now—the final
finishing touch." Pulls out a slim gold tube, which catches the
light and gleams.

"Let me, Maureen." Belle's whispering, like church or something's going on. She takes the stick and comes where I am,
touches my shoulder so I sit back down on the stool, tells me,
"Do like this," and stretches her mouth in a wide flat O. Then,
looking into my eyes the whole time, she commences to paint my
lips, me looking right back.

"Now do this," she whispers, backing away and rubbing her
lips together how I've been watching hoes do for eight long
years. Cream over cream, my lips glide. I take one more sip of
drink and see my mouth-marks on crystal, how I've seen so
many others before I wash them clean and put them away. Get a
shiver from up to down, stand to run, maybe, but just wobble
instead.

"Whoa, Minyon. Those shoes'll take a minute to get used to.
Just stand still." Maureen takes the mirror in two hands, getting
ready to show me myself.

Before she brings it up to me, she takes one last long look.
"Who'd of thought it?" Shakes her head. "Ab-so-lute-ly
smaaashing. You're gonna knock him dead, Minyon Madam."

"Min," Belle's in a state of shock, walking round every
whichway, checking angles, "you're, you're . . ." But she finally
just giggles and sips on her drink. Can't seem to grab hold of
words.

Looking in this long mirror Maureen finally sets before me,
I'm about past talking myself.

Ain't all that prone to mirror-looking, never was. You are what you are, I always figured, and what I've been, long's I can remember, is a short, skinny colored girl with frizzy hair pulled back tight in a best-she-can-do bun. I poke out in the usual places, but once I get my white blouse on and my long black skirt, it's not like I've got lumps that call attention to themselves, how Maureen and Belle and just about every other hoe does.

That's sure not the picture I see before me this minute. This slim dark girl's done up in one tight pink dress with black flowers blooming up and down it. Big old straps fit tight round her armtops, her shoulders're bare as bathing, ankles flashing trim over pink high heel shoes with shiny buckles that look like diamonds. This girl's got herself some bosoms and one fine behind, too. Hair's piled high on her head, and there's a bow, looks like three hot pink flowers, holding that hairdo in place. And the face on this one, oh, the face. Brown lids turned blue now, mouth red as raspberries, cheeks colored high on bones. Little spits of hair curled in all round. Who in the world's this face belong to?

"Don't look so scared, Minyon." Maureen laughs and starts packing up. "It's still you, under there."

Ain't so sure as all that. I try out a smile, white teeth next to slick red lips. I look dangerous, to myself.

"C'mon, Belle, we've got to make tracks—get ourselves gorgeous, too." Belle still stands frozen, her mouth gaped open. Maureen takes her arm to lead her off, hollering back over her shoulder, "Do us proud, Minyon. Remember what I told you."

Between what both of them's told me in this little piece of time, the perfumy pinkness fizzing round inside my head, and this strange dark woman grinning back at me from long glass, I'm lucky to remember my name good.

Now comes a door slam I know by heart. Frank's truck. I feel a cold quick flash pass through me—what if Winston didn't come with him today? What if that boy's already headed for New York City? A large sob catches in my throat, and I wobble toward the window, ankles bobbling every whichway.

There he is, though, all six feet or so of him, standing next to his uncle's truck. My knees go weak, and not on account of these shoes, either. All a sudden I wonder—how in this world can I cut Winston loose from Frank without that smart colored man seeing me and figuring something's up? Will he try and stop me? Don't know the answer to that one, and can't afford to find out the hard way.

Don't have to ponder long, though, because right this sec Frank's backing his truck out and Winston's raising one sweet hand bye, and I remember Frank has to pick up Sarah and Luella on account of Mizz Addie's being gone to Charleston. And I know this right now: the Lord's looking down on me and this, saying, yes ma'am, go to it. Which I certainly ain't fixing to shirk.

By the time I get this body locomoting and poke my head out the door, ain't no sign of Winston—disappeared like he'd never been here at all, was just a conjurement of mine. My lip starts trembling and I'm close to busting out crying before I see the tool shed door, half open. And I know I got to work fast, get that boy in here before Frank and those get back.

I open my mouth to call, but nothing comes out beyond a squeak, carried off quick on the cool November breeze. Meantime, here comes Winston, looking like he's got nothing but work on his mind, making for the back door of the main house with Frank's toolbox in hand. He's in and swallowed up before I can crank my voicebox again.

Ain't but one thing for it—I got to go fetch him. I take two steps out on my stoop and can't go further, something's holding me back. Looking down, I see one hot pink heel wedged in between boards. Tired of that, anyhow—I lift my feet from out both shoes, free that one up, and carry them by hand, tiptoeing across outback dirt like I might wake the dead, if I'm not careful. More got in mind waking the living, though.

The kitchen feels warm and safe. I lean against the door a sec, trying to clear my head of pinkness. Perfume floats up to my nose, reminding me—get on with it, girl.

Don't know what that boy had in mind to fix, but whatever it was, I believe it's gone straight out of his head. When I tiptoe up to the parlor door, there he stands, in the middle of the room, gazing first at that oil painting shows naked people lounging round, then at the brocade chair, up at the chandelier, round at the jukebox. His back's to me, but I know by how he holds his shoulders that he likes this, being in Hazelhedge's parlor, letting his head think whatall might go on in here, nights.

Quick and quiet as sin I set these hot pinks on the floor and straighten back up, my head spinning, my feet finding their places in lended hoe shoes. I put one hand on my hip and lean against the door frame, good for steadying. Praying my voice's working by now, I open cream-red lips, stealing words I once heard out Maureen's mouth, been practicing in my head: "Looking for a little jazz, honey?"

Boom—that heavy toolbox of Frank's shakes the whole house when it hits the floor, same sec that boy's feet leave it. He jumps and whirls, hollering out one high screech, face gone dead pale, mouth and eyes both wide as wide. Course I jump too, and got nothing to come down on but these rickety pink heels, which naturally don't hold, so the next thing I know I'm heaped on the floor looking up at one sweet boy's face looming over me, changing from scared to mad to puzzled—blink blink blink.

"Hey, Winston." I smile up at what I've been longing to see. "Just trying to surprise you."

Next blink looks pretty interested, and I take heart. This's gone turn out fine after all, maybe.

"Minyon? That's you?"

I lift one arm, slow and lazy-like, never taking eyes from eyes. "Help us up, honey, and see for yourself." Sound all the world like that Yankee hoe, ain't I?

One more look, then he reaches out and takes my arm, and up I come. He lets go and backs off, still looking. Seems nervous now, licking his lips. Not that I blame him—he's got reason to wonder. "What you up to, girl?"

I go to dusting my behind off slow, one-handed. "No good,"

I say, shocking myself at how the words come out like they been in there all the time, waiting.

That boy laughs one pure laugh then, throwing his head back, showing his strong white teeth. Two steps and he's next to me again. Putting both arms round me, he holds me to him and clamps that sweet dark mouth right down on mine. Just before I close my eyes I see one ray of sun shoot through and hit the chandelier, scattering light that stays inside my eyelids, even closed.

He bends me back some, kissing my neck and naked shoulders, running his hands up and down behind me. I'm no more than part of him, swaying here and there, moving to directions his hands give. I don't have to recollect about holding nothing back—couldn't if I'd a mind to. Back he tilts my head again, kissing, both us breathing so hard we hear nothing else till the truck door slams.

"Oh, Jesus," he groans. I don't say a word—no time for talking, far's I can tell—I just take his hand and lead him down the dark hall to the linen closet, open the door and pull him in behind me. There we are, in the cool dark sweetness I never shared with a soul before now, Ophelia's cleanness all round us. My head spins with pink fizz and Winston-mintness and Chanel.

I turn to him and he to me, and how I figure it, we're fixing to give each other everything, just how Maureen said. My knees're buckling some now, from kissing so, and Winston lets go of me with one arm long enough to grab some sheets off a shelf and throw them on the floor under us, then we both sink down there. Our breaths've got this closet warm already, near hot. He kisses the tiny curls round my face while his hands stay very busy too— unzipping's all he's got to do, but it ain't that easy, me on my back like this. He goes to lifting himself off me a minute to pull my dress down and it ain't but a eyeblink till I'm lying baby-naked before him, though how much he sees I don't know on account of this closet's dark as moonless midnight. He rests his weight somewhere on my bottom half, wrestling his own clothes now. My whole self goes to shaking while he sways up here above me, trying to get his pants down. And it is fixing to happen.

Don't hold one thing back, I hear Maureen telling me how to do—*open yourself up wide.* I try to fix on that, recollecting word for word what she said, trying to keep this bad shaking that's coming up inside me from knocking me and him both to kingdom come, while he hangs here above me trying to get his pants down and I hear his breathing. It's so hot, and I can't quit this shaking, feeling dead weight on my legs, and him on top, and dark all round. And from out the blue I all a sudden don't smell Winston-mint and Ophelia-clean anymore, but bad bootleg-breath instead, and outback dirt.

A pure wildness comes inside me, and in place of opening my legs up wide, how I mean to, I go to thrashing them round on account of my throat's closed up and I can't breathe, nor scream out, neither. Can't breathe and I'm hot way up in my head and can't scream because no air's in my throat and he's still trying to get himself loose and then he does and here he comes, lowering down onto me, and my head's filled up pink and hot in this dark close space. My one hand reaches out to fix on one smooth, hard hunk of something. I hold my mouth wide trying to breathe or scream, I open my hand wide to hold hard smoothness, I swing my arm wide to bring Ophelia's smooth hard iron upside a head so I can breathe, breathe—but still can't and he's fallen down on me now, breath coming ragged, but still breath, ain't he—and I smell a death-stench ain't cleared from my head in eight years—death and rot whiskey and that's all, coming up from inside me, can't be stopped no matter what, and in the middle of it all I hear Maureen's voice one more time, telling: *you're gonna knock him dead, Minyon Madam.* It's coming up from inside me, and I scramble out from under that dead weight lying on top me, so bad-familiar—and out it all comes. Can't even stand, on my hands and knees like a dog over the body of Winston Laurette, and it comes, covering him, Ophelia's clean whiteness, borrowed hoe-dress, all—pink it comes, pale blood out my insides—on my

hands and knees I throw it up time and again, hardly even knowing when the door opens and Luella's high-pitched scream rings
out, hardly even feeling strong Frank's hands lift and lay me on
the parlor sofa, hardly tasting the coffee Sarah forces down my
throat. Even when Frank lifts me one more time, carries me to
own outback bed and covers me up, I ain't got nerve to open my
eyes nor mouth either, though there's something I know I got to
know, sooner or later.

Dreaming now, seems like, and to my dream comes dark
gold-redness, Addie-colors, gleaming and hard, flashing words
hurtful as knives, telling about personal responsibility, boozing,
disgrace, scandal-mongering, law-trouble. About this being one
clean house, one well-run operation, world-famous, and if
you're not thinking about being part of it, then you might as well
be thinking about hitting the road too, like the rest.

In my dream I do—my feet slap one after one down on that
road, heading out, looking for what lies round the next bend,
past these loblolly pines.

In my dream, I do.

chapter 5

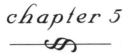

Sometimes you just got to put one foot in front of the other, Min, and keep going. Ophelia again, trying to teach me how to get on in this world. It's one piece of advice's surely been useful lately.

One foot in front of the other, I head into the loblolly pines behind Hazelhedge this Christmas evening, toting a gift I wish not to be. Ain't too cold, that's one thing to be glad of—just drizzly and gray, a sad old no-color world, not much a day to celebrate.

I did my life's share of celebrating anyhow, most likely, last month. Ain't had much to rejoice over since either, unless you count the fact that I didn't kill Winston Laurette, just knocked him cold, split his head wide open to where Doc Thayer took fifty-some stitches putting it back together. I'm sure not celebrating the fact that he was gone by the end of that week, his mama with him, plus skinny Luella to boot—which seems like must have been some redheaded somebody's plan all along—leaving me with more work and less will to do it. Got no call to be pleased about whoall else hit the road either. Faith, that very same day, while me and Winston were having our linen closet

set-to, ran off with a boy that peddles picture-book Bibles door-to-door, came in here for the first time the day before and got so full with the holy spirit he ain't figured to be able to live the rest of his life without Faith—so Belle told me all about, later. And then Maureen, that old hard Yankee hoe I sure don't miss one bit—she came in two weeks ago while I was finishing up my dinner and fixing to get to work, told me, "I couldn't leave without saying goodbye, Minyon. Jackie's come for me." And seeing all the hope writ on a face I knew deep down would be hopeless hard again by when the sun rose one day next week or next month or next year, I couldn't get my mouth round nothing past "Bye, Maureen. You take care, now." And she was out the door and in his car and down the drive before Mizz Addie'd got time to come to the back stoop and stand, hands on hips, glaring at my door, like everything that happens round here falls to me to answer for.

Belle and the other three hoes that's left's had their work cut out for them since, trying to take up the slack for those two disappearing girls till Mizz Addie can put the word out and haul in some more. Christmas ain't the best time for that, either. Feast or famine, she says, shaking her head, by which she means you're either turning them away or beating the bushes for them. That's one of the few times she's had much more to tell me than's absolutely called for. Been getting the silent treatment ever since last month. That's how Mizz Addie does—fills you up with silence till you can't breathe nor think about nothing else.

Anyhow, Christmas's generally slow round Hazelhedge, and up to about two weeks after. New Year's resolutions, Mizz Addie always says; we got to wait till they wear off. Doesn't generally take long.

It's damp in these pines, enough to seep right into my skin, sucking cool wetness in along. Not quite raining, but my face's wet. And I got to get on with this business quick, on account of loblollies ain't no place to be after dark. Daylight's tricky enough—too many secrets's hid out here, ain't they? And me fixing to give up one more, this day.

I have spent eight Christmases at Hazelhedge now, and some's been better than others. This one is the worst. We're pretty much closed up for the weekend, today and tomorrow, though Mizz Addie says if some stray lonesome somebody comes begging, we won't turn him away—everybody's due for presents this day, provided they can pay. Geraldine could take care of them, she's one hardworking hoe, keeps to herself, does her job, not a troublemaker, not since that once with Maureen. She's a West Virginia girl, but's got no family there nor anywhere else she's anxious to spend time with, she says. Doesn't seem too happy about spending time with us, either—here's just where she happens to find herself. Those two girlfriends Francie and Jeannine's already caught the bus to Charleston, planning to stay in a fancy hotel downtown, they say, and eat their breakfast in bed off silver trays.

And Belle, poor little girl, what's gone become of her? She planned all along to visit home this weekend, take the bunch of presents she bought for her mama and the rest. "Won't they be surprised, Min, to see how fancy I am?" Likely, especially since right after Maureen took off, Belle fixed herself up with a dye job, turned her sweet brown hair to hard white frost. Looks fancy enough, for sure. And two days later, cardboard-soled Charlie paid his visit, as usual. Afterwards, when I went in to change sheets, I found her still in bed, naked, all curled up, arms wrapped round her knees, rocking.

"Charlie ain't gonna marry me, Minyon. Why, he don't love me at all." She quit her rocking and stared straight out. "Said whores ain't meant to be mamas."

Nothing left to do then besides let Mizz Addie know so things'd be taken care of before too late. Doc Thayer generally takes care of that kind of thing right here; he stopped by two days ago and did his business. Belle's been taking it easy since, but ain't up to visiting home for Christmas, she said, so she called and told them the plant was working double shifts on account of the holidays, and she'd be sending a special big check, and maybe visit before long. She was too tired to cry, after, her face paler than the clean sheets she rested on.

Right round this very spot's where my brother Jesse rests—his body, anyhow. Visited here plenty of times since I last saw his dark face in the flesh—pulled along by those terrible nighttime visions of mine, won't let me sleep unless I pay my respects right regular.

It's darker than dark out here, though's not but around three in the evening. Always night in loblollies, ain't it?—dark stuff, secrets, buried under gold needles.

I lay Belle's gift, wrapped in a soft clean sheet, to one side, then take up the shovel I toted along with me, and go to digging. Won't take long, on account of the hole don't need to be much. And ain't it familiar, how this shovel slides in, turning gold up, finding wet blackness just under?

We had a little Christmas doings, this noon. Mizz Addie's idea—fixed up some food herself, called me and Geraldine in, we helped Belle to the parlor sofa. Mizz Addie had a gift for each one of us, though none of us three gave her one back.

Geraldine got two pair of silk stockings and some perfume, seemed to make her happy enough. Before opening my package, I watched Belle, hoping she'd get something to make her smile. From inside her big square box she pulled a large white fuzzy something—a teddy bear with a blue ribbon round his neck, shiny dark eyes, and a stitched-on red mouth. "A boy," she said, then whispered to Mizz Addie, "Thank you," and held it up to herself, tears streaming.

Then Mizz Addie turned to me, saying nothing, just looking, so I naturally went to opening my present. First glimpse I got of pinkness made my heart sink down and bob back up, beating hard. Couldn't stop now, though, could I—kept on, and sure enough, inside was one borrowed hoe dress, cleaned of pink insides'd been emptied on it, fresh as new. Hot pink shoes were in there, too.

Eyes stinging, I looked up at her. She stared steady at me. I blinked first, looking off. Then she said, "I've got a little Christmas bonus for each of you ladies, too," and handed out envelopes.

Just about then came a knock-knocking at the front door. It was Sheriff Dawson, who's not missed one Christmas in eight years, bringing Mizz Addie some fine present and planning to spend the afternoon in her room. He's never got over being stuck on that woman, these eight years, and she's come to tolerate him, too. The cost of doing business, I reckon, how she sometimes says about things.

In my outback room I found a fifty-dollar bill in my envelope, a whole month's pay. Didn't give me joy. I took the dress out of its box and hung it in one far corner of my closet. The shoes I lay on their sides on the floor back there, but they still shone too bright, so I put the box on top of them. But even when I close the closet door I know they're in there, just like she means me to. And I reckon that's my cost of doing business.

I was fixing to go clean the kitchen when in walked Belle, holding on to my door frame with one arm, had the other wrapped round that bear.

"Min, can you help me?" Lord, didn't I wish I knew how. I pulled that pale child into my room, set her down on the bed.

The fresh-faced girl who walked in here eight or nine months back didn't bear too much resemblance to this one, white hair crimped hard around a face that's lost its baby fat to hard-boned angles. Blue circled eyes, blue inside blue, stared up at me. She pushed that white teddy bear my way.

"Will you lay him down proper for me, Min? Bury my baby right? I just ain't got the strength for it, and it's gotta be done—going on two days now." She didn't blink those flat blue eyes. "Can you do it, Min? Somewhere safe and right?"

Ain't but one somewhere like that, and now I'm standing in it, opening Ophelia's death sheet to take one last look at Belle's baby, gleaming white, eyes black as loblolly woods, red-stitched mouth seems like grinning.

I hurry to cover that grin back up and lay Belle's babe down softer than I was able to do my own brother Jesse; go to covering white with black, covering and smoothing over with my hands, then spreading gold straw on top so nobody knows where any of this is. And maybe I could stay out here forever, on my hands and knees, covering things, mourning, dwelling on what was or might of been; but I got work to do yet, ain't I.

If I was to put a marker over this fresh dirt, it'd likely read *here lies Hallie Oakes,* on account of that's who I really buried here, and back there in Hazelhedge's nothing left now but a hoe named Belle.

Hard road to hoe, maybe—but mine, I reckon—and I'm getting smarter all along. Making my way back to Hazelhedge through loblollies, I know some things, weigh on my heart sad and heavy. I ain't no girlfriend to these Hazelhedge hoes, nor no sweetheart to some fine upstanding young man's headed for New York City, taking scrawniness along with. I'm not gone be whisper-touched, nor lip-licked, nor laid sweet upon. Ain't gone be but one thing: keeper of this house. Mizz Ariadne Fleming's Minyon. On account of she's been right about one thing all along: this *is* my place, after all.

PART III

1945

War's Hell, Ain't It?

chapter 1

"Did Useless poke his head out yet?"

Those're the first words out of my mouth after I bang through the kitchen door this cold winter afternoon. They're aimed at Sarah, who presents me with her back and doesn't bother changing it nor words with me, just keeps chopping. Girl is hell with a kitchen knife.

Ever since that Useless man first showed up around here, I've made it my business to know right where he is every minute. I don't want him getting round back of me.

Eustace Mason's what he calls himself—who knows if it's the truth? Around here, who even cares—nobody but us coloreds go by real names. Anyhow, me and Frank came up with a better name for him. Useless. Fits him from the top of his slicked-back head of hair to the bottom of his pointy-toed, spit-shiny shoes.

Of course, he looks a heap better these days than two months back, when he first came creeping up our road, conjured out of thin air one Sunday morning, dressed in a crumpled black suit, telling how he heard we might could use some help. Mizz Addie asked how he knew anything about that and he looked straight in her eyes, his shining beady blackness, said something like, "You'd be surprised how much I know, Miss Fleming." Which kind of smart talking doesn't generally set too well with her. But she took a bit to look his wiry little dark self over, head to toe, him staring hard at her the whole time. And when she raised her eyes back up to meet his, the words out of her mouth seemed to surprise her as much as they did me: "I expect we could do with some help at that."

Right then and there I got what Ophelia used to call foreknowing, a bad brassiness that lodged itself way in the back of my throat. Had to go round to the side yard and spit.

"Sarah." I'm tired of her uppity self choosing to speak or not speak, depending on how she feels. "I asked you—where's that Useless?"

She still doesn't turn, just advises me low, under her breath, "Best don't let Miss Fleming hear you call him so."

Lord, some things never change, I reckon. Sarah's still one of the preachiest know-it-alls I ever came across. Fixing to call her attention to it, too, when I hear a whispery rustling I know good as my own heartbeat. How that woman manages to move around without making any more noise than that, I ain't yet figured out.

I dread meeting her eyes, on account of I don't know how much she heard us before vice-versa. No need to worry, though, I see that right off. If there's one thing Mizz Ariadne Fleming's not worrying about this afternoon, it's her gossipy help.

She's sporting her Victory Garden getup, the one she's dressed up in for yard work ever since she decided we're going to jump on this war business bandwagon—it's an old pair of men's pants I believe must of belonged to Mr. Waldo, way back; a big shirt tied at her waist, laced-up shoes. These days, ever since Useless got here, she wears that fire-colored hair of hers down, too—bushy and wild-looking—and her forty-some years old, grown enough to know better. What in this world are we coming to, that's what I wonder sometimes.

"I'm going to turn the garden," she says, all cheery, like

somebody who believes she might could get out there and bring spring on single-handed. That chirpy voice grates some.

Kind of early for turning anyhow, if you ask me. She doesn't, though; just heads out. Even in those man-clothes, she keeps her rustle—I wonder is it skin and bones grating, that Addie-sound, or else fiery hairs, one scratching against the next? Glide-walking sighs.

When she gets to the back door, she turns half around, says: "Let me know when the new girl gets here, Minyon. I want you to sit in on that interview."

I feel heat shoot straight up into my neck when she says that, it surprises me so. Just like always when she gives me new things to learn, she's caught me somewhere between glad and mad. *Like I don't have enough on my hands as it is,* fusses one side of my head. The other side whoops: *She wants to teach me more about the business—ain't I something?* That's the voice wins out when I catch Sarah's eyes resting on my two-sided self. "Hmmpf," is all she says, then turns back to her sink.

"Sometimes there's just not sufficient hours in the day to do all a person's got to," I say, watching Sarah square her sharp shoulders and get back to work—chop, chop, chop.

Some puffed up with myself now, I head to the front parlor to see if Mazelle's doing her job right. Halfway down the hall when the door to Mizz Addie's room opens, and out *he* comes, pulling a sweater down over his head, showing that flat hard belly he's got, covered with long black hairs. The sweater's colored like thick cream, came all the way from Ireland—Mizz Addie pulled every string she knew getting it here, war or no war, so she could give it to him for Christmas. That's the kind of fool she's been over this one.

Out pops his head now, catches me gazing at that belly's bareness. He fetches up his grin, puts me in mind of how a copperhead must smile when he's scoping out a stretch of skin to sink his teeth to.

"See something you like, girl?"

For certain I don't. All I see's one thin mean white boy who's wedged himself in good around here. Useless. The army won't even have him, we heard—somebody claimed it's on account of flat feet, but Frank swears it's just because of general no-good-for-nothingness.

Mizz Addie finds him good for at least one thing, though—behind him I see the messed-up bed they spend way too much time in, and I know when I go to make it, the sheets'll be twisted like they've been wrung. That's how come she's so chirpy and he's so sure of his slick self. Shameful, ain't it?—especially when Mizz Addie's old enough to almost be his mama.

"Nossir, Mr. Eustace." I favor him with my best smart-face, the kind I practice in the mirror—smooth and secret and some stupid. "Just doing my job, sir."

Heading down toward the parlor, I feel his dark eyes push along my backside like fingers.

In the parlor is Mazelle Allston, polishing brass for all she's worth. She's the best worker I've had in sixteen years of day help around here—keeps her mind on her job without worrying about Hazelhedge being a hoe house and wanting to poke into things that's not her business, how most of them do.

"Hey, Mazelle."

"Evening, Mizz Minyon." She looks up a sec, then gets back to it. She is one clean colored girl, Mazelle; her blackness sparkles like it's been scrubbed and polished glossy, same as the brass table top she's sweating over. Cornrows're straight and shiny, too. She's round and dark and sweet as they come. I'm going to talk to Mizz Addie about a raise for this girl, come to think of it.

"When you finish up in here, I need you to check the linens, hear?" That's one job I dodge like poison, keep myself out of that closet if I can. "We're liable to have a full house tonight."

She doesn't look up, just nods. "Yessum."

I run my finger across the top of a picture frame. Not a speck of pale dust marks my darkness. I flip on the light switch, making her blink against it.

"Tomorrow, Mazelle, I'll show you how to clean these chandelier crystals, one by one. A hundred and twelve of them."

This time she looks up, straight into the sparkles of light, then—blind—over at me. "Yessum," she says again, and goes right back to rubbing.

Doesn't exactly run her mouth, does she?—I could get more talk from a stump.

Fixing to try to pry more than a yessum out of this girl, when here comes a car door slamming. By the time I get to the front window, I see the tail lights of Oneal Teal's pale blue Plymouth—Jameston's one and only taxicab—making the turn past pines. Standing in the drive, hitching up two big bags and a pocketbook's near as big is what must be the new hoe.

Whoo-ee—that's all my brain musters, at first glance. This is no run-of-the-mill one, for sure. Not that we ain't had our share of pretty girls over the past sixteen years—we've had plenty, even if the truth of it is most hoes're fairly everyday looking without the flouncy clothes, hairdos and face paint. But this girl's past good-looking; she's something else again. Her hair's red as fire—which Mizz Addie won't like one bit; we only had two or three redheads at Hazelhedge, who somehow never manage to last long. This girl's redness lays smooth on top of her head, then curves down on the side under her chin, almost covering up one eye when she leans forward, like she does right this minute to get a better grip on her bags. Then she gets to moving, one leg after the other—never saw such long legs, going up and up; this girl must be six foot tall, high heels or no—coming toward the house now, like a wildcat stalking dinner.

I move out to greet her. She catches sight of me standing in the middle of Hazelhedge's open front door—not what she's expecting, most likely—but she just blinks once and keeps coming. Then we both hear something from around the side of the house. She stops in her tracks to look; I step off the porch. Over in the side yard's Mizz Addie, big old man-clothes billowed out around her, hair every whichway, a stone rake in her hand, one dark dirt smear down her pale cheek.

The new hoe looks from her to me and back. "How about

one a y'all take you a little break and go fetch Miss Ariadne Fleming, tell her Georgia McDougal's reporting for duty."

I'm fixing to give this girl some news, but Mizz Addie moves forward, and something about her shoulder-set tells me I'd best hush. When she's right about up to the girl, she stops still, looks her up and down. Slow, no smile in sight. This Georgia-one's not a piece nervous about it, just stares right back. In a sec, she heaves first one then the other of those big bags right at Mizz Addie, so they land by her feet. "And, honey," she's got a long, drawn-out, drawly way of speaking, and a deep voice with some scratch inside it, "while you're at it, how about carry these bags to my new room, hear?"

All the cold of this January day seems like gathers in Mizz Addie's eyes, glittery green ice. I cringe for what's coming, already calculating how long Oneal Teal'll take getting back out here.

As usual, though, this woman's got surprises up her sleeve. She takes one more long study, top to bottom, then stoops and hitches up both bags. "Right this way," and she kind of bends at the knees some, like bowing, smiling with lips only, and walks on past open-mouthed me, tall Georgia strolling right behind.

"Minyon," her voice's sweet enough to coddle cream, "please show Miss McDougal to Miss Fleming's room." I turn to follow, glad not to miss whatever's coming next.

Through the front parlor we go, a three-woman parade passing by Mazelle, who at least's got sense enough to drop her jaw at the sight. Mizz Addie heads for the back door with the bags, not once looking back, and I get up enough voice to squeak, "Last door on your right down this hall, Miss."

Once in the bedroom, she gazes around: first at the rumpled-up four-poster, then Mizz Addie's fine walnut desk and brocade chaise, and finally me.

"Did she call you *Minyon?*" Her voice turns up at the end exactly like the corners of her full red lips. "What kind a name is that?"

"Perfectly fine one, far's I know." Some snippy answer, which I know, but I always was right sensitive about my name.

Two strides of those long legs bring her right up in my face. I got to crane my neck to look up into the near-about bluest eyes in the world, sparkling daggers down at short dark me. "You talking to *me* like that, girl?" Tough as hobnails, ain't she?

I blink up once at her red-white-and-blueness. "Nome." I give her a quick flash of whites to let her know there's no hard feelings. "Talking to myself."

Cranking my neck back to straight ahead, I step around her and start making up the bed. "Anytime you don't like what I say, Missus," I tell her, keeping my eyes on my business, snapping the sheet hard, then smoothing it, "you can rest easy that I'm just talking to myself. You don't have to pay me any mind." Just like I don't have to truck with high-faluty hoes, that's for sure.

She's fixing to let me hold something, her mouth opening to do it, when in walks Mizz Addie, still looking pretty ragamuffin, except she's pulled her hair up in a high twist that makes her look some taller and a whole lot more like business.

Georgia doesn't notice that, though; she's got somebody new to take her irritableness out on.

"I demand to see Miss Fleming right this minute," she says, "so I can ask her what the fuck kind of joint she thinks she's running."

Calm as an early-morning summer sea, Mizz Addie glide-walks over to her desk and sits.

"The finest house on the east coast," she says, picking up her pen and commencing to write in one her notebooks. "The kind where ladies live up to the name, where men get what they pay good money for. Where everybody plays by the rules," she stops writing and looks straight up at where Georgia stands staring, green glitter meeting blue ice halfway, "and I make them."

Now it's pretty quiet in this room, and I reckon I forget to breathe even.

"Do you think you're up to it, Miss Georgia McDougal? Because if not, I believe you can find your way out. Minyon will be happy to call you a cab."

Sixteen years later, and Mizz Addie's still offering a person out before she's in good.

Giving her credit, this tall redhead doesn't much more than swallow hard before she takes it all in and gets on the new track. "Well, that's why I'm here, Miss Fleming." She stalks over and pokes her hand out toward Mizz Addie. "I want to work with the best."

Ignoring that hand, Mizz Addie looks back to her writing. "Suppose you take a seat right there, then," she points her pen at the chaise, "and we'll get down to business."

Georgia tries settling herself, which isn't that easy to do, on account of the chaise being low and laid back and her having a lot of leg to fold up. Meantime, Mizz Addie sits tall and easy in her straightback chair. And I see right off that part of what gives her power's just being sure about how folks's situated. I sit myself quiet on the edge of the bed, fixing to get my first lesson in interviewing.

"Hazelhedge is a thirty-dollar house, Georgia." She doesn't tend to waste words. "That's the base price, covering half an hour, straight service. You get half, the house gets half. Is that clear?"

"What's covered by your half?" This redhead knows how to cut to the chase her own self.

"The roof over your head and the room to ply your trade in. You pay extra for board, laundry, doctor and incidentals. Here's a breakdown." Mizz Addie hands over a piece of paper, which Georgia glances at, then pouts out her bottom lip. "In Galveston, board was covered by the house take."

Just as well talk to thin air. "Supper's at five," Mizz Addie tells her, "and Sarah Besselieu's the best cook this side of the Mississippi. The rest of the time, help yourself to what's around, within reason. But no food in your room," she says. "Bugs."

Mizz Addie takes a breath, checks her writing pad, goes on.

"The customer pays up front, as soon as you've agreed on services . . ."

"Yeah, yeah, I know—no snatch before scratch."

Mizz Addie pays her not one bit of mind. "And you get the money to me before you take him to your room."

"To you!" Georgia sputters now. "In Galveston . . ."

"Fridays are paydays," Mizz Addie stays calm, taking her voice up one level, riding over Red like a locomotive. "You get one day off a week, three days off for your time of the month, one of which counts as your day that week.

"Jameston is off limits, without me or Minyon along. And wherever you go, you dress, act, smell, look—and talk—like a lady."

Mizz Addie looks up now. "One more thing, Georgia. There's a war on, you know, and at Hazelhedge, we do our part. We're proud to. That means a twenty-five percent discount for servicemen, split fifty-fifty. And we don't wear stockings."

"No stockings? Why . . ."

"Paint your seams on, like the other ladies. It's our patriotic duty."

Georgia seems plumb worn out with it all. But she manages to stand herself up to full tallness. "I don't know if you know this, Miss Fleming, but on Post Office Street in Galveston, I was famous as a specialist." She holds her head up. "What's the going rate for English?—that's my real talent. I do French and Greek, too, of course—but English's where I really . . ."

"I heard about your particular talents from Lena Harold, Georgia, when she called me about you. And about your troubles, too. Let me just make this clear: the sooner you understand that Hazelhedge isn't Galveston and that Ariadne Fleming isn't Lena Harold, the better."

Georgia's eyes go narrow and fiery. "Did the old bitch tell you about my *real* specialty—the one they'd pay over and over just to get a peek at?" While she's asking, she's unbuttoning her skirt. She lets it fall to the floor, unhooks her stocking belt and hitches up her sweater, showing neck to ankle's worth of white skin and something else besides.

"Great God Almighty." I can't help it, the words come hurtling out of my mouth. Even cool Mizz Addie sucks in her breath sharp enough to hear.

On top of this girl's pale cream skin, starting smack between two of the highest, roundest bosoms I ever did see and winding a couple times around each one before meeting up together between them in a straight path that takes in belly button and all and ends right over a wild puff of red cooter hair, this hoe's got the mark of the devil painted on her body—a large, fat snake, all shimmery blues and greens, his long tongue lost somewhere in fuzzy redness. Just before his hooded eyes, like a necklace made of letters, there's a word painted in a curve: *S A M.*

Georgia laughs once, deep in her throat—back in charge again herself now, and liking it. Then she moves her belly just enough to make that devil-serpent come alive, slither his bright terrible length before our very eyes. My neck hairs stand straight up, and she smiles and says, "In Galveston, they call me the snake-charmer, Miss Fleming. Did Mama Lena mention that?"

I reckon Mizz Addie's fixing to come up with some answer, though far's me, my voicebox's frozen solid. Just that minute, we hear a sound in the hall and both turn our necks at once, happy to have something else to rest our eyes on. Standing in the doorway is Useless, and where he's not looking is at either one of us—he's got sight for nothing but one Georgia McDougal and her snake-rid white self.

"Well, well. What we got here—an overeager customer, come early?" Georgia gives one more belly push, makes that serpent curl and swirl. Useless' eyes glow black—he stares like a man in a dream, and the air in this room is thick with something that almost sticks to the roof of your mouth.

"That'll be quite enough, Georgia." Mizz Addie's voice sounds almost normal. "Get dressed and go with Minyon. She'll show you to your room."

"Yes ma'am," says that tall redhead, reaching down for her

clothes but keeping her eyes on a dark wiriness that's not moved from the doorway. "I'll sure do that, Miss Fleming." She pulls a stocking up inch by inch.

Mizz Addie rises quick and walks stiff-necked to the door. "Ready for supper, Eustace?" By the look of him, he's ready for something, but not necessarily supper. Mizz Addie slips her arm through his, gives a little tug, and off they go.

Soon as they're out of sight, Georgia finishes dressing pretty quick. Myself, I ain't been able to quit staring, thinking all the time about what's under those clothes she's smoothing back on.

"Never saw anything like that before, did you, girl?" Seems like she can read my mind. "Never will again, likely, either."

She picks up her pocketbook. "How about let's get this show on the road—Minyon, is it?"

I nod, and lead the way to outback, trying not to dwell on what I can't see, thinking about what's following me, and what might lie ahead.

chapter 2

Listen to your bones, Min. Plenty of times, their aching'll tell all you need to know. When I get to missing Ophelia most, that's when her voice comes in my head, clear and sweet as life. Wonder what that large woman'd have to say about how things are round here today—with Useless and this new hoe Georgia, and Mizz Addie, gone fool with love. And all this business we got.

Tonight was jumping—two busloads of young boy soldiers, fresh from down Beaufort way, heading from one someplace to the next, randy and skittish as goats. Quick, too, what Mizz Addie calls a volume business—that little Coralie took eighteen pair of fresh sheets tonight, for one, and Rosemary wasn't far behind. I can hear Ophelia now, clucking her tongue and shaking her head, looking at all these sheets, saying—*poor, poor babies, how they gone keep on.*

Of course, like usual, the hoes'll all be moaning and groaning in the morning, but tonight, seems like they're the happiest girls alive—throwing their heads back laughing, showing their long young throats, sparkling diamond eyes, switching hips, leading one trick after the next to their outback or upstairs rooms.

This old war's been good to us, that I know. Hazelhedge never saw such business—last year we had as many as twelve hoes one time, some working round the clock, seem like. Down to ten now, but they sure stay busy. Us, too. Mazelle and Luna, the new part-time help I got for overflow nights, and me, some times, flat-out to keep up with sheets and towels, from upstairs to outback to the couple three trailers Mizz Addie put in back there to take care of this big business the war brought down on us, all these boys on liberty. Why they call it that I don't know— doesn't seem so much like free to me, more like folks with no say over what's going to happen next. Those boys must all the time think about dying, is how I figure it, and's doing their best to pack some good stuff in before, hard as they can. That's what we're here for.

I reckon that's the reason Mizz Addie's so crazy for this war business. "Doing our part," she calls it. She's been tending that Victory Garden of hers for going on three years now. We haven't had a new car in that long either—and even that doesn't rub her wrong. Plus we save paper and all kinds of scrap metal—bottle caps, old pots and pans. Once a week, Frank takes it down to the salvage people. We still eat good, though, rationed or no, on account of Mizz Addie's got her something special, called a X-ration card. "Got to keep the ladies' strength up, Minyon," she told me one time, "so they can do their part, too." Every once in a while, that woman tries her hand at funny. Sets strange on her tongue, mostly.

Now that Ophelia's passed, all our laundry business goes to Walker's. They do mending, too, which takes that chore off me—hoes're all the time popping spangles and such off their dresses, and I got neither time nor inclination to mess with that now. One thing about it, for sure—the sheets aren't the same now—they got a hot, burnt-up smell to them. When I close my eyes and try, though, I still can smell Ophelia's crisp-folded laundry. Brings back memories, good and not-so.

Hard to believe I haven't heard that woman's sweet, sure voice—other than in my head—for so long. Just a short time after our part of this old war started up it was, the morning she came in, hauling that laundry load easy as ever, bending over to set it down. I was up early that day, business was already picking up by then from the war boys, I had lots to do, and sleep never coming easy anyhow. So there I stood, waiting to hand her a cup of tea how she liked of a cool morning. She straightened up, grateful to see it, favored me with that wide smile I can still see so clear, that'd about split her dark face and warm anybody's insides.

But her eye clouded up even while I stretched out my hand, and she grabbed one arm with the other and took a gasping breath, gazing right in my eyes all the time.

"Min." She said nothing more—didn't seem able. One leg gave out then, and she crumpled hard to the ground, then lay back, eyes about to bust out, not seeing me anymore, looking somewhere inside. Under all that smooth darkness of skin, her color started fading to ash. Like a fool I stood there, couldn't even let loose of the teacup, spilled some on her arm and neck while I hovered useless over her. She didn't flinch, couldn't feel the heat of this world no more. She was leaving that pain, leaving me, and I all of a sudden knew it.

"Mizz Addie!" I screamed like something was torn from inside my ribs, standing over a mountain of dear dark flesh fixing to depart, screaming for the only other one I believed could help. "Mizz Addie!"

Wasn't but a sec till she came, but it was past too late, had nothing to do with us by then.

There was no way to save her, just like wasn't any way to save my Gan, so long back. I didn't get to tell Ophelia goodbye, though. Still, I'm happy for that last warming smile, glad I was holding my hand out to offer something. Lord knows, that woman offered me plenty. Took me up as family, most.

And family's getting harder and harder to come by. Especially after last year, when Big Robert sent word about us needing to talk, could I come to Little Town. Mizz Addie let me take her car on my afternoon off, and I drove over the bridge and through Jameston, right down Water Street, over the Waccamaw, and turned off the highway onto the big house road. First time I'd been back in going on fifteen years, and never behind the wheel of a car I was driving myself, a black Cadillac to boot. Drove slow down the road a ways, oaks on both sides, moss swinging in the breeze, looked like waving me in, whispering, *welcome home, Minyon Manigault.*

When I turned down the dirt road to Little Town, the first thing I noticed was, while everything else in the world's kept changing, Little Town seemed like it'd stood stock still. The same dirt road, same tar-paper roofed houses that'd been there since slave days, shanty front porches big enough for a rocker or two, barefoot children running loose. They all stopped and stared at that big black car I was easing down the road, kicking up puffs of dust behind. When I passed Gan's old house a big lump grew in my throat, and I saw again her face half-hid behind one screen door, in moonlight shadows, in ever-after dreams. Thought about my brother Jesse, with his sweet voice and mean eyes; my cuz Farina, that wild-headed city girl I'd never stopped missing; and Clarence, way too old for thumbsucking by then, doing who knew what. In my heart, I prayed to see that little brother of mine. Scared, too, wondering would he be mad with me because I stayed away so long.

All that was in my head while I sat in front of Big Robert's house, couldn't make myself get out of the car. Then he stepped onto the porch, still big, still living up to his name—but grayhaired all through his nappy head. Gave the Cadillac and me inside a good hard look, till I had nothing to do but swallow hard, open my door, and step out.

"Minnie," he said, calling me how Gan used to. He closed the door quiet behind him, climbed down off the porch. Had a hitch in one leg, seemed like. "How you, girl?" Smiled with his mouth only—not mean, just far off.

"Doing fine, Big Robert." I walked right on up to him and poked my hand out for shaking. Startled him some, but in a sec he took it, gave one quick up and down.

"Come set." There were two rockers on the porch and I eased into one. Wood curved round my back like it'd just been waiting on me to come set up my rhythms, back and forth.

"Lally around?" It'd be nice to see that woman's face, I thought.

"Feeling kinda punk today, Minnie. She's inside, resting." Robert's voice rumbled deep in his chest, trying for quiet.

He leaned forward, elbows resting on knees, and laced his fingers in and out, twisting around, all the time looking down like he was trying to figure out what they're up to. Finally cleared his throat and got down to it.

"I wanted to tell you face-to-face, Minnie, on account of you've been a good sister to Clarence all these years."

Two things happened to me then: I felt proud for him to say so and scared about why.

"All that money you sent helped that boy go to Miss Forshay's church school, get him a good start. Smart as a whip, too." Big Robert looked up then, had to give a grin about that.

I smiled back, staying quiet on account of my insides'd gone knotty. *Go on,* called my rocking chair, beating time to my heart. *Tell it.*

He did.

Clarence was so smart, Big Robert said, that he headed for New York City to look for work, instead of signing up for timbering at Arcadia. Didn't find any, though, so when the war came along he decided to sign up for the army. They took him, trained him, and set him to work in the kitchen.

My heart slowed a sec when I heard that part, because my mind said nothing terrible's going to happen in a kitchen—already forgot that's where Ophelia drew her last. Didn't happen to Clarence in a kitchen, anyhow, so Big Robert's voice told me as I sat there rocking, taking his rumble deep down into myself and storing it to bring out later and shuffle through, like cards that might hold some true something I needed to know.

Happened on a road somewhere in France, he said. Supply trucks were going to set up the next camp—one minute they were riding, the next they were blown to kingdom come. Wasn't time to know it, Big Robert said—they told him Clarence and the other boys never knew what hit them. Thank the Lord for that much, said Big Robert.

He got up heavy out of his chair, went into the house and came back with an envelope in his hand. I read the words on the telegram inside, started with: "We regret to inform you that your son, Clarence Manigault Tarbox. . . ." First I knew Big Robert and Lally'd taken my baby bub on as their son, and I was glad of it, even while feeling like I'd lost him again.

"They sent what they figure's his remains, and we're gone bury him at the Little Town cemetery, if that's good with you. He's the first veteran there ever, Minnie." Big Robert had some pride to his voice.

"It's Minyon, Robert," my voice said, surprising even me. "Not Minnie."

I handed back the envelope on account of it belonged to him. All that belonged to me of Clarence was what I could hold in my head; and sitting there on that Little Town porch in a rocker that was wanting to claim me for its own, I knew that wasn't sufficient.

Feeling family-poor and sad down to my bones, I managed to crank my voicebox to ask, "Anybody ever hear about Farina, Big Robert? Is she making it OK?"

He looked back down at his hands, fingers cradled round my brother's death news. He shook his head. "She's living, that's about all I know. Wild living. Had a couple younguns, died on her. Drove her to bad, is what we hear."

Before I left, I gave Big Robert some money and said I'd send more, to make sure Clarence had a good sending off. In that good man's eyes I saw Little Town's ideas about Minyon Manigault, how she's gone to bad, too, a hoe house girl driving a big black Cadillac. She was good to her brother, though, they'd say, that's one thing, at least.

On the road out, the moss wasn't swinging anymore, on account of the afternoon breeze'd gone stiller than death. It just hung like sad gray fingers, trying to latch on, while I drove underneath, back to my place.

I didn't witness Clarence's putting down. Wasn't any need to, far as I could see.

Didn't go to Ophelia's, either. Me and Mizz Addie did pay a respect visit to her daughter's house, though. A slim dark girl came up to me there, shy and serious-faced, asking quiet, "Are you Miss Minyon?"

In that face was a certain something that gave my heart a tug. "Yes," I said.

"I'm Lawtonette. Ophelia was my grandmama," she said, then handed me something small, wrapped in a cloth bag. "She left word with me that whenever she passed, I got to be sure you get this."

I grabbed hold of it, looking into eyes that put me in mind of some I'd never see again. "Thank you, child," I told her, and the heat rose in my head, trying to bust loose.

Soon's we got back to Hazelhedge, I went to my room, opened the bag, and caught my breath. It was Ophelia's rabbit-foot—her charm, mine now. The last little bit of her watching over me. Hasn't been gone from me since, except for bathing—I keep it next to my skin all day, hold it under my pillow, nights.

Driving home from Little Town and Big Robert's last year, I stroked that charm, prayed for some magic something that could turn time back to start. Nothing's that magic, though.

I kept to myself when I got back to Hazelhedge, didn't share the news about Clarence with Mizz Addie or anybody else. But she heard it someway—doesn't she always?—and said nothing to me, just sent what Big Robert said was the biggest, sweetest wreath of funeral flowers anybody ever laid eyes on. It was a fine burying, he told me, the last time we talked. First veteran, he reminded me again. But I don't picture Clarence as a soldier, all uniformed and tall. To me, he's still one dark small boy, shirttail flapping, milk-smelling, all eyes and red cherry mouth closed round a curved-up baby thumb. I remember how his cheeks worked it, hollowing in and out. Little bub, gone now, ain't he.

Bad nights like this one, I stroke my Ophelia charm, trying for sleep. Everything goes round and round in my head—all this dying, all this living—deviling me like the hag that rides poor sinners.

There's devils in this house now—that I know. Snake-rid Georgia, evil scratched right into skin; thin dark Useless, burny eyes ain't left that tall redheaded hoe in the two weeks since she first strolled in. Already I see how things're headed with their two bad selves—I catch eyes meeting when Mizz Addie's head's turned away, some oh-so-accidental hand brushing against hip in passing, one creamy neck arched just so, knowing it's hungered after. Thick enough to smell, what these two's hellbent on but ain't got round to yet.

Mizz Addie doesn't see it; she's not smart as herself these days—maybe blind with Useless' smooth-skinned young body, keeping her bed warm, staving off old. Hadn't had a soul in her bed since Sheriff Dawson passed on some years back, so I reckon she's feeling overdue for some skin on skin, Useless or no. Anyhow, she's all caught up with her Victory Garden, and running this busy house, and something else besides, something secret that's got her jitsy, not like her usual in-charge self. She spends lots of time playing up to the bigwigs that pass through here now from every place you can think of in this world, too—plenty from Washington, D.C., itself, come down to visit some of the rich Yankees that's bought up all the old plantations round here. A trip to Hazelhedge's always on their list; Mizz Addie says more government business gets done around here than most places.

They're all doing their part, and we do ours. Everybody's making money hand over fist while they're at it, too. Except the hoes, who pay out most of what they make before they got it good, and the soldier boys, who got nothing to lose and lose it all, spewing out ten- and twenty-dollar bills like there's no tomorrow.

There is, though. And who knows what it's going to bring.

Lying in my outback bed this early morning, when all the rocking and rolling round here's leveled off to a caught sigh or a half-asleep moan, I mourn my losses, stroke my lucky charm, hold Gan's old blanket close, and listen to my bones, like Ophelia said. They're warning of bad trouble ahead, and I wish with all my heart that large woman was here to get us through it.

chapter 3

"Hazelhedge is a thirty-dollar house, Pearl." Sitting in Mizz Addie's straightback chair, looking down at one of her notebooks and holding her slim gold pen in hand, I feel like she herself's in my body. My voice even sounds Addie-ish.

I sit straighter yet. "That's thirty minutes of your time, nothing fancy. Half for you, half for us." That "us" has a funny ring, doesn't it, and I can't make myself quit scribbling lines on this piece of paper in front of me to look up and see if this new hoe's surprised or glad. She's not said word one since she walked in the door and I brought her in here.

"Always collect the money up front, and let Mizz Addie have it before you take the customer off." Waiting to see if she offers up any smart-aleck sayings, how Red did, but all's quiet over there on the chaise. From where I got my head down I can see the tip of one white strappy shoe. It doesn't move, just points in at the edge of my mind.

"You get paid on Fridays, food's good, supper's at five, and don't eat in your room on account of roaches." Hurrying now, to get this over with: I figure anything else that needs telling can come later. All of a sudden, though, that white-tipped foot gives a little jerk and's gone.

"Where is the real madam of this house, please?"

She's pulled herself off the chaise and's standing poker-straight, holding her pocketbook so tight her knuckles're white. Either scared or mad, one—how I see it, there's not but an inch of difference between those two feelings anyhow.

I stand up, too. "Mizz Ariadne Fleming's in Columbia today on business, just how I told you."

She sets her mouth, which's fixing to quiver. She's no taller than me, this Pearl. Big pale eyes, curly light brown hair, and an ashy color to her skin, looks like it might feel grainy under your fingers if you touched it. Can't be much more than nineteen or twenty, I see that clear, and seems more scared than mad to me, the longer I look.

"C'mon, I'll show you round and take you to your room. Mizz Addie'll be back before work starts up tonight."

She sits back down, grabbing hold of that tiny white pocketbook like it's the only thing between her and perdition. "I'll wait."

"No, Miss, you won't." This girl just as well know who she's got to listen to around here before we get further down the road.

"You need to pick yourself right up out of Mizz Addie's chaise and come with me, so you'll know what's doing round here by business time tonight." I stand over her, hands on hips, looking down at her pale-skin self.

She's quiet a minute, not looking up, then out it comes: "I didn't come all the way here to take orders from a nigger." Her words ain't loud, don't have to be—they go off in my head like firecrackers.

"If you're planning to stay here, Missie, there's one you *will* take orders from—that's me, Minyon Manigault. I'm the house-keeper here, just so you know, and next to Mizz Addie, the one you *got* to take orders from." I hush a minute and watch her bottom lip shake. "If you don't feel up to it, Miss Pearl or whatever you call yourself, you'd best walk on out the door this minute. Got no time to waste on such, myself." Mizz Addie to the bone, ain't I?—offering out right off the bat.

It works, too. In a sec, she stands up and we look eye to eye. She blinks first.

"Where do I go?"

Just in case, I got to make sure she knows who's who.

"Wait in the hall. I'll be out in a minute." She picks up her one small suitcase and walks to the door. "And close it behind you, please."

The minute it closes, I sink back down on Mizz Addie's chair, feeling shaky-legged. This madam-business isn't easy as it looks.

I tear out my scribble sheet for trash and close Mizz Addie's notebook, laying the pen right back where I found it, on account of she's mighty particular about things being in their proper place. Stand up to leave when I see something doesn't look right about the table beside her bed—which isn't a table, but really her safe, which she keeps covered with a long lace cloth—handmade, she told me once, holding her palm under it for me to admire. She does have a sweet tooth for fine stuff.

I go to straighten the cloth, and see it's caught up in the safe door, which isn't all the way shut. Makes me suck my breath in sharp. Never saw this safe open long's I been here, not unless Mizz Addie was right next to it. Holding the cloth up, I reach out to close the door—got every intention in this world of doing just that. But my hand seems like's got its own mind—swings that heavy door out, instead of in. I smell the dark of steel, the oil that keeps it quiet, and secrets. Powerful mix has my head spinning.

Inside is neat as Mizz Addie's closet, where the shoes line up in plastic covers one after the next and dresses hang in one spot, blouses in another, skirts somewhere else. Just so in this safe: some few metal boxes stacked one on one, biggest to littlest, a stack of notebooks and papers, and a bunch of letters with a rubber band around them. V-mail, some of them, like the girls get from soldier boys sometimes. It crosses my mind to wonder who in creation's sending Mizz Addie such, and I pull them out to see they've got the name Fleming in the top corner and's addressed to Mizz Addie at our Jameston p.o. I flip through the stack of them, like my fingers might tell me what's what. I'm peering inside the safe the whole time, and all of a sudden I see, pressed way up against the back wall of it, that one special notebook, what Mizz Addie calls her Blue Book. Makes me forget about everything else.

My arm moves inside the dark safe, dark into dark, my fingers reaching for the biggest secrets Hazelhedge holds. That's what Mizz Addie told me once, holding that book in her hands like it was the Bible, tapping it so I could hear her nails on the leather cover, saying, "This is our Blue Book, Minyon, named after a famous one in New Orleans. It holds the key to Hazelhedge, no more, no less. Herein lies our future, our past, our safekeeping." Every time Mizz Addie gets talking so fancy, it gives me the shivers. I remember how she smoothed her hand over the top then, like she was holding something holy, before she put it back in the safe.

Now I touch that book myself, softer than skin, and draw it out to the light. The key to Hazelhedge. Aren't I part of that, and got the right to see?

Holding my breath, I open it to the first page. On a white piece of paper, in Mizz Addie's fanciest hand, is written:

The Hazelhedge Blue Book

and underneath, off to one side:

Ariadne Fleming, Prop.

In the middle of the page is printed a handful of words I can't read, must be foreign. I run my finger around their lines and points:

Honi soit qui mal y pense

and feel the skin on the back of my arm prickle, on account of they seem like magic. The key, like Mizz Addie says.

Too far gone to quit now. My trembling hand turns one page.

And stops. Then the next, then riffles through quick to see if there's something different. But there's not.

Mizz Addie must of lost her mind—this book's nothing but men's names, one to a page. Some I know right off—folks who've been coming to Hazelhedge ever since—and some I don't. After the names come some dates, then's written hoes' names, which get crossed off and new ones added. And sometimes there's a note or two: "Likes dressing up," one says. "Face man," says another. And then a few pages over, under Mr. George B. LaBruce, who used to be magistrate and sometime'd come for Saturday night doings in the back parlor: "Golden shower."

Still puzzling over how Mizz Addie thinks this mess's the key to anything, when I hear Pearl's voice start up out there in the hall, high and thin, then joined by a low one. Quick as eyeblinks, the book's back in place, lace cloth lifted up, door shut tight, handle pushed down. I got time to stand and whirl around before the door flings open and there stands Useless, his sharp eyes up-and-downing me.

"What you up to in here, gal?"

"Hazelhedge business, Mr. Eustace. Just how Mizz Addie said to do."

I step toward the door, but he doesn't move his wiry self for a minute, just stares at me while I fix my eyes on the door frame next to him. When he figures he's got me worried enough, he brushes by too close—I smell his sharp tangy meanness—and heads into the room. Standing in the hall is Pearl, who's lost that uppityness and looks more like a little girl, hoping for somebody to show her what to do next. Lord, ain't I seen sixteen long years of eyes like this?

"Come see the rest of the house, Pearl, and meet the other ladies." I flash one last look behind as we start down the hall, and see Useless standing next to that locked-up safe, looking glare-eyed at me; and in the back of my head something falls into place—*click*—like the door on a safe safely shut.

I show Pearl through the kitchen where Sarah favors her with a sharp look and one short head nod, and on to one of the new outback trailer rooms to leave her things. Then I show her on into what Mizz Addie calls the common room, set up in the next trailer, where all the girls sit and talk and listen to soaps while getting themselves ready for business. Yvette's in there now, doing her needlework same as always, and listening to *Stella Dallas*. She smiles friendly at Pearl. Then in wanders Faye and Doreen; they start asking the where-you-froms and who-you-knows, and I think Pearl's in good enough hands for me to get. So I get.

I pass by Mizz Addie's garden on my way from outback to the main house. It's not but mid-March, but things're already coming along just fine. Smells *green* out here in the early evening air, and stuff's stirring underneath. Change's coming.

I surely do hope it's good change, like all this green promises. But what's stirring doesn't seem so. And what worries me is, how come Mizz Addie's putting so much on me? She's not her old hard self lately, hasn't been since this war started, for some reason, and now with Useless, she's worse still. Going soft, seems like, wild-headed, between this garden and all that young skin. And careless—leaving her secret places open for anybody to mess with.

She gets all misty-eyed about the young boy soldiers, too, lets them get by with stuff she wouldn't generally no more put up with than fly to the moon. Like last week, when a blond-headed boy in his navy blues came knocking at the door round five of a slow Tuesday evening. I got there first, naturally, and was fixing to let him know he could do his business if he'd a mind to, but if it was a party he was wanting, he'd have to come on back around nine or ten. Just started explaining when Mizz Addie came up behind from somewhere, went to talking over me.

"May we help you, son?" Her voice was low and sweet as honey. That boy's blue eyes lit up when he got a look at her.

"We're just looking for a place for the one night," he said, nodding his head back at the car which I all of a sudden saw for the first time. A young girl was sitting in it, looking over at us, squinting against the sun, her forehead wrinkled and worried looking.

"Just for one night?" I swiveled my head around, surprised she even bothered to ask.

"Yes ma'am," he held his white sailor hat, turning it round and round.

"Where're you from, son?" What's that got to do with anything, I wondered, and a little sigh spit out from my lips.

"Wadley, Georgia, ma'am." He looked right at her, sky-blue-clear eyes. "But I'm shipping out tomorrow, and we, well, we just got married." He grinned, and a big old blush shot up from his white neck like it was being painted on while we watched. Meantime, he looked down again, round and rounding that hat of his. "We stopped in Jameston to see about a room, and somebody told us about your place here."

It was quiet on the porch a sec, and I was fixing to do the dirty work, let that boy know somebody'd played him for a fool—we ain't that kind of place. But Mizz Addie stepped by me, out onto the porch, and walked with the sailor boy over to his beatup old car; the next thing I knew, we went into action. The hoes cleared out of one outback trailer room, their doors shut tight, the room'd got fresh flowers from Siau's Flowerhouse and our softest, sweetest sheets on the bed, and those two newlyweds were behind closed doors, doing their business. Mizz Addie served them a couple of prime steaks that night herself, with all the trimmings, plus a bottle of Hazelhedge's finest champagne. The hoes had to shift for rooms, and a few boys had to wait, but nobody grumbled about it. The girls just sighed and mooned about how it was the sweetest thing.

Hard to figure what this world's coming to—Mizz Addie especially. Not that I got time to ponder it, do I. Got plenty of work that needs doing.

Coming up the back steps, I hear voices in the kitchen. ". . . gone off one more time and left us in charge. She think this place runs itself?" Sarah's voice isn't loud, but it carries.

"Acting different, that's for sure," comes Frank's low rumble. "Maybe we need to . . ."

I creak on the last step and open the door at the same time. Both of them look up sharp from their low, secret talking. Seeing them over by the sink, something strikes me all of a sudden about these two, how Frank's tall self towers over Sarah's smaller darkness, which seems to fit right up under him, like one puzzle piece against the next. They're standing close—not touching, but just *together*—in some way that makes my belly feel empty and my throat catch.

"Evening, Minyon." Besides his hair going whiter, Frank looks the same to me now as when I first laid eyes on him. A girl can't help but be glad when he's around.

"Hey, Frank."

Sarah seems further away from him now, without having moved a muscle that I see, and I figure my mind's playing tricks on me—and not for the first time, either.

She speaks right on up. "Who's that new one you were carting round today?"

"Name's Pearl," I tell her.

"Pearl?" She gives a little unfunny laugh. "Where's she from?" It's not like Sarah to be so interested in a hoe.

"Didn't ask," I say, and give Frank a little grin. "Ain't none of *my* business."

"Doesn't generally stop you," she shoots back, then gives one of her *hmmpf*s, and turns herself round to the sink. That's Sarah's notice, always was—she's through with us for now.

Me and Frank grin at each other. "Hear tell you're the new madam round here," he says. "Think you're up to it, Min?"

"Miss Manigault to you, sir." I pull myself up to a Mizz Addie shoulder-set, holding my chin high, sweeping my eyes over him, how she'll do sometimes. "Can I assume by how you're standing around talking that you've completed your tasks this evening?"

"Getting right to it, Miss Manigault," and he heads for the

back door. We laugh. By the sink, Sarah shakes her head and mutters.

Out he goes, and I head to the front parlor on account of it's a worse mess than usual—we had a crowd in this world last night, and there's a whiskey spill on the blue armchair I know'll take some extra work getting out.

Heading down the hall, I hear Mazelle in there cleaning, humming church music to herself how she sometimes does. Then I hear something else, behind me down the dark hall, coming from Mizz Addie's room.

Voices. All this day long's been one set of them after another beyond doors, just past my reach, and doesn't seem like it's going to stop now. Dark and whispery as shadows, I slip myself down the hall and stand before one thin slice of light that shows me all I need to see and more besides.

Stripped naked she is, spread out on Mizz Addie's very own bed, so tall those bare toes of hers almost dangle over the edge. He's on the bed too, dressed in nothing but dark pants tight enough to seem like skin, rocked back on his knees beside her, taking stock—reminds me of how a buzzard'll choose his spot before he goes to lunging in for lunch.

She's got both hands behind her head, and laughs up at him—I see the flash of white teeth between drawn-back lips—saying, "Like what you see, Mr. Mason?"

He doesn't say a word, just takes his hand and trails it backwards from her cooter up to her neck, slow and steady. Her belly arches up, then back down, and she ain't so much smiling now as staring at him, glazy-eyed. With one finger he goes to snake-tracing—I see it circle twice round one bosom, same round the other, then in a straight line I know's following that devil-mark she wears in her skin. He stops short of that orange-red puff of hers. She squirms, laughing low.

"Yeah, baby," he tells her, tracing circles on skin. "I like it just fine." His hand stills, then swoops down, grabbing hold of her soft belly flesh.

She jumps, her hands flying out from under her head. "Ouch! Shit, Eustace—that hurts!"

He goes back to tracing, a crooked little smile on his sly weasel-face. "Hurts me too, baby, thinking about all those other men, get to like it just fine. Hurts bad," and he twists his hand in her cooter hair, and she turns and groans, but doesn't reach out to stop him.

He's tracing again, and after she catches her breath, she tells him, "That's my job, Eustace. I got to let them."

Still he traces. She's quiet a sec, then says, "Besides, how about you and Madam Fleming? You think I like knowing what you two do in here?"

His hand slides down into her red puff, and she relaxes her legs some. My skin goes to tingling, my breath coming shallow, my head light. From way far off I hear sweet, slow gospel humming, like calling me from sin. But I can't any more move from this door than quit taking breath.

"You don't worry your head about that, honey girl. She's just my ticket to ride, and I'm just her baby boy." Nasty-voiced, ain't he? "We got us more important things to be thinking about now, don't we?" Soft and slick as oil he is.

Both of them's quiet a bit, then he asks her, "You let them do this, Georgia-girl?" while his fingers make rhythms she has to match.

"Yes, Eustace." Her hands're flung back beside her head now, eyes closed.

He scootches down and bends over her, licks his tongue once, slow and deep, where his fingers've been, then raises back up. "You let them do that?"

"Yes, Eustace. Yes." His hand goes back at her now, and he unbuckles his pants and sheds them quick, changing dark skin for white, never moving his hand from its rocking business. She's gone now, lost inside herself with what he's doing. His bare behind's facing me, muscles flexing down to legs, strong and wiry.

"We're going to have to figure out a way for you to get a different job then, aren't we, baby?"

She doesn't answer this time—too far gone, any fool can see that. Not him, though.

"Aren't we, baby?" Louder this time, and still no answer. He straddles her, takes both hands, grabs the softest belly skin down low, and twists.

Red's eyes fly open, glittery and strange. My heart, which's been beating in my chest to the time of their rhythm, stops short.

"Stop them from leaving their mess on you, writing their names on you—right, baby? Like Sam here." And while she watches, he jerks back from her, leans his face to her belly, and bites. I see his jaws working hard. I'm about to scream myself, but she doesn't, just stuffs the sheet into her mouth to keep from.

He raises his head in a bit and goes up close to her face. "That's *my* mark now, baby, on top of his. Deeper."

Then he takes that sheet out of her mouth and kisses her, and she goes to groaning and moaning again, and in a sec, he lifts himself into her and goes hammering over and over, making soft little grunts and causing Mizz Addie's bed to bump the window sill, like somebody's knocking to come in, over and over, making the same rhythms this old house's shook to long as we've been here.

My legs'll scarce carry me from there; I got to grab hold of the wall and creep back down toward the front parlor and Mazelle's sweet music, calling me back to light from the blackest bad stuff I ever laid eyes on. I sit myself in the armchair a bit when I get there. Mazelle fixes me a cool, damp washrag to hold to my face, which feels burnt-up from what it's borne witness to.

Barely got my legs steady, fixing to see about that whiskey stain, when I hear steps by the hall door and look up to see his own evil self, worse-than-Useless, staring at me. My insides start shaking, and I want to make a sign or spit to ward off badness, but I can't bring myself to move.

"Minyon." His voice's flat as a rock, ain't it—gives me the shivers, wrapping itself around my name. "You need to get Miss Fleming's room straight before she gets home."

"Yessir," I say, and get working on this armchair with seltzer water and a rag for all I'm worth.

"Now," he says. And I got no choice, do I. He stands aside from the doorway to let me pass, then his steps fall in close behind mine.

"You'll need to change the sheets," he says, his voice so near in the dark it makes me jump. I open the linen closet door and don't step all the way in—such bad old memories in there and now a hellhound on my heels to boot—just grab sheets off the certain shelf where Mizz Addie's stay. She doesn't use the same ones as the hoes, never has.

Nothing's messed up in her room but the bed. He leans against the wall by the door, arms crossed and one leg cocked over the other. Watching me.

My knees go to knocking again when I catch sight of Mizz Addie's bed. On top of her fine, white, lace-edged linens's a fair spattering of what must be belly blood. I'm about to get light-headed again, but I start stripping the sheets instead, not looking up.

"Just as well burn those things," he says, and when I look over I see he's pulled out the long silver toothpick Mizz Addie gave him and's reaming in the space between his two bottom teeth.

He nods toward the bloody sheets. "Cut myself shaving." He grins, and I swear by all that's holy, I must be in the room with a very devil. Hot enough in here for the sweat to bust out on my palms while I smooth on fresh new sheets.

He doesn't offer up another word, just fixes those flat black eyes on me when I pick up the old sheets and head to the door with them. Then he draws himself up by my face and whispers, "I expect a girl like you knows how to keep secrets, isn't that right?"

He's got me now, I can't tear my eyes off his, so dark and flat, that could swallow a colored girl up and never leave a trace she'd been at all. "That's right," I whisper back. And then he takes that toothpick out of his mouth and presses it, spit-wet, against my cheek, up near my eye. I don't blink.

"That's good," he says, giving that pick one sharp jab. "That's real good."

Then he moves it and swings the door open for me to pass.

Don't remember getting here, but I'm all of a sudden in my own outback room, holding these sheets up to me like they could save me from something, laying myself down on the bed and drawing my knees up against things way scarier and realer than haints, trying to rock away badness, call back Mizz Addie or Ophelia or some somebody to take care of things before they go too far.

On my face I feel his mark, still see his jaws working on Red's soft underbelly skin, blooding these fine Mizz Addie sheets, which I stuff far under my bed for now on account of I can't curl up here forever, can I? After all, there's business needs taking care of—men aching to prove it, hoes ready to let them. Drinks to pour, glasses to wash, sheets to change, smells to cover up, stains to clean or hide. And devils to watch. No turning back now.

chapter 4

─────── ✍ ───────

The sun beating down on the back of my neck feels more like late August than early June. The tomatoes show it, too; they're past being juicy and firm and a bunch's fallen off the vine since I last picked. The parts that's been on the ground have gone mushy and soft, hiding their rot till I go to pick them up. My fingers push through red skin, and I leave them lay, seeds spilled out on dark, dry ground. Gives me the shivers, and I move on to the crooknecks and peppers, too tough to kill.

Gardening's just one more chore's been put on me these last few months, since Mizz Addie lost herself. She doesn't do a thing these days besides flit—from her bed with Useless, to town two or three times a day, to Charleston or Columbia every now and again. Won't light long enough to see what's what. Got her a new laugh, too, high and skittish, goes with all that moving she's doing. If I try to stop her long enough to ask something, like what we're serving for Saturday night doings or who's going to town shopping, she's got but one answer: "You decide, Minyon."

I'm the one decides about everything these days, and it's not near the fun I reckoned. The thing I'd most like to decide is what's gone wrong with that woman, and how to fix it.

Puzzling over it hard as I can, I can't figure it. I don't believe it's this war, on account of if so, then ever since they told us last month we got it half whipped, she'd of been better.

Lord, we did have us some celebrating that day—town folks and sailor boys and soldiers all together out here. *Free drinks all around,* Mizz Addie called—though nothing else was free—and it was the biggest party Hazelhedge ever saw, till past ten the next morning. Looked like a war'd been fought right here, folks passed out and heaped up every whichway. Luna and Mazelle and me were all day cleaning up, just to start over again that evening.

Mizz Addie's no better since that news, though—frazzled worse than ever, maybe.

In the corner of my mind I hear a rustling by the far edge of the garden. Don't have to lay eyes on it to know, but when I half stand, my creaky knees grumbling, I see him: a black snake, winding over this outback grass, hunting him some cool shade anyplace he can find it.

Snakes. Could be that's what's got Mizz Addie going. Even though it seems like she doesn't know what that pair of two legged serpents're up to, deep down she's got to, smart as she is. Any fool can see it, ain't a Hazelhedge hoe doesn't know it. Those two take every chance she gives them, and that's plenty— slipping off to some outback room, the cool dark linen closet, her own bed—time after time, like wild starving things they are, who can't fill up. Even when Mizz Addie's in the parlor of an evening, and he's helping out with drink-making and Georgia's on the sofa entertaining one of her tricks, they'll pass their hungry looks right before her eyes. Which just get shinier than ever. And blinder, must be.

The hoes aren't afraid of Mizz Addie like they always have been, either—she'd have a hard time bossing them, if it was her doing it. Which it isn't—it's me. And I'm pretty much hard as nails with them, got to be, and they mostly don't give me grief, colored or no. All except Georgia, who I keep far away as possible from, and Pearl, who doesn't pay me a bit of mind, acts like no sound's coming out of my mouth when I talk.

My sweat showers these vegetables as I lean over them, and I reckon to be through picking for this day. Putting my basket on the back stoop, I look to the woods and feel a beckoning how I sometimes will—these windless loblollies's still got voices that can call my name, paths my feet can follow blind. Got to go, don't I?

The coolness welcomes me like an old friend, offering gold needle-mat underneath, green shade above, and a sharp piney smell to fresh my head, make me clean and new.

But Pearl still's lingering on my mind. Sarah believes she's got that girl figured out, told me one day last week when I was grumbling on about how funny that hoe acts, how she doesn't fit in with the rest, how I sometimes catch her with a look on her face that strikes my heart cold. "Seems more like she's scared near to death, than mean," I told Sarah, for lack of anybody else to tell.

"I don't doubt she's scared," Sarah said, without troubling to turn from the counter where she's making cornbread muffins.

"Think this's her first house?" We've had first-timers before, but they generally loosen up pretty quick. Pearl does her share of business and we haven't had complaints, but she hasn't relaxed in three months—strung tight as a drum, and no girlfriend round here to cut fool with, trade secrets, and laugh at the tricks, how the rest of them will.

"Maybe it is her first," said Sarah. "But that's not what she's afraid of."

One know-it-all, ain't she?—forever was.

Riles me, too. So last week I just left those words of hers hanging in the air and went on about my business in the front parlor. After about an hour of cleaning and thinking about Sarah maybe knowing something I needed to, I finally dragged on back to the kitchen, started fixing myself a glass of water.

"Sure can work up a thirst today." It was burning up then too, like now. It's been one hot, dry summer, for sure.

Sarah said nothing past *hmmph*. I stared at her back, where sweat'd wet through her starchy white shirt.

"How you know what Pearl's scared of, Sarah?" I finally broke down and asked. "You been talking with her?"

"Don't have to. All I got to do is *look*."

"Huh," I said. "Hard as I look, can't see nothing but what she *ain't* scared of—me."

"No, Minyon, you're dead wrong." Sarah turned from where she was cleaning vegetables and was going to tell me finally, on account of she saw no work'd get done otherwise.

"It *is* you that girl's scared of. And me, and Frank—all of us." Wiping the wet from her hands with a dishtowel, she studied that, not me. "She's scared we'll know one of our own."

Her face went hard, and she looked straight over at me, her mouth twisting: "That girl's *passing*, fool." Then she turned herself right back around and got busy, leaving me gape-mouthed.

Ever since, I study on Pearl every chance I get. One minute I think she's way too pale-skinned, and's got those light eyes; the next I notice the curl of her hair and that slant of cheekbone she's got. Mostly, though, I just see a sad, scared little girl, whatever color she happens to be. So as soon as I get around to some of this other business that never seems to get finished, I'm going to have a talk with that girl, before too late gets here, and something bad past helping happens.

I'm thinking so hard that, before I know it, my feet've found their way to my own dark place, marked by only memory, but sure as if a line was cut clear through pinestraw and dirt and hard earth below forever, separating this one spot from all others. It's cool in this place, pure joy on heated-up, sun-soaked skin. I slip out of my shoes, then off comes my blouse and skirt and underthings. The air strokes my bare skin, sweet as lover's breath. I lay me down on these cool gold needles and close my eyes, and this secret-saving ground seeps up through dirt and takes part of me into it, leaving some of its own dark self in me.

My brother Jesse's bones're under here and some part of my baby brother, too—his old brown army hat, given to me by Big

Robert to remember Clarence by, he said. Buried deep now. Hot pink dress and borrowed hoe shoes, too. And blooded sheets, and more. Secrets, turning black under all this gold—part of me, me part of them.

This loblolly burying ground holds so much of me and mine, it's like church for me. How Ophelia used to say the spirit of Jesus'd get in her blood and give her peace down to her soul—that's how here does me. I lie still and quiet, my soul soaking up the secrets of my earth, till seems like it rises out of my body and floats above.

When I'm full enough with that, I rise and dress again, breathing slow and clear now, and head back to Hazelhedge.

I'm not but halfway there when I hear something that stops me still. Right off, I think the loblollies're tricking my ears, but in a sec I know clear through skin and bones to my core: it's those same voices that's been hiss-whispering round corners and past doors for going on six months now.

The first thing I feel is mad—these're my loblolly woods, they got no business bringing their badness here. Just two beats pass before curious takes over, though, and something else besides, drawing me to them.

I bind myself to shadows and slip soundless off the path toward their voices. My feet fall on soft needles that won't tell on me, the cool dark air wraps my skin in a secret cloak, and my body finds one old rough pine to keep safe behind. Invisible, I bear witness.

In a clearing not but scant from me's Useless and Red. They've been at it a while, I reckon, on account of they're both buck naked, pale skins shining through piney shadows. He's lying on his back this time, she's a-straddle, looking down. That woman looms so large over him, seems like she could break his back if she was to buck her hips just right one time. She doesn't know about being strong, though, does she—she'd swear she's weak—I see it in the hang of her head and shoulders. Useless is running his mean mouth.

". . . opening your legs for every one of them, night after night. Doing whatever they tell you—right, Georgia?"

Her dark red hair hangs forward, covering this side of her face. She nods, hair swinging like a curtain.

"Hump me," he says, his voice flat as a rock. And like he's pulled a string somewhere, her hips push forward into his, blue-green belly snake slithering to the rhythm, keeping its own time.

"That's how you do *them,* isn't it, Georgia. Any old one that wants it—fat, ugly, short-dicked, hairy—there's nobody you won't hump, is there?"

Still gyrating hips, she shakes her head back and forth.

"Stop it, whore!" He reaches up and slaps her face, knocking her head hard enough to where I catch a glint of one eye. Her hips go still, her head hangs further down.

Inside me's rising mad. Georgia surely's no favorite with me—she's too cold and strange—but still I want to jump out from my place, holler to her: *Girl, quit hanging your head—can't you see you the one's got the goods? Get up for yourself, Red!* But I do nothing, just keep my dark watch, got no voice or power. Invisible.

"Get off me, slut." He hitches one leg; she loses her balance and falls to the side, then crawls off. Huddling up, she makes herself small.

He sits halfway up, spits his words. "If you loved anything besides your own sweet ass, you'd quit."

"I love *you,* Eustace." She says it, though far's I can hear, there's not a stir of love in her voice. "But there's no way in hell to quit, sugar. Got to eat, don't we?"

She holds self to self, her knees drawn up, her back toward him and me. He takes one gold pine needle and strokes it across that curved white back. His voice goes softer, but not sweet: "How many times I got to tell you, baby? Of course there's a way in hell to quit. We just get us a little place, a few good girls, and open our own house."

She says nothing, and he keeps tracing patterns, gold on white, in time to words.

"How do you think any whore quits flatbacking and starts running things? How'd the old bag do it? Money, honey. What separates a whore from a business. She had her a sweet setup, and it's our turn now. Don't you see that's right?" His voice rises and falls like conjure talk.

"All we need is a stake, baby—a good start—and then you can save your loving for me, right? Just me and you. And plenty of the green stuff. Doesn't that sound good, baby?"

"Yes, Eustace." But she doesn't turn around.

"All we have to do is figure out how to get the start we need." Slides that needle all around now, whorling. If it was me, I'd be jumping every whichway with that tickling, but she stays still as death. "You know how, Georgia?"

"No, Eustace."

His moving hand stops. He says nothing, nor she, and all I hear's my own wild heart.

"You don't?" His hand gets back to business and his voice goes coaxier. Makes my hairs stand up to hear it, thick as molasses, dark as pitch.

"Told you before, baby, how we can. Time and again—you got to start listening to me." He plays that pinestraw over her behind now, round her hips and waist curve and the shadow cleft between.

"We do it on a Monday morning, right, Georgia? When all the week's deposits are locked up in that safe she thinks nobody but her can get into. Round four or so, when all's quiet, the whores are sleeping the sleep of the damned, that nosy nigger too, and you and me got the run of the house—just like we've had for months. It's our time, right, baby?"

"Yes, Eustace." Voice comes muffled now, like a hand's clamped tight across a mouth.

"Maybe I'll slip her a little extra something that night, and while the old bitch sleeps," he slides that gold straw straight up Red's spine, clearing the hair off her neck with his other hand,

170

"you take that stupid little silver toothpick she gave me," he points that straw at her bare nape, "and drive it in at the perfect angle, just so." At *so,* he jabs that needle straight into the spot where her neck and head go together.

He jabs and I jump, my skin going hot and cold all at the same time. Sweat breaks out from head to toe, and I start shaking, my heart hammering for all it's worth. I hold tight to this loblolly now, for dear life.

But Red hasn't once moved; she might be dead as he's planning for Mizz Addie to be.

He goes to whorling again. "In the meantime, I'm getting the cash together and those bonds I found. Our nest egg, baby. And then we're out the door and down the road. We can ditch that old Caddy of hers along the way. And then it's California, Mexico—our own place, baby, wherever you say. Simple." He draws circles, tighter and tighter, around that spot on her naked white neck. "Sweet and simple."

"I can't do it, Eustace." She doesn't turn round. "I'll do all the rest, everything you say. But not that."

He tosses the straw to one side, takes her neck between his two hands, and presses his thumbs there. "I can't do it, Eustace," his nasty voice mocks hers. "Anything but thaa-at, Eustace."

He drops his hands and turns away from her. Looking pure disgusted, he paws around in his heaped-up clothes, finds a cigarette and lights up. The red match glows on his flat mean face like hellfire. He lies back down, propped on one elbow, and looks her over.

"Guess I'm going to have to find me a *real* woman, then—one who knows what love is. Not some old hand-me-down whore with another man's name scratched into her belly." He blows smoke toward her back. "Fucking yellow belly, at that."

She finally stirs. Sitting up, she moves closer to him. "You're the only one I ever loved, Eustace."

He takes a long draw off that cig, lets all the smoke loose on her face. She doesn't blink.

"Prove it," he says.

She stares at him, and even in the piney dark, I see her eyes go to glitter and shine. Then she's on her knees beside him, rocked back on heels, her cooter not but a breath away from his face. When he brings that cig to his lips, she takes it out of his fingers.

"I can," she says, her voice tight and catchy. "I will," she says.

Then she takes that burning end and turns it round to her belly. Holding it right over the first curve of the letter *S*, she lays that hot tip to skin. Seems like I hear it hissing, red on white. Or else it's him making that noise, sucking air through his teeth. Or else her. She pulls it away in a sec, breathing hard, her eyes gleaming in the dark; then she sticks it back down, right next to the black circle she just made. When she pulls it away this time, she says: "There's nobody for me but you, Eustace."

He doesn't budge nor change words, just fixes his eyes on that inches-away belly while she burns letters from flesh, one black circle at a time. His face's close enough to feel the heat.

When the smell comes my way, my hours-back lunch rises in my throat, begging out. Swallow, swallow, swallow—I got to get loose from this place first, before my insides give me up, and I get myself buried out here along with the bits of me and mine these woods keep now.

My legs won't hold me, though. I drop to my hands and knees and crawl, baby-like, quiet as I can go, trying to hold moans in, and lunch. Trying to stay alive long enough to get back to Hazelhedge and Mizz Addie. Oh Jesus, let that woman be back from town.

Good thing these hands and knees know their way from memory, on account of my head's too full with black burning flesh and gold-silver needles and naked necks to think. No telling how long I wander four-legged through these loblollies—I just all of a sudden look up, see a light at the edge of the woods, and know that outback's just beyond.

Hauling myself up hand over hand against one of my sweet tall pines, I stand. My head's spinny and light, and the lunch that's kept its peace long enough comes spewing out. Then I walk to the back door, my shaky legs calling—*move on, sister, move quick.*

Up the steps, open the back door. No Sarah in here, and should be. The house is bad quiet. Even wild as I am, I feel it.

The parlor's empty, too. Looking around, I hear a high-pitched drony noise, sounds like it's coming from Mizz Addie's bedroom. More bad feelings heap on the worst ones I've just about ever felt, but I got to put one foot in front of the next to see about it, ain't I.

Her door's half open, and when I walk up I see Sarah and Frank in there—they've never been in that room before in their lives, far as I know. They stand together, looking down at whatever's making that noise. I push the door open and step in.

On the brocade chaise is Mizz Addie, still wearing her go-to-town clothes. Her hair's bushed out wild around her bent-over head, and even while I watch she takes both hands and pulls on it, hard enough to where some comes away in a hank. She's folded herself over her knees, and's rocking, pulling her hair, and keening; reminds me of how some of the old ones used to do, a long time back in Little Town, to mark loss.

I look at Sarah and Frank, who seem frozen in place. Then I see it on the floor by Mizz Addie's feet, torn open and crumpled. Not likely to forget the look of that envelope. I reach down and pull out the paper stuck in it, knowing the first few words by heart, for sure: "We regret to inform you . . ." It's the next ones I study not once but twice, before they stick in my head, already full with too much badness: ". . . that your son, Clifford Earl Fleming, was killed in action . . ." Still puzzling out who this boy is, when we hear a hateful voice from the doorway that causes me, Sarah, and Frank to whirl around: "What the hell's going on in here?"

We're struck dumb. Mizz Addie stops her keening one sec when she hears his voice, then goes back to rocking and hair-pulling. This time she puts words to her wail, hard to make out at first, then clearer, over and over: "They killed my baby, my Earl, oh God, they killed him, they killed him, my baby."

chapter 5

Quiet as a grave round here this afternoon. Dog days. Can't hear nothing past the whirr of this fan that's just stirring up hotness, and the scritch-scratching of my ballpoint pen as I pay the few bills Mizz Addie doesn't give cash for.

Reckon tonight'll be one more slow one around here. Ever since last week, when they came on the radio telling about how the war's finally over and done, this house's been quieter and quieter. Some of the hoes took off, on account of their daddies or husbands or boyfriends's coming home. And I reckon soldier boys got more on their minds than rocking in this house.

What keeps popping in my mind's those folks over in Japan where that new bomb got dropped and laid them flat—whole big cities, they say, full of people just walking round, minding their own business, not even looking up to see what's coming and's now blown them to what one girl calls smithereens. So everybody over here's whooping and hollering, blowing horns and having parades, celebrating—while over there's wandering mamas looking for what's left of their babies, sisters hunting for dead baby bubs, folks wringing hands, torn every whichway.

Still, I don't reckon any of us especially knows what's coming before it hits us, do we? Or how we'll act when it does.

I have practiced enough to where I can sign Mizz Addie's name pretty close, but on these checks I don't bother. I'll just poke them in front of her and put the pen in her hand and she'll sign them without paying much mind, the same as she's done ever since her boy died.

Her boy. One pure shock, wasn't it?—finding out she all this time had a son, tucked away in Charleston, going to private school and then off to the war, same as my own Clarence. Except her boy stayed alive till almost the very end, then got his head shot off in some place nobody ever even heard of before, called Okinawa, and the war finished up but scant weeks later. Our in-town p.o., those tied-together letters in her safe, so many trips to Charleston these past sixteen years, her craziness about this war business and Useless' young wiry self—all that came clear to me, after. That woman is one good secret-keeper, that's for sure.

She can't keep much else, these days. Not this house, not even herself. Doc Thayer calls it a nervous breakdown, says Mizz Addie needs rest and time. She doesn't seem nervous to me, though—more like dead, just getting through the motions of one day and the next.

Right after she got the news, seemed like it was just too much trouble to get up in the mornings, so she didn't, just lay abed. She wouldn't let anybody do for her except Useless—held tight to that wiry man, stroked his arm or shoulder, murmured and cooed over him like he was her own boy she'd lost and found again. And I was the only one knew she was clinging to death himself. Besides Georgia, that is, who stayed clear the first few days after.

What to do? I couldn't tell Mizz Addie—she was too far gone to fetch up her name, much less the truth of something that'd finish her off, for sure. And the new sheriff's not a regular out here like Sheriff Dawson used to be. Besides, I worried what might happen if folks saw the way things are around here—how Mizz Addie is, who truly's running this house. I was too scared to tell Sarah and Frank, on account of believing Useless'd just soon kill somebody as look at them, especially coloreds.

So—what to do? I asked myself that time and again, while I walked a circle in my outback room, did my chores and saw to business, when I opened my eyes every morning. Not that I slept much, on account of having to keep watch—just took little cat-naps when I could. The rest of the time, I blended myself to shad-ows and was the watcher, the listener. The keeper-alive of Mizz Addie.

The way I figured it, Useless had made up his mind to make Red do the killing. As long as I could keep space between her and Mizz Addie—too much space for one thin silver pick to reach between—I reckoned to have time to plan the next move.

How things turned out, though, planning didn't have a whole bunch to do with it. More like happenstance, grabbing what's in front of you and making do with it.

Like the afternoon I passed by Mizz Addie's bedroom and saw her in there alone for once—who knows where Useless'd got to, getting with Red, most likely. In I tiptoed, meaning to make sure she was still taking breath, when I saw once more the safe door open, like before. Quick as a blink, seemed like without even thinking, I opened the safe, bent to look inside, and grabbed up some papers I thought might be the bonds Useless planned to make off with. Plus the Blue Book, which Mizz Addie swears's the saving of this place.

I swung the door to, just so, exactly how it'd been. My knees were wobbling, and I knew I had to get that stuff and myself out of there quick. But I took one sec to look down at Mizz Addie.

It was middling dark in there; the shades were drawn down tight. She was lying on her side, her hair all wild and mussed-up on the pillow, her legs bent towards her body, one arm under her head and the other cradling her chin. Her mouth hung open some. I heard her breathing. She all of a sudden seemed like a sweet, helpless baby to me, needed taking care of. I almost cried, seeing strongness turned so terrible weak. And on account of being bone-scared my own self.

Wasn't time for crying or feeling sorry, though. So I slipped quick and quiet through the house to my outback room, where I shoved that secret stuff up under my bed and stepped back out into the heat like a woman with no more on her mind than every-day business. Felt pretty proud of myself, being smart enough to figure that Useless ain't going to do the deed if it doesn't gain him. But I didn't step more than about two feet before something brought me up short, when I all of a sudden realized that under my bed just wouldn't do at all. Wasn't but one place I knew that was safe enough.

Still nobody stirred, and it was early for Frank and Sarah yet. I slid myself into the cool darkness of the tool shed, where all Frank's gardening and carpentry things hung neat on big high wall hooks, like stiff sides of meat in a salt cellar. I like the dirt and sawdust smell of that place, but had no time for such that day.

In one dim corner was a pile of croker sacks. I chose one, lit out quick for my room, stashed the papers and book inside, and stole through the bare yard to the comfort of loblollies, where secrets stay put.

It was good I did, too, on account of Useless didn't waste any time. While I was in the parlor that night doing Mizz Addie's job plus seeing to Mazelle and Luna and all the hoes and their tricks, I'd feel an every-once-in-a-while cold shiver start at the bottom of my spine and sweep itself up my backbone. I'd look around and sure enough, there was Useless, taking a break from Mizz Addie's bedroom, staring a cold hole through me. Red took stock, too, in between tricks. Neither one of them changed words with me, though.

On my way to outback round four that morning, after all the business was done for the night and nothing left but echoes and stains and smells, I was wishing hard for eyes in the back of my head. Every sound stood my neck hair at attention. All was quiet, though. Feeling safe, I closed my door behind me and leaned against it, breathing hard a minute before turning on the light.

When I did, a pure sight greeted me. The place had been turned upside down and left so—mattress half across the room, closet doors wide open and not a piece left hanging, clothes spread here and yon.

Soul-tired, wasn't I, from all the not-sleeping and worry. Too tired to dwell on that mess or even be surprised—just went to clearing enough space to walk by and get in the bed. Inside me was flat, gray, used-up. I was past scared, I thought, till I picked up the fancy hand mirror Mizz Addie gave me some few years back for Christmas. The glass was broken—their bad luck, not mine, I hoped—and when I turned it to me, my face stared back, looking like it'd broken into three or four pieces, jagged edges that didn't line up with each other. I dropped the mirror like it was on fire and held my hand across my own mouth to keep from hollering.

Later, holding Ophelia's charm in one hand and Gan's blanket in the other, I fell asleep in the middle of that mess, but not sound sleeping—light enough to feel the devils and hags riding my worn-out body, till I woke.

Which even now, weeks past, sitting here doing no harder work than sliding a pen across paper, my whole self feels tireder than ever in its life—fingers, eyes, skin, teeth, even hair—all about done in, between Mizz Addie's sick self, that Useless and Red business, and poor Pearl.

Pearl. She's the one who got lost in the shuffle of trying to keep Mizz Addie and Hazelhedge going from day to day. In the back of my mind, I knew she had problems that needed tending to, I surely did. Hadn't conjured what to say, was one reason I didn't go on and have a heart-to-heart with that girl—even if I did have time, which I surely didn't.

Then came the afternoon I knew I couldn't wait any longer. I was on my way to the common room with a load of clean laundry. I stepped quiet into the trailer and was fixing to leave it lay, when I heard whisper-talking from the far back room. With things around here like they were, I was having to make whisper-talking my job, too. So back I crept.

Through a crack in the door I saw Pearl and two other hoes. The new one, who calls herself Jasmine and's from around New Orleans, had her face right up in Pearl's, whispering hard and mean enough to where I saw mouth spit.

". . . can't fool me, girl—nothing but a high-yellow, passing. I know, I seen enough to know." Laurie Ann, the other girl, just stood there looking mean, not saying a word.

"We fixing to show you how bad we hate working in a mixed house, nigger," said Jasmine. Pearl didn't change words, just backed against the wall, dead-pale, like she was waiting on something she'd been knowing was on its way.

"Fresh clothes, ladies," I called out at the same time my foot knocked open the door. "Take your choice." Laurie Ann and Jasmine swiveled and froze, and Pearl broke through the middle of them and was out the door in two secs flat. She didn't lock eyes with me, but what I saw in hers when she brushed past made me know I couldn't put off that business any longer.

But in the meantime, wasn't life and death going on all around, and me doing the best I could?

Later that same afternoon, when I was walking to Hazelhedge from outback, I saw Pearl. Just out the corner of my eye I caught her disappearing into the tool shed, and in a corner of my mind I told myself that soon's I finished checking on Mizz Addie I'd get back out there, find out what that girl was up to, and see if we couldn't have us a serious talk.

But Pearl was out of my mind like a speck of dust in a whirlwind by the time I got to the hall. Halfway down, I heard it and stopped dead, every worn-out nerve standing straight up: that whispery devil-voice that'd been hatching up badness so long I could scarce remember the time before. It was coming from the linen closet, that place of used-to-be Ophelia smells and old bad memories.

Took a sec for the whispers to make words in my head. Then: "I say we're out of this joint tonight. Me and you, on our way. You know your part?"

It was quiet a minute. All I heard was the blood thumping

through me, made my head throb. Then came her scratchy whisper.

"But Eustace, what about the bonds? Can we . . ."

"Goddam nigger." Sounded like he was fixing to spit. "Shit, we don't need them anyhow, baby. Her jewelry's probably worth twenty grand—and there's a big hunk of cash, more after tonight. The last night you got to do this, baby. Then just us." He waited a minute, and I could hear them both breathing. "Not backing out on me, are you, Georgia?"

"No, Eustace. But . . ."

"OK, then. This is it. After all's quiet tonight, meet me in her room—she'll be out like a light, with those pills the doc gave her." He laughed, quiet and mean. "Hell, the old bitch's half dead, anyhow—look at it this way, we're just putting her out of her misery."

My heart pumped blood through my veins so hard I thought they'd hear it, come rushing out of that dark closet and do me in, too. Couldn't breathe, seemed like, nor think too clearly. Backwards down the hall I slipped, touching my fingertips to the walls like they were old friends that would guide me out safe. Through the kitchen I went, and out the back door, where the screen door screech rang loud as screaming in my ears.

I wasn't thinking about anything when I headed for the tool shed except finding the nearest safe place outside that house. Inside the shed was quiet and cool, pitch dark after the bright August afternoon I just raced through. Still trusting hands, I let them make their way over rough-sawn walls to the furtherest corner, where I slid myself down, my back to the wall, held my knees tight up to me and tried to still the shivering deep in my belly. I pressed my head down a minute and closed my eyes, trying to collect myself, thinking: *it's time now, Minyon Manigault. You got to do something, girl.*

When I opened my eyes, they'd accustomed themselves to the darkness some, started questing around the inside of the shed like some answer might present itself, hanging up on the walls alongside the rakes and clippers and hoes. Just in front of me, turned on its side, was one of Mizz Addie's good dining room chairs, got busted up some way or another, which Frank was supposed to fix when he got around to it. My mind dwelled on that a bit, grateful for something different to linger on, when I saw, lying beside that chair on the dirt floor, one white, pointy-toed shoe.

Slow as dreams, my head started inching itself to the side, my eyes still memorizing the chair and the shoe lying next to each other, even while they took in the next thing. By the time that head of mine was turned flat sideways, I found myself staring at something scant inches from my face. Took some long space of time, seemed like, before my brain got the message to my eyes: it was one more white shoe, and next to that, a bare pale foot, all just about eye level.

Everything in me hollered *don't look up,* but my eyes had their own job to do, and did it. Up, up, up they traveled, taking in slim pale legs, a flowery dress, limp hands, and a head of wiry light hair.

My legs had their own mind, too, and before I knew it, they'd lifted me off the floor and turned me to look that hanging thing full in the face. Pearl, wasn't it—made stary-eyed ugly, blue-faced. Stone dead, hanging by one short thick rope slung over a heavy, high wall hook.

Great God Almighty—maybe I said it, maybe just thought it, reaching out at the same time, like with a touch I could wake her and say, come on back down from there, girl, and let's us talk. Her pale arm was still warm to my fingertips, her skin glimmering in the shadows like it was giving the lie to what might of vexed this poor child plumb to death.

It was too much for one soul to bear up under. My legs gave way, I fell in a heap to the floor, and everything I'd held inside so long came pouring out. In my life I never felt poorer nor sorrier nor scareder, and I set to crying like there wasn't going to be no tomorrow. Buckets came forth, wetting my hands, my skirt, the dirt floor—spring rains don't flow so free and hard.

But smack in the middle of all that crying, something inside me took a turn. And by the time I was through, I knew this: there truly wasn't going to be any tomorrow around here, not unless I made it so. Wasn't any Ophelia or Mizz Addie or any other body to do it. Just me. And hanging before me was proof of what happens when somebody does nothing.

Huddled up, dry-eyed, and quiet on that tool shed floor, sitting next to the chair she kicked over and the shoe she flung doing it, I studied on sad dead Pearl, till the whole thing fell into place in my head.

Just then, exactly when I had it writ in my brain like a map of someplace I hadn't been but had to head for, I heard the door of Frank's truck slam. Fast as lightning, I scrambled up from there, tore to the door, and motioned him in, a finger to my lips. Quick, before his eyes could see what they'd soon have to, I told him everything: what happened up to then, what just happened, and what was going to have to happen that night. All through it, he didn't change words, just drew his breath in sharp once or twice and listened to my wild whispering till I was finally done with it—winded, head-hanging tired. Then he put his arms out, drew me to him, held me a good long minute, and said, "Great God, girl, you been carrying yourself one load." And then together we lifted Pearl down off her hook and covered her over with croker sacks. Her pale skin was already chilled as the tool shed air, but we didn't remark on that or anything else—both of us fixed on what we had to do to save Mizz Addie and Hazelhedge and us all.

Looking back even through this little piece of time since, it all seems like something that happened to other people. Thinking how we did what we did, it plumb amazes me. But I reckon it's how Ophelia used to say: *keep putting one foot in front of the other, child, and before you know it, you got yourself someplace.*

That was sure enough a night of putting one foot in front of the next, best we could. Got us where we had to go, too.

By four or so that morning, the place had cleared out. I was in the hall by Mizz Addie's bedroom, blended into dark, hardly breathing, thinking how everything'd gone like clockwork up to then. Frank had slipped some bit of laudanum into the glass of watery champagne Red's last trick bought her, and we both watched while she tossed it down, throwing her head back after, laughing with only her mouth. Me and Frank were careful not to meet eyes, but we both knew that girl would be some kind of sleepy before long.

When the last trick left, Frank took off in his truck, too. Parked it down the road and ran back, where I let him in the front door. Just then, knowing he was in the parlor was the only thing that kept my bones from knocking together hard enough to wake the dead, much less evil Useless, just beyond the door, lying quiet in wait for his she-devil helper.

Directly I heard a stirring in the room. I tucked myself back into shadows, thinking he'd go fetch Red now, and we'd spring to action. But he didn't come out, just kept rustling around. In my head came a picture of what he might be up to in there— latching hands around a bare white throat or holding a soft down pillow hard to one sleeping face—and I was just before busting in when I heard him pad quiet to the door, cussing under his breath. Invisible, I watched him pass through the door and down the hall, on his way to one outback trailer and tardy Red, who must've been sleeping the sleep of the dead. I had time to let out one relieved sigh, then hopped to, on account of we had but scant time to get the job done.

I fetched Frank and he headed out to the tool shed and his part of that bad business. Meantime, I had to see to Mizz Addie. Turning on my flashlight, I slipped in, shining that round white- ness before me. She was on her back in the bed, mouth gaped open, and for a heartbeat, I thought she was done for. Then she squinted against the light and moaned, and I quick hitched her up to me, whispering, "Come with me, Mizz Addie, I got to show you something real important." She moaned and groaned, but swung her heavy legs over, habit keeping her moving.

Right before we headed out, my light swung around to show the safe door open. On top was Mizz Addie's jewel box, and inside that I saw, the silver and pearl of it gleaming up at me like a prize for the taking, the little revolver Mr. Waldo gave her so long back. Into my pocket it went, and nothing else, for there wasn't time, was there?

Half dragging Mizz Addie through the kitchen and out the back door, I headed for outback, passing Frank and his burden on the way. "Where we going, Minyon?" Mizz Addie mumbled one time, and I said, "Don't you worry, Mizz Addie, we're just about there, you'll be resting in a minute," and by then we were to my door. I got her into the bed, where she turned right on one side and went to sound sleeping. Between whatever of Doc Thayer's drugs Useless fed her plus her bedside sipping whiskey, she didn't much know what was going on. Which was good for us right then.

By the time I got back to her room, Frank had Pearl situated in the bed, lying on her stomach with the covers pulled way up, hiding all but her hair, which's wild enough to fool them, we hoped, though some lighter.

We'd not but two secs past slipped back to our own dark places—me my hall corner, Frank the parlor—when I heard the *scree* of the back door hinges. Here came those two—creeping badness, slinking through, him pulling her, razor-sharp mean whispering, she slurry-voiced. They stopped in front of the bed-room door, and he cut off her excusing: "I don't give a good goddam about you think somebody slipped you a mickey. Just get in there and do your part, or I'll do it for you and leave your whoring ass here to take the blame."

They were so close I heard the sound of her neck snapping when he shook her. "You got that, Georgia?"

"Yes, Eustace."

"Take this, then." Couldn't see what he handed over, but didn't have to—I'd seen it in dreams so long, that slim silver pick; in waking dreams I'd felt that sharp tip press in on my own nape, and'd come to, shivering and shaking, sweat-soaked. Standing there, but scant feet from their badness, I felt all of a sudden ready to do that battle, on account of I wasn't going to lay still for such anymore. Had to fight, and I was ready, my skin hackled up and heart pounding to beat the band.

In they went. Now my ears worked harder than ever, while I moved silent to the door. I heard sounds, must of been him riffling through and trying to pack up. Then came a thud, and he cussed under his breath, hissed: "Shit, I can't see a fucking thing." Directly something else dropped to the floor. "Get it done, Georgia, so I can turn the goddam light on."

Red didn't make a sound, but I could almost hear her gathering up to do it. Useless must have, too, for he quit his rummaging. The air all around us seemed somehow charged-up, the room went quiet as a grave, and we four were fixed in that place while time and us seemed like holding our breaths together.

When it came, what I'd been waiting for, it still struck cold every nerve: a high-pitched, wavery scream it started out, then switched right off to a full-throated holler even Useless' "what the hell" couldn't hush.

That was our signal. In a sec I felt Frank beside me, and we two stepped like one into that bedroom, me flipping on the light switch as we came.

It was one pure tee mess. The suitcase was open on the floor, clothes spilled half-in, half-out; jewelry box stuff was strung here and yon; the safe was open, the cash box and papers spread over the chaise. And there were Useless and Georgia, frozen in the light—him glaring black-eyed at us, her half-risen from the bed, hands held to face, steady screaming, till as we watched, his hand shot out and clamped itself over her mouth. She looked at him, wild-eyed, then turned to see where he was looking—at us.

"Get out," said Useless, his voice flat and thin. "Now."

"Nossir," said Frank, not using his shuffle-voice, sounding strong and steady. "Not even thinking about doing that."

Useless started to tell Frank something, when Georgia twisted her mouth away from his hand, jabbered high and shaky: "She's cold, Eustace, she's already stone cold." She moved over to the chaise, sat on the edge and buried her face in her lap. "Stone cold, already. Cold."

"Seems like we got us a problem here." Soon as Frank left my side, a shiver ran through me. He went over to the other side of the bed, pulled the covers back, and turned to me. "Minyon, you'd best call the sheriff. I believe this girl's dead."

He turned to Useless, who was standing stock still, staring. "Where's Miss Fleming—what have you done with her?"

The question hit Useless like a knock in the head—I saw it from where I stood by the door. Then he slow-motion looked down, and it hit him again—it was the first he saw it wasn't Mizz Addie lying there dead.

What happened next went so fast I hardly had time to take it in—just saw that meanness reach in his pocket and quick lunge across the bed toward Frank. Then Frank was holding his arm, red, red blood spurting every whichway. Frank's mouth opened in a wide, surprised O, and Useless was climbing over the bed to finish him, when I all of a sudden felt a cold hard weight in my own hand, heard my voice say: "Move one inch more and I'll kill you."

It was quiet enough, but the words had their own weight, didn't they, and that thin white boy locked himself careful in place, halfway across the bed, knife-toting hand still raised.

I raised the pistol to a point just between his eyes. "You got two secs to get your behind and hers out the door, Eustace Mason," said my shaky self. "Or I'm going to shoot first and ask questions later." Heard that once in a cowboy movie down at the Camelot, and it was out of my mouth before I knew it was coming.

He narrowed his bad old beady eyes, backed off the bed, and faced me. My hand wasn't exactly rock-steady, and I saw his eyes focus on that. Then he came creeping toward me, molasses-slow, silver blade by his side. His eyes told me he didn't believe I could do it.

I cocked the hammer back, how Mizz Addie taught me a long time ago. He showed his whites at that, but crept on, moving so slow I couldn't see it, only felt him nearer. All the time he gazed straight into my eyes, till I felt like I was fixing to fall into darkness and drown.

Must of been some kind of tranced, on account of I didn't hear one thing, not even a rustle—the only way I knew somebody else'd come into the room was by how his eyes shifted to behind me. Then time slowed to a crawl, while things happened inside it bam-a-lam: I turned to see where he was looking, he lunged, I raised the pistol, wild-haired Mizz Addie rushed past, grabbing my arm, screaming, "Don't shoot my boy, don't kill my baby," and flinging herself right at Useless. They started falling just as the gun went off, a short, sharp bark that set time to tracking regular again.

Mizz Addie and Useless were on the floor, him trying to get out from under her; Georgia was still as a statue on the chaise, mouth agape; and Frank looked on, holding his bloody arm. Took us all a bit to see that the bullet had gone straight through the wall without touching a soul. While we took that in, I stepped forward and picked up the knife Useless dropped when he went down.

Meantime, he'd got himself free of Mizz Addie and was backing over toward Georgia.

My voice didn't shake now. "I believe I said two secs, Mister Mason. Now you're on borrowed time." I did like the sound of that.

He didn't much care for it, though. Blinked those black eyes and didn't move.

"Frank," I said, cool as a cuke somehow. "How about take care of Mizz Addie and call Sheriff Cato."

At that, Georgia started pulling on Useless, whining and jabbering: "Oh, please, Eustace, let's go, let's go while we can, please."

And go they did, didn't they, without changing another word, me and Frank watching every move. Leaving behind their things they went, scuttling off into the dark they came from. While I watched them disappear down the road, still looking to make sure they didn't come slinking back, the pink and red of morning showed itself, and I knew then they were gone for good. We still had a mess to take care of. It was a miracle and a blessing that none of the upstairs hoes'd heard all the commotion and come running, but they hadn't. I gave Mizz Addie another of Doc's pills and put her back in my room, near-about dead to this world, then tended to Frank, whose arm'd got slashed pretty good—a long cut, though, not deep.

Then there was the question of Pearl, and how we were going to explain the whole thing to the sheriff. That's when we knew— it wasn't going to work that way.

Together Frank and me carried that poor child back to the shed. We got a shovel and some clean sacks, then down my lob- lolly path we went. I chose the spot, and Frank went to readying a resting place while I covered that poor pale hoe with sacking that smelled of the same tool shed she took her life in. And out there next to so much else that belongs to me, we put Pearl to rest, me claiming her in my heart from that day on as one of mine. It's the least I can do, seeing as I failed her when she was living.

Almost done, we near sleep-walked back to Hazelhedge. Frank helped me get Mizz Addie to her room. Tired as I was, I couldn't let her lay on sheets where the dead'd been, so while he held her, I quick changed the linens. When I was gathering them up to throw in the closet, I found a slim pick in a fold of sheet, its thin silver gleaming in the early light. I put it in my pocket, we got Mizz Addie to bed, and Frank went home, both of us know- ing not a word of what happened would ever be spoken of again.

That's one man a girl can count on—I remember thinking that before I climbed my aching self into bed. Don't remember anything else till I woke what turned out to be two days later to find that Sarah'd been taking care of business, and Mizz Addie, though she was some better, didn't remember a thing. I knew then we'd somehow keep going forward together.

I'm worn out now, from all this bill paying and recollecting.

Best go check on Mizz Addie, anyhow, and see how Mazelle's getting on with the silver polishing.

From my outback door I glimpse what's left of Mizz Addie's Victory Garden, makes me remember looking out last week to see her standing smack in the middle of it. The garden'd been dead since early August, shriveled by heat and lack of tending. And there in the middle of that deadness was Mizz Addie, gazing over at me, looking surprised. In her hand were the short clippers from the tool shed, and all around her on the dirt lay her wild red hair—she was shorn as a boy. While I watched, the wind kicked up and carried a tangle of it, rolling, toward loblollies.

I went to her and took the clippers before she could do herself more hurt. We stood together out there, one raggedy-headed crazy white woman and one worn-out black one, holding on to each other for dear life, crying till we had no tears left.

And all I know is this: we fought our own private war right here at Hazelhedge, and I reckon we won. But it surely does leave a bitter taste, for all that.

PART IV

1957

Winds of Change

chapter 1

"We've got a big night ahead, ladies, and I just want to be sure you're ready for it, one and all."

From where I'm leaning against the door frame, none of these three lined up on our long red couch look even close to being ready for more than a handful of aspirin and a good night's sleep. It's past three in the afternoon, and Mary Lou's hair's still in curlers, a large blue scarf wrapped around to hold them in. She's rubbing one eye, yawning her mouth so wide I see teeth-silver gleaming. Fawn's slouchy, as usual, that white-blond, poker-straight hair she's got falling like curtains on either side of her thin flat nose. Even Monique, that new one who calls herself an actress and's generally done up to the nines, doesn't look too appetizing right this sec: half her makeup's puddled under one eye like she's sporting a right smart shiner.

Not that any of that seems to faze Mizz Ariadne Fleming, never has. She just proceeds to tell how things're going to be, same as usual. Reckon that's how come she's who she is, and they're who they are. And me here, taking it all in.

"You three have been chosen for this little party tonight because you're the top of the line at Hazelhedge, the cream of our crop." Monique wides up her eyes some at that, and Fawn leans her head to the side, enough so I catch sight of one pale eye, blinking glassy at Mizz Addie. Mary Lou just yawns again. And I calculate to myself that if these three are the cream, I surely would hate to behold the curdle.

"They expect you at the house around eight-thirty, which means you'll have to leave here about eight. Mary Lou's been to Greenfield before, so she can drive."

Mary Lou stops in mid-yawn at that, and Mizz Addie beams tender in her direction, like a teacher upon her A-plus student. "You can take the new Cadillac, Mary Lou, if you'd like." Mizz Addie's got three automobiles for this place now, and she lets the hoes use one of them every now and again, sometimes for business, sometimes not. But she generally reserves the newest one for just herself alone.

"The new Cad? Whoa." Fawn lifts one limp sheet of hair and folds it behind her long, narrow ear. "Who are these cats, anyhow?"

Peering over her glasses like she's doing right this minute, her hair pulled back in a bun, her white shirt tucked prissy into a long black skirt, Mizz Addie resembles one of those old-maid schoolteachers this town seems to have an abundance of. And if Mary Lou's her prize learner, Fawn's the troublemaker, sitting in back of the class, making remarks.

Mizz Addie's eyes go steely gray-green, her lips thin out, her voice gets quiet and cold. "These *cats,* as you call them, are some of the most influential men in this state—maybe even this country." She narrows her flinty eyes. "Suffice to say, tonight's important not only to your future here, Fawn, but to ours as well."

Fawn's not one bit worried about all that; she gives Mizz Addie back her stare, beat for beat, looking bored as all getout. Finally she blinks, unhooks her hair so her pale face's covered up again, and says, "That's cool."

This girl's from California, the first one of those we ever had here, and far's me, she might as well be from China, she's so hard to figure. She stopped off on her way to what she calls the Big Apple, anyhow, just long enough to earn herself some traveling cash, she says, so we won't have to put up with her forever. In the meantime, though, she sure stays busy. Men around here's partial to something strange, I reckon, like that Mexican girl Conchita a couple of years back. Exotics, Mizz Addie calls them.

"Well, you've got about five hours to rest up and get pretty," she tells them, and her face's got a look saying she believes it'll take every bit of that. "Fawn, you wear the long black gown and your highest heels. Mary Lou, how about the red chiffon."

Big doings indeed—Mizz Addie doesn't generally pass out dressing directions.

"Oh, and Monique, you'd better plan on packing your full setup. Just in case." Monique's what we call a specialist. She nods, all business.

"That's it then, ladies. Don't leave without checking in, though. I want to see how you look, and make sure about any last-minute changes."

They get up to leave, and I'm thinking, class dismissed—till she swivels those glinty greens my way. "See to them, Minyon. I don't need to tell you: tonight has to be perfect, to do the trick."

All the time doing tricks around here, ain't we?

"Yessum," I say, on account of having to say something, and yessum falls light on her ears.

"And see that the rest of them get out here in good time to-night. No stragglers."

I give her one more yessum as she passes me and sweeps down the hall to her room. Stiff walking, how she gets when she's worrying. Quiet too—she's misplaced her used-to-be rustle for going on twelve years now, ever since the war got over and she lost her boy and her hair and almost her mind to boot.

I start straightening the parlor some, even though Portia'll be here directly and get down to the brass-tacks cleaning. Still, it helps me think. I get the polish and a clean cloth from the hall cabinet and go to rubbing the walnut side table Mizz Addie bought last year. Upgrading, she says—something she's all the time doing at Hazelhedge. "Always the finest, Minyon," she tells me. "Fineness begets fineness."

Oh, we are fine around here all right. Aside from this government mess Mizz Addie's stewing over now, trying to fix up tonight. Do the trick, make the federal boys look somewhere else for trouble, turn the other cheek.

I rub wood till the swirls shine. Round and round, trancing myself, till the slam of a car door brings me up short. It's not Frank's truck—I know that sound by heart—and besides, whoever it is, is pulled right up front.

On my way to the door I catch the faintest sound of whistling, makes me know right off who it is: Blue Ballard, moved here a couple years back and set himself up as Jameston's one and only colored taxi driver; that man'd just as soon whistle as breathe. Though what Hazelhedge business he's got this time of day I can't figure—we're not expecting any new girls and it's early yet for trade.

Just as I step off the porch to see what's what, he helps some somebody from the back seat. Her back's to me, so all I see first is hair, wild and witchy, frizzed out past her shoulders. I speed up and round the back of the taxi, fixing to ask Blue what he's thinking about, this's no mixed house, never will be either. About which time I see that bushy head's attached to a long skinny neck and a body that's got more bones than flesh to cover it, dark skin all angles and sharp shadows, bare arms and legs thin as dry sticks, and one bright-colored slash of dress in between.

"Blue Ballard," I say, almost upon them now, fixing to take charge of this situation, give this boy what-for and set the two of them on their way. Her face is still turned to his, and seems like she's grabbing hold of his arms for dear life. Then she turns her head and here's a small dark face, all sunken eyes and poked-out cheeks and browbones inside a circle of wild black hair's got some gray mixed in.

My mouth opens to say who knows what, because before anything comes out, her dark eyes stare into mine, then blaze like the sun's lit behind them. She quick lifts her arms from where they're gripped tight to Blue and throws them around my neck. Now my face's buried in that frizzed-out halo of hair, seems like I can't hardly catch my breath, and she goes to sobbing on my neck, calling over and over: "Minyon, oh Min, oh Min." And it's not by the hair, nor the face, nor the bony black body that I know her, but by the old good smell that hasn't changed in the twenty-eight years since we last touched flesh. It's Farina, my long-lost cuz, my sweet Farina, and as my eyes and nose believe it, my arms go around her tiny self and my heart leaps like it's going to bust itself loose.

Then I reach up with both hands and pull her head back some, on account of needing to feast my eyes upon a face I never figured to see again besides in dreams. Tears run down her cheeks and mine, too, steady streams. I relocate familiarness, so long absent: eyes, nose, mouth, cheekbones, chin. While I gaze, her dark eyes all of a sudden roll up, showing nothing but whites, then close, and she goes limp as death in my arms— about pulls me over, even slight as she is. I cry out a little and stumble, and Blue jumps to take her from me at just the same minute Frank's truck pulls into the yard, Sarah and Portia riding along with. They're milling around, Blue's clutching Farina up to his chest like a daddy holding his baby girl, I'm trying to collect breath and thoughts, too. And into the middle of us all comes Mizz Addie, not saying a word, just hands-on-hipping it, taking in the commotion on Hazelhedge lawn, then question-marking her eyebrows over at me, the one who's got to offer up some explaining for it all.

I tear my eyes from the rise and fall of Farina's chest long enough to say this much: "It's Farina Ward, Mizz Addie, my cuz from Little Town I haven't seen since, since . . ." I can't pry more words out of my mouth on account of sad and happiness catch up together in my throat.

"She's sick," I manage, which's surely clear enough to us all. "I got to take care of her now." By the time those words finally manage to tear loose, I'm in sufficient charge of myself to direct

Blue around the side of the main house to where my very own outback trailer sits small and neat on the edge of the piney woods.

He lays Farina soft on my flowered sofa. Her eyelids flutter some, she takes a deep breath, then turns on one side. Looks like she's sleeping now. I cover her with the bright green afghan a curly-headed hoe named Rosie gave me some years back, and turn to Blue, who's standing by the door watching me tuck her in.

Quiet, I walk over and whisper, "Where'd you find her?"

He looks down at me, and it's hard to discount the sweetness of his brown eyes. "Got off the two-forty-five. I saw her and noticed, on account of her looking so frail and all. Said she'd been traveling three days, all the way from New York City." His eyes flick over to the sofa. "She's your cousin, Minyon?" Deep-voiced whisper's soft as touch.

"Only kin I've got in this world, Blue, far's I know." I look over at that tiny lump and turn back around to find him gazing at me, making my face go hot.

"Now I got work to do, and you've got a living to make, too," I say, turning to the table and fishing in my purse, feeling him watch. "Thank you for your trouble." I hold out two dollars, even though I know it's not but a dollar ride to Hazelhedge from the bus station.

"No thanks, Minyon." He smiles down at me. "It's not every day I get to bring a family together—this one's on me." And he's out the door and headed for his cab, whistling to beat the band, before I can muster a proper thank you.

From behind me comes a moan, and I'm beside that cuz of mine quick as quick, wanting to make sure my face's the first thing her eyes light on, once she decides to open them. She settles back down without blinking, though.

I reach out and push back that wild wiry hair, study some on the lines of a face I've not beheld in so long, see a curve of cheek that brings back the sixteen-year-old I recollect plus a little of our old Gan mixed in for good measure. Remembering our Little

Town times together, my heart grows so big in my chest I don't hear a thing till her voice comes, and I look up to see Sarah standing beside us.

"That girl's going to need a doctor, Minyon, soon as she wakes up. She's hurting, in more ways than one." For once, Sarah's voice's missing that old hard edge that usually lurks under.

"What you figure's wrong?" Sarah's got the gift of knowing about sickness or trouble brewing, especially about our hoes, and generally'll let me or Mizz Addie know. It galls me sometimes, but I have learned to listen when she talks.

She bends down, lays the flat of her hand against Farina's cheek, picks up one limp hand and studies on ragged fingernails, then gently sticks her finger inside Farina's mouth, pulling her lips down and checking out her teeth and gums. Standing back up, she wipes her finger on her apron, says: "Drink, most likely, else something kin to it. About killed herself with it, looks like." She walks to the door, holds it open. "Want me to call Doc Larkin?"

"Yes, please," I say, grateful enough to where my eyes sting with it.

"One more thing, Minyon," Sarah's half out the door; I can't even see her face, just hear her voice floating back on the spring afternoon air. "If she ain't careful, she's going to kill that baby she's carrying, too."

Her words and the screen door slam come together, raising me clean off the sofa. Farina doesn't even flinch, though. I reach down and pull the afghan back past her middle part. This slim dress's tight enough where I can make out her hipbones poking sharp against shiny yellow cloth. There's not the first curve of belly to give Sarah's words weight. So how come I suddenly feel the truth of them, even though this cuz's not but skin and bones and's my own age, forty-three, time to best be past baby-making?

Still sleeping, Farina takes up a shaking while I watch, seems like it starts at her toes and works directly up to her head, sets her teeth to clattering loud enough to wake the dead. I cover her back up and stroke my hand down her arm, whushing and humming soft till she quiets, all the time thinking about what to do.

After some little bit, here comes Portia, tap-tapping on my screen door and sticking her head in timid, still new enough to think I might be something to be scared of. "Mizz Min, Mizz Fleming said fetch you. She's in her room and wants to see you."

First I realize how time's passed along, because when I step outside I see evening's right upon us, darkness fixing to spread her cloak, one star winking on even while I look. As I go through the kitchen, Sarah doesn't turn from the sink, cleaning up after the girls' supper and fixing snacks for the evening. Portia scoots on past me to the parlor, where I hear Frank's familiar sounds, setting up bar. Everything seems the same but isn't—it's been turned turvy by one slim somebody lying on my outback sofa.

I push open Mizz Addie's door. Her back's to me as she sits before her dresser mirror, pushing a gold hoop through one ear-hole.

"Come in, Minyon," she says, not turning round. And by the set of her shoulders and the tenseness of her voice I know she wants to play the old game, the Madam-to-housekeep one, which I figured we put behind us a long time back.

Takes two, though. I close the door soft, cross to the chaise longue angled sideways to her chair, and lie back, putting my feet up. Looking over at her—who doesn't crane her head my way one time—I lace my fingers together, stretch my arms out, and rest my head back against my hands, elbows high in the air. "I'm in, Missus."

She doesn't see a bit of funny in my doings today—doesn't see anything but her own mirror-face. In the quiet I study on it, too, that face I know the outside of about as good as my own. Inside's something else again, for sure.

While I watch, she smooths her hair back tight and starts wrapping it in a bun. It's still red, that hair, but now it's on account of Lunette McKenzie, who comes out here from town once a month or so to do a root job. Underneath is gray as iron, has been ever since she sheared herself most bald and lost her rustle, all those years back.

"Are the ladies ready for their evening out?" She's all business.

Truth is, I haven't given those girls the first thought. "Didn't check, Missus. I'll be glad to go see."

She jabs in a couple of hairpins, still doesn't turn around. "And the rest of the ladies, Minyon?" Her voice's fair frigid.

"Didn't check, Missus."

Now she swivels that head around, glaring icy green at me. "Do you surmise that this house can operate *sans* supervision?"

All that cold and those fancy words don't bother me how they used to. I swing my legs around and lean towards her. "It can sure enough operate itself one afternoon, *Missus,* while I tend to the one and only blood kin I got left in this world. That's what I surmise."

She leans up, too, eyes narrowed, words near spit out: "If tonight doesn't go well, Minyon Manigault, you may not have a roof over your own head, much less a place for some . . ."

Just that sec comes a tap-tap-tapping on her bedroom door. Holding her eyes level with mine, she sits straighter, calls out, "Come," and in they do.

In twenty-eight years I'm yet not used to it, how these hoes can go from sow-belly ugly to spit-polish pretty in the space of a few hours. These three no more resemble their earlier selves than fly to the moon; they look more like the glamour girls in the *Screen Romance* books they're all the time mooning over.

Fawn's in first. Just like the Madam ordered, she's done up in her long black gown, cut so low at the bosom and high at the leg, there's not but scant cloth between. Her pale skin and hair look paler still next to all that blackness. Her eyes're all darked up too, lashes out to here, pale pinkness on her lips.

That flat black and cool whiteness set off fine next to Mary Lou's fire-red dress—its layers shimmer, seem to give off a rising heat. Her honey brown hair's pulled back from her face, then tumbles in big, loopy curls down to bare shining shoulders. Her curvy self's perched atop hot red heels, pointy-toed as arrows. Her mouth's painted to match the dress, a slash of flame; her cheeks're colored high, eyes sparkling.

After her comes dark again: Monique's in black leather, what she calls her catsuit; a second skin, smooth and dark, that even stretches down between her fingers, leaving ten palenesses that look like claws. Her dark hair's spitcurled around her face, reaching in toward catty eyes darked out in points. On her feet are short leather boots with silver studs and narrow heels, higher than Mary Lou's even, and in her hand's what she calls her bag of tricks, which she's not ashamed to show, I've seen it—holds handcuffs, some leather leashes, a couple of rubber hoses, and a small-handled whip, for starters. That's one scary woman, if you ask me. Whoever wants to mess with her is beyond me. But there's plenty that do, and they pay extra, too.

Standing there each next to each, these three are enough to clean take your breath.

"Very nice, ladies." Mizz Addie's not one for overpraising. "Very nice indeed."

Fawn gives a little bow, her black dangly earrings and hair falling forward when she does. "All we need now's a set of wheels," she says, straightening and tucking her pale hair back behind one ear, "and then we're off to see the wizards."

Mizz Addie doesn't favor her with even a glance, just reaches for her purse, fetches the car keys, and holds them out. "Mary Lou," she says, and that girl steps forward to take them.

"Park around back, right, Miss Fleming?"

"Just like before, Mary Lou. And do take good care." Mizz Addie's generally got a favorite hoe, and this go-round, Mary Lou's it, maybe because she sends money back home every pay-day, regular as clockwork. Mizz Addie's a great admirer of family values, she always claims.

Mary Lou steps back with the others, and Mizz Addie takes a deep breath. "I can't overemphasize the importance of tonight's rendezvous, ladies. What you must give is nothing less than your absolute best." She goes over by the safe, opens the door, and pulls out a stack of what look like twenties from here, with a rubber band wrapped around them. "And if you do your best, ladies, and if all goes as planned, ladies, there'll be a very sweet bonus." She fans the edge of the bills so we can hear the swushy sound of it. "One thousand dollars—for each of you."

The room goes still as still, on account of it might take these girls a couple three months to put that kind of money in their pockets. All three stare at that stack, dreaming about how far ahead it could put them, maybe. Maybe Fawn's halfway to the Big Apple, Mary Lou's thinking about money she could surprise home folks with, Monique's eyeing Hollywood. Their dreams, rich as syrup, thick up the air in this room till it's hard to breathe.

Then Mary Lou gives a little laugh like she's catching her breath and says, "We surely will do our best, Miss Fleming. You can count on that." Monique gives a cat-grin and purrs, "the performance of our lives," and about licks her lips, eyes still locked on that stack of bills. Fawn stares at it too, then turns and goes out, the others following right behind.

After the door closes, Mizz Addie keeps staring at the space where they stood, still and concentrated, like she could *will* them to what needs doing. Then she takes a deep breath, recollecting herself, and when she lets it out she seems smaller to me.

"You know what the price is, Minyon, if tonight doesn't do the trick?" Her voice's soft, almost like talking to herself, and she doesn't face me. "A hundred and seventy-five thousand dollars, that's what." She folds her hands in her lap and stares down at them, then laughs soft and bitter. "All the things that could've put us out of business all these years, and it might come down to something as, as, *inane,* as senseless, as *stupid,* as taxes. Back taxes, twenty-eight years' worth. Like we haven't paid our dues every other way from day one."

She breathes deep, stares straight ahead again at the space where those girls just stood, then gives her head a hard shake. "Well, in the meantime, we've got a house to run, haven't we,

Minyon." And just like that she's the Madam again, strong and hard, her mind on business. "Check on Frank, see that Sarah's set, and get those ladies into the parlor. No dawdling tonight."

I rise to get going. At the door I stop and turn around, figuring to say it now or never. "My cousin Farina's going to need to stay with me a bit, Mizz Addie, at least till she finds a place. She can help out around here, she's some handy."

She looks at me a sec, and both of us might be pondering the unlikeliness of Farina being some handy. She blinks first, though, looks to the side, and says nothing except, "Just see she doesn't cause trouble, Minyon."

I don't give her chance to draw one more breath nor word at that; quick as a heartbeat, I'm in the hall—the door closed behind me, the night stretched out before, and my own sweet cuz Farina safe and sound in outback.

Seems like this night speeds on after that—men come and go, strangers and old hands, short ones, skinny ones, nervous ones, loud and bold; Portia scurries with linens, and me too, part of the time, meeting in halls and between outback and the main house the girls and their tricks backing and forthing, or sometimes just a hoe alone, carrying herself along to the parlor and her next-in-line; Sarah finishing up kitchen work and catching her ride home; Frank busy drink-making, grinning and cutting fool with the tricks; Mizz Addie making her rounds, spending time with this one then that one, laughing and talking, turning sightseers into paying customers by looking right into their eyes, making them feel like they're the only and best man that ever was, taking their money with a smile that never stops. Hazelhedge's parlor is clean and sparkly and fine, the dark wood shining, the chandelier lit. Around us are all the usual smells of here: liquor and Listerine, cigars and sweat, perfume with woman smell just under. The jukebox never stops either, one fifty-cent piece after the next slipping in, so the quiet can't catch up and jar us loose from stepping one step after the next. We're in our places, doing our jobs—smiling, serving, hustling—one big smooth ship sailing through a cloudless windless night sky.

Seems like any other night around here for going on thirty years, except for two things that float on the top of my mind: worry about my new-found cuz and wonder about that Greenfield Plantation party and whether it's doing the trick or not.

It's near dawn when the last tail lights round the bend of pines. I'm heading through the kitchen to outback when I hear the purr of Mizz Addie's new Cadillac, then see it swing by the back door and glide into its parking place. I thought she'd gone to bed a while back, but all of a sudden here's Mizz Addie next to me, both of us looking, side by side, like the future's riding on what we'll see.

Nothing but three tired hoes come dragging out, though, Monique and Fawn on either side of Mary Lou—red sandwiched between black—all three walking close, like if they don't, one's likely to fall and bring the rest down, too. Their shoulders droop, they're weary clean to bones, looks like. It's light enough to see their faces now, as they walk by on their way to outback rooms: old woman faces, ain't they, tired and drawn, shadows hugging deep-creased lines, lips and cheeks pale-faded into skin, eyes no more than dark slashes in a face. Mouths like bruises.

They don't look up, just one foot-in-front-of-the-other it. And bad as I know Mizz Addie needs to find out how things went, she doesn't make a move, nor me. We just stand here watching, till those three ugly sad girls're in and gone.

We both draw breath in, and then Mizz Addie whisper-walks away, just as well be a ghost for all the noise she makes. In a sec, I head for my own place and sleep, feeling whipped past words, but knowing this: for the first time in years, seems like I got something worth waking to.

chapter 2

I pour a glassful of ice cold water from the pitcher we keep in the fridge and take a big draw, letting it glide cool and sweet down my throat. Outside the kitchen window the late May sun glints bright, heading for afternoon. Ain't had us much sweet spring yet to speak of, and this day looks to be stoking up as hot as the one before.

Fixing to head out the back door when I hear voices from the front parlor. Nobody's generally got business in there this time of day, so I hitch my big black pocketbook onto my shoulder and head down the hall to make sure everything's what Fawn calls copasetic before I get myself to town and errand-doing.

Halfway down the hall when I hear Mizz Addie's voice, her friendly, taking-care-of-business one.

"We're happy to help out, Earl, you know that. What would you suggest?"

He coughs and clears his throat. That's Mr. Earl Winchell Junior—I'd know that cough blindfolded—he's all the time hacking and generally's got a cigarette in his hand, mouth, or halfway between. Mr. Earl Junior runs the hardware store on Bay Street just like his daddy did before him. And just like his daddy, he's a Hazelhedge customer, though not near as regular. President of one those men's clubs Jameston's got a mess of, too, that's named for animals—moose or lions or elks, can't recollect which.

"Well, we're sure hoping to have our best parade ever, maybe bring that brass band up from Charleston this year, Mizz Fleming, don't you know, if we can raise the funds."

"That's good, Earl. I like brass," she says, and I hear in her voice that she likes playing with this boy some, too. "How much?"

He pauses to work up to it, then croaks out: "Three hundred?"—voice rising on the *dred* to a near squeak.

Longer pause from in there this time, and should be, far's me, asking for that big bunch of money for some fool parade or other. Then comes her voice again, even more businessy. "Fine, Earl. Let me write you a check."

"A check?" He goes to coughing again, and in my head comes a picture of his daddy, old Mr. Earl, right before he died, eat half up with the cancer, but still coming out here for his pleasure. Coughing, too, like his boy out there. Kept coming till he couldn't drive himself any more, even though the girls said he wasn't up to much, just liked to watch them undress and have them fiddle with him some.

Mr. Earl Junior's caught his breath again, seems like. "Surely you . . . is it possible to . . . under the circumstances . . ." Who knows how long he might go on like that, but Mizz Addie sees fit to stop it there.

"Or maybe cash is better?"

I hear a drawn-out sigh, and can almost see his head nodding up and down. I don't move when I hear her get up. She pauses a sec when she sees me here in the hall, but doesn't say a word, just goes on into her bedroom, stays a while, and comes back out with a roll of bills. They say their polites, him coughing in between, and when I hear the screen door slam, I go stand next to her and watch him drive off, the big fins of his car catching the sunlight and glaring back at us.

"Heading for town, Mizz Addie, to the laundry and Goldstein's to pick up those new dresses. Anything else you need?"

She reaches up and settles her glasses, still looking through the screen. "I liked his daddy better," she says, then turns and walks back to her room, the door closing firm behind her.

In one of her moods again, must be. I don't have time to worry about such, though; got my own business to see to.

It's quiet out here in the Hazelhedge yard as I head for the carport. The hoes're still sleeping off last night, dreaming who knows what. As I drive past my trailer I strain to see can I catch a glimpse of Farina's head, maybe she's stirring. But all's still and quiet there, too. My foot presses harder on the gas, already thinking about needing to get back before I get gone good.

As I round the corner I glance in the rearview mirror. Hazelhedge shows trim and fine behind me, white boards gleaming in the sunshine, porch stretching out gracious and wide, trees offering up cool shade, yard green and close-mowed. Picturebook. No sign from here about what goes on in there.

Pulling out onto the highway, though, my mind doesn't dwell on Hazelhedge, this road, nor my errands, but on my sweet sick cuz instead.

"This woman is lucky to be alive." That's what Doc Larkin said after he checked her over the first time. "She's severely dehydrated, malnourished, probably anemic." He took blood out of her arm, made her pee in a jar. She didn't offer much fight about any of it, either, too sick to. Soon as we walked into the next room, I whispered, "What about the baby, Doc?" which gave him a start. But the next time he came out to check her, he took me to one side and told me that's right, we got one on the way, most likely'll show up in October or November. The baby might or might not be all right, he said, on account of Farina's being so sickly, and with her drinking problem. Which hasn't had a drop to feed it since she set foot in here.

"I need your help bad, girl, all you can give." Those were the first words out of her mouth, the morning after she showed up, her lying still as death under my afghan, me bringing her coffee which she couldn't get to her mouth on account of hands that shook too bad. I finally held the cup for her, listened to her teeth clink on china while she swallowed some, along with a biscuit. Even which little bit she couldn't keep on her stomach long. Not that day.

The whole first week, as a matter of fact, not much would stay down. I put her in my bed and tended to her during the day, in between chores. Mostly she stayed there, not so much sleeping as tossing and jerking, moaning, whimpering. Sometimes she just cried quiet into my pillow.

It was funny who-all else helped out, without my asking one time. Sarah kept trying to fix some kind of food Farina'd hold onto, conjuring up vegetable potions to get her strong. Frank moved her when I needed him to, days she'd sweat-soak clear through sheets, me and Portia quick laying fresh linens down while Frank stood by holding her littleness in his big arms. Blue Ballard's kept checking in too, whenever he brings trade out this way or even sometimes not, whistling and cheery, wanting to know what he can do, resting eyes kind on me while he asks. And all through, Mizz Addie's not raised one word about this extra time and work folks're spending, which I know is her sideways way of helping, best she can muster.

The unlikeliest help of all's from that hoe Mary Lou, who showed up on my doorstep a day or two after Farina got here to say she'd see to her while I did my afternoon chores. She'd just as soon get herself fixed up and ready for evenings in my trailer as in her room, she said, if I wanted the help. Whatever worrying I had about her disappeared after I once watched her tend Farina, leaning over and murmuring soft down at my cuz, gentling her.

It surprised Doc Larkin too, the first time he came out while Mary Lou was there. Of course he knew her, he knows all the girls on account of he's the one checks them every month to make sure they're free of the clap or syph or some other woman-part infection, which isn't so big a deal as used to be, now they got that penicillin drug that cures most of it. After Doc checks them, he stamps the health cards that every girl keeps under the glass on her bedside table. So he knows Mary Lou most of her whichways, even though he doesn't mess around with the hoes, past examining them, that is. He's got what Mizz Addie calls ethics, which she claims's in short enough supply in this town as a rule.

So now Doc Larkin talks to Mary Lou about how Farina's coming along, explains things to her in a quiet voice while she listens hard, staring into his eyes and leaning her head toward him. I heard her tell him one day that her daddy'd messed with her and her sisters till he finally drank himself to death, and how her mama's broken up over it and fixed on that same road. Heard him say, "You poor kid," and look at her soft and kind.

Anyhow, Doc says Farina's getting better on account of all this good nursing, and it's true enough, she's got a little flesh on her skinny self now, and can get up to creep around the trailer and fetch what she needs. Still doesn't talk much, though—seems like she's holding her strength and story in, scared to lose the one if she lets go of the other. I'm not pushing either, just every day thanking the Lord for this kin-gift he sent.

I'm thinking so hard about all that, I almost run the new red light at the corner of Water Street and Fraser, stop short enough to squeal the tires on the car behind me. As I turn and head for Goldstein's, I see Jameston's showing off all its stuff this fine May day. I pass Cooler's Electric Supply with its brand new green-and-white-striped awning, then Hazzard's Hallmark's window that's decorated red, white and blue for Memorial Day, which they generally leave up till the Fourth. Right next is the new jewelry store, its watches and bracelets and diamond rings sparkling and calling attention. Every trip our girls make to town, they spend some time in there, mooning around and some-times even buying, or else marking what they want, to see can they sweet talk one of their steady customers into a little some-thing extra. Fact is, I heard Mizz Addie say this jewelry operation plus half the other stores in town'd go broke if it wasn't for the business Hazelhedge brings them, one way or the other. Especially in the hard times a few years back.

I know they big-time believe that down at Mr. Hamilton's car lot. Those boys'll practically blind a person with their big old grins, every time they see Mizz Addie coming. Cash. They like cash around here, and that's how she tends to do business. Twenties, generally. I saw her plunk down seven thousand dollars worth of them for that last Caddy she bought, watched Mr. Jimbo Hamilton's eyes get bigger and bigger as she opened her black bag, pulled out a wad of them, and went to counting out three hundred and fifty bills. It was his first day working on his daddy's lot, which Mizz Addie knew—she chose it especially for just that reason. Breaking his cherry, she called it. That'll give him something to tell his grandchildren, she said, smiling into the rearview mirror at me when we drove off.

Goldstein's got plenty of business even on weekdays, on account of being the finest department store in Jameston, so I have to park around the side, next to the old Jeff Davis Hotel, which somebody's bought and is fixing to turn into a fancy seafood restaurant.

As I get out the car, tuck in my shirt and straighten my hat, I snag a few stares from some strollers-by. Which I pretty much expect—folks aren't so used to coloreds driving such a car, and this isn't but Hazelhedge's third best, our two-year-old Buick. Doesn't bother me much anyhow; I reckon I know where my place is, and whether these folks do or not's no concern of mine.

Inside the store smells rich to me, always has: the perfume and leather goods counter's what greets you once inside, expensive smells flying up your nose first thing. Then comes shiny leather shoes on racks and behind them, way in the back, ladies' lingerie, every color of the rainbow. The hoes love to browse back there, whenever Mizz Addie lets them come to town. Women's clothes're on the left, men's on the right, all the jackets and shirts and dresses and suits hanging fresh and new on their special green Goldstein's hangers. Rich, for sure. The light's not bright in here either, soft enough to shine sweet on oak walls and floors, gleaming like a smile; soft enough to make just about anybody look good.

I breathe this air in deep, and go hunting Miss Floride Hinkley or else Mr. Isadore, since I got a special order to pick up. Neither of them's in sight, so I head for the back till all of a sudden right in front of me steps a white girl I never saw before. She cuts me off, standing so close I nearly bump her, so close that even in this light I see the makeup clumped under her eyes and the flat round pits in her cheek-skin. She's got the face of one of those Kewpie dolls they sell over at the county fair, punched in some at the center, eyes a trifle too close, and two of the coldest blues I ever had the misfortune to look into.

"Where you think you going, girl?" Keeps her voice low, still so close I feel the wetness of her whispery breath; smell it, too. Her eyes narrow up, snake-mean.

This girl must be new in here, and fool as she looks to boot. Mizz Addie and Hazelhedge's kept this store running through some of the worst years ever, and they're plenty grateful for that. We are quality trade in here, me included.

Keeping my eyes steady on hers, I draw up tall as I can: "I'm going about my business, Miss, if you'll step yourself aside."

Her pasty skin goes red as hellfire at that, flares up from neck to ears in an eyeblink. I'm marveling at that colorfulness so hard I don't know what hit me till it does—*whack*—one flat white palm upside my dark cheek, hard enough to jerk my head sidewise, the clappy sound of it ringing in my ears. I don't cry, but tears jump to while I stare amazed and that mouth of hers comes close till I've got eyes for nothing else and she spits out: "No niggers allowed."

Inside me goes still and white-hot. Rooted to the spot, I don't budge or even blink when Mr. Isadore bustles up and takes that girl rough by the arm and moves her out of my face, hissing at her and smiling around the room to let his customers that's stopped dead still in their tracks know that everything's just fine, thank you, no problems at all here, showing his pointy teeth all around and handing her over to Miss Flo, then taking me by the arm and leading me to the back where the office and dressing rooms are.

"The whole order came in yesterday," he says, his voice reasonable and oily-sweet as ever. "We've got them all ready to go," and he points over to a rack full of clothes wrapped in see-through paper. I turn my head to look at him, my neck stiff, but he doesn't look back—just slides his eyes to one side, showing his teeth and talking fast: "Where're you parked?"

His boys, Jake and Lewis, load the car up from the back of the store and Mr. Isadore walks me out to it. I get in and look up at him. The hot May sunlight's bright behind him, outlining his head and darkening his face to near match mine. He leans in and I think he's going to say something about it all now—to say, she's new, she doesn't know any better, *something*—but instead he says: "You take care." Then he walks off, not looking back, slapping his hand on the car hood. As he rounds the corner and disappears inside, I think about all the times I've watched his narrow behind slip round Hazelhedge corners and disappear inside one room or the next.

My mind's not but a blank white slate, but still smart enough to steer my hands where they've got to go. At Walker's I park by the side door and his people hang the clean pressed clothes alongside both back windows. Mr. Walker himself comes out and stands by the car when they're done, shading his eyes against sunny brightness. "Linens'll be delivered by four, tell Miss Fleming, same as usual. OK?" Everything's business as usual, ain't it—except I can't clear the sourness of that white girl's breath from my mouth, and the burn of her hand across my cheek keeps getting hotter and hotter.

Sitting there trying to make small talk with Mr. Walker like this day's no different from any other, I glimpse Blue Ballard's taxicab rounding a curve down the road, cutting across the Piggly Wiggly parking lot. My heart gives a jump and I stop mid-word, wanting nothing more than to start my car and chase that man down, just to hear his deep calm voice, feel those brown eyes lingering sweet on mine. Instead I say my polites to Mr. Walker and head back, my cheek flushing harder than before.

At the Five Points stoplight in the middle of Jameston, I take a look around me. Over by the ice house's a mess of cars, same as usual, folks milling in and out. Jordan's Esso across the way's got cars at the pumps, service people round and about. The parking lot in front of Squeak's Cafe is full, too—through the glass I see customers' heads inside, hands guiding food into mouths. Everywhere I look's nothing but cars and white folks' business and white folks. And me at this red light stuck smack in the middle of *no niggers allowed,* with nothing but four thin walls of this Hazelhedge Buick to keep me safe.

All the way home I'm thinking about something Sarah said a while back, talking about how the N double A and Dr. Martin Luther King's stirring everybody up, about how things're going to get a whole sight worse before they get better. Frank's nodding while she talked, and we all three were likely recollecting that boy that just got himself killed over in Orangeburg on account of smart-mouthing some white church woman—but we didn't bring that up, Frank just said *mmm hmm* under his breath and nodded. Then I said I reckoned maybe it was time to stir things, which words caused Sarah to jerk her head around and Frank to quit his humming. Then she said: "Girl, you got next to no idea about real life, and don't even know it. You've been out here so long," she said, her eyes flashing with the old anger she doesn't generally heap on me nowdays, "you believe Hazelhedge is the *world* and you got some say or place in it." She snorted then and turned back to her work: "You are dead wrong, Minyon Manigault. Best stick to your own business and don't be making trouble, because you will reap way more than you're equipped to sow. You can believe that, girl, and you'd best study on it good."

Studying on it so hard right this minute that I nearly miss the road to Hazelhedge, got to about stand this car on end to make the turn. As I pull into the yard, I trail along behind me the dust and dirt I stirred, going so fast.

In the drive's a pale blue Lincoln I know belongs to Mr. Parker T. Sutherland, Mizz Addie's Jameston lawyer and one of our Saturday night regulars. I pull on around back and unload the clothes at the common room, so the girls can sort through and lay claim to what's theirs. Half a dozen of them're in here by now, starting to stir this time of day, watching *Guiding Light* or some other of those TV stories they get so wrapped up with. They're eating sandwiches, drinking coffee, doing their nails, and watching. Hardly even glance up, still half lost in their dreamtime selves.

Watching them, my mind sees a parade of their sisters, in and out of here going on thirty years, never stopping long enough to make much of a mark, most of them. Even their names start to repeat, like there's not but just so many that sounds sexy or sassy enough to do. I try not to think too hard about how these girls end up, though one bitter hoe named Bridget told me the ones that stay in more than a year or two mostly die young. Young's the only way we take them, anyhow—much past twenty-nine and Mizz Addie refers them on to some house ain't so choosy as Hazelhedge. Not that I ever heard one announce her age past twenty-nine; these girls make up ages right along with names.

Time to go check on Farina, but before I do, my stomach tells me I got to decide something about food for us two. I slip through the kitchen door, on account of my own pantry's near bare, and I plan to borrow some lunch.

Quiet as I am, though, it's not quiet enough. From the parlor floats a putting-on-for-company voice: "Is that you, Minyon?" My stomach gives a large growl, like it's answering back without my say-so, and I'm calculating how quiet I can get this door shut and myself down the back steps. Like she can read my mind, here comes that voice again, just calls the one word: "Minyon?" which wraps itself round and round me till I've got no will past closing this fridge door and opening my mouth to answer, "Yes-sum?" already starting to walk down the hall to where she is.

In the parlor she and Mr. Parker T are cozied up on the love seat by the window, having themselves a sip of some gold-colored something out of our best crystal. When I walk in he looks up and gives that big old grin he's famous for around these parts, shows all his teeth. "Afternoon, Mizz Manigault. How you doing this fine day?"

That's Mr. Parker T—always the same kind of friendly and overpolite, whether he's talking to Mizz Addie or one of the big shots he brings here from time to time, or even me. It's nothing personal, just his way. I recollect a big slow gator used to laze by the river at Little Town that had a grin like this.

"Fine, Lawyer Sutherland, thank you." I nod my head, then turn to Mizz Addie and see right off that trouble's up. Nobody but me's liable to know it, to look at her—she's still and pale as usual, comporting herself like a lady, as she calls it. But there's a tightening around the eyes and a small moving of mouth that means she's tearing tiny bits of skin off with her teeth. It makes for an ugly knitting of lips she's not generally prone to.

"Bring me the red cash box from the safe, would you, Minyon?" she says, her voice calm as the turned-up palms of her hands lying still in her lap, like this is something she might ask me to fetch any day out the week instead of for the first time in twenty-eight years. I manage to stay steady on a yessum as I head for her room.

I have to haul out a box or two and shove files to one side to get to the bottom of the safe. Letting my fingers shift easy over the back corner on the right-hand side, I feel blind in the dark for a small break in the steel, how she showed me some years ago, whispering: "This is our fall-back money, Minyon, for emergencies only," as she pulled out a slim metal box, gray on top to match the safe, all the rest fire-engine red. When she lifted up the lid, I saw stacks of bills, all hundreds, seemed like. "I don't expect we'll have to use it," she whispered, "but you need to know where it is."

And so I do. My fingers find the spot and push till one edge pops up. I lift but don't open it, just walk back to the parlor and hand the box over, looking into Mizz Addie's eyes as it passes between us. What I see in there makes me cross to the hall closet,

get a cloth and some polish, and set myself to rubbing the mahogany on the bar, which already gleams sufficient to near re-
flect my face back to me.

These two aren't talking now. The only noise is her opening
the box, laying its lid flat, and starting to count. Small sounds,
aren't they—the crisp slide of money on money, whispered num-
bers, cloth rubbing rich wood—but seem plenty large enough to
fill this room full.

Then: "As agreed, Parker." I bend over my work, glancing
sideways to see her hand the bills over. His grin breaks out again
when he takes the money, cracking his face almost in two: "As
agreed, Ariadne."

She stares till that grin of his wavers and closes up, shutting
off the light that never did make it all the way through his face
anyhow. "I trust this will resolve the situation," she says then,
folding her hands and leaning back some. He stands, fishing up
his grin again, and says, "I trust so, too." And I'm thinking trust
is the last word I'd conjure about either one of these white folks
across the room, taking care of their white-folk business. Got
nothing to do with me.

By the time I put up the polish and cloth and go stand beside
her at the door, Lawyer Sutherland's nothing but the dust he left
swirling in the drive. "If that doesn't do it, Minyon, I don't know
what will," she says, holding the empty red cash box and looking
out at the swirls like maybe they'll settle into some pattern that
will give her a sign. "We might be lost indeed," she says.

I watch her white face while my mind jumps around a mess of
thoughts at once—Hazelhedge being lost, my sick cousin in outback, the tail lights of Blue Ballard's cab, real life outside of here.
My cheek stings, fresh-slapped.

There's lots of things I might say, but all I do is, "I'm going to
get some food and see to Farina," and leave her standing there to
chew on her problems while I go tend to mine.

chapter 3

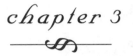

Farina slumps against the car door, as far from me as she can get across the pale leather of this seat. When I glance over, she slants her head some, angling that sharp cheekbone away, making sure not to look at me.

"We're crossing the bridge into Jameston," I report, my voice cheery as a brush salesman's. "Paper mill's cooking today, for sure." I take a deep breath and say, same as everybody who lives here: "Smells like bread and butter, doesn't it?"

She still has no comment. I reach over and switch the radio on to the new station in town. "I'm all shook up," I sing, humming right along and tapping my foot, just like we're having us a good old time. But in my head I hear Doc Larkin's words the last morning he paid us a visit, after he motioned me out to the living room and told me Farina's not coming along like she should, even though she's passed the danger point now with the liquor poisoning. She still eats next to nothing, still's not talking. She's reached what Doc calls a plateau and's got no ambition to leave the bed, seems like.

"The thing is, Minyon," he told me, leaning his head down

close enough to where I caught the clean smell of him, "Farina's going to have to *want* to live—to want her baby to live. Until and unless that happens," and right then he turned his head to look out the window instead of at me, "I don't know if either of them will survive the birth."

I don't believe the Lord sent Farina and this baby-to-be just to give me a taste of happiness and then snatch it away. So it must be my chore to make sure something different happens. I've been conjuring how to do that, and this morning, soon as I opened my eyes on the day, the answer was waiting like a hag that'd slept the night perched on my chest to jump straight into my brain first thing. That's how come I'm carrying my cuz back to Little Town, to see can we find what's lost before it's too late.

Beside me Farina shifts, pulls a pack of cigarettes from her back pocket, and lights up, sighing the smoke out. She's not exactly thrilled with this trip and wants to make sure I know it. "Why would I want to go there, Min?" she asked this morning when I came jostling her sound-asleep self, saying we got a visit to pay. "That's ancient history," she said, "it's got nothing to tell me—or you either, girl." Then she turned her body away and closed her eyes. "I just need to sleep, Min, OK?"

Her kind of sleep's too close to the kind's got no wakeup at the other end to suit me, though, so I kept at her till she pulled on some clothes and got in the car. This is the first time she's been off from Hazelhedge since she got here, almost three months ago. And she's not purely mad at me, just tired and sulky-acting, more like a baby girl than a forty-three-year-old woman who's got her own baby inside her, finally showing itself, barely poking out from that skin-and-bones belly that doesn't resemble any too safe a keeping place.

I turn down Water Street, where all the stores're showing their red, white and blueness, fixing to celebrate the Fourth. "Jameston's ready for Independence Day," I say, pointing around, inviting my cuz to sit up and take notice. She stays slouched, though, takes another draw off her cigarette and reaches one hand up to let the wind flick the ash. "Aren't we all," she tells me, in that gravelly, tired voice of hers. But when I look over, her mouth's curved at one corner—just enough to make my heart lift about the same amount.

"First, the tide," sings the radio voice, smooth as silk, as we take the curve heading out of town. In the distance I see the wide new Waccamaw bridge, rising from the flat of land like it's going to bear us two cousins heavenward, or if not there, at least to Little Town.

". . . rushes in," I join my voice to the radio one and put my foot to the pedal, hope flooding. Farina says nothing, just leans back and closes her eyes.

In the middle of the bridge I slow down enough to take a look. On one side's my sweet Waccamaw, the sun dancing on its white-curled edges, making blinding points of light a thousand strong. I see the curve and flex of river rounding a bend to the old rice fields and cypress stumps, meeting up somewhere with the Little Town beach where we used to bathe and swim. On the other side, the land stretches and thins out, the river widening itself to bay. Seems like if I tried hard, I might could see some bit of ocean past it, lapping its waves on the sand. I can't, though—water and sky just slip off together to palest blue.

"Best watch the road, girl," says Farina, "unless it's some place else than Little Town you're planning to get us." Still doesn't open eyes, though, just lazes back.

The Arcadia road's not but a few miles from the bridge. It's been a while since I was out this way, though I do come pay my respects to Clarence's resting place every now and again, and try to keep up with folks.

The road to the big house's been paved, but the turnoff to Little Town's still dirt. Mr. Waldo's granddaughter owns this all now, but she mostly tends to business up north and's got some local folks running things for her. Keeps the Little Town coloreds busy, those that's left, anyhow, tending the grounds and helping run the tree-cutting operation. But the big house sits empty, aside from three-or-four-time-a-year visits. Lally told me about it, on one of my visits. She said her granddaughter Sylvira and a couple of others go up there once a week to keep that big old empty place clean. "White folks's something else, ain't they?" she asked me, nodding her head and tutting her teeth, not looking for an answer—me thinking she doesn't know the half of it.

It's Lally I check in with now that Big Robert's gone, along with most of the others I knew—dead like him, or moved off. They're still plenty of coloreds that's lived out here all their lives, though, and never left except for trips to town once in a blue moon or so.

Quiet this morning, not but a few children stirring and one girl on a porch shelling beans. I drive slow down the road so's not to kick up too much dust, and say to my still closed-eyed cuz: "We're here," even though it seems like the smell and feel of the air'd make her know without me telling.

At that she finally rouses, pushes herself up with one foot and looks around, first to one side and then the other. When we pass Gan's old house—*our* old house—she sucks in her breath sharp one time, but doesn't speak. I stop in front of Lally's, three doors down, and Farina lights a cigarette, her hands trembling bad as they used to, till she can hardly hold the match.

Lally steps out on the porch. She always was a substantial-sized woman, and's more so since Big Robert's heart gave out a few years back—like she's looking to eat her sorrow before the other way around. Fetches up a big grin when I step out the car, and comes on down the stairs, one hand on her bad hip. "Min, honey," and then both arms swallow me up, folding me in to a large warm body, covering me head to toe till her voice only comes muffled, like from far off: "Been too long, child." Then she holds me back from her and tuts: "Need some meat on those bones, Min. How about share a little something with me?"

"Nome, Mizz Lally," I say. "We can't stay, just coming to pay respects." At that *we*, her eyes shift over to the car. Can't see much of Farina except that wild head of hair framed against the light and one slim outline of arm as she reaches up to draw hard on her cigarette.

Mizz Lally bends down. "Who you got in there?" and goes to walking over, so Farina doesn't have much choice but to step out, which she does, with a tired smile—but still a smile, looking all of a sudden like my cuz of old—saying: "It's me, Mizz Lally. Farina Ward."

One whoop, then Farina disappears same as me, lost in arms and bosoms and belly. It's not till she can deliver herself from that and catch breath, and Mizz Lally stops exclaiming and shaking her head about folks coming back from the near-forgot-and-dead, that we're able to take leave, and then only by swearing up and down to come back soon and stay a while.

We ride slow past Little Town's shanty houses, some empty now, plywood slapped across windows, porches sagging—ghost-looking and sad. Just past the last one, the road curves down to river, and that's where we head a bit till we come to the rise where our little white church's sat ever since slave times.

I pull in front and look over at Farina, who stares out the window, maybe remembering all those Sundays we spent in there from morning till past suppertime, singing and praising the Lord, me and her and Clarence and the rest of us children, Jesse too, and Gan and Preach and Lally and Big Robert and all them.

The church is boarded up now, too, paint peeling and wood warping here and there, on account of they've had nobody to lead since Preach passed. Most folks go to the A.M.E. in Jameston, Lally says, those that go.

I step out and walk up to the front stoop, which looks too shaky to stand on. In a sec I hear the car door slam, and next to me's Farina, both of us hushed and still, like we're inside there instead of out here under this midday sun.

"Remember the first time we walked in there wearing our new pink dresses, the ones Gannie sewed us?" I whisper to her. My hands drop down by my sides, and I feel eight years old again, pretty and proud.

"Yes, I do, Min," she answers back, her voice borne on the wind of its own breath, sweet in my ear.

"And how Mizz Mabel Tarbox used to faint, every time that

visiting preacher from Charleston'd come and get talking about the ecstasy?" I could see Mizz Mabel right now, how she'd grab hold of her chest and start gasping, eyes rolled back in her head, and people all around her getting set to break the fall.

Farina laughs, soft music I haven't heard in going on thirty years. "I do."

Her hand catches hold of mine, slim fingers twining, and she says, "Remember how we'd laugh at that—our shoulders'd shake trying to hold it in, and Gan would thwack us good with her fan?"

Standing next to my cuz I feel it again, that terrible laughing coming up from inside me. I hear the preacher's voice, see folks making way for Mizz Mabel's fall, feel this cuz sitting next to me, thinking my same thoughts. My shoulders start shaking while we stand here hand in hand, and I can almost hear the whistle of Gan's fan through the air before it lands on a shoulder or a wrist, which just makes us hold in harder and harder till we can't hold anymore and she finally has to lead us out of church, one on either side of her, her looking straight ahead and walking fast.

Seeing it so clear, I bust out right now, just like that eight-year-old in my head, just like Farina does, too, standing here by me. We laugh and laugh, and in a minute we're not holding hands anymore—we're hugging instead, knees weak, trying to keep each other standing up, gasping and clutching same as Mizz Mabel used to, till we finally give up and fall in a heap on the grass in front of the church, then flat on our backs looking up at the cleanest, bluest sky I ever witnessed. Both of us quiet. The tears of my laughing stream like spring rain.

After a bit we collect ourselves, I take Farina's hand and lead her to the plot of ground next to the church, where lots of our folks lie buried. Some's got no markers anymore, just low spots or a sinky bumpiness to the ground to show a body's resting place. Others have wooden crosses held fast with leather twine. There's plenty of old stone markers, too, on account of in slave times and years after, Gan told me, Little Town had a stonemason named Sorrow Bartholomew who made such sweet markers white folks'd come from miles around to buy them, Sorrow's markers.

In the back center, next to Gan and her Cap, is Clarence's place, with the marker they bought in town on my Hazelhedge money, that shows his true Manigault name right alongside his adopted Tarbox one. He's the last one's buried here, Lally said, on account of the law closed this cemetery down right after.

We stare down a while, then Farina tells me: "I saw Clarence—did you know that, Min?—when he came to New York, before he joined up. He came to see me."

I feel like the breath's been clean knocked from me, and can't think of anything to say past, "How . . . ?"

"Folks could find folks in the city, back then, specially in Harlem. Still can, but it's different now." Her low voice bitters up, and in a minute she goes on. "Anyhow, he asked around and asked around till he found me. I was doing pretty good, waiting tables in a club then, before the real badness came."

I say nothing—can't—just look over, marking the lines, bones, angles of her face.

"I sure was surprised. He looked so *good,* Min, grown tall and filled out so—a big, strong, *sweet* man."

In my throat rises a terrible fullness, so big it presses hard on all sides, aching, trying to bust loose.

"He told me about how Lally and Big Robert'd been good to him, about how you sent money all those years to help him get the right schooling, about how you never came to visit on account of working at the whorehouse. He wanted to go see you before he left, he said, but didn't, on account of he was afraid to shame you."

My heart goes still and frozen, thinking about all those years I missed of my baby bub, seeing him grow, wondering what he thought about his disappeared sister. Now I don't know if I can stand knowing, and anyhow, the question won't get itself out of my mouth.

But Farina answers, like she hears it clear as spoken words.

"Know what he said about you, Min? Said you'd always be his sister, and he was glad of it."

Now ain't that simple, ain't that small—but it sounds true, and it fills me with a gladness so large I can't grab hold of it.

We're quiet a long time, then she asks: "What about Jesse, Min? You ever hear what became of that boy?"

I think of telling her now, opening my mouth to say what I've kept all this time, to tell how the breath came out of Jesse as he lay on top of me, how I smelled his death stink, how his soul flew out when I freed that knife, how his head bobbed on the ground till I picked him up, too, and helped carry; to tell that dark, bad secret's been binding me and Mizz Ariadne Fleming together all these years. But I don't—it's in there too deep, and let out, it can't do anything but spread grief wider and deeper.

"Wherever he is," I say, seeing in my mind by the light of a lantern the dark rich dirt covering his dark cold skin, hearing the thrust of a shovel into soft piney ground, and conjuring the Jesse-haint that's visited my dreams so many times since, harking me out to loblollies, "he likely isn't resting peaceful."

Her sigh's rich with colors of memory. "You know that's right, girl."

She seems very tired again, but I don't believe we've finished our business here just yet—I've got to get this girl done with it once and for all. I take her hand and walk towards the piney woods across the way. "Where now, Min?" she asks, but doesn't offer much fight, just lets her legs and my hand carry her.

"You'll see," I promise, my feet finding the old paths like it was yesterday they last touched this dirt, made their way through the tall pines to a clearing and our used-to-be meeting place. Grown as we are, this old stump's still got room for two; it welcomes us to sit a while, talk like in the old days, till's nothing left to say.

Farina's not even surprised enough to remark it, just climbs up and curves her small self around the high half, propping her head on one hand. I take my old seat just below, resting my back against the high part of the stump and angling my head where I

225

can see her face good. The breeze's sufficient to keep the bugs busy battling it instead of us, and the sun beats down hot, bright in her eyes now, which she closes against it and starts talking, taking right up where we left it.

"That thing inside that made Jesse so mean, it's one of the reasons I left when I did, Min—that, and you and Gannie being gone." She gives a little chuckle's got no laugh in it. "Funny thing is, I found that same meanness, and worse, almost every-where I went—even in myself. Couldn't outrun it, far's I tried to go."

She opens her eyes a bit, just to slits against this bright sun. Doesn't look at me, though—starts tracing the whorls of tree veins round and round with one finger, her voice going sing-songy, like those patterns and the patterns of her telling have one same rhythm driving them.

"Left here with a boy name of Sammy Watkins, passing through on his way to the big city. I hadn't seen Jesse for a while, but I was carrying his baby and I knew he'd be back on account of that, if nothing else. So I lit out while I could, without a word to anybody and everything I owned in that old cloth suitcase Gan used to keep under her bed." She sighs and's quiet a minute before starting back up.

"Up around Baltimore I started getting sick, terrible aching and weakness, then finally bleeding. Somewhere around Phila-delphia Sammy got scared enough to quit driving and find me a doctor, but it was too late—that baby was coming, too early to live, don't you know. And the doctor Sammy finally did fetch said it was better that way, the baby was bad messed up. So we stayed a day or two in a motel there while I got some strength back, then headed out for New York. But Sammy wasn't the same after; he didn't care to touch me anymore. About two weeks later, after we got to the city and found us a place to live, he left one morning to look for work and didn't come back, leav-ing me holding about thirty dollars and a place to live for two more weeks, which seemed pretty bad at the time, though now I know he could've done me much worse." Her voice runs down and she quits whorling and closes her eyes again.

"What'd you do, Farina? Why didn't you turn around and come home then?"

"I didn't know where home was anymore, Min. It sure wasn't here." She opens her eyes and they stare flat and tired into mine. "What I did was the best I knew how. Went out job looking. It was hard—uptown stores didn't hire coloreds, so we had to get ourselves downtown to get work. Got me a job in one of those big hotels down there, started work at four in the morning, doing laundry, changing sheets, cleaning up after white folks' mess."

Isn't that funny—my cuz halfway across the country, and us doing the same thing at the same time.

"Later I did other things—kept house for some folks, waited tables, washed dishes—always was some kind of work like that, if you knew how to look.

"Days weren't much fun at all, but nights, well, they were something else again." Farina's voice goes dreamy now, and a smile settles in. "Nights I'd go to some club or other just down the street from my place, listen to foxy music, and dance. Times were hard, and lots of folks were hurting, but there was always some jive-talking boy or other round, had a few coins in his pocket, glad to pick up a girl's drink tab—the girl too, if he could. Which he generally could." Lets out her bad, unfunny chuckle.

"So that's how I got found by Mr. Jimmy Z. Jones Esquire, my Sugar Hill sugar daddy—on a real splurge one night, sitting at Small's Paradise, listening to jazz, and sipping on a vodka collins." She looks sideways at me, her mouth held crooked. "Know what Sugar Hill is, Min?"

I shake my head no.

"Sugar Hill's where all the rich Harlem niggers live. Big old houses, grander than most white folks'. Jimmy Z had one—and he was crazy for me. Said mine was the sweetest brown sugar he ever had—so sweet he didn't want to share it. So he moved me to my own little uptown apartment, where he'd visit almost every night of the week—at first, anyhow. And I'd stay in all day waiting on him, going nowhere but the store to get food and liquor, cook him up something good. And then wait. He'd take me to fine restaurants some nights, girl, and shopping, buy me clothes I only wore for him. Oh, I lived fine." She pulls out a cigarette, lights up, and draws in deep, laying her head back against the stump.

"Years we went on like that. Sometime in between, I carried and lost two of his babies. Hard as I'd try to hold on, I never could seem to get one to stick. After a while I started going crazy, holed up in that place waiting for him, and by then he was coming less—once or twice a week—but still didn't want me going anyplace else. Wouldn't leave enough money but for food, which sometime around then I started spending on whiskey instead, to keep me company and pass the time.

"That's when the meanness started creeping in on me, Min. I felt cornered, desperate; I wanted a real life. Kept thinking of Jimmy Z's big old house on Sugar Hill and his wife, sitting up there so fine and respectable and free.

"So one day I showed up on the doorstep—in the afternoon, when I was pretty sure he wouldn't be home. He wasn't. She was. I told the maid I was a friend of Mr. Jones', and in a minute she came back and showed me to the parlor. After a while in came Mrs. J. Z. Jones, Esq.—that's what her card said—she had a card, girl, with that name printed on it so deep you could *touch* it." In my cuz's mouth lies a bitter taste that same kind of deep, poisoning her voice.

"I didn't know what I was going to say till I got started saying it. I was about half gone anyway, I'd been drinking all morning to get up my courage, and the card finished me off. I told her everything: the apartment, the presents, the dinners, the promises, those two lost babies, the one I was carrying."

I raise my eyes then, and Farina opens hers halfway, saying, "yeah," then closes them again and draws the hot fire of her cigarette down into herself, lets the ashy smoke out slow.

"She didn't say much the whole time. Got a stone-faced look and sat stiller and stiffer while I talked. When I finally ran down, she just got up and left the room.

"I was so tired, Min, I couldn't move. It's hard work being mean."

"What did Jimmy Z say, Farina?"

"Didn't say a word—didn't show up at the apartment, didn't call. I was waiting for it, but when it came, it wasn't words, and it was so fast I never knew what hit me.

"I went out to the package store and to pick up some groceries a few days after my Sugar Hill visit, and when I got back to the apartment, it was locked and my key wouldn't work. I beat on the door, I hollered, and after a while, I threw the bottle of booze at it. When the landlord came, saying that apartment didn't belong to me, it belonged to Mr. James Z. Jones, Esquire, who had the perfect right to it and everything in it, why then, I turned my attention to that boy, picked up part of the broken bottle and went for his ugly black face. Got some of it, too, before it was over."

She laughs, low and bitter. "Should've kept that bottle in one piece, though; it was the last whiskey I'd see for a while.

"Spent the next week or so locked up. Lost Jimmy Z's third baby while I was in there." She stops and swallows hard, then draws deep on her cigarette.

"When they put me on the street again, I didn't have but the clothes on my back and about ten dollars in my pocketbook. It was raining; I had no idea where to go—I'd lost touch with my old friends, all those years with Jimmy." She looks up at the sky, but the sun's too bright and she closes her eyes against it and heaves the tiredest sigh in the world.

"What'd you do, Farina?" Figure my job's nothing more than pushing her along when she gets herself stalled out.

"What I did was find me a bar, girl—what else? Perched my

narrow ass on a stool at eleven in the morning and ordered two
shots of Beam, straight up. Somebody bought me a third, and by
the time he ordered up number four, we were pretty friendly.
Before the night was over, he found a flophouse and I found
enough money for a week's rent. And a new job. Flatbacking.
Easy on the feet, but a killer for the head and stomach. It paid
rent for my old shamble of a room and kept me in booze. Long as
I had enough of that, I could mostly do all right, keep from
thinking too much.

"Then one early morning I got up feeling real bad; my insides
shook so hard that when I reached for the bottle next to the bed
I couldn't hardly get it to my mouth. I sucked on that a minute
and then a voice came from right beside me—didn't even know
anybody else was in the bed till then—some john's voice, not real
mean but not nice either, more like he was discussing whether or
not it might rain that day—that voice said, 'Why don't you just
slit your wrists, sister; it's quicker and don't hurt near as bad.' I
didn't say anything and he got up out of the bed and put on his
clothes and walked out without another word. I sat there all that
day, thinking without even knowing what I was thinking. But by
the next morning, all that thinking'd turned into something, and
I knew what I had to do: I had to come home. And that was to
you, Min, the only home I knew."

I breathe and draw those last sweet words in deep; they settle
down alongside old scarred-up spots. We neither one say anything for a while after that, both quiet here together, my cuz and
me, lying against this old tree stump's seen and heard all this
mess and much more besides.

By the time we rouse ourselves sufficient to walk back
through the woods to the church where our car's parked, it's
already getting on to late afternoon, and into my head comes
thoughts of the work that's waiting on me. They don't weigh too
hard, though—I feel light right now, empty of some stuff and
filled with other that's not near as heavy.

And who knows what Farina's thinking as we ride slow back
through Little Town, up the road away from the big house and

across the shining Waccamaw, heading back to Hazelhedge. On the radio a smooth sweet voice sings "Chances are." And I don't know for sure what ours are, me and my cuz here and that unborn kin of us both inside her—but I reckon they're some better now than when we started this day out. As we ride, I hum right along with.

chapter 4

"Why can't we?" Mary Lou's cheeks fired up hot smack in the middle of each and her pale neck flushed red after supper last evening, when she stood face-to-facing Mizz Addie, right before Wednesday night trade started up.

"I love parades, Miss Fleming. We'll be quiet, we'll be good. Nobody'll even know we're there, I promise." Her face went pleading then, looking like a young girl begging her mama for some favor or other.

"Of course they'll know you're there, Mary Lou." Mizz Addie's voice was that patient one she gets, grates like nails on glass. "This is a small town, as you're certainly aware."

Mary Lou flounced herself over to the long sofa and sat down hard next to Fawn, who leaned back, tucked a long blond hank behind one ear, and fixed a pale blue eye on Mizz Addie, saying, "What's the big deal? Why can't she go to the fucking parade— she's as patriotic as the next."

Mizz Addie's not crazy about Fawn and doesn't care for that kind of talk, so she didn't even favor that girl with a sideways look, just concentrated on her favorite. "It simply won't do,

Mary Lou. As I've told you before, Hazelhedge has a definite place in this town, and we have to be very careful indeed to keep to it. It's not public, dear. We're not parade material."

That's about as close to nice as Mizz Addie gets, but it didn't faze Mary Lou—she just kept her head turned toward Fawn and her lip poked out, till Mizz Addie heaved a big sigh and left the room.

And now here's sitting me and Mizz Addie in our big black Cadillac, parked in the first parking spot off Water Street, right next to Rose's dime store, primed for parade watching, on account of, like she says, she paid for most of this, not just this year but every one since she can recollect, and she figures it's high time she came down here to see how her money got spent. Besides, she likes brass, she says.

She's sitting up front—nobody else's going to be driving, for sure—and I'm here in the back, the sweat streaming on account of she's got the windows up—for propriety's sake, she says, like rolled up windows're going to make us invisible—and it's twelve noon on the Fourth of July, likely inching up on ninety degrees out there, maybe more in here. Every so often she'll start the car and let the air conditioning cool us some, but it's not by a long shot sufficient.

Around us mills the folks of this town—the white ones, that is, the coloreds're three blocks over, crowding around the corner of Willow and Water, on account of that's where all the colored stores are. That's their place. Far's I can see, I'm the only colored in this world, trying to keep invisible in the blackness of this car.

Just when I feel like I can't draw another breath for the heat, Mizz Addie reaches out and turns the engine over, and at the same time I hear sirens, and here comes the brand new Jameston fire engine, glittering red as flames and covered top to bottom with dressed up, suntanned white girls, waving first to one side, then the other, baring their shining shoulders and large white teeth. Chief Luquire's driving, and while I watch him go by, grinning to beat the band, I all of a sudden see his page in the Hazelhedge Blue Book like it's a picture in my head, going better than fifteen years back, one girl's name and the next written in, then crossed off, them coming and going, never staying long enough to be anything but young and slim; him coming and going, too, but older now, and some fatter, his tastes staying pretty much the same, though: —*strictly a missionary man; —prefers petite blondes; —likes dirty words whispered during the act; —no rough stuff; —45 min. max.; —good tipper.* Mizz Addie still does the Blue Book writing and keeps it in her safe, but for years now, I make time to study on it every week, gathering those words to memory, in case anything ever happens to that book— the key, as she calls it, to Hazelhedge. I hold it in myself. *Honi soit qui mal y pense.*

The Chief's eyes rest a sec on our big black car, angled to the curb, Mizz Addie at the wheel. She reaches up to settle her little straw hat, and he turns his face to the river side of the street, showing us the back of his hand as he waves to the crowd and sounds the siren again.

I hear music now, and right after the fire trucks comes the Jameston Gators High School Band, it says so on a long white cloth three young girls carry. Behind them's more, twirling sticks round and about and lifting their legs high, showing pale thighs, wearing silky-looking shorts and high boots, their hair pulled back in long swingy ponytails, most of them. They're not that different-looking from our girls, except their faces're fresher and full of something ours've lost along the way. They're hot, too, I see the wet glistening on them.

Watching them makes me dwell on those girls of ours, Mary Lou especially, and be sad they can't even sit on a side street in a closed-up automobile and watch this. Wonder again how come Mizz Addie brought me along with, instead of maybe Mary Lou or another one of them. When I said that question out loud this morning to Farina, she looked at me a minute, smiled that little smile she has, where one side of her mouth curves up and not the other, and said, "That's because having you along's no trouble— ain't no different than having another one of herself for company—just colored different and sweeter-natured, that's all."

After she said that, she turned her attention back to break-fast. That girl's got her appetite finally, and's showing right large now. Doc Larkin says her chances and that baby's are getting better every day.

I interrupted her in mid-chew this morning, though. "What in this world're you talking about, Farina?"

She swallowed her cereal and sipped orange juice, then looked straight into my eyes, no smile in sight. "Girl, you're so in the middle of this place you can't see clear as you might." A Sarah-echo, for sure. Then she put her spoon down and leaned back in her chair, crossing her arms. "Who runs this house, Min?"

I can play along good as this cuz of mine. "I don't know, Farina," I said, hands-on-hipping it. "Who do you think?"

"Who keeps the books?"

She knows the answer, on account of she watches me do it, but I said it anyhow. "Me."

"Who hires and fires the help?"

"I do."

"Who bargains with the liquor salesman? Who orders groceries? Who buys supplies?"

I said nothing. She took a deep breath and kept on. "Who keeps the girls straight? Where do they go when they need somebody to talk to? Who is it they trust?"

I reckoned I could play this asking game good as my cuz. "Who sits down to Saturday night suppers with the movers and shakers?" I asked, taking Mizz Addie's very own words. "Who politics to keep the sheriff from this door and has been doing so going on thirty years now? Who knows every madam from one end of this country to the next, keeps our girls fresh and up to par?"

Farina was quiet now, just looking at me, and inside myself came rising some mad kind of feeling that made my voice louder and higher. "Who's got the money, girl, tell me that? Who signs those checks I write? Who thought and dreamed and planned this place? Who started this, anyhow? Tell me that."

Then my cuz rose up from her seat, came around to me, took hold of my arms and kept me still. "Doesn't matter who started it, Min. The question I'm asking is, who's keeping it? Who runs it now? Whose place is it, really?" Her voice was quiet, and I quieted some, too, and listened.

"You're the one who said it, Min—nearly thirty years together. You and Miss Fleming're more like one than two now— you even look alike."

I snorted at that. She turned me around, keeping her hands on my upper arms, steered me down the hall, and made me stand in front of my bedroom mirror. "Look," she said, and let go, standing to one side. "Long dark skirt, white tucked-in blouse, slicked-back bun—that's your everyday getup."

She stepped back a minute while I looked at my sorry self, something I haven't done in who knows how long. Then she went on: "What's *her* everyday getup, Min?"

I saw, and said nothing, just lifted one shoulder.

"And that," she said, touching my arm again, "that shoulder shrug—*she's* got the very same one."

I turned my head then, fixing to tell Farina she must of lost her mind.

"That look!" she cried. "How you dead-level your eyes when you're fixing to bless somebody out—that's Miss Ariadne Fleming to the life, girl.

"You walk the same, talk the same, eat, sleep, dress the same. For all I know, you even dream the same. Y'all are twins, Min, grown that way. You're the one runs this house, much as she is: her in the open, you in secret; her public, you private; her white, of course, and you black."

She ran out of breath then, stopped talking and just rubbed on her belly, plumb winded. I was through listening anyhow.

"No," I said, taking myself out of that room, picking up my straw hat and pocketbook, heading for the door. "No, no, no," I said again, shaking my head and walking out, not looking back even, just keeping on shaking my head and whispering the word all the way across the outback yard and up to the main house. *"No, no, no."*

Mizz Addie turns off the car again, and the band music clears my head some, makes my feet want to move to the drumming of it. She doesn't turn herself around to me, just keeps looking out the window, so I can see her sideways face, the passing-by parade colors reflecting in her glasses. Then she says: "Minyon, I need to talk with you about Hazelhedge."

Here we are in the middle of my first-ever-in-forty-three-years-of-living on-this-earth Fourth of July parade, and she can't leave that place be for even one minute?—got to carry it around on her back like it's part of her?—in her skin, her hair, her lips? Can't we once just be two women doing something as simple as sitting in a car watching a parade go by?

I reckon I know the answer to that well enough, and out of my mouth it comes, automatic as breathing: "Yessum?"

In front of us now's riding two carloads full of Shriners, with their tall, tasseled hats. I recognize Francis Marlowe and Jimmy Ray McDaniels, red-faced looking enough to bust. Mr. Jimmy Ray's famous at Hazelhedge for being the noisiest trick we ever served—you can hear him grunting and hollering clear to outback, and him in one of the upstairs rooms. Fawn's his favorite, nowadays, and before her it was Angelique, who's moved on now, we heard maybe to Atlanta.

Above Mizz Addie's top lip I see sweat popping. She reaches out to turn the car on again, but far's I can tell, it's not helping much. Feels like more hot air to me. She takes a white handkerchief with lace edges, the kind she's got about a hundred of, and pats the spot between her lip and nose.

"Minyon, I'm sure you know there've been some problems at Hazelhedge in the past few months. Government problems." She clears her throat, still looking out the window toward the parade, where just now's passing a big something looks like a railroad flatcar, that's got flags and more red, white and blueness than I ever saw before in one place, with a banner that reads

"VFW" and a bunch of Jameston men, young and old, dressed in their service uniforms. I see familiar faces and flashes of Blue Book notes at the same time: —*likes English;* —*face man;* —*fast and straight;* —*welsher;* —*needs coaxing;* —*around-the-world every time;* and on and on, with girls' names attached, too: Rosalie, Maude, Zelda, Gilda, Hilda, Lila, Zoe, Chloe, Veronique.

"Specifically, IRS problems, as I believed I've mentioned, to the tune of nearly two hundred thousand dollars. Which would seriously jeopardize our survival, Minyon. Very seriously indeed."

Another band marches by, this one from Red Hill High School, with more young girls showing thighs and swinging hips, more young boys blowing brass. Behind them's one flashy red convertible with little Jimbo Hamilton at the wheel and sitting up in back a blond-headed girl in a no-shouldered evening dress—and it the middle of the day!—carrying red, white and blue flowers in one hand and waving to the crowd with the other. She's got a little crown on her head, a sign draped around her that says "Miss Jameston," and a mouth full to near overflowing with long, white teeth, sparkling hard as diamonds. I see Mr. Jimbo see us, but his eyes slide right over our Cadillac like he never spied it nor us before in his life.

"Mr. Sutherland's been working on it for me, along with some other friends in high places, Minyon, and he thinks it may be taken care of. But he's come up with something—a legal sort of maneuver—that may just confuse the issue enough to ensure that it is truly behind us, once and for all."

Cattycorner across the street from us's Goldstein's, and I see Mr. Isadore and his boys standing in front of the store, trying to stay cool under the green awning with their name writ white across it. If he sees us, I can't tell it. I feel like waving, but don't. By now Mr. Isadore's just one more soul in this town we can see who can't seem to return the favor. So maybe Mizz Addie was right after all, maybe keeping the car closed up does make us invisible—for propriety's sake, like she said it.

While I stare, Mr. Isadore and his boys go kind of wavy in

front of my eyes. Inside my head's fuzzy, too, maybe on account of the heat in here—the blower's making a whooshy noise, but there's not a bit of cool to be found. I'm soaked clean through, and Mizz Addie's glasses's slipped down on her nose, her cheeks slick with wet. She's still talking, though, something about Mr. Parker T, I hear it through the buzz in my brain: "Mr. Sutherland thinks, he says it might be a good idea," she pats a sweat drop at the corner of her mouth and angles her head just a tad more my way. "He thinks it may just cinch it, if we, if I . . ." Now she turns her head a little more toward me, and instead of eyes I see light reflected off her glasses and the parade still going on beside us.

"If I, if we, that is, if Hazelhedge is put in your name, Minyon. Temporarily, that is. Just until this thing blows over, he says."

I stare at those glary blanks where eyes're supposed to be, and my mouth gapes open—partly in surprise, partly trying to suck fresh air in from somewhere. None to be had though. Around my chestal region's a drum beat I can hear and feel in my ears, too. My whole self's awash, and I can't make my mouth say anything.

Cutting through that drumming in my ears comes some new sound now—sweet and sassy, brassy. Mizz Addie turns her head to the parade and I do, too—like we're both summoned to it—just in time to see Mr. Earl Winchell Junior glide by in a baby-blue T-bird, and right behind him that Charleston brass band he bragged so on, fixing to finish up this parade in style. Through the powerful thrumming in my head I hear that music, and out the corner of one eye I see Mizz Addie's hand raise up. Mr. Earl Junior clamps his eyes right down on her just as her hand starts rising, and even though I'm amazed to see it, I believe it: she's got the right to at least wave. At which Mr. Earl Junior's face goes red as fire and he takes a terrible coughing fit, then turns his head. And directly here comes the brass and Mizz Addie's raised-up hand's doing nothing more than straightening her hat on her head after all, so maybe it's just too hot and I'm dreaming things.

Must be dreaming for sure, because right across the street, in the parking lot between Goldstein's store and the old hotel, I all of a sudden spy a couple of folks I sure didn't expect to: Doc Larkin and our Mary Lou, standing next to his car where they must of been all this while. Mary Lou's face's lit up like I never saw it before, watching that brass band march by. Doc's is angled down to hers, and even from here, there's something about that angle that sends a lump to my throat and a rise to my too-hot head, and I close my eyes or maybe I don't, but can't see anything anymore, nor hear that brassy sound even. I reach for the door handle, got to get me some fresh air, on account of can't breathe and can't see and can't think. All I hear, like an echo of something's been said but not taken in, are the words I've held off from me as long as I could: *if Hazelhedge is put in your name, Minyon; in your name, Minyon; your name, Minyon.*

"Minyon, Minyon!"

Must be rousing from bed—overslept, time to get to work. "Wait a sec, wait," I say, trying to push those hands off me. "I'm getting up," I say, or try to: don't hear the words myself.

I slit one eye open. The light's enough to pure blind me, but in a sec I see the outline of Doc Larkin's head. "Turn the light off," I try to say, but it doesn't come out so clear as all that. My head aches near to busting, and I can't think for a minute, but then when I do, I think of Farina. I start rising up out of bed. "Oh Lord, Doc, is it Farina? Is it my poor sweet cuz?" And in my head I can see her rubbing that belly, looking up at me, saying, "You got to help me keep this one, Min. You got to."

From far off I hear music. Doc Larkin puts his hand gentle on my arm, saying, "No, Minyon, take it easy, everything's all right," and I lay back and open my eyes again, my head splitting, and see to the one side of me the wheel and tire of Mizz Addie's black Cadillac, which doesn't make a piece of sense for a sec, till I turn my head the other way and see a mess of white folks' feet and ankles cutting a wide path around my head, and know all of a sudden this isn't my bed at all, but the hot hard Jameston street against my back. Over me leans not just Doc but Mary Lou, too, and from somewhere out of thin air comes Blue Ballard's sweet face, his brown eyes all worried looking. Between their three heads I see Mizz Addie; she's got the front door of the car open and her legs dangling out, peering over where I am, mopping at her top lip.

I know I got to get myself up, on account of this's what Mizz Addie calls a scene, close on to a scandal, but my mind's not as in charge as it might be. Now comes cool water to my lips and that's better, and then Doc Larkin says maybe they can raise me. Arms come under mine, I smell Blue's good man smell, and I am lifted up. I hear Doc Larkin tell Mizz Addie in what sounds the closest to mad I ever heard out of his mouth that he doesn't know what she was thinking, she could've killed us both. Then he says he's got to get me taken care of, and he and Mary Lou and Blue start carting me off.

The brass band's passed, and the parade's about done, but just when we go to cross back over the street, here comes one last car, honking its horn something fool and scattering folks every whichway. This one's a convertible, too, a brand new one, jam-packed with girls grinning and waving side to side. None of these wear banners or crowns, but they're dressed to the nines. At the wheel is Salters Bouchette—the dentist's son, a college boy, whose daddy gave him his first trip to Hazelhedge a few years back for his eighteenth birthday—he's a wild one that folks say's got more money than sense. Right next to him, dressed in her best red dress, sits a long blond drink of water, cool as a cuke, waving one arm slow and pushing a hank of hair behind her ear with the other hand. In the seat behind them's three more, with two others perched alongside the back of the car—all done up in their finest hoe fixings. When they pass, Fawn gives us a long, slow wink, then keeps waving as they glide on by us four and Mizz Addie's big black Caddy parked right behind.

Round us the crowd's set abuzz. A couple of men're fighting to hide grins, and I see one thin-lipped white woman go even paler and teeter, like she might keel over in a dead faint. I don't look back at Mizz Addie, don't have to—I can see her face in my mind clear as if I was looking in a mirror.

My head's about to bust wide open, seems like, and right before they put me in the back of Blue's taxicab and I close my eyes, praying for cool and quiet, I hear one more time her voice, and my hot, tired mind tries to make sense of what it means. I finally go to sleep with it running through my head, singing in my poor fried brain, a chorus from a tune I can't fathom: *If Hazelhedge is put in your name, Minyon.*

chapter 5

I jerk awake, and hear nothing at first but the wildness of this heart of mine, thrumming deep in my ears. Pitch dark, so I can't tell if my eyes're open or not, I have to reach one hand up through this black soundless air to feel.

They're open. My mind's closed, though, and my whole body lies still, waiting to know the story. Am I dead? No—breathing, beating, feeling, eyes open. I'm not dead. Then what? I breathe some more, and try to crank my brain past the noise of this yammering heart.

On my chest rests some pure heaviness, solid as life. Doesn't seem to be my too-familiar Jesse-haint—but what? Lying flat on my back in this darkness past memory of light, I raise one hand slow and careful up the side of my leg, onto my belly, up, up. And in the sec before my hand connects with this weight on my heart, memory kicks in and everything comes back, playing in my head like a movie show, but real.

On the radio we heard about it first—no, the TV. It was TV, the one I have in my trailer, the one I bought with my own money last Christmas, which Sarah says's likely the one and only

TV any colored person in this county owns, besides Thomas Delacroix, the undertaker. Anyhow, me and Farina's been watching a lot lately, ever since earlier this month when those colored children in Arkansas started trying to get into that white folks' school, and everybody gathered round outside shouting and shoving and screaming meanness at those young ones—way too young, if you ask me, to be having to do that hard thing. And the governor and the president and everybody else's in it, too, and who knows where it'll end. It was on that same six o'clock news that we first heard it, from silver-headed, sweet-faced Charlie Hill who tells about the weather on the Charleston station. Tropical depression was all, he said. Nothing out the ordinary for fall, he said. Next I heard, though, they'd made up a name for it, same as hoes do—Diana—and by then Charlie Hill was calling it a hurricane.

Course, we went on about our usual business. After all, we know about hurricanes around here—they come close enough every few years or so to give us some substantial wind and trees go down and sometimes Water Street floods. I remember Gan telling about a storm when she was young and first married to Cap that carried off whole houses over at Arcadia beach—one full of white folks at a big party, she told me, and them all still eating supper and dancing, not knowing one thing, while the old ocean swept them off to what Gan called their watery grave.

A grave. That's where I'm lying, maybe. Still and dark and quiet enough. And this heaviness on my heart might be all my sins, weighing me down, the dirt piled atop them and me.

I know better, though, don't I? But this brain won't let me get ahead of myself.

The last few days, every time I passed by the TV while doing chores, or later when Farina and I'd get a bite in front of my little TV in the trailer, we'd watch. One minute there'd be *Queen for a Day*—the hoes love that one—or *What's My Line?* or some other fool show they all the time watch, the next'd come the faces of those colored babies, set like stone while around them raged grown folks' white hate-faces, and in a minute'd be

Charlie Hill again, talking about Diana, which he'd got around to calling a killer storm and said was beating up on islands where poor folks had no place to hide. Plenty of people were dying, Charlie Hill said. And the storm was maybe headed here, they didn't know for sure. Unpredictable, he called her. Isn't that just like a woman, he said, but his smile had more tight than funniness in it. Stay tuned for more news and possible evacuation notices, he told us, and about then's when some of our girls got jittery.

Fawn's the one started it, far as I recollect. She said she could stand an earthquake or two, being from California, but this hurricane business was something else again. Talked about tidal waves and such. "I'm splitting," I heard her tell Marlene, the new hoe that came here from a place in Tennessee called Pigeon Forge. "I don't know where I'm headed, but out of here." Fawn hadn't been too popular with Mizz Addie since the parade, anyhow. She tucked a hank of hair into its usual place, I saw Marlene nod, and in a sec here came two more girls, and one of them, Rochelle, says they can go to her family's farm in Olar, about three hours off and inland, where nobody lives but her crazy brother. That's when it started, catching as a flu bug, and pretty soon every trailer in outback buzzed with it, and hoes were stashing clothes and jewelry and stuffed animals into bags and calling the bus station.

After a while Mizz Addie got wind of it and called us all into the parlor for one of her lectures. "This is not a time for panic," she declared, pacing back and forth in front of the passel of us, me and Portia and Farina and Frank and Sarah standing together over by the door, the rest of them sitting or standing—all of us together about filling the room full. "In the unlikely event that this storm does hit here, we have a way to stay safe." She stopped her backing and forthing, pointed one arm toward outback. "The Kidde Kokoon," she said, and hushed, like she'd settled the matter once for all. They stared at her blank as boxes, and after a sec she blinked and huffed, and said, "Our backyard bomb shelter, ladies. Eight feet down and all the comforts of home. If it'll protect us from an atom bomb, I imagine it can handle a Lowcountry hurricane, don't you?"

I sure knew all about that shelter—Mizz Addie had me checking behind that young contractor from Charleston who sold her on the notion and then did the work, about four years back. Three thousand dollars she paid for it—more money than lots of folks make in a year's working—plus a little trade on the side, to make sure he did a good job, Mizz Addie said. After they finished up, we stocked the shelter just like the book said to: canned food, water, a radio, batteries, flashlight, first aid kit, cots, blankets, tools—I can't recall what all else—plus a little box that's supposed to let you know when you can come out for a breath of real air—all in a low-ceilinged space about as big as the living room in my trailer.

Most of those girls still looked blank, though, so before we could blink, we'd all been marched to outback, Frank'd opened the door leading down into the ground, and Mizz Addie said, "Anybody who wants to, go on down and take a tour."

The afternoon was still and steamy, and standing there staring into that hole in the ground I had trouble conjuring a wind so bad it could cause anybody in their right mind down to it.

"Really," she said, "feel free to have a look around." On the second go-round of her invite, a wave went through those fifteen girls—two got coughing so bad they had to walk off, a bunch started mumbling about needing to fix their hair and put faces on, others got so hot all of a sudden they had to hurry inside to cool off. In no time flat, wasn't but me and Farina and Mizz Addie standing there.

"Well," Mizz Addie said. The three of us peered down a few minutes more, then she turned without another word and went back in. Soon as the kitchen door slammed behind her, I stole a look at my cuz and she at me, and both of us busted out laughing. Then Farina rubbed her poked-out belly and made a face, said she was feeling kind of poorly, let's us go take a rest and see if Charlie Hill had something new to say.

Thinking about Farina's face and that belly-rubbing and how

we did laugh, tears flow up in these eyes of mine, opened wide to darkness. I feel them spill over and roll down the sides of my face, into my hair, into my ears, soaking down through this cot I'm lying on, from there to the hard concrete floor, and through that to the black rich dirt. But I don't move, and can't stop re-membering, can I?

Later on the same evening Charlie Hill did have something new for us—he said Diana was headed north, looked like, and maybe would just blow on out to sea. That night we had the fullest house we'd seen in some time, kept us hopping, and glad to be.

By first light next morning, though, looked like that fickle storm was still full of her tricks, teasing us and poor Charlie Hill, deciding in the dead of night to make a turn against nature and head straight for Jameston after all. Coming fast and hard, too, once her mind was made up.

The hoes got wind of it early, before most them were used to waking up, on account of Fawn made it her business to go around telling each one. Mizz Addie went close behind, trying to talk them into riding out the storm right here, in the Kokoon, but after getting no place fast with the first handful of them, she gave up. By noon they'd about cleared out, leaving behind one pretty big mess, looked like a storm'd already blown through—drawers and closet doors agape like open mouths. On one of my trips through the main house trying to keep order, I found some girl's red high-heeled shoe smack in the middle of the dining room table. A shiver ran straight through me, and I swept that shoe off the table fast as I could, hoping I was the only one saw it, but knowing deep down it didn't matter one whit who saw—a shoe on the table means death in the house, seen or not. Soon as I knew it, I forgot it, or tried to.

Directly, the only hoe left was Mary Lou, who Doc Larkin took off with him soon after. Frank spent the morning boarding up a few windows and tying down loose ends, then headed off to take care of his own business. Sarah stayed home, seeing to her mama and those. By the time the still gray of day started picking up wind, it was down to us three, me and Farina together in my trailer, Mizz Addie in the main house alone.

When I saw Doc carry Mary Lou off in his car, I turned to Farina and remarked it, wondering how come he's so good to that girl, her being a hoe and all. She looked at me a sec, then laughed and told me, "Girl, you're smarter than you know about some things, and dumber than you think about others."

I don't take all that kindly to being called dumb, so I said nothing, just looked out the window. She came over next to me, said, "Min, that boy and that girl's in love with each other—you didn't know that?" No, I didn't, but I wasn't about to let on, just kept looking out the window. Treetops'd started bending, and the bushes by the house had set to dancing.

"It's love you don't get, isn't it, Min? You probably don't know a thing about Sarah and Frank either, right?" I couldn't keep still at that, turned my head to look up at where my cuz stood beside me. She rubbed her belly, gave a sigh, said, "I don't know if they ever *did* anything about it or not, girl, but those two's as strong in love as any I ever saw."

First my mind said *no,* and I was fixing to open my mouth to echo it, till flashed in my head twenty-eight years of walking into a room full of interrupted silence, and those two bending in the same direction, not touching, sharing some understanding I never understood. Struck me how in all those years I never much heard them sharing home tales, Frank of his wife, Sarah of her mama and all those sisters and brothers she raised up. And I all of a sudden felt sad, for some reason, and lonelier than ever, even with my cuz standing there next to me.

She wasn't through yet, either. A gust of wind swooped and howled, the outside air darked up, and Farina said to me, "You probably don't even know about that Blue Ballard being sweet on you, do you, Min?"

That made me turn my head quick over to my cuz, heart thumping wild inside my chest, maybe on account of the low howl of wind, maybe something else. Opened my mouth to tell her she's gone too far now, but no words came out. She looked straight into my eyes, smiled crooked, told me: "It's there for you, if you want it, Min. If you got the heart in you to go for it." Farina leaned back and closed her eyes; her face twisted with pain that made her gasp soft, like she's surprised. When it passed, she opened her eyes back up, said: "I hope you do, sugar. That love's so sweet, when it's right."

Just then came a crash of something somewhere out there Frank must've left untied, a screen door banged hard once or twice, and there wasn't any more time to dwell on such.

Me and Farina must've headed for the main house at the same time Mizz Addie came looking for us. We met in the mid-point of outback just when the sky decided to open up, the gray air blackening in a heartbeat, rain not just falling, but more like *propelling* itself towards the dirt and us. And just that quick, things looked dead serious.

"Min, we need to collect a few things and get down to the shelter." Mizz Addie had to shout over a gust of wind, and the rain already had her soaked, wet streaming down her face like a river. "I need your help."

I turned to my cuz, who wasn't so much noticing the rain and wind, seemed to be looking more inside than out. She put one hand on my arm, brought her mouth near my ear so I could hear, said, "I'll see about our things. You go do what you need to." Might be she said something else, too, but the wind took her words beyond me.

When Mizz Addie opened the screen door to the kitchen, it flattened itself against the side of the house. I tried to pull it shut behind me, but strong as I am, it wasn't budging. "Minyon," from inside the house she called, so I quit fighting the screen door, pushed my whole self hard against the other to close it, and followed that sound, same as I've done near long as memory.

In her room I found her, kneeling before the safe, gathering papers and files, stacking them to one side. Without a word I headed to the kitchen, got the vinyl cloth off the small table, and came back. Together we wrapped those papers. Last of all she put in the Blue Book, and we made a bundle.

From upstairs came the sound of glass breaking, then the wind whushed its wild self down the stairs, through the hall, and into Mizz Addie's bedroom, swirling around our ankles, howling low: *hurry hurry hurry.*

Funny, ain't it?—how your memory plays tricks, speeding things up so fast you can't hardly recollect them later, or else slowing them down to where you got to view each and every speck of what went on, want to or no. From the time that wind went to knocking our knees till me and Mizz Addie were out the back door is no more than a blur when I try to catch it. We looked each other in the eye half a sec, then our legs or the wind or both carried us hurly-burly along, heading for that safe space in outback ground. Next thing I knew, Mizz Addie's hand was reaching for the door and it banged open so hard she had to jump back and the water and wind followed behind, making themselves right at home. The lights went out before we could push through to stand on the back stoop, and in the gray darkness they left I saw it: smack in the middle of outback, where we three'd stood scant minutes back, was a heap of something on the ground, not moving.

Now as I blink up into this black stillness and think back on what seems like some other somebody's life and time altogether but must be my own and yesterday, this heart of mine speeds up while my mind shifts into slow as slow.

Like walking under water, I turned to Mizz Addie and handed her my Hazelhedge bundle, which she took without a word, then I headed straight for that lump of something, pushing myself against wind and rain, so slow seemed like walking backwards, and then there she was, my sweet cuz, legs drawn up to curl herself in a ball away from the storm. I reached down and picked her up like she weighed nothing. Her eyelids fluttered but stayed shut.

When I stood and started walking, I saw Mizz Addie'd got the shelter door open. While I watched she disappeared into the hole, and time really slowed up then, along with my heart—near stopped, while I walked with my cuz in my arms, the wind hard at my back, wondering would that shelter door maybe close up now and leave me and mine up here at the mercy of this wind. All around us, loblollies bowed to the storm, and still I watched that hole in the ground and walked on like in a dream where my steps never take me where I'm heading.

Then up through the hole comes Mizz Addie's soaking wet head, and she motions me to hurry, which I all a sudden can, and in the next sec I'm there and she helps me get Farina down, lighting the way with a flashlight, pointing me to the cot in the corner of the room. About halfway down the stairs the storm noise lets up some, and my cuz, whose head rests on my shoulder, whispers, "I fell, Min, I'm sorry, but I did, I just fell."

I lay her on the cot, and Mizz Addie starts up the lantern, which casts a flickering, ghosty light. When it falls on Farina's face, I see she's breathing ragged and hard. A terrible pain seems upon her and she curls herself back into a ball, keeping her eyes shut tight and clenching her teeth, saying, "I think it's coming, I think it's coming now."

It's not the hurricane she sees inside her eyelids, I know that, though it most surely is coming, too.

I look up to find Mizz Addie staring straight at me, and I reckon my eyes're wide and wild as hers. My mind calls up Doc Larkin's name, then lets go it just as fast. How can we get him or anybody else here now, in the middle of all this? We're not about to, that's a pure fact. And in the flickery shadows, this shelter all of a sudden's like a cave to me, from time before memory, and we three's all the folks left in this world.

While that runs through my head, Mizz Addie grabs the flashlight, jumps up, and starts for the stairs, not changing words with me. She opens the door, and the storm blusters its loud self down to me and Farina's corner, then hushes back up when the door shuts behind Mizz Addie. I don't know where that woman's heading, and got no time to ponder it, do I?—on account of my cuz's doubling herself up again, biting hard on her bottom lip, and when she quits that and relaxes, I see blood there.

Farina whispers something now, and I lean near. "Not going to give this one up, girl," she says, and I see one mouth corner curve, old sweet smile trying to flex itself. "It's early, but it's really coming this time. I feel it fighting to." She opens her eyes full for the first time since I found her outside. I smooth her wild hair back and make whushy sounds, how Gan used to when one or the other of us came crying to her in the night. Farina says not a word, just sighs one time and keeps her eyes fixed on mine. She's comforted, though. Both of us are.

In a little bit comes the pain again, I see it gather; first her eyes get tight at the outside corners, her mouth tenses up, her body starts into that familiar curl. Then her forehead, ears, lips, nose, neck—all, every muscle, nerve, bone of my sweet cousin's body—gets pulled and stretched till she's got to holler out to make it stop. It does, finally, and she pants and gasps at the end of it, like a runner that's reached the finish line. "It's coming, girl," she tells me, and in her weary voice is pure joy. "Not losing this one."

When I help her out of her wet clothes, I see blood on her underthings. It gives me a terrible feeling, scares me bad as a huge wave coming down over my head for a sec. I breathe deep and turn my back to collect myself. After a minute, I cover Farina with a blanket from the linens stacked alongside one shelf. While she rests I fetch a jug of water and pour it up into a pot and get the burner going, on account of the one thing I know about having babies is everybody's got to stay clean.

In between one of the spells that's upon her, after her panting's quieted and she's got her breath, Farina says, "Just in case, Min." I go quick and sit myself beside her, trying to hush her before she can say more, scared of words foretelling their own truth. She won't stop, though.

"Just in case," she says again, closing her eyes and then opening them full back up, looking steady into mine. I look back and my head nods—has to—at which she closes back up and sighs deep.

I wet a small cloth, sit back down on the cot, and lay that

coolness on her dark, shining forehead. She opens her eyes one more time—and if I'd known it would only be that one more time to look into them, could I have looked harder, seen more?—and leaves me these few sweet words: "I love you, Min, and I thank you, too."

And though I'm here in this still blackness mourning, I'm there again, too, hearing right after those words the door opening back up, the storm banging down once more, screaming its promise, *I'm coming, I'm coming,* then quietened again, but still yammering.

Here comes Mizz Addie, her arms full of our best soft white linens covered with a sheet of plastic, plus the book she always looks in when one of the hoes is ailing and she doesn't feel the need to call the doc. The storm's pulled her hair loose—it's flying every whichway, same as it used to—and she's soaking wet, but's got a calm look to her. Spying the pot of water I set to boiling, she says, "Good, Minyon," then takes a knife and goes to cutting and ripping some linens in strips. When Farina slips into one of her sessions, I comfort her while Mizz Addie watches without saying a word. Soon as it's over, she sets herself by the lantern, opens the book she brought, and starts reading hard as if she's in a room by herself instead of an eight-by-ten hole in the ground with one woman birthing a baby, another one trying to help, and a storm named Diana fixing to let loose the wind and sky and maybe even that old Atlantic Ocean on top of us all.

Farina cries out, and I turn back around to find her head thrown back, her knees drawn up, every piece of her straining, the scream piercing out through tight-together teeth, lips drawn back to show just about every shining white one of them. I see a dark gap I never glimpsed before, where a back tooth used to be, and something sweeps through me, a sad bad wave of it, but before I can figure what or why, Mizz Addie's next to me, pulling the blanket back from Farina's legs and having a look.

"Bring the lantern," she says, and I do, and shine it over those two bare, wide-apart legs, feet planted hard, one on either side of the cot. Right between my cousin's thighs some huge dark something's partway out, and I almost holler myself, looking, but even while we watch, her legs go slack again and that thing pulls itself back into hiding some. Not long, though, on account of right on the heels of that push comes another, and that dark roundness I know now is the head of this baby comes urging forth again. I glance over at Farina just once right in the middle of this push, but I can't see her face, just the underpart of her neck, and it's all long dark strings standing out against thin skin, fixing to pop themselves loose, seems like. At the next push Mizz Addie reaches her hands between Farina's legs, trying to turn that baby and get it loose, and I can't tear my eyes away from the round darkness coming out and Mizz Addie's pale hands down there in the middle of it, me steadying the lantern and holding my breath and willing it right so hard that I don't know how long passes before I hear how quiet my cuz's got. The head's free now; Mizz Addie's turned it some and's slipping her bloody hands in to pull it the rest of the way out, but Farina's not making her cries now, her legs're slack now, Mizz Addie having to use her own body to hold them open and get that baby out. And my hands beg to tremble, but I got to hold this lantern still; and here comes the rest of that babe's little eel-slick body, quick now, so much littler than that large circle of head. Mizz Addie turns the baby upside down and it spews out a tiny cry, sounds like a baby kitten, then she lays it right up on Farina's belly. From its middle still trails the cord holding that baby to its mama, my own sweet cuz.

"Pull that table over here and set the lantern on it." Mizz Addie doesn't look up at me and her voice sounds so businessy I don't even think, just do what she says. She's got a few things laid out on a clean cloth, and soon as I set the lantern down, she reaches for a knife and goes back to between Farina's legs.

I take the flashlight from the table, flip the switch and guide its round white circle up the side of my cousin's body till it reaches her face. I go slow, on account of already knowing no amount of hurry's going to matter.

"Cuz?" Farina's lips're together now, so dark they look

black, and her face ain't straining anymore. Eyes're shut. I hold the flashlight steady on that sweet face with one hand while the other reaches out to feel of her wild wooly hair. My fingers move on their own across that face, tracing cheekbones and jaw and straight-down nose; eyelids, forehead, lips—right where her smile-curve used to lie. Then comes to my ears a terrible high-pitched sound like a fierce wind, keening, coming out of my self, purely without say-so from me.

"Take this." I hear Mizz Addie's voice but don't look around, on account of I can't take any of whatever she wants me to nor nothing else. Nothing. My one hand keeps life, smooth-stroking the lines and angles of Farina's face, but the rest of me's gone dead heavy.

"Minyon." Her hand reaches out and lifts mine from its chosen path across my cousin's colding face. "Take the baby."

But I don't hear those words so clear—too busy gazing at the blood on Mizz Addie's hand—Farina's this time, not Jesse's—and seeing we have come full circle, now that I've given over my last scrap of blood kin to Hazelhedge dirt.

My limbs come to life; I whirl and back off from Mizz Addie. Still she glides nearer, offering in her outheld hands a baby, darkness wrapped in soft white linens. It doesn't make a sound now, maybe it's dead, too, which doesn't matter, that baby's nothing to me. I got nothing, and here stands before me the reason why.

"Take her," she says. My back's right up against the wall now, standing here eight feet under, and inside me rises a strong, bitter surge, a tidal wave swelling so large and quick and dark it pushes everything else aside, leaves room for nothing beyond its own terrible self. It fills me up, lifts my hand from my side, into the air, sweeping through it so I feel the breath of it against my palm right before it connects with Mizz Addie's face. Her neck jerks sideways and she closes her eyes. My hand stays suspended in the air, inches from her face, out of my power. I can't swallow nor breathe, and all of a sudden hear the roar of wind outside, joining up with this terrible noise in my ears till they're one and the same.

Mizz Addie opens her eyes; they glitter in the lantern light. And still she holds that sheet-wrapped bundle out to me, not saying a word, just staring glitter-eyed, her face gleaming ghost-pale. My arm swings itself back again, and again I feel the rush of air and again the smack of dark flesh on white. This time when she opens her eyes, she opens her mouth, too, says, "That's enough, Minyon."

And it is and it isn't, but anyhow after she says that I let my breath out in a long, sad sigh that seems to go on and on, till I got no wind left in me at all.

This time when Mizz Addie offers up the baby, my arms reach out on their own and take it. "It's a girl," she says, then turns her back on us, lifts a sheet from the linen pile and draws it over Farina's body so we can't rest eyes on that sight further.

And still my eyes stay busy tracing the lump of sheet I know's my cousin—feet, knees, belly, bosom, face—till I feel a moving against my heart and look down to see a babe so tiny I can hardly feel her in my arms. While I gaze, she sets up a mewing and goes flailing, then reaches one little fist to her mouth, cheeks working. "Lord have mercy," I say, my knees weakening so I have to set myself down. "She's hungry," I say, and in me rises something else now. "I believe this child is hungry."

Mizz Addie's already heated more water, which she mixes with some canned milk and sets on the table by me in a bowl. I dip one finger in the whiteness and bring it up to this small wrinkled face, offer it to tiny working lips. They open and draw my finger in, sucking life. The warmth of that mouth brings tears to me, and I sit and dip my finger and offer it, over and again, till everything else fades off, time slows to a crawl, and there's not but me and this small dark life, hungering.

After some time I got to rocking in that straight-backed chair, and humming, too—just quiet, under my breath, some long ago Gan-song. And those things along with that suckling babe got my eyes to watering again, salt trailing quiet down my face. I looked over at Mizz Addie, who'd set up two more cots at the far side of the room. She lay on her side, just watching, and in the lantern light her face was sad and wet as mine. We two stayed there mourning this and that, the muffled storm howl our only background music, till that babe tired of sucking and Mizz Addie told me come lie down, try to rest some. I didn't think I could, but I must have.

Now my hand comes to rest upon this baby on my chest, my deep breathing next to her shallow; my slow, steady heartbeat beside her quick one. She's light but heavy, happy burden. And in my head comes her name, in Ophelia's voice, who once wished me grace, which she called "letting yourself receive." *Grace Ward Manigault,* my lips shape themselves around the words in this dark still air, *I receive you.*

I sleep again, must be, and sometime later wake to a lit lantern and the sound of Mizz Addie astir. I rise and together we change this baby's linens and I once again finger-feed. On one side of the room lies still cold Farina, while here on my lap is warm sweet Grace. Between is me and Mizz Addie, tending to business like we always do.

After a bit she says we might as well go see what's left, and it's not till just that minute that I realize the wind-roar's gone from outside. Mizz Addie goes up before me, lifting the shelter door and stepping out, disappearing. Halfway up the stairs I raise my head to see a square of gray without a cloud in it. Up we go, Grace and me, till we stand on solid ground next to Mizz Addie. All around us is what Diana left, or didn't; and in the half-light of just before day it's hard for my mind to make sense of it.

The main house is still standing, mostly, though part of the roof's stove in on one side, a raw ragged edge of pine tree poking through. The top of the shed's peeled back, there's not an out-back trailer in sight, and trash and tree limbs're heaped in piles everywhere we cast our eyes. Turning around slow, I see my loblolly forest, my secret woods; and my heart about stops, on account of half those tall thin trees that stretched most to heaven are changed to wet brown sticks, tilted every whichway.

I turn back around. Mizz Addie starts laughing low in her

throat, gazing at this mess, and says: "Well, Minyon, looks like your house needs putting in order."

In front of me is this laid-open house; down in the shelter lies what's left in this world of my sweet cuz, needing to be buried proper and said last words over. In my arms is sweet Grace, my charge, looking to be fed and cared for; standing next to me with the mark of my hand on her face is Ariadne Fleming, a woman I have known longer and less than anybody else in this world, who I owe everything and nothing. And before me is work to do. So I'd best be about it.

Grace stirs; my useless bosoms ache like they might spring to life. One bird calls a song. And here rises the sun.

EPILOGUE

1969

Endings and Beginnings

HAZELHEDGE, 40 YEARS OF TRUE SERVICE TO
MANKIND.

JAMESTON—This state—perhaps even this na-
tion—lost one of its finest yesterday around
noon as South Carolina Law Enforcement Divi-
sion officers closed the doors one last time on
the house that made Jameston famous the world
over.

Hazelhedge was born in 1929 and thrived for
forty years, remaining active in the community
until the end. Mourners are many, though none
were present during the final moments.

Services will be private. There will be no calling hours.

[From the *Charleston Observer,* April 2, 1969]

Still as a cemetery, dark as a grave, is my loblolly wood this
clear cool December day. But even moonless midnight wouldn't

worry me—I've followed this path for forty years, so my tired feet find their old, familiar way, and happy to.

Touching this ground for the last go-round, likely, and that's fine, too. Time to move on, I reckon.

That's what Addie said. She said it back in March, just before she called Sheriff Forshay and told him the exact date—April 1, no sooner, no later—to let the state boys come in and close us down. She said it again two months later, close on to drawing her final breath, lying in her bed amongst clean fresh linens with nobody but this old Minyon Manigault beside her. Now I say it, agreeing: time to move on.

Time for last respects, too, which I aim to pay today, all around. Out here in the dark of my loblobby woods, I walk in a circle, stepping off my goodbyes. No Sorrow's markers lie in this ground; they're all in me.

First to first, I say them. To Jesse, my sad old, bad old brother, just a child, I see now, whose meanness took over his good, gobbled him up with hate—I say rest now, sleep now, take peace now. Leave off from my dreams. And on top of the ground where my memory lays claim to his bones, I take a handful from this funeral home box I carry and scatter part of Addie, dust and ash and bone bits, to mix with my blood kin below this ground. Bound in life by death, bound by me now with this wish: rest, both of y'all. Take peace.

To all these others lying here, bits and parts, I say my byes, too, spreading Addie-dust as I go. Over Pearl, scared little mixed-up hoe hung halfway between white and black, who stood in for Addie and helped save us all: know yourself now, girl, and rest. Out here's the soldier hat of my baby brother Clarence, who gave his life to his country, whose life I gave up, thinking I was doing him right; still can see clear the smooth hollow of his cheek when he sucked on that thumb how he did, and the silky curl of his black lashes when he slept: lie still, sweet bub; be proud of yourself. Right next to Clarence lies one more stand-in, that white stuffed teddy bear one sad girl mistook for her own lost babe. Buried out here alongside might as well be Hallie

Oakes, who got lost inside that hoe named Belle and never was seen nor heard from again, like too many others to name or even think about. I buried Ophelia's rabbitfoot out here one fine day not too long back, on account of even way after she passed, that woman kept teaching me, and I sometime learned enough about luck to let it go.

All under this ground's more to let go, clues to where we all been these last forty years: a fancy hoe dress that might still smell of Winston-mint and pink foolishness; one thin silver pick and a handful of Addie hair; a blooded sheet and a birthing book. Bits and pieces, remembrances of us who lived here and the girls that came and went, some mourned, some not.

When the newspaper folks heard the famous Ariadne Fleming died and left some old black woman the house and twenty-some acres plus just about all the rest of her worldly goods, they swarmed around here like a pack of wild dogs, trying to get me to tell them stories. I didn't, though. If there's one thing I learned from Addie, it's close-mouthedness.

They let me be for a while after, till they got wind of the deal made me by Mr. Robert E. Lee French, that developer from up-state who's going to build a Winn-Dixie and some other stores out here along the highway and portion off the back acreage for apartments. He made me a fair deal, one that'll keep me comfortable for the rest of the time I got in this world, and Grace, too; her children even, when they come along. And he agreed to the only two conditions I laid down. First, that they had to name either the shopping center or else the apartments Hazelhedge, so something around here can keep the name and memory besides me. I remember he laughed and gave me a look to see was I serious, then straightened up his face pretty quick and said, "Yes ma'am, Mizz Manigault. No problem." Turns out they're going to name them both that—Hazelhedge Plaza and Hazelhedge Villas—which suits me fine.

The second one he did hand me some argument over—it's going to cost him money—but he gave in, finally, on account of this land's what the real estate boys call prime. So the deal we'll sign later on today's got a special part that marks off three acres slap in the middle of this property, right about where I'm standing now, that will stay loblolly woods through all time. Runs with the land, is how the lawyers say it. That's the part the papers picked up, and one Charleston paper, the same one that ran the smart-alecky obituary, called and wanted to come talk with me about it. They claim I'm a conservationist—even wrote me up in a national magazine. Funny, ain't it? But conservationist is just another name for keeper, how I see it, so maybe they're right in ways they don't mean to be.

I don't plan to open my mouth to a one of them, though—the stuff I got to tell isn't likely to be what they want to hear. And it's not that I'm mad or even sad about how they act, just that I see things clearer now than I used to.

Hazelhedge has always been out here on the edge of town, the edge of folks' lives, here but not here, only called on when things were needed—something for folks to either snicker about or else whisper tales of. Not many ever stopped to think it was just *us*—folks not much different than them, out here putting one foot in front of the other, making the best of what we've been given.

The papers came up with all kinds of stories about Miss Ariadne Fleming, too. One said she left a husband and six children in French Lick, Indiana, the day her clothesline broke with three loads of wash on it—just walked away and never looked back. Another claimed she murdered a man back in Chicago and the mob'd been looking for her ever since. One of the trashy supermarket ones swore they found evidence that the famous South Carolina madam was really a man in disguise. Not one of them was smart enough to find out about that boy of hers that she lost to the war, or heartsickness, or just plain hard work and natural toughness. But Addie'd of liked the mystery, on account of she was all the time making up where she'd been and who she was, till I had to wonder sometimes if she herself knew anymore.

I leave these loblollies now, and haints, pieces and parts of lives. In times to come, folks that walk in this wood'll likely feel a breath on their neck or a whisper at their ear, and wonder, and walk harder.

At the edge of the woods, loblollies behind me, I stop and fill my eyes. Not that there's so much left to see—just the three same buildings that were here back so long ago—the main house, the shed, and outback. All the trailers've been sold and carted off except mine, which they're moving tomorrow to the piece of land I bought alongside the highway near Little Town. Maybe I'll build a house there later, maybe a fine brick one, but for now, my trailer'll do me.

It's there I head now, glad to rest in my one safe haven a sec or two before finishing the task that lies before me, my last day of keeping this house called Hazelhedge. Off by itself my trailer stands, which suits me well, close to loblolly woods and at a fine remove from the rest of this place.

Work still to do, and not much time to do it; but I got to rest these old feet a minute, ready myself. And when I stretch out here in my easy chair and close my eyes, I can almost believe that when I open them, Farina'll be lounging her skinny self over on my sofa, old green afghan pulled up round her neck like in those first weeks after she dropped back into my life, when she one minute couldn't keep warm enough and was the next pure sweat-soaked. And maybe we'd sit and talk about our old days together like we did when she got better—how Gan raised us and lots more of our kin besides, remembering the Little Town Saturday evening gatherings and our lazy summer days, when we did our chores and escaped off on secret woods walks. I squint my eyes up and almost do see the outline of her wild-haired self, whose face at the end put me so in mind of our Gan.

If my sweet cuz hadn't of come back to give me Grace and something more before leaving this world and me again, maybe I wouldn't feel much like keeping on right now myself. But she did, and I do.

The gift of Grace was the one thing kept both me and Mizz Addie going, I think, in those bad old days after that mad wild wind came through and left us holding the biggest mess this side of creation. We might've given up then—both so tired, don't you know, and me with a soul-deep sadness I longed to lean into. But babies got their own way of doing; and what Grace needed I flat couldn't say no to.

It was for that new babe I bought the rocker across this room, closest resemblance to the one fixed in my memory as money could buy. And it was there I held her and my lips remembered those old croony songs from Africa my Gan used to sing, songs I didn't know I knew anymore, must of been keeping just inside my mouth all those years between, waiting for a reason to spring forth.

My girl had fine things, on account of even then, I had more money than a person could rightly spend on herself. But the thing she loved best was one of the few I managed to salvage after that hurricane blew us most to kingdom come. Didn't find it till a couple weeks after, snagged and hid in the low branches of a bush by the main house: my old blanket, the one thing still left in this world of what I brought here with me forty years ago, which I washed and mended and passed along to Grace. In those days, time would every now and again get all mixed up in my head, while I fed and held and rocked that baby, grieving for what's lost and celebrating what's not; and it sometimes seemed like I was my own Gan in the very flesh, rocking and crooning, and that baby holding fast to a soft pale blanket was me.

Time's funny still: it's hard right now to think on that baby and then my Grace today, her thin twelve-year-old self perched on legs she hadn't yet grown into, smart as a whip and knocking them dead down at St. Cecilia's School in Charleston. And it's not just that gift my cuz gave me, though Lord knows, it might be enough. It's something else Farina left along with—not that she ever out and said it, just that her being here brought things back to me fresh, what our Gan raised us to know. It's believing about family, helping each other, and loving—stuff that makes the whole thing worth doing. After Farina passed, I saw that clear. My soul grew stronger on account of it, and took in not only my sweet niece but Addie, too, and Sarah and Frank, and a good number of our hoes—all family, in a way. All of us needing one and another. That was Farina's gift to me—that and Blue Ballard, who I might would've hardened my heart to, if she hadn't kept on at me about how bad it was to bury that part of yourself, about how too late can come sooner than folks think, about how sweet such man and woman love can be.

And sweet it surely is, which knowing is no less than a miracle, far as me. Blue took his time, for certain—man's got the patience of Job, Sarah one time remarked; needed it, too. But when we two finally lay ourselves down together, in my back room right through this narrow hall, it was as right a thing as ever was. Soft and slow; fingers lingering, eyes feasting, lips and tongues and mouths learning new ways; the pure sweet joy of skin against skin. Born again, was how I saw it; still do, and rejoice it every day.

Sitting here now thinking on that, I find myself so hungry that my feet propel me up right out of this chair and away from those memories. No time for daydreaming, on account of I've surely got work ahead. What's sweet is knowing I got other stuff yet to come, too.

Before I leave here, I slip one large box of kitchen matches into my pocket, to help me keep things proper round here one last time. I take my box of Addie-dust, lighter now, soon to be lighter yet.

Walking across the back yard towards the shed, I stop still over the spot where that old underground shelter used to be, where Farina lost life and Grace came into it. Neither me nor Mizz Addie ever set foot back down there after they hauled Farina's body out and took it to the A.M.E. cemetery for a proper putting down. Mizz Addie had the hole filled in later, and I couldn't help thinking, as I watched that backhoe turn fresh dirt, that that very ground held the blood of my brother Jesse, too, and now Jesse and Farina's blood was mixed in together, along with my tears and the sweat of Mizz Addie and some of her old

Victory Garden dirt and a bit of red-gold hair. And who knows whatall else. For good measure, I add one handful of Addie ash, swirls soft round my legs to dirt.

Standing in the mid of this yard and looking round, seems like forty years have come and gone and we're back where we started. Ready for the wrecking crew that'll be out here at first light tomorrow, according to Mr. French. And even though lots of folks came after me hoping to get bits and pieces of this place to hold onto—one Charleston hotel offered me five hundred dollars for our crystal chandelier, and I thought about it, I did— the fact is, I don't need the money now, and something didn't set right, so I told them, no, thank you. Other folks came calling about buying this and that piece of furniture, especially our long couch and that jukebox whose music we all danced to so long back, for what they call a conversation piece. But I made up my mind that nothing from the main house would be sold off, on account of there's no place else it belongs. Folks'll just have to find themselves something else to converse about, far as I'm concerned.

When this place goes, then, everything left in it goes with— living room sofas, chairs, rugs, pictures, lamps, tables, all. Same with all that's in our fancy dining parlor; upstairs, too, and out- back, where not that much is left—just beds and dressers and glass-topped tables, the hoes' clean-bill-of-health cards still taped underneath for anybody to see we ran one high-class house. Lots of dressers're still missing their drawers on account of some girls didn't have sufficient suitcases and got so hurried at the end that they hauled the dresser drawers along with, filled to the brim with all their personals, black and red and pink spewing every whichway, leaving a lacy trail.

Of course, the newspaper heard about how the house and its belongings are going to be destroyed what they called intact, and wrote that up in one of their articles. Lawyer Mercer says there's likely to be a crowd out here tomorrow, to witness it. Which I fretted myself up good about till I conjured a different ending.

My feet move me forward; walking over dead-and-goneness, I head for the outback shed. Cold and dark in here, but even so, it holds sweet summer smells, lawn mowing and garden tending. I breathe that in once, then fetch the can I left in here yesterday, fixing to get down to it. Got to move along, on account of I told Blue Ballard and Chief DeBlois a close-to time for this event, and have to meet it.

First to first, I make my way one last time. Starting where I stand, in this shed that still holds hard to the memory of one Frank Washington, the first to show me a kind face here, and never stopped, after. He had riches inside him, that man. When he dropped dead five years ago, it was right in here, him lifting this heavy wagon like believing he was still thirty years old instead of seventy-some, believing himself so strong as'd live forever. Which he will, long as I have memory, anyhow, and Sarah, and after us Grace, who loved him too, and after her maybe her own. Family passing family stories, living on that way. It's my job now, to see to that.

I heft this heavy can and head for the pile of cleaning rags in the corner, which I soak straight through. My eyes rest light upon the place where Pearl finished herself; I feel sad and sorry once more, then let her loose. Taking a few rags along, I head into the carport—all that long parade of cars we had us gone now but the one Cadillac I'm keeping, parked this morning way behind my trailer next to loblolly woods. I soak these, too, and leave them lay.

Outback's next, where I spent more than half my life at Hazelhedge, peeking out the window, listening to hoe talk, dreaming, rocking. Where I saw Bess and Chantal walk out of all those years back, and men froze, and time stopped, and I saw stars and knew where I was. Into each outback room I go with this can, and the smell of gas's got my head light, till I'm almost dizzy with it. I soak each mattress good and say bye, remembering pieces and parts of girls—faces, arms, legs, feet, hair—and names I can't always connect them to—Lila, Maura, Babe; Andi and Scylla and El; plain Jane, pouty Katrina, plump Nanette. Handfuls of Addie-dust grace each bed, pale icing soaking into what I pour.

Crossing the yard to the main house I remember many times of such crossings, but especially when Mr. Waldo came to tell about Gan passing and I couldn't keep my eyes from spilling sorrow. And that other, the one's dogged me forty years, when life spilled from my brother Jesse. Still spilling, I sift Addie bones and bits behind me.

Up the back steps I go, and into the kitchen. The door slams shut behind me, sounding pretty lonesome, and this house's still and quiet as that first morning my fourteen-year-old self came tiptoeing in here, scrounging around for food, scared of haints, not yet knowing how much else there was in this world to be afraid about.

This kitchen belongs to Sarah, always will, in my mind. She's retired now, living with her niece, well seen to by Addie's will. Still, I can picture her here right now if I squint my eyes up some—her back to me, working away at the sink, offering up one sharp comment or other, telling me the truth, whether I want to hear it or not. Keeping to herself the one truth she chose to, which was plain enough anyhow for a person with eyes to see; how she loved Frank and he her, though he stayed married and she stayed tending to her mama. And who knows if they ever did more than love and take care of each other; who cares, either. Except in my heart I hope they had something like me and Blue's blessed with.

The air in here all of a sudden's filled with the rich smells of Sarah's plain, good food, and my stomach growls like it thinks suppertime's close. But I got other business to attend to, and I cover memory-smells with this strong gas scent, and keep on.

In the living room, the chandelier catches one bit of sun through the window and lights like splintered glory. My hands remember years of taking down those crystals, one by one, and washing them till their glitter was near more than a body could bear; my eyes recall a time those crystals lit behind Ariadne

Fleming's fiery hair and made hoes believe they were ladies, and had themselves a mission.

Which I do, now. I douse our long red couch that's seen the backsides of who knows how many hoes, how many tricks, fine upstanding citizens of Jameston and almost every other place else you can think of. I hold my breath against this strong gas smell, smelling instead jasmine and liquor, smoke and polished wood. Closing my eyes, I hear tunes old and new, and high strange laughter; if I listen harder I hear groans, too, and whispered lies. Oh.

Up the stairs I go, into dark still bedrooms, more and more of them, soaking those beds straight through. Lightheaded for sure now, and light, too—near dancing through I go, this gasoline can and the box holding Addie lighter and lighter.

Back down and through the dark hall now, and don't stop to open the door of this linen closet I still dream dreams about, bad and good. Instead I lean myself against the wall beside it, and let Ophelia's wide face come to mind. She's smiling, and I smell sweet clean laundry soap, hear her telling me wisdoms that linger still in my brain. In the middle of all this letting go and leave-taking, Ophelia brings me comfort right this sec, same as she always did, living. That's the good part of here. But in here too's the mint of Winston, that boy I almost killed for trying to take me someplace I wasn't ready to get to. The murdering whispers of Red and Useless—they're in here, too. But I don't dwell on such, not this day, not ever again.

Addie's room, finally, where stands the poster bed she died in, same one she lay happy as a girl in with Mr. Waldo, shared some less joy in with Sheriff Dawson's whorly-eared self, and almost lost her mind in with Useless, whose memory still makes my mouth want to spit. Lost her rustle after that bad business, too, and never got it back. But then I reckon big things have a way of changing us, all through life, like we shed one skin and grow the next, tougher, to keep alive. All the time changing, ain't we.

For sure, if there's one thing that's stayed steady at Hazelhedge over these forty years, it's change. Too much, in the end, for Addie. She spent the last few years fussing about it.

"Things are getting out of hand, Minyon," she'd tell me every once in a while, when she'd get herself worked up, especially in the evenings just before trade'd get going good, when she'd have a couple of shots of Scotch whiskey to warm her insides. "The moral fabric of our society is unraveling." That's how she talked.

It wasn't just that our business kept getting stranger and stranger, Addie said, which it did—we finally had to stock more than a half dozen specialists to take care of what she called the *outré* trade. Folks got to where there wasn't but a handful of them cared for a straight half hour anymore, which used to be the mainstay of our business. Too much out there for free, Addie claimed—for a hundred dollars folks wanted something they couldn't get so easy on the street or in the back seat of their cars.

"People have lost their sense of propriety," she'd say, and what she meant was something like how those teenage boys from Jameston got to sneaking out here in the early morning hours to steal liquor out of their daddies' cars. One Halloween they wrapped every automobile out here in pink toilet paper. But the worst was the time a bunch of them dug up the new sign from in front of the Piggly Wiggly one night and put it up on Highway 17 by our Hazelhedge road, where it stayed two-and-a-half days before anybody worked up the nerve to tell Addie. WE GIVE GREEN STAMPS, the sign said—it was a large one, too, white with big green letters. Got written up in the state paper, with a big picture, and after that Addie patrolled the road first thing every morning to make sure folks didn't pull another fast one on her.

Our girls changed, too—turnover nearly doubled, and a bunch of them got to using dope—smoking or sniffing or swallowing one something or another to get them through the night. College girls, a lot of them, so they claimed, just doing this till they could get enough money to do something else. So they claimed.

Tired now, ain't I. Down I lay this burdensome box I've carried long enough. Right in the smack center of her bed I lay it, and sit myself in her chaise, and lean back.

Whatever else Ariadne Fleming was to me over our forty years together, in the end, in this bed where she lay dying, she was just who she was, or had come to be—just Addie, who I never did get to the bottom of knowing, or even close. Just a woman, far's I could finally figure, sometimes a bad one, sometimes good, doing her best to get on.

The biggest surprise of all came late, when she was so sick, and we'd had our April Fool's Day shutdown, as she called it, all our girls scattered to the winds, our only visitors stragglers who hadn't yet got the word. I'd fix food she couldn't eat, and'd sit beside her wasting-away self—the cancer'd got into bones, Doc Larkin said—he came up from Summerville where he and Mary Lou moved after they got married—and wasn't nothing for it but to wait, he said. While waiting, me and Addie'd get talking about how things were around here in the old days, and remember funninesses, and laugh. But every time I'd start recollecting something sad or bad, she'd skit right off, close her eyes to sleep, or take a coughing spell.

Finally, one day right near the end, I made up my mind to say out loud my memory of Jesse, and loblolly woods, and we two grave diggers—to unbury and speak of that bad old secret that'd bound us together so long. But directly I started with it, her face twisted and her eyes shut like a curtain'd fell upon them. Looking down at her, it came to me all of a sudden clear: how Addie got by all those years was to bury the bad memories, every single last one of them, down so deep she didn't even know they were still there, or ever had been.

When she opened her eyes up again, the look inside there put me in mind of star-watching with my Gan, oh so many years gone now, and feeling like I might could get lost, looking into black. Addie's eyes were that empty and full, too, a same dark night sky without end. I closed my own eyes against them, and that's when I knew: I was more than just keeper of this house; I had to keep the memories, too.

Something else I knew that minute was a sad truth about Ariadne Fleming—she didn't know much about truth at all; she'd spent so many years adjusting it—changing it to make every hoe feel like they shared some something in common, sisters under the skin, which somehow made what they had to do able to get done—that in the end, she lost the truth of all that her life held, the truth of herself, even.

I didn't open my mouth to speak of it further that day, just let it go—along with Addie herself, a week or so later. After that was a bunch of business to see to, and me the one left for it.

Close on to being through with this now, but before I leave Addie's room, I go over to her big closet—where's still stored her clothes and those shoes she took such pride in, right to the last, all lined up neat in rows—and haul out the Blue Book. *Honi soit qui mal y pense*—which words I finally did ask her about and which she said just meant that things are only bad if folks think so. Seems like it must be more than that, or else different, but I don't know why or what. The key to Hazelhedge, she called this book. It surely isn't, though, never was. We were, just us, all the time.

I lay this heavy book in the mid-spot of her poster bed, right on top of that funeral home box with whatever yet remains of Ariadne Fleming. I soak them both, the bedclothes, too. My head's so full it's almost empty, and I am nearly through.

From Addie's bed I walk backwards, trailing in front of me a thin stream of what gas's left in this can. Down the hall, past the linen closet, into the living room. When I step out on the porch where a long-ago girl named Minyon Manigault lay her head that first night, I almost expect to see that child, but don't. Back in I go. The gas smells so strong I hold my breath as I step light through the dining parlor, into the kitchen, and down the back porch stairs where I stop still, take the matchbox from my pocket, draw my breath in deep once more, strike, and throw.

Whoosh—red flame follows quicksilver the path I made, but I don't have time to watch, not yet. I run to the shed and carport, taking care of that business with two quick strikes, then on to outback, one match to each bedroom, leaving the doors open to let the wind do his part of this business, too. By the time I get myself back to the middle of this yard all's ablaze, and my job now's to witness the finish of what I saw born all those years ago.

Inside the main house I watch a lick of flame peek out at one upstairs window, waving down at me like it knows I'm the one gave it life. Inside Sarah's kitchen glows red as a hot stove, and a curtain melts while I watch.

I turn to see Frank's shed doing itself proud, too, crackling and popping, and turn again to check outback, blazing good. The red of these fires is all round me, my head's light as air. I twirl myself two times, then three, standing in the center of that fiery place, then stop, winded and dizzy, just as a loud pop comes from the kitchen and the window blows its glass outward, some near reaching where I stand.

Starting to heat up here now, and I know I got to move myself, but don't yet. Instead I watch the fire reach high, red fingers craving sky, and know that I am through burying things down deep in a dark earth beneath loblollies. Things buried come back. I'm burning secrets now, for all the world to see and smell and know before I'm done, for ashes to rise and sift back down, make themselves into something new.

I have been keeper of this house, and still am keeping it, yes I am, keeping it by letting it go, all those years true and clear as when they happened: girls' gossip, randy man smells, fancy French wine and Johnnie Walker Red and bit-off stubs of Havana cigars. Saturday night doings, dirty money under plates, taking just about anything out in trade. Ophelia's omens and Frank's steady, strong back and that deep-down love he shared with stony Sarah, the finest cook this side of Christiandom. Hoes' tears, and letters home. Pink fizz, silver picks, lost babes. Lies and sighs. Alibis. Lysol and Listerine. Perfume, every kind. A blue-green belly snake, words writ on skin. And sheets—oh

Lord, mountains of sheets. All, all, risen now and gone, secrets kept to us that lived here.

Too hot to stay now. I turn and take myself to the side yard past the driveway, near where my trailer edges woods. From here I see a window in Addie's room bust out, just before comes a sound like a bomb that rumbles this very ground I stand upon. Fire and smoke pour forth together, and the red of these flames looks like the ruby-fire dawn light I waked to this morning.

As I watch I know one more thing: there's not a bit of use looking back on Hazelhedge further than this, on account of that's just history, and we made it, we surely did. But like Addie told me once, so long ago now it seems like a dream—what had to happen, happened. And it's true; life will go on from this place and time right here and now.

Like that thought conjured him, I see Blue Ballard pull his taxi into our driveway. He drives onto the grass, stopping a good ways back and leaving the road clear. And even though I don't turn my head yet from this I'm bound to witness, I see him get out of his car and stand, waiting for me to be through with one part of my life so I can get on with the next.

The walls of the top floor go wavy and start crumbling in on themselves, and I hear the noise of the fire's roar, and more. Up and down stairs, back and forth to outback, I hear feet passing, tricks talking, high heels clicking, clicking. Hear liquor pouring into glasses, and down gullets. Laughing, moans. Music—ain't we got fun, and cry me a river. Sly whispers, oh-so-funny jokes, sad secrets. And that rock, rock, rocking of beds, night after night.

Now I hear something else besides—sirens, meaning Chief DeBlois's good as his word. Before me flames and smoke twin black as sin, and rising above them's the red and goldness of Ariadne Fleming, light as air, always watching, seeing, knowing. And somewhere in amongst is Minyon Manigault, too, keeping house.

I turn and start over to where Blue waits, my feet firm on the ground. On account of I'm through with here; forty years's plenty long enough to keep this house. Just going to keep myself now, and Blue Ballard standing here before me, and sweet Grace, long as she'll let me. And this story, long as I choose.